GLORY DEPARTED

By Nora R. Hobbs

Glory Departed

Copyright © 1997 Nora R. Hobbs All Rights Reserved

Cover by R. S. Hayes

First Edition Spring 2004

Library of Congress Control Number: 2004103501

Published in the United States by
Youwriteabook.com
P.O. Box 905
Snowflake, Arizona 85937
http://www.youwriteabook.com

ISBN 1-932373-38-1

Dedication

This book is dedicated
to those who have ears to hear
what the Spirit says unto the churches
Then and now
Revelation 4:1;3:22

Table of Contents

GLORY
DEPARTED

Forward

The Hebrew name for our Heavenly Father is "Yah" or "Yahwah", meaning "I am" or "I exist" or "the existing one". The Hebrew word for God is "Elohim". The name Christ should properly by rendered "Messiah". Messiah means "The Anointed One" or "The Anointing".

Aramaic is the language used at the time of the appearing of the Messiah. I have chosen to use the Aramaic names for cities, towns and people to add a flavor of the area. YahShua Messiah was the name and title the disciples used when addressing our Savior, the Son of Yah.

I have strived to keep this writing nonsectarian by using only the basic belief in the death, burial and resurrection of the Messiah to tell the story. It is my hope that everyone regardless of their religious affiliation or spiritual standing can find pleasure in the pages of this book.

DAY ONE

"My lord." The soft voice of my faithful personal servant drew my attention away from the scroll I was studying. I knew it was important for him to disturb me. I looked up to see Benren standing in the doorway to my study room. He did not wait for me to ask him what he wanted. "Elsan and Yochanan-bar-Yhosetha have arrived in town and sent a boy to tell you." He hurriedly informed.

Many rumors had reached us from Yerushelayim about the Man, called YahShua of Natzeret, whom many believe to be our Messiah, the Son of Yah. Some of His followers came on several occasions telling us of many miracles He performed and preaching that the kingdom of Yah is at hand, the time for Israel's deliverance had come. We have been waiting for many years to hear this and now our hopes have soared as on the wings of an eagle. Just how many of these rumors are true we have no way of knowing.

The small village of Beitorah hidden away in the mountains of Galil was alive with excitement when I arrived. A large throng had gathered at the Synagogue. We had heard that this YahShua had gone to Yerushelayim for the Posach so we sent my son Elsan and young Yochanan with word for this YahShua of Natzeret called the Messiah, to come and let us hear Him ourselves. We were enthusiastic about the miracles and the idea that He was the Messiah, the Son of the Living Elohim. But, for Him to be the true Messiah, He must and will surely fulfill all the prophecies spoken by the prophets of old concerning the Messiah.

Abidad, the Rabbi of the Synagogue, was calling for quiet just as I pushed my way through the press and entered the building. The Synagogue was on a knoll on the edge of town. It was a large building supported by several heavy beams. The roof spread out far beyond the walls of latticework making a porch like structure all around the

3

building. The men would go into the Synagogue proper and the women would remain on the outside of the lattice under the porches and listen to the Torah being read. Women were not allowed into the Synagogue proper.

Elsan wore a coat of dust from his travel, but grinned broadly at me and shoved a stubborn lock of hair off his forehead. Abidad finally succeeded in getting the drone of voices to still and he spoke with a loud voice where all could hear for the throng spilled out onto the street.

"Men and brethren, Elsan and Yahanan have returned from Yerushelayim with sad news." It was now so quiet that even the bird's singing in the near by trees seemed loud. "It seems," he continued in a troubled voice, "…that the man on whom we based our hopes was crucified on the Day of Preparation and buried before the Posach."

Believing He may just be the one, our hopes were all dashed to pieces as he told of His blood falling to the ground at the foot of a Roman cross. And this on the very Day of Preparation for the Posach Feast celebrated by devout Israelites everywhere. He was crucified by the order of that Roman tyrant, Pontius Pilate, Governor of the Providence of Yhudah, at the request of the Chief Cohanim and elders of Israel.

A great mourning went up from the men that stood by to hear the words and my heart sank. With much weeping and mourning we sitting in sack clothes and ashes until evening, our hopes for deliverance vanquished.

It was related to us the fact that the Sanhedrin including the P'rushim, Tz'dukim and scribes not only brought charges against this Man before Pilate, but also condemned Him as a heretic, blasphemer and liar. They accused Him of being a false prophet, and possessed of the devil. It is reported by the Elders and cohanim that He blasphemed the Elohim of Heaven by speaking His holy name in the very presence of the Council. A charges of which under our law carry the penalty of death. I know that

4

by the laws of the Sanhedrin it is considered blasphemy to speak Elohim's holy name, but it is used freely in the Tanakh and the writing of the Prophets. Therefore, it is almost impossible to get a written copy of them. The P'rushim and Tz'dukim guard them carefully. The true holy name of Yah is lost to most, and known only to those who study the Tanakh.

Even while the night air was still filled with sorrow and deep anguish a rider from Nain in the valley at the foot of the mountain came by camel. He begin to tell of our hoped Messiah's last sermon, 'How He would be mercilessly killed and rise again, coming forth from the cold clutches of death, the third day.' That rumor haunted me that night tormenting my mind and bringing much distress upon me. Yet, within my heart a glimmer of hope had sprung to life, telling me that this Man still may be the one to deliver Israel from the bondage of Roman rule and establish again the throne of David. The promise of this YahShua, called the Messiah, to raise from the dead the third day may mean that Yah will, as the Man has said, still deliver Israel at His hand.

I have knowledge of Yah that makes me understand He is infinite in wisdom and His ways are far above our ways. Sleep had fled so I sat down with pen to list the rumors that came to us through many sources about this Man. I felt I must to find the truth of these rumors leave no stone unturned, both in the searching of the Sacred Writings of the Prophets and even expending all my wealth if needs be. This is not my choice, but some inward force that torments my mind seemed to be driving me.

On the dawning of the day after the Posach's Holy Sabbath, the first day of the week, I decided to travel to Yerushelayim to see if these things be true. It was now the third day, the day in which He was said to say, - "I will arise again the third day". So I took Yered, the son of my concubine, with a company of servants and set out for Yerushelayim. In a compartment under the driver's seat of my carriage, I brought a copy of the Writings of the

Prophets each in a doe skin cover and searched them again to see what they had to say about this latest information.

It is common knowledge that YahShua, the Messiah, was from Natzeret. Yet, the prophets declare the Messiah would be born in BeitLechem of Yhudeh. Furthermore, it says, -"*I will call my Son out of Egypt,*" not out of Natzeret. Upon finding this passage of prophecy, my heart sank and I wept bitterly. While I wept, it occurred to me that according to what was heard of the man YahShua, He had chosen not to speak of Himself, so it might be profitable to search out His background.

This idea set well with me and I told Yered to command the servants to change directions and head back for Natzeret. This would mean a delay in getting to Yerushelayim, but unless I could connect this YahShua with BeitLechem, my going would be in vain anyway. The true Messiah must be from BeitLechem of Yhudah.

One of the earliest rumors of YahShua, the Messiah, was rude but bore some interest to me. The rumor was that wherever He relieved Himself, even in sand or on hard rock, the ground would burst to life with foliage and trees. This was an intriguing rumor because Yah is the giver of life and therefore, His son, also, would hold this power.

With my course set for Natzeret, I went back to the prophetical writings to see what I might find about this rumor. As I read about the Messiah, I found that everything about the Man was to be human, fleshly and natural. So to fit into the plan of Yah, the Messiah must be fashioned in the likeness and similitude of a man. All His bodily functions would be no different from mine, only to rid the body of impurities. With this in mind, I became interested in the prophecies of His birth, reading them over and over.

Being a breeder of the finest, most spirited, chariot horses renowned in the Roman Empire, I could understand clearly how the birth of the Messiah has to be by the act of a living Elohim, not by a fleshly man to produce a true Son of Yah. It is a known fact that the pure bloodline flows through the male, from father to child. I, myself, am from the lineage of L'vi.

Now my trip to Natzeret was twofold. Did this thing happen? How could it be? If he was truly the Messiah, by what means did Yah bring this about? Imagine a living Elohim, a Spirit, producing a child in the womb of a woman. I knew Yah could bring this to pass, but just how I knew not.

As the golden sun hung low in the purple sky on our first day of travel, we entered the outskirts of the small village of Natzeret, nestled in a plateau of the Galilean Mountains, not many stadims from where our journey had started.

The village sits on staggered levels, as do most of the cities and towns in Israel, because of the contrast of high ridges to low ravine that forms the land. Stones hewn from the nearby mountainside or bricks made from mud and straw are the materials used in construction of buildings. They have flat roofs of beams, cross-layered with sticks and covered with a thick rolled layer of the same mixture as the bricks. There are few windows and usually only one entrance. The roofs provide a safe place to set a cot for the hot summer nights, a place to offer devotions undisturbed, and to build a booth for the Feast of Sukkot.

The market place was silent and almost empty by the time we arrived. Only a few people coming to draw water from the stone well in the center of the Village Square near the market places were about.

"Stop here, Yered," I said to the son of my loins from my concubine Athera. Riding beside my richly crafted cisium of hand rubbed cedar on one of my finest horses, he was tall and handsome to look upon. I was as proud of him as I was of Elsan, my son in whom my wife Sarepta bore me. Yered was a fine, obedient son and I watched as he dismounted and saw myself in his movement. I could not help wondering what predestined course in life Yah had planned for him.

7

I climbed from my carriage and Benren, my personal servant, came to my side awaiting my instructions. However, I directed it to Yered. "See to it that the horses are well watered and cared for".

"Yes Father," he grinned with a patient tolerance. I smiled knowing from the look on his face that was his intention before I spoke.

Then I said to Benren, "I will talk with one of those at the well. We will spend the night here. Send someone to find us accommodations."

"Yes my lord". He bowed his head slightly.

I turned my attention to a young man drawing water. From the appearance of his clothing he seemed to be the servant of a merchant or a noble.

"Excuse me." I interrupted his chore and awaited his full attention.

Then he looked up from the well and replied, "The market place is closed, Sir."

"I can see that." I realized my voice was sharp. Correcting my tone, I continued. "Are you from here?"

"Yes Sir."

"I am looking for someone who knows YahShua, the Messiah. Do you know Him or someone who does?"

Immediately a scowl gathered on his brow and he spit on the ground at my feet. "No friend of His is welcome here."

I was dismayed at the bitterness in his voice. "I do not know the Man. I would only like to talk to someone who does."

"No one will talk to you about that lying blasphemer. You came to the wrong place," he growled angrily, turning to pick up his urn filled with water.

"Then you do not believe the Man was who He claimed to be."

"Huh!" He tossed over his shoulder as he turned away.

I stared at him, as he went his way, not believing the anger and bitterness he holds for the Man. Maybe, He was a blasphemer. Then an elder in scribe's apparel came from the side door of what I guessed to be a synagogue. I debated within myself whether to approach the scribe about this YahShua, but the desire to know something about Him drove me on and I hurried to catch him.

"Master," I called as I drew near. He turned to face me. "Could you help me? I am looking for someone who knew the Man YahShua, called the Messiah. Do you know Him or someone who does?"

The man's dark eyes narrowed and I sensed the question annoyed him. His beard was long and grayed but trimmed neatly, showed years of service. Surely, he knew Him, being an elder of the community. But, will he answer me or reject me as one of His forlorn followers? He did not respond immediately and what was only a short degree of time seemed like an eternity. I anxiously watched as his mouth made several slight uncertain movements, and then he spoke.

"I had no use for that heretic and I am glad Elohim saw fit to rid us of Him." He waved his hand in a casting motion.

"But He did miracles for the people and was well thought of until He started pointing out some sins of the elders." I caught myself defending Him. Where did that come from? I have said something I know nothing about. I know not His teachings. Have seen no miracles. This disturbed me greatly and while I pondered it, he began to exhort me.

"My son," he laid his hand on my shoulder and spoke in a teaching tone. "...Not everything that seems good on the surface is really good. It was by the power of Satan that He performed these deeds and led many astray causing them to rebel against the teachings of Moshe. Good that comes to an evil end is not good, but deceiving. That is why it behooves us all to come together and learn the Torah

9

so we may know when someone is leading us away from the path of righteousness."

His brow rose over one eye. "The only good that came from this Man is to make us to stand even firmer in the laws of Moshe. I believe, ...that is why Elohim allowed him to continue as long as He did."

Standing before me was a man with years of study, and wisdom gained by experience. A scholar, ...a man of high position and his words stung my heart like the lashes of a Roman flail. Surely, he was right. Who knows the laws and teachings of Yah better than he does? The scribe must have seen in my eyes the struggle of my soul, for he gave me a warm smile and I sensed his annoyance had subsided.

"Do not let your heart be troubled." The master's voice was tender now. "Many were deceived by the devil in this Man. Many other people have asked the same questions. Take this opportunity to learn of Elohim and do not be disheartened. Elohim always takes care of his own. Go offer the sacrifice for the sin of your heart and rejoice that you have learned not to be deceived."

Still, racing through my mind was the unusual way I reacted to the scribe's accusations against this Man I did not even know. I nodded my head in response to his last words and hid them away in my heart.

"Son," he continued, "that blasphemer grew up here, sitting before the teachings of the Rabbi. He was a good Man until a demon entered Him while He sat in the very midst of the sermon. I remember it well. He asked to read the writings of the Prophet Yeshayahu and then boldly declared before us all that in Him all the prophecies just read were fulfilled. I was taken back in astonishment and dismay. The Rabbi and I, myself, ejected Him from the synagogue. We escorted Him to the edge of the village and there denounced Him, casting Him forth. His brothers stood shamefaced and they, too, condemned Him. Only His cousin did not condemn Him."

He twisted his face into a frown. "Now, there was a strange young man that came to a tragic end," he continued.

It was apparent that he was finished with talk of the man YahShua. "Herod put him into prison and lastly beheaded him. He was held in high regard by the people as a prophet, saying, - 'repent and be baptized'." He sighed deeply, "As though mere repentance and the water from the Yordan River could cleanse sins. Foolishness, sin sacrifices must be made according to the laws of Moshe. It is a sad story...sad story indeed." The old man shook his head slowly and turned to go his way.

I stood numbed for several degrees, shaken, grieved and disillusioned. Two conflicts struggled in my breast: the words of those who testified of YahShua bearing witness of His miracles and the words of the scribe, a learned man of Yah. Slowly I returned to my company at the well.

The young adventurous spirit in Yered had drawn him away to explore the village, and the servants had not returned with word of lodging yet.

I spoke with several others as they came one by one to the well, but received either cold stares with no answers or harsh rebukes that made a sick feeling build up inside.

The turmoil in my soul must have displayed itself on my face. For, as I paced back and forth wrestling with the many thoughts that pressed upon my mind, one of the young men in my troop came near to me.

"My lord, you seem very troubled. Is there something I may do or get for you?"

With my emotions ebbing and flowing like the waves that lap the shores of the Sea of Galil, this simple concern of the lad touched me deeply. I forced a smile scuffling his curly locks.

"Yes," I returned, "Bring me a cup of wine." The request seemed to please the boy and he hurried away.

To relieve my mind of its torment, I again picked up a scroll of the Prophets and scanned it. It all seemed so confusing, vague and futile. In a fit of anger, I threw the scroll back into the carriage. The scroll, however, determined to try my already thin patience came tumbling back out and fell at my feet on the dusty stone street. When

I stooped to pick it up, the young servant returning with the wine, bent quickly trying to spare me of the task and picked up the scroll with haste. In his haste he grabbed the partly unrolled script and held it out to me. It was crumpled in his grasp and the unrolled end dangled from his fingertips. Any other time this careless disregard for the Holy Writings would have brought the severest scolding. But, because I understood his intentions and stood guilty myself, I merely frowned in displeasure. The boy's servitude smile faded as his eyes followed mine and he stood shame faced staring at the hand holding out the parchment that had done the awful deed. I could tell he was expecting some form of disciplinary action for his carelessness, but I merely took the scroll and wine from him.

"I am sorry my lord, I only wished to serve you well." The lad began trying to excuse his error.

"I will overlook it this time," I replied to put his mind at ease. "But, hence forth remember to treat the Sacred Writings with the utmost care and reverence."

"Yes my lord, I will remember." The boy returned gratefully with a release of his breath and I waved his dismissal.

I will remember it also, for this was Yah's way of showing me my own disrespect for sacred things. Carefully, I examined the crumpled scroll to see if it had received permanent damage and sighed with relief to see that it had not. While I was rolling it back onto its stay, my eyes fell upon the passage that read; *He was despised and rejected, forsaken by men, a man of sorrow and pains, acquainted with grief and sickness. As one from whom men hid their faces. He was despised and appreciated not for his worth or esteem.*

This statement shocked and dismayed me. That was all I could stand to read. My understanding was dulled by all the tormenting thoughts and things I had heard this day. "I am tired," I told myself. "On the morrow when I am refreshed, I shall read further." Yet, the passage returned to me many times. While I was waiting, through the dusk of the evening, I noticed a woman with a vessel approaching the well. I wondered if all here reject him? She began to draw from the spring and I studied the maiden with the words of the Prophet still echoing in my mind. I must know if this damsel believes in the Natzeret or if she, too, hates Him. Going to her, I opened my mouth to speak, but my courage fell as I reasoned within myself. What real difference would to make if she did hate Him or for that matter believed in Him. The Man was dead and only Yah could give life. I now regret having not continued on to Yerushelayim, but even that seemed to be a vein thought now.

"Excuse me, daughter?" I heard myself say, as though I were no longer in control, but detached from it. "Do you know the Man, YahShua, called Messiah?" When she looked at me, I wished I could have taken back the words. The dark eyes still visible behind her veil shot hot daggers at me.

"No!" She spit at me and turned away. I stood there as if in a daze and watched her fade into the darkness.

Then I became aware of someone near, standing slightly behind me. Turning, I saw an aged woman with almost white hair in common clothing. Her eyes were deep hazel with a hint of sadness in them. Surely, she had heard the words of my question and the damsel reply. She turned away, letting down the draw into the cistern.

"Here, let one of my young men help you." I came and took the rope. "Why do you come so late to the well?" I asked. However, that was not the question in my heart. She looked at me and smiled slightly.

"My family has gone to Yerushelayim to celebrate the Feast." She spoke softly. "It is too much of a travel for me." She was avoiding my question. A lad standing near by came at my beckon and took the rope. He seemed aware of my intentions so I turned to look at the woman. "Do you know Him?" I blurted out, no longer being able to refrain.

Her eyes moved slowly from my face and flowed to the boy's hands as they worked the draw rope. She was beautiful in her youth, but now many years and hard times had taken its toll. However, she seemed to be soft in her tone and manner leaving me with a sense of her inner beauty years could not mire. Who is this woman? Will she speak of YahShua? I suppressed a sharp pang of irritation at her seeming lack of interest in my words. I too, stood watching the boy draw. Then I could feel her eyes turn upon me and linger there. I suppose she is wondering what I am doing asking about Him. She did not speak, and when the vessel was filled, I said to the young man that was drawing, "Take it to the house for the woman."

While my attention was turned to the boy picking up the pitcher, I heard her say, "I knew Him."

Looking at her inquiringly, our eyes met and in searching her face I found it troubled. But, my curiosity about YahShua was overwhelming. I had to find out about this Man who had done so many wonderful things and had now become despised, even in His own hometown.

"Will you tell me about Him?" I ask pleading. "I must know."

"You will find no rooms for such a large party in Natzeret," she informed, ignoring my words. "You look tired as though you have traveled far. Come take meat at my house. There is room for you and your company."

"That is very kind of you. I will be glad to pay." I studied her further. She had a way of ignoring things she did not want to deal with. It was her sanctuary, I suppose, but it is very irritating. Something told me that she was one of His followers.

"That will not be necessary," she returned. "This way."

I called Benren and said to him, "We will spend the night at the house of this woman." He nodded and went to bring the company along. I then hurried, taking several large steps, and came to the woman's side.

"What is your name?"

"Eliseva."

"I am Timon of Beitorah, on the slopes of Mount Tabor."

"Why have you come out of your way to this small village?" she asked cutting her eyes up at me curiously. She was assuming I had gone to Yerushelayim for the Posach and was now returning.

"Because I had determined to go to Yerushelayim and see if this YahShua of Natzeret had truly raised from the dead. In my going, I felt compelled to come here to find out about the Man."

She smiled half-heartedly, but continued to look down the street. Finally, she said, "Why bother with that? If He is dead, ...He is dead, … if not, you will surely hear the news."

"I have heard too many rumors already. Now I want to find out for myself. I am full of rumors. Do you think He has risen?" I looked for some response, but found only the discipline that comes with years.

We walked on silently and I found myself becoming irritated again at her lack of respect. She could at least answer me. Then I looked at her the second time. Well, ...I guess the wisdom of her age afforded her the right to speak when it pleased her. Nonetheless, the walk through the ever-darkening streets, nearly empty now, seemed to take forever. I had so many questions. We came into an area where there were several houses. She turned through the gate of one and I went beside her.

"This is my house. Your servant may make camp here." She made a motion with her hand to the lower level where we stood.

The lower level was roomy and lit with several torches. A small wooden fence made an enclosure suitable for the horses. A cow of the herd stood tied near a manger that was cut into the rock wall below the upper level of the house. In one corner, a family of sheep milled around nervously. Several steps lead to a narrow walkway running along the west wall with a doorway at the far north end leading into the upper level.

I turned to Benren standing near by, "Send someone back to the well to wait for Yered." He nodded, and I then said to the young man with the pitcher. "The woman will show you where to put the pitcher."

Elisheva turned and ascended the steps to the walkway. The boy and I followed. Beyond a thick woolen drape hung over the doorway at the end of the walk was a large room and in the middle of its yellow stone laid floor was a beautifully crafted, hand rubbed table with several lounges around it. A long service table with carved billows and fig leaves were against the wall to the right of the door we had just entered. I wondered how she could afford this fine furniture. It was obvious she was not well to do. Another doorway was on the north wall across the room near the east wall. This one had long dried reeds individually hanging close together by colorful beaded leather straps fastened to the upper part of the doorway.

"Be seated," she offered with a swing of her hand, "please, excuse me." Lowering her head slightly, she then led the boy through the other door and the reeds made a dull musical sound as they banged and crashed together. I watched her and the lad disappear and was grateful for the warmth of the room. Surely, she must have been one of His followers.

Offering her humble abode so graciously did not really strike me as a strange thing for her to do. I wondered how many pilgrims and strangers had found refuge from the chill of the night air in the seclusion of this wonderfully warm house. I was sure there must have been many.

Settling on one of the lounges, I noticed on the wall a banner of the tribe of L'vi. The colorful woolen rug covering the floor was well worn and the lounge covers were thin in several places. In my mind, I tried to visualize the Man, YahShua, sitting where I sat, talking about the Kingdom of Yah to a room full of followers and Elisheva caring for their needs in her quiet manner. I wondered if He had been here one or more times.

As I amused myself with that thought, the servant boy returned and stood before me waiting further orders. I waved his dismissal and he went back out through the way we came in. Elisheva came again now carrying a foot basin and a towel was about her waist. She said nothing but squatted before me and began to remove my sandals.

"You do not have to do that. My servant will be here in a few degrees and he will wash my feet."

She looked at me, and in the light I could see that she was much older than she appeared at the well. Lines etched by experience revealed her many years of wisdom gained. The hard lines melted into a tender smile that brightened her whole face. She did not know me, but her love went out to me with no restraint, no hypocrisy.

"Please allow me. It is my duty for I have no servant."

I could see in her eyes the flames from the candelabra that lit the room with a mellow glow. They were like reflecting pools, sharp and clear. As I hesitated, she continued with a soft voice. "He has said, -'Love one another, do good one for another. Wash one another's feet to show your love, for this is pleasing to Elohim', it would please me very much to do it."

He had taught this? These are not the words of a blasphemer. Her kindness was sweet as honey from the comb making this simple task of hospitality an act of love. Something so commonplace and accepted all my life as routine, now, took on a whole new light. I was humbled and deeply touched. I wondered if all His followers were like her or was she just a rare woman. Here in a simple abode, this woman of soft countenance had taken the humbling work of a household servant, not merely for tradition sake, but as an act of love. Her hands, though wrinkled, moved with skill and tenderness. She was in no hurry and seemed to take a good deal of pleasure in her task. A lump appeared in my throat and I swallowed hard to keep from choking. Never had I been so richly received, not even in the finest homes while in Rome.

17

I was now totally convinced that she knew Him well and was one of His followers. I watched as she tenderly washed the red Galilean dust from my feet and dried them roughly with the towel to relax them. She knew the ways of a servant but, somehow, I found it hard to believe that this precious woman had never served any man being compelled to do so by servitude. This woman has surely washed His feet, maybe, repeatedly and now mine. There is no real way to describe what I was feeling, but it brought a glow of inner warmth.

"Tell me about Him," I begged. "Is He the Son of Elohim?"

She picked up the basin and stood. "I will bring you something to eat and when you have eaten and are well refreshed, we will talk." Her words were firm with authority like that of a mother. I simply nodded. So, she handed me a sweet smelling damp cloth and went back through the reed curtain.

I washed the dust off my hands and face and began to study the curious wooden candlestick that sat in the middle of the low richly carved table beside the lounge.

The candlestick had seven candles, three on each side of the middle one on a central carved column. The six side candles were sitting on up turned stems branching out of the center column arranged so that each candle was the same height. On the stand was carved designs of almond blossoms with knobs and leaves. A cup at the upper end of each stem, like upturned almond flowers, held each candle. Now it came to mind that this was like the menorah in the Holy Place of the Great Temple at Yerushelayim.

This brought to me the words of the Prophets again and the words of those who testified of the miracles and words of YahShua. However, that which the scribe had spoken kept pushing them away and I felt the confusion returning. I then realized that while I talked with the woman, Elisheva, the confusion had subsided, but was now beginning to return.

The curtain clattered again and I watched as the woman carried in a large platter filled with sweet meats, nuts, pomegranates, figs and other fruit. She set it down on the table in front of me and went again into the adjoining room. I must have been very hungry for this simple meal looked delicious and its aroma danced in the air around me. Then the woman returned with a cup and pitcher of wine.

She sat down on the lounge across from me and poured the wine in the shiny brazen cup. Unfolding a cloth napkin, she handed it to me, her eyes searching my face.

"I find the fruit of the vine refreshing." I commented after a sip of wine. She just smiled at me, which seemed to smooth her face. I could feel her uncertainty. If she was a follower of YahShua and with the village so full of bitter hatred for Him, I could surely understand her uneasiness. It might prove to be dangerous to talk freely about Him. "I sense your concern regarding my questioning you about this YahShua," I said to her. "I want you to know that I only wish to find out if He was really who He claimed to be." I paused to get her reaction, but found little. Then I continued, "Anything you say will go no further than this room. I, Timon, son of Philorah do swear this oath to you in the hearing of Elohim." Now, her expression softened and I saw the concern melt slowly as I spoke but the sadness remained, hidden in her eyes.

"You speak with a Greek accent." She responded.

"Yes, does that offend you?"

She looked down and did not respond, so I began to eat in silence, after all she had invited me and had heard my speech at the well. Eventually, she spoke, "I was far into a late pregnancy..." She sighed, "My husband and I lived in the hill country of Yhudeh at that time, and Miryam, my cousin's child, being espoused to Yosef of the house of David, came to me for she..."

A soft knock at the curtain doorway that leads down stares stole her words. She got up quickly going to the curtain and pulling it open. Her age had not slowed her. She seemed as agile as a young maiden. I heard Benren ask to enter. He had come to attend my needs. She bid him enter and he slipped past her into the room.

"I have no need of you now, my friend," I told him while he was still coming.

"Very well my lord," he responded with a slight bow of his head, "I thought you might like to know that young Yered has returned and has news of the matter at hand."

"Good! Good!" I replied.

"He may come in and speak with you here." Elisheva offered.

"Very well..." I nodded, "Benren, send him in."

"Yes my lord," Benren bowed again and departed through the woolen curtain.

"Thank you for your kindness," I said to Elisheva. "Yered is the son of my concubine. An adventurous young man I am afraid." I smiled with understanding, remembering my younger days.

"Your son may take meat also. There is plenty." She offered in her motherly way, echoing my smile. She seemed to somehow understand.

"You are a fine woman," I returned her smile. "We are grateful for your hospitality."

The curtain rustled softly as Yered pulled it back and peered into the room. His eyes found me, then flowed to Elisheva standing near the table.

"Shalom!" He set forth his greeting to the mistress of the house.

"Enter, come, ...sit! There is plenty." She offered, moving her hand to the platter prepared before me.

"Thank you." He bowed slightly to her. "But," He turned back to me, "...there is an urgent matter at hand."

What was so urgent that Yered would refuse a chance to stuff himself? He is usually always ready to take meat. I sometimes wonder where he puts all his appetite demands.

"Elisheva, this is Yered." I remembered my manners. "Yered this is Elisheva, who has so generously offered her home to us." Yered nodded to her and she returned it.

"I have found out something of importance, Father. We must go now, before it gets any later," he insisted.

"Very well." I reached for my sandals. "I will come with you."

"I will wait with the servants." Yered replied turning to Elisheva, bowed again and then took his leave.

"When you have finished with your business and have returned bring the young man. Your meal will be waiting," Elisheva ordained.

"Thank you." I nodded and went out and down into the lower level where Yered waited near the campfire.

"What have you been doing?" I asked when I approached.

"I have been about my father's business while he entertained himself with a woman." He returned with a sheepish grin.

I knew this was only meant as a jest, but I was not in the mood for his foolishness and have great respect for Elisheva. "Is that any way to talk about your father and the woman who has offered her hospitality?" I scolded sternly.

His face sobered quickly and he looked ashamed. "I apologize, Father. My words were not to show disrespect to you nor the woman."

"This is not the time for foolishness," I replied with a sigh. But, I knew for a young man, foolishness is as much a part of him as his breath.

"What is it that is so urgent? What have you found out that could not wait until morning?"

"It is about the Man, YahShua. I have found that He has four brothers, two of which have a carpenter shop at the edge of the village."

"This is great news, Yered." I laid my hand upon his shoulder to let him know I was not angry with him. He always tries so very hard to please me and, sometimes in my haste, I forget to let him know how much it means to me. His boyish grin returned accompanied by a twinkle in

21

his eye. "I thought you might wish to go speak with one of them before the night was too far spent. I had your horse made ready."

"Good, let us be going." My heart was not in going, but Yered was so pleased at his discovery that I did not want to make him feel that I was ungrateful. So, I turned to Benren and said, "Tell the woman we will return shortly."

"Yes my lord," he nodded and turned to ascend the steps.

We rode through the dark empty streets of the small town and I could feel the desolation of the place. Nothing stirred and the buildings cast dull moonlit shadows on the cobblestone streets. They were built in the typical flat roof style, some two and three stories tall. Though the place seemed peaceful enough, only a dog's bark could be heard somewhere far away. This would not be a place I would want to live, too full of hatred and bitterness.

As we drew near the edge of the village, we came to a carpenter's shop where a dim light made thin lines around the closed shutters at the back of a large porch like structure that was the work area.

Yered pulled his horse up in front of the steps that went up into the shop and dismounted. Catching the reigns of my horse, he held it while I stepped down.
"Father, I will go see if the man will receive us."

"All right," I agreed. Even with Elisheva's warm welcome, I was not particularly anxious to be greeted by another angry face.

I was feeling the weariness of the day's travel and did not really believe that this visit would be fruitful. Besides, the Man was apparently a deceiver, just another Messiah to rise up in these troubles times.

On the wall of the house and on the support posts of the porch that made up the carpenter shop hung all manner of small finely hand crafted wooden items for sale. The shop itself was crowded with tables, chairs, lounge frames, oxen and horse yokes, wooden barrels and water buckets plus other useful items, several barrels full of tool handles

22

for working the ground and many other furnishings. On a table near the steps to the shop was an unfinished high-backed chair. Its curved legs pointed upward and the smell of fresh cut wood perfumed the air. Beside the porch on the ground was a pile of tree trunks, a splitting stump with a hammer and wedge lying on it.

Galil is not known for its safety. It is a matter of common knowledge that it probably has more robbers, thieves and murderers than all Israel. I wondered why the carpenter was so careless with these things and why, especially here on the outskirts of the village, he did not have a way to protect his good, and make it harder for those who might pilfer such things.

Yered returned promptly and with him a small boy. "One of the brothers is at home and will talk with us, Father. This boy will look after the horses." I nodded wearily and went with Yered.

A big man with large arm muscles and a short beard greeted us at the door. He looked to be in his late twenties.

"Shalom!" His voice was hearty. "I am Yaakov, the carpenter."

"I am Timon, a husbandman of horses from the slopes of Mount Tabor and this is Yered, son of my concubine."

"Shalom," Yered nodded.

"Enter." He bid huskily and stepped aside. "The shop is not open at this hour, but because you are strangers and this is Posach season, I will sell to you." I was aware of his tremendous size as I passed by him.

"I have not come to buy," I informed.

The man's eyebrows raised slightly and he looked inquiringly at us. However, he did not forget his manners. "Take your rest." He showed us some very fine lounges, like the ones in Elisheva's house. This must have been where she bought hers.

Almost before we sat down, a lovely young woman came through an open doorway with a foot basin, girded with a towel. She knelt before us and began the ablution.

23

"So, what brings you here at this late hour?" He began with a curious look.

"I understand you are the brother of the Man called YahShua, the Messiah." I went straight to the point. His expression changed quickly into a frown, as he seated himself looking uncomfortable.

Yered's eyes followed the woman's every move until she had finished the washing and without looking directly at either of us disappeared through the open doorway again.

I studied the man for a degree and then opened my mouth to say something when the woman returned and placed a tray on the table in front of us. There were three cups, a pitcher of wine, some bread sticks and a bowl of sop upon it. She poured the wine and handed one to each of us without a word. Yered watched her with deep curiosity and our host smiled at him.

"This is my wife, Sarah." He answered Yered's unspoken question and Yered looked somewhat embarrassed.

"She is a fine wife." The man smiled at his woman. She smiled back and promptly went back into the other room.

He looked at us inquiringly and then dropped his eyes to his cup watching the rich red liquid as it caught the light from the burning oil bowl hanging from the ceiling by a chain.

"I..., am one of the brothers of YahShua." He spoke slowly. Then looking up at us he continued. "What do you want?"

"Tell us about Him." I prompted.

"He was a good Man with a feel for the wood and, ...He is dead. Why do you ask?"

"Is He who He claimed, the Son of Elohim?'

"Are we not all sons of Elohim?' He replied.

"But, He is believed to be the Messiah," Yered injected.

"So some have said." His voice was filled with doubt.

"But, he did so many wonderful miracles." Yered insisted.

"I have seen no miracles, though they say He did many." He moved his head from side to side slowly and took a drink of wine. Sadness was in his manner, but I sensed no hate or bitterness there. "I am sorry you traveled here for nothing. I cannot help you."

I nodded, "So I guess, ...we look for another Messiah." The glimmer of hope was only a dying ember now and I was content to let it go out. "Thank you for speaking with us. The night is far spent and we must travel on the morrow." I stood up.

"Shalom!" Yered bid and I nodded.

"Shalom," he returned and showed us out.

If His own brother, who grew up with Him and knew Him better than any others, did not believe in Him... I must have, because of my desire to see Israel delivered, been disillusioned by all the rumors just as the scribe had said. Yet, ...I couldn't forget how my heart sang for joy as I sat and heard the witness of those who claimed to be His followers.

When we returned to Elisheva's house, the servants took the horses and I said unto Benren, "We will return to Beitorah at first light." He nodded and went to tell the other servants.

"Will we not go to Yerushelayim, Father?" Yered said in a disappointed tone.

"I see no need of that now. We have much to do at home." I returned. "There will be another time to see Yerushelayim. Perhaps, we can make the journey for the Feast of Harvest after the spring foaling." I tried to take the sting out of his disappointment. He nodded but I knew it did not really help.

"Come, Yered, the woman has bade you to take meat for there is plenty."

I turned for the steps that went to the upper level. He caught my stride and said nothing. I knew he was eagerly awaiting our stay in Yerushelayim. It is an exciting experience to go there for any young man. I still remember the times when my father, brothers, and I traveled there for many Pesachs. The feast days with all their pomp and splendor at the Great Temple were always overwhelming.

I knocked and Elisheva appeared at the door, pulling the curtain back for us. Enter, she beckoned with her hand. "I trust your business was fruitful."

"Unfortunately not." I reported with a sigh.

Elisheva smiled warmly at Yered. "Your father neglected to tell me how very pleasing you are to look upon."

"Thank you." He reddened at her words. "I see true beauty comes with age," he recovered quickly. His voice carried a high tone of respect and I knew it was for the thing he had said by the campfire. It was proper and I gave him a pleased glance as I sat down on my lounge.

She reflected a degree on his return and then said, "You must be hungry. Sit, I will pour you some wine."

He took the lounge beside me while Elisheva went to the long table against the east wall and returned with a foot basin, already prepared, kneeling at my feet again. I said nothing this time while she washed our feet. When she had finished she went and replaced the bowl on the table. Yered began to eat and I said, "You were telling me of a visit from your kinsmen's daughter, I believe."

Her eyes quickly darted to Yered, busying himself with the delicacies. She came to stand beside the table and poured wine into our cups.

"Yes," she finally said, "well, ...she stayed with me for some time." Setting the pitcher down, she took the lounge across from us.

"How many children do you have, Timon?" She did not seem interested in talking about YahShua of Natzeret, so I did not insist. I guess it was not really important now anyway, after finding He was a blasphemer and had paid the penalty.

"My wife, Serepta, has borne me two children. Elsan, a fine young man, is at home tending the business. A beautiful daughter, Miryam and Yered's mother is heavy with child. How about you?"

"I had one son, Yachanan, whom Elohim gave me in my unfruitful years to take away the reproach of my barrenness."

I saw in her eyes the hidden sadness present itself boldly now and I could tell that it was not easy for her to talk of him. She had used a past reference to him, which probably meant he was dead. He surely came to some tragic end, as he should still be in his prime. I did not wish to bring her any further pain, so I did not ask about it. Instead, I tried to change the direction of our words.

"Is your husband in Yerushelayim?"

"No", she shook her head. "He is with Avraham resting from his labor." There was no regret or sadness in her answer.

I looked at the young robust Yered and thought, also, of Elsan, Miryam, Athera and dear Serepta. I could not imagine the depths of anguish the loss of any of them would bring and made a quick prayer for Yah to spare me that fate and allow me to go to be with Avraham before any of them. The sound of wine being poured brought me out of my thoughts. I quickly held up my hand and Elisheva stopped pouring into my cup.

"You must be very weary. Come! I will show you where to sleep." She arose and beckoned with her hand.

Yered made a loud gulping sound as he swallowed the last of his wine. "I will sleep with the servants." He stated.

"Please," the woman insisted, "there is room."

"I prefer to stay with them. Something might come up and Father needs to rest undisturbed."

This was Yered, always trying to spare me any undo disturbance and I recognize his need to fulfill manhood by taking part of the family responsibility. This is a natural way for him to feel, but sometimes in his zeal he forgets, that I do not mind these disturbances. However, he was right this time about my needing undisturbed rest, so I just smiled to myself and let his words stand. While they talked, I drank the small amount of wine Elisheva had poured before I stopped her and set the cup back on the table.

Elisheva nodded to Yered, turned and led the way through the noisy reeds covering the door and I followed her. At the doorway, I turned back to Yered who was putting on his sandals.

"Sleep well Yered," I bid.

"Dream well Father," he returned with a glance.

The woman was waiting patiently on the other side of the doorway in what was the preparation room. A table sat against one wall and several shelves held the utensils and service items. There was a linen closet, with a cloth covering and a few pottery containers with lids setting on the table. Hanging from the ceiling near the wall were several cords with vegetables and fruit on them. In the center of the floor was a dug out fire pit for cooking and the roof had a small hole for the heat to escape. The hole itself had a small roof above it to keep the winter rain at bay.

"This way." She led through another curtain, made of thick wool.

We entered a narrow hallway with two woolen curtain covered alcoves on the side opposite the entrance. On the wall beside the doorway was a tapestry of a Posach Feast. At the end of the hall were steps to the roof, but Elisheva stopped before the furthermost enclosure and moved the dividing curtain back for me.

This was a small bedchamber with a finely carved bedstead and a small table sat beside it with an oil lamp burning on it. A thick mattress of fleece made the bed look restful and enticing.

"Good night," she bid and let it close between us, leaving me alone.

28

I should have been able to fall asleep quickly for I was tired, but alas, ...the conflict of my mind wouldn't allow sleep to come and all the things of the day tormented me.

"Dear Yah, why is this happening? The matter is finished." I muttered in desperation and then heard the soft clink of wine cups. The woman was in the preparation room, most probably washing the utensils. Since I could not sleep and being the type of man whom dislikes leaving things undone, I slipped on my tunic and went in where she was. As I came through the curtain, the woman turned quickly to face me. I must have startled her.

"I have found sleep flees from me." I explained my presence.

She smiled understandingly. "These are trying times," she consoled me. "Some warm milk might help."

"No, ah, but..." I hesitated.

"Yes?" She urged me.

"Maybe we could talk further, if you are not tired."

She dried her hands on a cloth hanging from a peg driven into the wall beside the table where she had been working. "Sleep is not easily found for anyone these days," she returned.

"Many things trouble my mind and I do not understand why Elohim does not ease me of them."

She drew near and touched my arm, "Let us go into the lounge and talk there."

I looked into her eyes, so tender, loving, yet sad. I had been so concerned with my own troubles that I had failed to see hers. She was one of His followers and had probably listened to the Man speak His deceiving words and if I have been deceived, what of her? Surely, her wish to understand was as deep and probably even more tormenting than mine. I nodded and followed her into the first room. We sat down across from each other.

Trying not to sound too bold I asked, "Elisheva, ...were you one of the followers of YahShua?"

"I believe in Him," she confessed with a sigh, "I do not understand the happenings of the past few days. I always depended upon Zkhrayah, my husband, to explain these things to me. I am afraid I do not know much about what has happened." She paused and pondered something a degree of time and I waited. Then she continued. "I still believe in Him, ...even now."

"But the Sanhedrin and the scribes all say, - 'He was a blasphemer and a liar, deceiving many and turning them away from the Laws of Moshe.'" I found the words hard to say now, for the writings of the Prophet Yeshayahu raced through my mind. *'He was despised and forsaken of men; and like one from whom men hide their face, He was despised and we did not esteem him.'* "I only know when Miryam, my cousin's child, came to me in the mountains of Yhudah and had greeted me something very strange and wonderful happened. It had never happened before and has never happened since," she related the story.

"While her greeting still sounded in my ears, the child in my womb leaped with joy as the Spirit of Yah came upon me. Raising my voice, I began to prophesy saying, - 'Blessed, favored of Yah above all other women are you! And blessed, favored of Yah is the fruit of your womb! How have I deserved this honor that the mother of my Adonai should come to me?'"

Elisheva had a far-away look in her eye as though she were reliving it all again. "I pulled her to my breast," she was saying, "...and my tears flowed with joy. Then Miryam said, 'Elohim has looked upon this handmaiden for, behold, He who is mighty has done great things for me'. Then she continued to speak and prophesied of great things to come that would bless generation to generation, age after age. She told me of a visit from an Angel of Yah who told her that she would bear a holy seed and his name would be YahShua. She stayed with me three months. Until her espoused husband Yosef, of the house of David, decided not to put her away as it is his privilege under our law. He had, also, a visit from an Angel and was told not to be afraid to take Miryam to be his wife and so he did."

I was so taken by the woman's words that I did not speak for some time, trying to put this wondrous story in the right perspective with all the things I had read and heard. Suddenly, it became clear to me that this gracious woman is related to this very YahShua. But, was He the Messiah or just a Prophet? I pressed her further. "But the prophets have said that the Messiah would come from Betlechem, not Natzeret. And, He would be called out of Egypt." I sensed the importance of the story about her sister's daughter.

Then I recalled the words of the scribe and saw that she surely must be the mother of Yachanan the Immercor, whom we heard about that preached repentance in the wilderness. Now the reality of it all hit me like a bolt of lightening. He was the one beheaded by the treacherous Herod! Now I understood the sadness in her eyes and the pain of his memory.

"Yes, this happened," she assured me, pulling me out of my thoughts, "Miryam was nearing time for her delivery when Caesar Augustus decided to take a census of the people. So, they had to go to Betlechem, the city of David. While there, the child was born and they continued there for some time. When Herod understood that the Messiah was born, soldiers were sent to slay all the male children born around that time. He felt his throne in danger because of the prophecies about Him." She frowned, and I guessed, she was remembering the time. I have deep remembrance of the event and the hatred it spawned in the hearts of all Israel.

I could feel a glimmer of hope begin to glow. Surely, Yah will still fulfill the promise. Maybe, He did raise YahShua from the dead. And this may be the reason I could not rest, because of the things that I had heard. I will make haste, I determined, and go on to Yerushelayim to see this thing for myself.

31

"Miryam and Yosef took the child and fled into Egypt until word reached them that Herod was dead by the hand of Yah. Then they returned here where they sojourned."

I became very excited and joy filled my soul as it had when I heard the great things of those who bore witness of YahShua. "Then He is the Messiah and has raised the third day as He said!"

"That I do not know," she returned with a hint of doubt. My heart sank and my hopes came tumbling down once again. "When YahShua talked with us," she continued, "He only said to us, He was the light of the world and that Elohim had sent Him to proclaim the Kingdom of Elohim was at hand. He said nothing about His death or his rising from the dead, nor about breaking the yoke of the Romans."

"He spoke only of love and taught us to be kind one to another. By it, we would please Elohim and if we believed Him, we could have everlasting life." She paused thoughtfully, as though pondering His sayings. "He could not preach openly here," she sighed, drooping her shoulders.

"He went away, telling us, 'A prophet is never accepted in His own country', I could not travel to hear Him speak much in the latter part of His ministry because He was on the move most of the time. All I can do now is ponder all the things I hear and believe Elohim will not forsake Israel forever."

"My heart aches for His mother, I know her loss." Elisheva offered. Yes, I could see how she would after having lost her only son at the hands of King Herod. She sighed deeply and almost whispered, "Elohim be with her." Then looking up at me she said, as though I did not hear her little prayer, "I would have gone to comfort her, but she is in Yerushelayim. Yaakov will probably bring her home now and satisfy her last years."

"A messenger came to Beitorah and told of His last sermon, how He would be killed and then after three days

come out of the tomb." I eagerly told her watch her closely
for a response. She looked at me with a blank expression.
Either she did not believe this would happen, did not care
or knew something I did not know. "That is why I am
going to Yerushelayim, to see if this thing has come to
pass." I waited, but was puzzling the dullness of her
expression at such news.

"Perhaps he did," she finally ventured. "He did raise
up Elazar of BeitAnyah."

"You do not sound very convinced." I suggested.

"If it was the will of Elohim that He die, why would
Elohim then bring Him back to life. I only know that He
was sent from Elohim, but perhaps not to be the Messiah as
some think."

This was why I could not sleep. I had the very same
thoughts, but why did Yah send Him? Only the Messiah
could bring the deliverance we needed.

As I lay again upon the bed of sleeping, I too
pondered all the things written by the prophets, the scribe's
words, and those who bore witness of YahShua. I thought
about His brother, Yaakov, and how the words of Elisheva
burned in my heart. Why was Yah making it so hard to find
the truth? Why was my mind so disturbed by this matter?
Why had YahShua said He would rise again from the dead?
What was the purpose of it and His death? Did Yah have a
weightier purpose in mind, something far beyond our
understanding? Did Yah raise Him from the dead? Will this
Man, like Moshe, deliver Israel from Rome as when Yah
delivered Israel out of Egypt's bondage? Could this Man
only be the forerunner? Was He the promised Messiah or
just a Prophet as Elisheva said He claimed to be? Had this
wonderful woman fallen prey, also, to the deceiving words
inspired by a devil? I must know the truth of these matters
and that truth surely lies in Yerushelayim with His
disciples.

DAY TWO

At daybreak, much to Yered's delight, we set out for Yerushelayim. I shall not long forget the visit to Natzeret, the warmth of the woman Elisheva and her kind hospitality. She came late to the well for water because of the bitterness of the people for the followers of the Man, YahShua her kinsman. Her beautiful inspiring story has given me the encouragement I needed to continue my search for the truth. In Yerushelayim, I hoped to find the answer to the many questions that haunts me and talk with His disciples about the events of the past few days.

I can still feel the weariness of thoughts that struggles in my mind, which caused my sleep to come only after much tossing and turning. Anxiously, I went back into the writings of the Prophets to read further what they had to say about this YahShua Messiah. I was as a child in the market place, running to and fro, looking at this and at that. The words of the Prophets about this Man were so intriguing I could not get enough. I read them and read them again, not understanding much of what it all meant, but I felt sure it was important. I hid them away in my heart as a man would hide a treasure of great value, but I did not know why.

The lush mountain valleys and rolling rocky hills are just beginning to put forth buds, showing signs of life. Mountain springs bubble forth in musical notes bringing out its hidden wealth. It pours sparkling cold out to quench the land of its thirst as well as the throats of weary travelers. The birds called to one another with cheerful sounds sending greeting from the boughs of trees and grassland hideaways. If Yah had brought life out of death, He had chosen the perfect time for even nature was waking up from its sleep.

A herd of fleecy sheep on the nearby slope flowed like a white stream down to the fertile plains of Esdraelon to feed upon the fresh sprigs of new green shoots that push their way up through the rocky soil. A hawk soared on feathered wings overhead in wide circles sounding a warning to the bold intruders who rumbled down the dusty paths paying no attention. I sympathized with its frustrations, knowing the feeling well and wondering if the course I had set would end up as the flight of the hawk.

Israel is a land of sharp contrast carved out by many hundred of years of winter rains. Rough knolls jet upward hundreds of feet and then slide away drastically into deep vile gorges. Low weather scarred plains crawl their way toward the horizon and the rugged mountain plateaus beyond which can be seen high peaks. Cities and villages have to be terraced as often as the terrain requires with ascending and descending streets. The beauty of the land on occasions would capture me for serene degrees of time taking the torment from my mind giving me the feeling of oneness with Yah and the land. I could again appreciate Yah's blessings to Israel and know the bounty of life.

It was about the sixth hour when we came to the crossroads where Yaakov's well beckons weary travelers to stop and rest.

"We shall rest the horses here for a while," I called to Yered, "We will have a quick meal and continue."

The procession stopped and he gave instructions to the servants. I had given orders not to rest the horses hourly. I wanted to reach BeitHal, if possible, before dark overtook us. We had traveled relentlessly all morning for I knew here we could replenish our water supply, relieve ourselves and rest before continuing.

Yered, however, seemingly never needed rest. He took this time to unsheathe his shiny sword and take on two or three imaginary enemies to defeat in cunning battle. I watched with delight remembering the days when I too fought mystic foes and defeated many adversaries making quick work of them. Now the enemies are not so easily defeated. I no longer fight unseen foes. I find my battles are in the finding of truth.

Truth? What is Truth, ...the results of knowledge strong enough to build a life upon? Or is it more than that? Could truth simply be the tool Yah uses to move man into His divine will? If so, what will the truth of this Man, YahShua, bring? What purpose or work will it do in my life? Where shall that truth lead Yered or Elsan, or for that matter any of us? There is one thing for certain, when truth avails itself there will be change.

"Yered," I called to him while he was in mid-swing. "Behind you!" He dropped down quickly on his heels spinning around on the ball of his sandals, cutting the air fiercely. "Good move," I acknowledged, "...but, had I been your opponent I would have been expecting that."

"You only say that because you were not behind me," he returned with a grin.

"Maybe, ...but I have defeated you anyway."

"How is that?" he asked putting his hands on his hips. "Well, as you stopped to talk with me your other enemy you were first fighting in your front has run you through." I teased with a smile.

"Not so, Father! My last swing cut him asunder while I turned to strike your enemy."

I laughed aloud. "That had to be quite a feat young Yered, to destroy both enemies with the same blow."

"Not for me! I know the strength of my arm," he smirked confidently. "Besides, ...I almost had him down when you called the warning." Yered proudly sheathed his weapon and came near to me.

"Well," I scoffed at his arrogance. "Since you managed that feat so masterfully, see if you can manage to get this troop to BeitHal before dark."

"I will, Father," he declared. "You will see." He then called out the order and went to his horse that was tied to the wheel of the coach.

We traveled until evening stopping only a short time to refresh ourselves and water the horses. The servants set some folding chairs and brought out the woven woolen cloth to make a covering for us.

That evening as the road brought us to a rise a small band of men was standing under the shade of some large bushes a short distance down the hill. By their motions I could tell they were talking excitedly. When we drew near they began to argue with loud voices, but I could not make out what they were saying. Just as we came near the spot, two of them began to be shoved about by the others.

"Stop brothers!" I called from my carriage while Yered quickly dismounted and ran that way. "Is there not enough death and destruction at the hands of the Romans without Israel tearing at each other's throats?'

Yered came between the two groups of men and poised himself to defend the two who were out numbered while they watched me climb from my cisium.

"Elohim forbid that brethren should fight against brethren in these trying times," I spoke sharply as I came near. "What evil has entered your hearts to cause you to want to bring harm upon your fellows. Has the spirit of Cain come forth in this hour, also?"
The men's eyes fell and they stood shame faced with their heads down. None of them offered to answer or made an effort to rise up against us.

"What disagreement has you gnashing at each other and near to do violence?" I asked after a space of time, and one of the two being pushed around by the others stepped forward.

"It is about the Man, YahShua," he confessed. "In Yerushelayim, we saw Him die upon a cross at the hands of Pilate by the insistence of the elders of Israel and," he pointed at those doing the shoving, "...they say, He was a false prophet, but we say, He was the Son of Elohim."

"These questions have disturbed the heart of every true Israelite who looks for deliverance from the Roman yoke." I assured them knowing the confusion of their souls. "But, that is no reason to fight among ourselves. What is the news from Yerushelayim concerning this Man?"

"YahShua, the Messiah, has risen from the dead just as he said," one of the two, but not the one who first spoke, blurted out with enthusiasm, "Some of the women have seen Him in the garden."

"You would believe the words of a woman over the report of the guards?" One among the others mocked.

"Yes!" He returned in a snort. "I would take the word of any Israelite anytime over that of a Roman swine."

"Sir," one of the others said. "The women saw only the gardener. The guards who were set to keep watch at the tomb say, they fell asleep and His disciples came and took His body away so it would look like He had risen."

Now, the one who spoke first replied. "That is a lie. Roman guards are crucified for falling asleep on duty. It is a story the guards and the chief cohanim made up for the fear that this truth of YahShua would spread even further making more trouble than before His death. He did raise as He promised."

"Lies!" One among the others shouted with a raised fist. "He does not deserve this glory! Leave Him in the tomb where He belongs. BarAbbas and the zealots have taken His body to stir up Israel against Rome and we shall all end up in the tomb if this nonsense is not stopped."

"How can you say that?" The second of the two responded. "You were there when He was teaching, ...everyone of you." He swung his hand in their direction. "You heard His words! You, of all Israel, should remember how His words burned in our hearts and we were filled with the joy of the Adonai, yet now you doubt? How right He was when He said, 'Even if one rose from the dead and went unto them, they would not believe.'"

"What other words did He speak?" I asked longingly.

The second one answered and said unto me, "He said, '*I am the light of the world, but men love darkness more than light because their deeds are evil. The Kingdom of Elohim is at hand; repent and turn from your evil ways and receive me. If you receive me, you are receiving Elohim for He has sent me and we are one and you may be one with us.*'"

"Yes," the other chimed in, "...and He told us He must die, but on the third day He would rise again and that He did. Furthermore, some of the disciples testified that He appeared to them in a closed room and talked with them."

"Then you believe that YahShua, called the Messiah, is the Son of Elohim?" I challenged the one who just spoke.

"Yes," he returned.

"Then where are you going?"

He replied, "To tell that He has risen as He said."

The first stepped to his side. "I will go with you. In the mouth of two that witness, a thing is established."

Then Yered spoke up. "But, have you, ...seen Him so your witness be true?"

The two men looked at each other a space of time, and then shook their heads with some embarrassment.

There was dead silence for some time, then one of those who had been arguing said, "I tried to believe, ...but I no longer know the truth of the matter."

I looked at these men and knew the turmoil in their hearts. "Where are you going?" I addressed my question to the man who had just spoken.

"Home to my family, ...if they will have me back," he returned with uncertainty.

"Can you find the truth there?" I asked.

The man thought a degree of time. "No." He shook his head.

"Then why are you going there?"

While he thought about that I said to the others. "Where are you going?" But they too had no answer, so I said to Yered, "Come we must make BeitHal before nightfall." He nodded and went for his horse while I went back to my cisium.

As we went down the road the men stood there and looked after us. I do not know where they went or what they did, but I believe they parted in peace.

While I pondered the things I had just heard, my mind went back to the times around the fireplace my father

40

would tell us the stories of our forefathers. I always listened breathlessly as he told of the great leader Moshe, who parted the water so the people could cross, and how Yah drowned the soldiers and chariots of Pharaoh in the midst of the sea.

He would tell about Yah giving the laws and how the people refused to go in to possess the land of promise. Then I remembered the story of the twelve spies sent by Moshe to spy out the land. How that when they returned, they carried a large cluster of grapes so large that it needed to be supported on a stay between two men. I thought about how there were, also, pomegranates the size of a boy's head.

"A land flowing with milk and honey,'" the spies said, but there were also huge giants in the land and ten of the spies said, "They are too much for us, we will surely die." While the other two said, "Yah has given us the land. We can take it because Yah will go before us." However, the people believed the ten who discouraged them and they did not go in.

Suddenly, my mind came back to the present and I thought about the two men that we had just left behind and the others who stood against them. Were they right and the others wrong? Maybe Yah was trying to show me that just because many say a thing is a certain way does not always mean they are right.

There was the time all the people demanded a king like other nations around about them. The man of Yah said it was not Yah's will, but they too did not listen. And there was Noah, who said it would rain, but he was laughed to scorn by most of the inhabitants. They did not believe him for it had never rained before.

"Yah," I cried out in the depths of my heart, "...if this thing is of you then help me to believe."

As we entered BeitHal, the streets were dark and empty but there were many travelers who had set camp beside the well, near the edge of the village. I was thankful that at this time of year the days are very long affording us much travel time. I was, also, glad we had good strong horses that could be pushed hard in the heat of the day. We refreshed ourselves at the cistern and I had Benren send three servants to find lodging for the night, although I knew the effort was futile. Yered being youthful and restless went to find the evening entertainment.

Never had I seen so many coming from the Feast. It was like there was something very special about this Pesach. Maybe, they came as I had hoping to see the Man, YahShua. Or maybe, they just felt compelled to come by some unseen force. Whatever the reason even this small village some distance away was so full that travelers set their camps near the city well.

When the servants returned it was as I suspected. There was not room in the inns, so we set our camp beneath the black velvet, star spangled, sky along with all the others.

That night around a common campfire used by all, the talk was about the happenings of the past few days and we heard many things about this YahShua. Some said, 'He was a wonderful Prophet who did miracles and proceeded from Elohim.'

Others said, 'He was a false prophet, deceiving the people with lying wonders to turn them away from the teachings of the elders and the laws of Moshe, receiving His just reward.'

Still others said, 'The zealots were behind it and YahShua was just a rebel trying to incite an insurrection.'

And still others talked about a man named Yhudah, who had led the soldiers to arrest YahShua. How he was a betrayer for he was one of his disciples and an Israelite.

Some were saying, 'There were some members of the Sanhedrin who believed in Him but could not convince the others that He was not an enemy of Elohim.'

Then some spoke of His disciples, Kefa, Yaakov and Yachanan, men of K'farNachum and fishermen by trade. Others told of Him being laid in a tomb in a garden near where he was crucified.

I heard someone say, "The Centurion did not break His bones for He was already dead, but he pierced Him to make sure." If this truly happened more scriptures were fulfilled. 'Not a bone of Him shall be broken.' The words of the Prophet echoed through my mind, and again in another place; 'They shall look upon Him whom they pierced.'

There was much arguing as to whether He raised from the dead or if His body had been taken away by the disciples, as those soldiers guarding the tomb had said. Many believed BarAbbas, and his rebels were behind it all. Some kept insisting that the Man had appeared to some of His disciples.

By the time I went into my tent that night of all the things I had heard only two were agreed upon by all. One; BarAbbas, a convicted murderer was freed instead of YahShua, and two; YahShua was crucified and laid in a garden tomb. There was much confusion and debating about everything else. I would continue to Yerushelayim and see what I could find out about the other stories.

One thing is for certain, if the body of this YahShua was truly stolen, the rebels could use it for the purpose of starting an insurrection that would have repercussions even in Rome itself. The events of this Posach had created the perfect atmosphere. If they moved swiftly while everyone is in the state of confusion, the Rebels could influence many people to rise up against Rome. However, that idea did not set well with me because the people are not trained soldiers as are the Romans, there would be a large slaughter of the people for Rome could send many Legions of heavily armed men.

My knowledge of Yah's ways would not allow me to believe He is for such a thing, much less behind it. If He has truly raised YahShua from the dead, there had to be a higher purpose in it than to stir up the people against Rome. But, what purpose? What were all the miracles about? Did YahShua ever raise a band of zealots? No! Was this Man the promised Messiah or just a rebel with a plan? He had fulfilled some prophecies, but because of my lack of understanding a good deal of them was I jumping to conclusions? Then there was Elisheva's wonderful story, so powerful I could not ignore it. Did He rise from the dead as He promised or was His body stolen? I must know the truth of this matter, and I must follow it to the end, discounting length of time or cost. I am perplexed in my soul and will not find peace until I have found for myself the answers to these questions.

After Benren had seen to my needs, before I dismissed him for the night, I asked, "Benren, ...what do you think of the things we have been hearing about this YahShua Messiah of Natzeret?"

"There are many strange tells, my lord. One would be a fool to believe anything one hears these days. I only believe what I know."

"And what is that?"

"Elohim does not create confusion. That is the work of an enemy."

"Yes, ...and only evil things come from confusion; - bitterness, fear, hatred, anger, turmoil and unbelief." I thought aloud.

"My lord," Benren said after a space of time. "Truth dispels confusion and all its evils."

"This is so Benren, but what is truth?"

"Peace, my lord! Truth is peace."

"Perhaps so," I said thoughtfully. "Perhaps so."

DAY THREE

Daybreak found us setting out again for Yeruselayim and a touch of excitement could be felt among the troop. The hustle and bustle around the well slowed our departure somewhat, but we were soon leaving the small village of BeitHal behind, to face the long narrow road that winds its way through Yhudea's hill country.

The sky spoke friendly tones of a beautiful day, but not without a warning of the heat that it would bring. I was thankful my cisium had a cloth canopy to keep the sun's hot rays at bay. However, that did nothing for the wind swooping down the hillsides parching our lips and drying exposed skin.

Yered came to the side of the cisium after we were well down the road. "Father," he said, turning sideways on his horse to face me, "...we should reach Yeruselayim by the ninth hour unless something happens to detain us."

"Good." I could see the anxiousness in his fair youthful face. He was full of life and adventure, excitement flashed in his eyes like the rays of a noonday sun.

"While we are going you should consider now taking unto you your bride." I said to him. He looked startled at me a degree of time. I had not mentioned this to him before.

"What if I told you... I am just not yet ready for that?" He answered quickly.

"Well..." I mused at him. "I guess that excuse will do for the present."

"That is not an excuse," he defended, "I could have Nebra any time I like." He looked confident.

"She may decide she does not want you," I teased. "You are far to mischievous and there is too much adventure in your heart."

"Not so, Father! She would not want someone dull and uninteresting. I, on the other hand, am exciting, full of..."

"Spare me!" I raised my hand to silence him, and he just grinned with satisfaction.

Nebra, the daughter of Ishbak, had been espoused to Yered since he was twelve years old and her nine. I have seen to it over the years that they were together a good deal of time so a love could enter their hearts for each other and begin to grow. Nebra is a lovely young maiden with chestnut colored hair and hazel eyes. Her mannerism is well pleasing and when she smiles her face glows as the light of a candle. Yered seems to be delighted with her and that pleases her father who has been a friend of the family for many years.

The sun slowly moved across the deep blue sky and as it began its descent into the west, we drew nigh unto Yeruselayim. I had been deep in the study of the Sacred Writings as we traveled and was paying little attention to my surroundings. Would knowledge come with study and time?

"Please Yah, I cried out within myself, make me to know these things. Leave me not desolate and empty, void of understanding." I knew that whatever the truth of this matter was, it had to lie in the writings of the Prophets or there was no truth in it.

Yered pulled his horse up sharp beside the carriage, creating a cloud of red dust to boil around us in angry curls. Coming fast from the front of the procession, the horse tossing its head and prancing nervously wanting to run, but Yered had a firm hand and kept it under control.

"Father," he excitedly exclaimed pointing up the road ahead of us, "Roman soldiers are coming."
I looked and could see a mounted troop of about half a score of men riding in formation of two. "They are none of our concern," I replied, "just give way and let them pass."

"Give way! Give way!" Yered ordered the servants and signaled for the troop to move aside. He galloped to the head of the column again and soothed his horse as the Romans drew near.

I could tell that the one in front, apparently in command, was a Centurion. The scarlet colored lacerna hanging over his shoulders was fastened to the shiny breastplate of his uniform by gold symbols of Caesar. He moved gracefully in rhythm to the beat of his horse's hooves on the hard sun baked ground. This was highly unusual for these were ground troops. What were they doing out here on horses? Dust rolled and twisted into the air in a great stream kicked up by their coming. A horse here and there blew residue from its nose and stared with unconcerned eyes.

When they approached within hearing distance I called out, "Good day!" I tried to sound friendly for I did not want trouble from them.

The Centurion halted his patrol and advanced to the side of my cisium. "Do you know the man, BarAbbas?" He spoke in a hearty voice.

He was a large man with strong arms and a square set jaw, clean-shaved with heavy eyebrows now reddened with dust. His eyes were deep brown, without the hard look most Romans have and I could tell he was tired.

"I know not the man," I replied. I had, however, heard his name around the campfire at BeitHal.

"He is not tall but stout, black hair, with a scar on his cheek." The Centurion drew a line just below the right eye but behind the cheekbone with a gloved hand. My eyes fell upon a blue Israelite robe thrown across the front of his saddle. I wondered what a Roman soldier of his rank wanted with a common garment of that sort.

"No, I have not seen one like that," I assured him.

"What is your name?" He demanded in a voice of authority.

"Timon, son of Philorah," I returned.

"Where are you heading?" He asked. There seemed to be a sudden change in his manner.

"To Yeruselayim."

"You are too late for your Holy Days," he said causally. "You have missed all the excitement."

47

"Unfortunately," I sighed.

"BarAbbas was set free on your Pesach in accordance with your tradition. However, he wasted no time in making trouble at a tabernae, and when some soldiers tried to stop him he picked up a knife from the table and killed one of them. Pilate has offered five silver shekels for him dead or alive."

"I will tell my servants to watch for this man and if anyone sees him I will summon the nearest soldiers immediately."

He had relaxed by this time and seemed very friendly, so I ventured, "Sir, I could not help noticing the robe. May I ask how you came by it?"

He looked down and grinned, "I cast lots for it in a gamble beneath a cross."

"Why Sir?" I asked in amazement. "Of what value is it to a Roman of your standing?"

He shook his head and shrugged. "None, I suppose. It was something to do while we waited for the man to die." Laying his hand on the robe, his fingers worked the woolen cloth, then he laughed. "It belonged to the King of the Yews."

"Who, Sir?" I had not heard this before.

"Have you not heard of the Man, YahShua the Messiah, who claimed to be the King of the Yews?" Suddenly, a scrawl came across his face and he looked stressed.

Instantly the words of the Psalms came to me, "They parted my garments among them and over my apparel they cast lots."

"I am glad these Holy Feast Days of yours are nearly over," he was saying.

"These are trying times for all men," I agreed and found sympathy for him. "Sir," I added after a thought, "would you like to step down and rest your animal. I have some very fine wine and prepared meat."

He looked puzzled at me a degree, then returned, "You would eat with a Roman?"

He was well acquainted with the customs of my people. It was well know that Yews did not eat with a gentile, but for him to be aware of that was intriguing to me.

"Would a Roman eat with a Yew?" I countered, meeting his gaze.

I disliked referring to myself as a "Yew" for I am of the tribe of L'vi. The term Yew is short for Yhudah, only the tribes of Yahudah and Binyamin go by that title, but there are twelve tribes of Israel. However, these Romans keep insisting on calling all Israelites, regardless of the tribe, Yews. It is being widely spread through the Roman Empire and I fear the whole Gentile world will begin to use this word for us and the other tribes will loose their identity over the years.

The Centurion turned in the saddle and called to his troop, "Dismount and rest the horses." He then stepped down looking at me. "I will have some wine."

"Benren, set the shelter and bring us some wine." I commanded before I climbed out of my carriage.

Benren went to the supply cart and in a short time there were some traveling chairs set under a shade made of heavy cloth. The make shift Sukkot was held in place by servant boys. The Centurion took off his helmet and seated himself wearily. The shade seemed to be a welcome relief. Then one of the young maidens, who traveled with us, brought to us a tray with wine in silver cups.

We sipped our wine and said nothing for some time. Yered stayed near the carts and kept a cautious eye on the Centurion's men.

"Did you know the Man, YahShua?" I eventually broke the silence.

"No," he said, watching the wine as he twirled it around in the cup. "I talked to Him once and I was there when Pilate judged Him, ...and at the cross when He was crucified. I saw the way he died," his voice trailed off, "...and," he recovered quickly, "I know very well all the trouble He has caused. My men and I have not had a good

49

nights rest since He came to Yeruselayim. And now," the Roman made a gesture with his hand, "...my men are disbursed over the entire country side, for Pilate has demanded the capture of this zealot murderer, BarAbbas."

"Some believe that YahShua was the Son of Elohim," I informed. "The Prophets have much to say about a promised Messiah. I wonder if He was the one."

"If He was your Messiah, He is dead." He paused a degree, then asked without emotion, "What good is a dead Messiah?"

"Some say He has raised and Elohim may still fulfill the promises."

"I have heard that, also, ...foolish talk," He sighed. "I saw the Man die on that cross and I for one do not believe in ghosts." He thought on that a degree of time and continued. "With talk like that and the temperament of the people being what it is, all I see ahead is more trouble. I do not know where it will all end."

If the prophecies are being fulfilled as I hoped, I knew it would all end with Israel's freedom form the Roman Empire and a new Israelite kingdom, but I did not say it.

He finished the rest of his wine and stood. "I must be going. Thank you for the wine." He handed the cup to Benren. Picking up his helmet, he turned to me and struck his breastplate with the fist of his right hand, giving a Roman salute. Then went to his horse, climbed up and turned back to his troop. I stood amazed. He had given me the highest honor a man of Rome could give. He was unlike any Roman officer I had ever met.

The Centurion rode forward to where his men were waiting and ordered them to mount up, while I climbed back into my cisium. As the soldiers rode past on their way, the Centurion dropped out of their ranks and stopped beside me. He looked down at the robe a degree, then tossed it to me in the carriage. Our eyes met and I saw a hint of sadness in the man. What did it mean? He turned his horse without a word and galloped to the front of his patrol, while I watched them go.

Yered then came to the side of the cisium, "Why was he so friendly, Father?" Taking my eyes off the road, I looked up at him and he, too, was watching them ride away.

"I do not know, Yered," I replied, "...strange, very strange."

He had seen the owner of the robe die. Maybe, he knew something I did not know. "When truth comes, it brings change." I muttered softly, letting my eyes drop to the robe I held in my hand.

"What, Father?" Yered asked.

"We must get under way," I returned without looking up.

There were several dark streaks on the back of the robe. I fingered them and they were thick, coarse and stiff. Blood. It was dried bloodstains. A Roman whip had scourged the Man. Then the words of the Prophets came to mind; *"He was wounded for our transgressions, bruised for our guilt, iniquities, chastisement for us was upon him, with many stripes we are healed."*

Another prophecy fulfilled, surely this was the Messiah. He had fulfilled so many scriptures, but there were still so many questions, so much to be answered.

Yered signaled for the column to continue and I tenderly folded the robe, placing it in the compartment with the scrolls. I pondered for many hours the things I had heard and seen as the carriage wheels sang of the miles they had covered in a dull blend of notes. I remembered that the earth trembled and it was unusually dark the precise day that YahShua gave up the ghost at the hands of the Romans. I remember wondering then if for some reason Yah had become angry with us. I could certainly see why Yah would be angry if this Man was His Son and the Romans had killed Him. Now, Yah is Elohim and He could have stopped it, if He wanted to, but He did not. There had to be some reason He did not want to stop it. This thought

51

sent me back to the scrolls for I remembered reading something in Yeshayahu's writing. It took me some time, but I found it and read it aloud. *"Yet it was the will of Elohim to bruise Him, making Him an offering for sin."*

Sin? What sin? As long as I could remember Israel had made the proper sacrifices prescribed in the Law of Moshe for sins. Now, the words of the two men under the bush who had spoke concerning Him came to mind. Yes, the sin referred to here could be rejection of the Son of Yah. But, no Israelite would reject the true Son of Yah. If this YahShua was the true Son of Yah then why was it all so mysterious.

Yet, the writing continues to say; *"He shall see His offspring, He shall prolong His days. The will, the pleasure of the Adonai, shall prosper in His hands."*

How can this be, if He is dead? Maybe He is not dead, and will yet deliver Israel by this Man, YahShua. My dwindling hope sprang to life within me at the thought, sending a shout of joy into my heart and for a fleeting degree of time I knew peace. If this happened, it would surely have happened in Yeruselayim and I will soon know.

Shortly, we began to see the towering Palace of Herod built into the west wall and beyond that the wonderful walls of the Great Temple. Yeruselayim is the most beautiful place in the whole world to me and I never tire of seeing her. She stands on a hill as a sentinel to all of mankind that the Elohim of Israel reigns. The pomp and splendor of the Temple is His glory, the people of Israel His pride. The gates of the city stand open wide to welcome all that would enter and comfort all whom have traveled far.

Yered's excitement increased as we wound our way to the city gate. The road was filled with those who were going home from the Feast. They seemed almost like a river emptying itself out onto the side of a mountain. Carts and wagons of every description along with those on foot poured out the gates. Some carried their belongings tied to their backs and on their shoulders, while others seem to be bearing no noticeable burdens. The women mingled with the children to keep them moving along and from straying.

Merchants still hoping to sell some wares sat along the sides of the roads calling out their prices to attract the attention of any possible buyer. There were many voices, many merchants, but they all had the same message to spread, last chance, best price. Near the gate the congestion coming from the city was almost impregnable. We made no small stir as we forced our way through the flow almost running down a fellow with a donkey at one point, so I called a halt some distance away.

Yered, who had been leading the way, came to the side of my carriage and followed my gaze to the gate. "Father," he said to me with enthusiasm, "...we should have no trouble finding lodging now for many people are leaving the city."

"Yes," I agree. "Take the servants and the supply cart on into the city and find lodging for us. Leave my driver and Benren for I will not go in now. I will go to the Place of the Skull and try to find the garden tomb of YahShua. Set a servant here at the Genneth Gate to bring us to the inn where you have found us rooms."

"I will see to it." Yered grinned widely, and I caught a flash of adventure in his eyes.

"See to it that you stay out of trouble." I warned with a shake of my finger.

"I will, Father," he returned and called out the order.

I watched until they disappeared into the oncoming throng and then said to Benren who rode beside his son Semone, the driver of my cisium. "Take the north road," I directed with my hand.

Then I smiled warmly as I again saw the generous hands of Elisheva as she used them to express herself while we talked.

I settled back in the seat and thought of the story she had told, while the driver carefully merged the carriage with the resilient flow of the travelers leaving the city.

Towering above the heads of the crowd some distance away, set against the blue dazzle of the sky, and pointing heavenward, were the tops of some crosses on the hill of Golgotha. Some poor souls would soon rest in the arms of Avraham.

In my mind's eye I could see the place already, for I had been there several times in my youth. I know my father would have been very disappointed in my brothers and me had he known what we did. But then, we were as full of adventure as young Yered.

We would sneak away from the Great Temple Court while the Sacred Writings were being read in the hearing of the people. The reading of the Tanakh would last for the better part of the day before the Holy Sacrifice was offered. I am not sure about my brothers, but the restlessness of my boyish spirit found this teaching long and boring. After a short time my desire to explore the city overcame me.

I remembered the very first time I found enough courage to slip through the press in the Temple Court, through the Court of the Gentiles, and then into the city. Soon I realized my brothers, Philip, the oldest, and Yachanan, were not far behind me. They called for me to wait and after much arguing and threatening to tell Father we came to an understanding.

Putting it in their words, "If you are going to roam around the city, then we should come along to keep you out of trouble." They also wanted to explore, but had been afraid to do so. I, being more foolish than they, had found the courage they lacked. So, the three of us set off to explore the wonders of Yeruselayim, making plans to be back inside the Temple Court before the Holy Sacrifice was offered.

Each year, from that time on, when we went to Yeruselayim we would steal away and explore some part of the city we had not explored before. Occasionally, we found ourselves in trouble, but somehow always managed to escape or get away with it.

On one such venture we found ourselves outside the city walls and there was a hill, which from the gate looked like a skull of a man. There were several caves in the side of this hill, in the exact location of the holes in the face of a skull. Well, they looked dark like caves and intrigued us, drawing us like bees to the flowers. The thought of high adventure took us captive.

In wonderment and with challenge in our hearts we started the climb up the face of the hill where the beckoning gapes of darkness stood silent as death. The pebble like rocks were loose and we had only gone a few cubits when a man's voice from further up the hill warned us to go back saying it was dangerous and no place to play.

We squinted in the sun and placed our hands above our eyes to see who was calling to us. I could scarcely make out his form through the brilliant glare of the sun that was behind him. He stood, arms folded, on the crest of the hill. Instead of putting fear in us, the warning just seemed to have stirred our curiosity, but the man could see the whole face of the hill. Reluctantly we descended again to the road and followed it on around and up the hill hoping he would be gone by the time we got to the top. He was, but what we found there took the caves from our minds. There were several thick upright posts about six cubits high with similar cross braces fastened from post to post making a peculiar wooden maze.

We walked all around the looming structure, which covered a good part of the top of the hill. As my eyes flowed up the tall posts, they seemed to spiral and weave in the luminous blue over head. The maze seemed to call to me in unspoken words. I looked at my brothers who, as I, were captivated by the sight. After a degree we grinned at each other. Knowing each other's thoughts, without a word we mounted one of the cross braces.

After a time of climbing around we began free walking from post to post with arms spread out for balance. When we grew tired of that, a game of haptomal began. Laughing and teasing, we twisted and wound through the structure trying to tag each other to be free of the haptomal. Suddenly, Philip catching me by surprise, made a tag on my head that unbalanced me and I tumbled to the ground with a yell. Reaching out my hands to break the fall, one landed close to the base of one of the upright posts. My brothers just laughed knowing I was not hurt for my fall was only a few cubits.

My hands were stinging, but I scrambled to my feet because of my brothers. I shook my hands and looked to see how badly they were hurt and there on my left hand was a reddish brown, sticky substance covering the palm. I had seen it before at the killing place for lambs for a feast and knew it was blood not completely dried by the sun's hot rays. It gave me a strange feeling and my brothers looking at my hand with interest. We looked around and there was more at the foot of each upright post.

That was enough exploring for that day. We raced back down the hill, stopping at the spring pool of Amygdalon where I washed my hand and then we returned to the Temple Court. Several other times we went to the mount in the years that followed, but for some reason or another we never saw a crucifixion or made it into the caves.

Once when we were leaving Yeruselayim, I ask Father about the caves and he told me they were just crevices in the rock.

I was suddenly jarred out of my daydream when the cisium wheel dropped sharply into a deep hole, worn in the road by the many travelers. As we moved with the flow of the throngs, a narrow side road jetted off from the main road on the right toward Golgotha.

"There," I pointed up ahead, "take the side road to the hill." Semone nodded and slowed the carriage to turn away from the main stream and in doing so caused quite an interruption. The on going masses streamed out around us until we were out of the way.

A cold looking Roman soldier stood on the edge of the hill watching us climbing the upward grade leading around the hill to the top. For a degree I thought I had seen him there before. I wondered if he would stop us, but he did nothing except follow our progress with an icy stare. There could be clearly seen, silhouetted against the sky behind him, four limp naked bodies. Rounding the top of the hill we could see they hung nailed to crossbeams that were then hoisted to the top of the upright posts, on a structure such as my brothers and I had played haptomal upon as lads.

Two other guards stood watch to keep the sympathizers from taking down the dying men. A small huddle of people stood some ways off, obviously friends and relatives of the crucified. Some wept while others shouted curses and insults at the "Roman Dogs" who stood unimpressed at their posts.

"Stop here," I commanded and Semone pulled up the horses. They stomped their feet in the air at the smell of death, blew through their nostrils and flounced nervously while Semone wrestled with the reigns to control them.

I climbed slowly out of the cisium, my eyes filled with the scene of misery. Never had I seen the horror of crucifixion and the sight sent a sick feeling through me. I swallowed hard to get control of myself and went forward driven by an unnatural need to know about such a ghastly death. This was the way YahShua suffered in dying and I felt some kind of kindred to this agony. It was so strange and I did not understand what I was feeling.

Upon drawing near one of the crosses, I could see an iron spike protruding from the man's wrists at each end of the crossbeam holding him spread abroad into the open heavens. A crimson stream from the ruptures ran down his arms to mingle with the blood oozing persistently from the flesh torn asunder by a single large spike driven through both anklebones. They were nailed to the upright post, one on top of the other. Gore pooled in scarlet cascades from his pain-racked body at the foot of the cross and caught the reflection of the afternoon sun.

A low agonizing groan came from the man's dry peeled lips and he quivered weakly and made a feeble effort to relieve the stress on his joints. They looked strained and out of place from the dead weight of his form. Quickly, I looked up into the twisted expression of pain in his face. His eyes fluttered while tears coursed down his cheeks to drip from his short matted beard. Losing in the effort, he swayed again, sending forth a new surge of blood from his wounds.

"My Elohim!" I cried out within myself.

It seemed as though every bone in my body screamed out the pain I saw on the man's countenance. My knees weakened and my stomach wrenched sickly. I knew that if I did not turn away from his torment I would succumb to its trauma.

Then I felt a strong hand upon my shoulder. "Step back!" A voice behind me commanded in cold tones. Shocked by the violence and paralyzed by the horror of the scene, I stood wide-eyed and pale. "Get... back!" The Roman soldier ordered again, shoving me aside. He was the guard who watched us up the hill. His face was sober, set with no emotion and in his hand was a large heavy wooden club.

I stood like in a daze and watched as he drew it back and then he sent it crashing with force into the legs of he man on the cross. I felt myself cringe. When he found his mark the full thud of the club did not drown out the loud sharp crack as bone splintered. The scream of the crucified gripped the pit of my stomach like a huge fist. I stopped my ears with the palms of my hands to shut out the suffering, gasped and turned away with much effort. Running to some shrub brush growing on the edge of the hill, I emptied my stomach with violent jerks and stood for some time weeping. No man, regardless of how vile, deserved a death like this.

I thought of the words of the prophets who prophesied about YahShua and knew a bitter anger of despite for these Roman barbarians. Nothing but the treachery of a Roman mind could have devised such an evil. At least YahShua had died before they could break

His bones. I rent my garment, cursed them silently and begged Yah to avenge the blood of the many who had died here.

With the wails of the family member bombarding my ears and the vision of the indifferent Roman's dreadful deed still in mind, I turned slowly for my carriage.

Then I became aware of faithful Benren standing near me. "Here, my lord." He handed me a cup with some fresh water in it. "This will wash the taste out of your mouth."

"No Benren," I assured him taking the cup. "Only Israel's deliverance from this Roman tyranny will do that."

I washed my mouth with some of the water and spit it out in distaste. After drinking the rest of the cup, I handed it back and we turned toward the cisium.

We had only taken a few steps when I felt something crush under my sandal. Looking down, I saw a most peculiar thing. I stooped and picked up a crushed wreath made from the twisted runners of a thorn tree. The few remaining thorns that had not been walked off were covered with dark bloodstains. I cast it from my hand wondering what it was doing here and why there was blood on it.

There came another loud crack and those standing by cried out and their voices drowned out the man's anguished reply. Without looking I knew one of the others hanging on the crosses had met the same dreadful fate as that of the first. I wasted little time climbing into my carriage.

"Let us leave this place of misery," I commanded almost before I found my seat.

As the carriage rolled back down the hill, I tried to shake the things I had just seen from my mind and return to the thoughts of YahShua and finding His disciples.

On the side of the road opposite the hill was a small ravine and on the top of it across the way I could see what appeared to be a man, a gardener by his apparel. He was working with a ground tool beyond a low rock fence.

"Stop the cisium!" I cried out and Semone acted quickly.

"What is it my lord?" Benren turned in his seat.

"Maybe nothing," I returned, but scrambled out of my carriage.

The ravine was not deep and the footing seemed good so I went over to the other side where the stone wall stood. The man spotted me for he was nearby and straightened himself from his work and smiled at me.

"I know," he said with a sigh. "You want to know of the sepulcher where they laid the Man, YahShua."

"Why, ...ah, yes. How did you know?"

"Many have sought to solve the mystery of the tomb," he returned. "Come! I will show you where they laid Him." The man waved his hand to a gate up around a corner in the fence.

The man was waiting and I followed him down a winding pathway through the small garden and there in sight of the very hill where He died was a tomb with its stone rolled away from the opening.

"Did He raise from the dead as He said or was His body moved in the night by His disciples or some zealots?" I asked as we drew near the entrance.

The gardener laughed lightly. "I said I would show you the tomb. The mystery is yours to solve."

I looked at his tough, weather ridden face behind a mass of beard and saw the gleam in his eye that told me that he was enjoying this so called, "mystery". I could tell he was delighted to be a part of it all and did not really care whether it was ever solved. This was probably the first time in the man's life that he felt himself to be important, something besides just a man who tends a garden. I acknowledged his laugh with a smile and went into the tomb.

It was empty and bare. Nothing remained to testify of the happenings that had taken place here. The room was small with a stone slab against the left wall to hold the body. The words of the Psalmist came to me as I stood there; "For thou wilt not abandon my soul in Sheol; neither wilt thou allow the Holy One to undergo decay."

The avalanche of questions I had been holding at bay came crashing in on me and I spent a considerable amount of time in the tomb. I meditated on everything I had heard, read, seen and felt the past few days. There was more than one mystery.

If YahShua was the Son of Yah, and sent to die as a sacrifice for sins, would another come to deliver Israel from Rome? Was the deliverance we had been waiting for so long, not a deliverance from Rome at all, but from sin so grievous that it called for a sacrifice of the very life of Yah to cover? Did Yah intend for His resurrected Son to sit upon the throne of His father David as the Prophets have prophesied, or is the Man just a pawn in the hands of the rebels? Did Yah have something more in mind than what meets the eye in the whole thing, a hidden purpose not made known to us now?

Why can I not rest this thing in my soul and be content to leave the understanding of it all to the scribes and leaders of Israel? Why instead of finding answers, all I was finding was confusion, so very much confusion. Would I ever find the truth of this Man or as the hawk have I just made one senseless circle? I had as many puzzling thoughts as when I started.

When I emerged from the tomb of YahShua who claimed to be the Messiah, the Son of Yah, I noticed that the gardener had apparently gone back to his work up the pathway. The sun was low in the sky and the once brilliant white clouds were now cast with colors fading from fire red and orange to amber yellow. The sun's rays fell earthward like golden threads through the clouds. The air had cooled and the garden was pleasant. I would have enjoyed the stroll back up the path had it not been for the thoughts that muddled my mind. I raised my voice as I came near the gardener.

"Sir?"

He stopped working the ground around an olive tree, leaned on his tool handle and looked at me with a twisted smile.

"What can you tell me about the Man's disciples?"

"Not much." He gestured with his hand. "They are common men, mostly from Galil. It is said they left their families, businesses and trades to follow this fellow, YahShua, for about three years. They, as now, always seemed to cause much disturbance here in Yeruselayim. I heard they sometimes went to Gethsemane to hear Him preach and to pray, but since this happened," he shrugged, "I have heard nothing."

The gardener took a deep breath letting it out slowly and then began to speak. "The chief cohabim and elders persuaded Pilate to set guards at the mouth of the tomb because of the Man's words, for they feared the disciples would take His body to keep His teachings alive even after His death. The guards say they fell asleep and that very thing happened, but His disciples swear He is alive and has appeared to them."

"Did you see a woman in the garden early the morning He reportedly raised from the dead?"

"I saw no one that morning until Pilate sent the Captain of the Guards to find out what happened at the tomb. I was questioned at length and then told to say the disciples stole the body and carried it away."

"I see," I nodded, "Thank you."

"Do you think you can solve the mystery?" He inquired with an amused expression.

I could feel a wrinkle form between my eyes. I had to face the question I did not want to think about. The thought of not finding the truth disturbed me greatly, but I had to be honest, if not with this man then at least with myself. "I do not know, but I must try."

"Why?"

His reply was simple and just as disturbing. I have asked myself this same question repeatedly and found no real satisfying answer. I just know for some strange reason

I feel pressed to find the answers. It is strange, so very strange.

"For the sake of the truth, and because I must know for myself."

The gardener shook his head and a light smile escaped his lips as he went back to work.

Upon returning to my carriage, I said to Benren and Semone, "Let us go to Gethsemane, some of the disciples may be there."

If I were one of His disciples and in view of what has happened I would most assuredly want to go somewhere to pray.

We set out down the road for the garden of Gethsemane three furlongs from Yeruselayim to the east. The outflow of travelers from the north gates had almost stopped as it was nearing evening. Only a few merchants remained beside the road.

Leaving the city wall, we turned east and up ahead some soldiers were doing something just off the road a short distance under a twisted old cypress tree. When we drew near, I could tell they were removing a body from a cord that hung in the tree. A shallow ravine separated the road from a sloping hill where the tree grew. It looked to be no wider than a few reeds and apparently not very deep. Three soldiers wrestled with the rigid corpse and two others stood on this side of the ravine watching. I said nothing to Semone intending to pass on by. I watched them carry the dead man out of the crevice to the horses waiting near the road. I took in the fact that the body was clothed in common Israelite garments.

I must admit this pricked my interest. It was highly unusual for Romans to hang criminals in such a manner usually they crucify them. One of the soldiers who had been watching the proceedings turned to face the cisium as we made to pass by and held up his hand to us. Semone complied with his wishes and drew the horses to a stop. The soldier looked over the carriage with a curious eye coming up to it. "Are you a follower of the Man, YahShua the Messiah?" He demanded to know.

I opened my mouth to reply but found the words hard to form. "I am not!" I managed to say. "What has happened here?"

"We have just found the body of Yhudah Iscariot who led us and the chief cohanim to the Man, YahShua, the night we arrested Him. He has apparently hanged himself. Unable to live with being called a betrayer by the others, I suspect. You are a Yew. Do you wish to claim his body?"

"No, I do not want the body," I shook my head. "It is customary to return it to the family."

"Him?" The soldier looked surprised. "Even if we knew where to find his family, they would not want him after him betraying an Israelite to the Romans. The whole region has knowledge of it by now."

"Then what makes you think I would want him?" I returned a little irritated at the soldier's arrogant attitude. "Maybe, ...you should take it to the chief cohanim and elders of Israel seeing as they take such pleasure in him." I added as a second thought.

This seemed to amuse the soldier and he began to laugh and the others within hearing joined in. I did not find my suggestion the least bit funny, so I just stared at them while they entertained themselves with the thought.

"I shall do just that." The soldier talking with me replied between laughs. Then he turned to the ones with the body. "Put it on a horse. We shall deliver his body to the Council." Then turning back to me, "Be gone!" He waved us away. "I have no further need of you."

As we drove on, I could still hear the soldiers making sport with the idea of returning the body of the betrayer to the elders. I had heard talk about this Yhudah at the campfire in BeitHal. He came to a fitting end as far as I was concerned. What a low depth Israel has sank when an Israelite will betray another Israelite and that to Romans. What is sadder, the chief cohanim and elders of Israel conspired with this man to lead the soldiers to YahShua. I was heartsick and groaned deeply for my beloved country. I could now see as the Prophet had seen when he wrote down the words of prophecy saying, "Yet we considered him stricken, smitten and afflicted by Yah."

If there was ever a sin so great that the blood of lambs and oxen could not cover, it would have to be the killing of Yah's anointed one, the Messiah, the Son of Yah. I prayed that this did not happen and for the first time I found myself hoping this YahShua of Natzeret was not the Messiah. Israel must not kill its deliverer.

Another portion of the Prophetic Writings came to my mind; "Yet it was the will of the Adonai to bruise Him, making Him an offering for sin."

Maybe, this is precisely what Yah had allowed to happen. I have to speak with His disciples. I must find out what the Man taught.

The carriage came to a stop and I found myself sitting in front of a small opening in a rock fence about waist high. Beyond this yellow stone fence were the budding olive trees, which filled the garden called Gethsemane. The sound of songbirds and turtledoves echoed through the tree boughs while the sweet smell of clover mingled with that of honeysuckle that grew on the rock wall. Another time it would have been a welcome sight, but this evening I just wanted to find the disciples of YahShua and talk with them about the things that struggled in my breast. Maybe, it would help ease the scene of tragedy and misery that stood still vivid in my vision. This has been one of those days that I will be glad to leave behind.

After searching the garden and found not even the gardener. I went back to my carriage where Benren and Semone waited for me. The strain of the day and having not found His disciples must have had expression on my face.

Benren came to meet me saying, "Will we go into the city now, my lord?"

In his dark eyes I saw the years of faithful service and loyalty. He was aged now, streaks of gray mingled with

65

his brown crop of thick well kept hair and short beard giving him a look of wisdom. Wisdom I had drawn upon repeatedly.

He had cared for my needs since I was a lad and we had shared many of life's ups and downs. He stood beside me through my mother's death, my marriage and then the death of my first born son. I almost did not make it through that one. Then there was the time when I lay nigh unto death after being kicked by one of the big stallions. I was there when his house burned to the ground and when his wife died. That was a hard time for him, but he had Semone and the other children.

I remember his plea to stay in my father's service the day his debt was paid and he was released. There was no hesitation. He just stated he did not know how to do anything else nor how he would care for his family. He would just worry about me being well cared for if he was not around to do so himself. So, Father honored his request and set him a more than generous salary for his duties. That was thirty years ago and he has been seeing me through one scrape after another ever since.

If I was tired and this travel had taken its toll on me, it must have been extremely hard on this precious man who was many years older.

"Yes, my friend," I agreed, my heart going out to him, "We will rest now."

The gate to the city was a welcome sight as well as the young servant boy Yered had set to watch for us. He waved his greeting with a big smile while we were yet some distance away. Getting through the gate was no problem now for there was hardly any traffic. The streets, however, were still flooded with the endless streams of people.

There were women in embroidered hinations followed by veiled young women in colorful dress with shopping baskets or pitchers on their head. Cohanim in long fringed robes walked along with haughty looks greeting merchants with their wares. Store keepers in light

66

tunics putting away their goods for the night. Beggars in worn or ragged clothing sit on corners and cross streets begging alms from those who pass by. Tax collectors sit in the doorway of their booths counting their coins while men and women in common clothing moved in endless procession up and down the streets. In a profusion of color people of every description went along their way, short ones, tall ones, fat and bald ones, women with child and without. Children scurry about laughing and playing.

Occasionally there could be seen a shepherd with a small sheep. He would dash this way and that to rescue or retrieve the wayward beast. Camels laden with goods led by dark skinned nomads with turbans on their heads pushed their way through the mass of people. A man was struggling futilely with a donkey that was stubbornly setting on his haunches refusing to budge, while others lead docile beasts of burden peacefully down the street.

There were cobbler's shops, market places, mercantile stores, vegetable booths, synagogues, tabernae and Roman bathhouses. There are banks, where moneychangers sit just outside or just inside the doors. Metal working shops, leather shops, porched eating establishments, Inns and hostels, ...many, many of them. Most of the businesses have private living quarters over them for the owners. Then there are buildings with rooms to let out.

There were homes made of fine marble or yellow limestone rock to simple ones of mud and straw bricks that were scatter through out the city. There are few windows in the buildings, to help keep the heat out and usually only one or at the most two doors to keep thieves at bay.

Here as in most town and villages, the wealthier homes are built with several rooms surrounding a central well-kept garden. The children play in safety there and where aged men may sit under his own vine or tree. These houses are large for there are usually several generations of the family living in different parts of the residence surrounding the garden. There are even special rooms for the servants and animals in the nicer houses and in the poorer ones like Elisheva's humble abode the animals get the lower level and the upper level or levels are for the family.

Yered was right, there were plenty of rooms now and he had found accommodations for us at an inn called, "The House of Yhudah", in the upper city near the market place and just off the bridge road.

When I shut myself into my room I found it large and comforting. There was a lounge with a low table in front of it. The bed occupied most of the east wall having the table on the west near a window. Benren followed me in with the sacred scrolls and stacked them neatly on a table beside the large bed near the window. Semone followed him placing the blue robe carefully beside them before going out. The view from the window was of Golgotha on the far left and the Great Temple on the right. We were on the second floor and a cool breeze, which comes with the declining day made the corner of the robe dance to the music of the city drifting on the wings of soft passing. I went to the window and stood transfixed before the beauty of my beloved city and thought of all the wonderful times I had with my two older brothers when visiting here. I watched the city darken and wondered if there was another light besides the natural light going out in this city. My mind was so tired, how could I stand any more. I needed to rest, if only I could find sleep tonight. Yah help me!

Then the door opened softly and I knew by the sounds that Benren was there to see to my needs. "My lord," Benrens voice was soft as his manner, "I have brought you meat."

"Very well," I acknowledged and kept my vigil. "Benren, call the servants unto me. I wish a word with them."

"Tonight, my lord?"

"Yes, quickly now."

"As you wish, my lord," he replied and the door opened and closed again.

My thoughts turned once again to the things I had heard and seen. All those I had talked with and the horrible scene on the mount of crucifixion. The laughter of the soldiers echoed in my mind as I again saw the cold glassy stare of the one called Yhudah. I tried to visualize the man YahShua walking the crowded streets of my beloved city, doing the miracles I had heard of Him.

Once I heard tell, He raised a friend named Elazar from the dead in BeitAnyah not far from Yeruselayim on the east. How in the world could someone who does these things be evil? How could a man who cared enough to heal blind eyes, open deaf ears and cure those who are sick and crippled be worthy of death on the cruel tree?

Time had escaped me for I was still standing there when Benren returned with the servants and brought me back to my senses. Four fine young boys and three young maidens with proper veils.

"Children, have you heard any rumors about the Man, called the Messiah or His disciples?"

"My lord," one spoke up, "I heard this fellow say the disciples were hiding in the cave tombs."

"It is said," one of the young damsels spoke up, ..."He cast demons out of a little boy".

"He came into Yeruselayim riding on a donkey and all the people and the disciples went before Him throwing palm leaves and their garments on the ground shouting, 'Blessed, Blessed is the King who comes in the power of Elohim'."

A timid voice said softly and then grew in confidence, "I heard, He wept when He saw Yeruselayim and pronounced a curse saying, 'An enemy shall lay her waste and her children with her'."

Now they fell silent and after a short while I said unto them. "Listen carefully my children for any further news of this Man or His disciples, and if you find out something tell Semone or Benren and they will bring me word. I do not know how long our stay here will be. It may be quite some time and I will be very busy." I looked at the son of Benren standing near his father.

"Semone, I will hold you responsible for these children." I motioned to the servants with a swing of my hand. "This will be your duty."

"Yes, my lord," he returned with a pleased look, then glanced at his father smiling with approval.

I nodded and turned to my lounge to be seated and Benren said to the servants. "Be gone with you now, and mind your manners."

After Benren tended to my needs and I had taken meat, I again went to the window and looked at the small mellow lights that burned in a thousand windows. It brought to mind how they told around the campfire at BeitHal about the Chiliarch and many soldiers, including the chief cohanim and elders, going out by night with lanterns, torches and weapon to arrest YahShua of Natzeret. A man who did no violence, raised no army, nor did despite to any man.

As I thought on this, all the window lights turned into lanterns and torches and I could see a great multitude with angry faces and hateful looks. They entered the garden through the stone wall gate led by a man with a twisted frown. They laid hold of one whose face I could not see, dragging Him off by force toward the lights of the city. Now the torches and lanterns faded into the quiet glow of window lights.

The rumor about this Man cursing the city and her children did not fit my impression of YahShua. This was very disturbing, the beloved city destroyed! Yah forbid! Curses come out of anger and hate, ...but He wept. Why did He weep? Then the thought came to me, ...maybe, He had spoken a prophecy instead of a curse and the thought of it made Him weep. Just the thought of it sends a stinging pain into my heart, even now. I again remembered the earth trembling and the sun turning dark on the day He died that horrible death. Was it a warning from Yah? A sign of His rejection of Israel as they rejected His son? Was He really

70

going to destroy Yeruselayim? If this happened there would be no throne of David upon which for Him to reign. No Great Temple to offer sacrifices for our sins. What would become of us? A dark cloud descended upon me and the night wind cooled my cheeks moist with tears. I began to pray for Yeruselayim and for her children, but was almost immediately interrupted by the door opening.

I turned as Yered's voice greeted me. "Good evening, Father." His eyes showed the glint of the lamp and his broad smile faded quickly, a scrawl replacing it. "Why has your countenance fallen, Father?" He asked tenderly. "Do not despair, I have news for you."

"That is good Yered," I patted his arm. "It is just that I have heard a rumor that is heart breaking."

"What is it, Father?"

"I have been told that the Messiah cursed Yeruselayim saying, 'She will be destroyed and her children with her'."

Yered's sharp gaze dropped to the floor and he was quiet for a long space of time. "I..., I do not believe Elohim will let that happen." He raised his head again.

"I am sure you are right." My hope was feeble at best. "What news do you bring?"

"I have found a man who made the Pesach for YahShua and His disciples." His enthusiasm returned. "I have, also, met a zealot who knows BarAbbas. He told me some of the disciples are hiding from the Romans with them in the tomb caves. I think he can be persuaded to take us there for a price. Is that not good news, Father?"

Any other time I would have been delighted to hear it, but I was still disturbed about the curse or prophecy, whichever, YahShua spoke concerning Yeruselayim and it seemed as though nothing else was important now.

"That is good news, good news indeed." I tried to sound impressed for Yered's sake and I gave him a warm hug.

"I have also heard some rumors," Yered injected.

"Good!" I struggled to be cheerful. "Sit and tell me of them." I seated myself on the lounge.

He sat down and turned to face me. "Father, I heard that the Council tried YahShua in an illegal tribunal the night they arrested Him and a Prushem named Nakdimon argued His innocence but was overruled. I believe he is a follower, but a secret one for fear of the Council. A chief Cohen and Council member by the name of Yosef of Arimathea gave his very own newly hewn tomb as a place to lay Him. I also heard that when taken to the Romans, they put a purple robe on Him and mockingly calling Him, 'King of the Yews'."

"King of the Yews." I repeated his words. "That was what the Centurion had told me earlier on the road. Would it not be ironic if He really was the King of the Yews? The last laugh would be on them."

"Yes," Yered grinned, "...what an insult it will be when He overthrows them and takes the throne of David."

"Yered, your spirit has overcome you." I shook my head. "What will He do that with? A pitiful band of disciples or some zealots?"

"The young men of Israel will join Him. We are ready to fight to the death."

"Death is exactly what you would get," I assured him. "It will take more than a band of rebels and the arrogance of youth to remove the Roman yoke. Even if you did manage to take Yeruselayim, they would come with hordes of well trained soldiers and what chance would any untrained, undisciplined army of Israelites have against that?"

"Are you saying He will not deliver Israel?"

"I have very serious doubts that it will happen now, Yered. I am convinced something much deeper may be happening here. If deliverance from Rome was Elohim's purpose, why the cross and what about the resurrection? Of what value are they?"

"To stir the people and show the Romans that Elohim is with us. To put fear and confusion in the hearts of the Romans and to let them know we can conquer even if it takes death."

I could feel my spirit rise up within me. "Confusion is upon Israel, as well, wise one, and it has set brother against brother. I see no forces gathering or no weapons being forged. All I see is the evil hearts of the Romans and Israelites likewise bringing death and destruction in the place called Golgotha. Do you not see? Israel has allied herself with the Romans to shed innocent blood and to destroy the Romans would be to destroy ourselves."

I was shocked and amazed at the words that came out of my mouth. I knew I was speaking them, but did not know from whence they came. This is now the second time I spoke without reason. It was very strange and I pondered all the words.

Yered must have been thinking on them, also, for we sat a long time without saying anything. "What is the deeper purpose in these things, Father?" Yered broke the silence.

"I do not know, ...but we shall find out. It is late and we have much to do on the morrow. Get you to your bed and rest for we know not what it will bring."

Yered sighed and raised himself from the lounge. "Sleep well."

"That would be a change," I returned as he went for the door, "Shalom!"

I had just settled in when the sound of a multitude coming down the street aroused me. I rose quickly and went to the window to see what all the trouble was about. Some Israelites were being pushed and shoved along down the street in the direction of Herod's Palace by a troop of soldiers. There were several men and two women, obviously prisoners, lives to be sacrificed to the elohim of death on the cold rock of the skull. One of the women stumbled after being shoved hard by a guard and fell to the stone pavement. He caught a large hand full of hair, dragged her to her feet, and shoved her on down the street. I shall never forget her words nor that of the soldier for they were directly under my second floor window making me well within hearing range.

"I forgive you and will pray for your soul." The woman said in a tearful voice, but there seemed to be no bitterness in her words.
The soldier laughed heartily. "Pray for your own soul, rebel. You will need it more than I."

"I am no rebel and my soul is in the hands of the Adonai," she returned.

"Wrong, wench," He jeered mockingly. "Your soul is in Roman hands." He shoved her again on down the street.

I could bear no more and turned away from the window taking only a few steps when I began to hear singing. It was weak at first but grew in power. A song, ...a song of victory? They were singing a song of victory! That is a strange thing for them to be doing. What victory could they possibly find in being arrested? I turned back to the window and looked down the street where they went. Listening to the words of their song until it faded into the sounds of the night. The song was about love, forgiveness and peace dwelling where love is displayed. About the King of glory and how He makes them to triumph over evil. These must surely be some followers of YahShua. These are the things I have heard He taught His disciples. What a strange power He has over these people that even after His death they still sing a song of victory knowing they will surely share His fate. I have never seen such courage, no not in all of Israel.

DAY FOUR

The morning sun melted the sleep from my eyes and I woke to the sounds of the busy street below. The squeaks of wagon wheels, cracking of whips, and the clinking of metal against metal, mingled with the thud of horse hooves on the cobble streets made a chorus accompanied by the hum of many voices. A rooster somewhere added an interlude and the smell of breakfast in preparation drifted past my nose arousing my appetite.

I wondered what this day would hold and dreaded the barrage of thoughts that usually arrived with my breakfast. I have too many questions with so few answers. I loathe myself for being driven by them and longed to be at home with my family. I envisioned myself there, kissing Sarepta awake and sniffing the fragrance of her hair. The morning sounds there would be that of children at play and the call of a mare to her foal. There would be the smell of honeysuckle from the wall outside our window and fresh baked bread drifting up from the preparation room. I sighed deeply, but alas, I am not there and I must face the day with courage. Courage? I do not even know what courage is. Until I can face the evil hand of death and still sing the song of victory I will not know true courage.

The door opened softly and Benren entered coming to my bed. "Good morning, my lord."

"Mornings are getting harder to face," I grumbled as I sat up. "Listen to your courage, Timon. You are unable to face the sunrise without complaining." I said out loud to myself.

"You just miss home and your loved ones, my lord," Benren responded, "after you have had breakfast, you will find courage."

While he attended to my needs, one of the servant maidens came with a prepared platter and set it down on the table beside the lounge, poured fresh milk into a cup and then turned without a word and went out.

"Where will we go today, my lord?' Benren ask, as a matter of fact.

"Today, you will stay here my friend and take your rest." I took a morsel from the tray. "I will go alone this morning to see the Chief Cohen named Yosef and later Yered and I will search for the disciples of YahShua."

"Yes my lord." Benren picked up the scrolls I was reading last night before sleep came and placed them with the others on the table by the window. Taking the blue robe, "I will see to it that this robe is well washed and cared for my lord."

"No!" I almost shouted and nearly choked on a bite I had just put into my mouth. Benren batted his eyes at me in astonishment. I swallowed and softened my tone. "I wish it left as it is."

"But, my lord, it is dirty and there are dark stains on the back." Benren did not understand. I was always one that insisted on things being clean. Therefore, I was not angry at his defiance.

"I know, but it was His robe. I do not want it disturbed."

"Very well, my lord," he submitted, putting it back on the table. "I will make it my very own charge and guard it with my life."

"Good, now bring my clothing. The day is wasting." He carried out my order without a word, and after I was clothed, he took the platter and went out, only to return shortly.

"Do you wish the carriage prepared and a young man to drive it?" He asked.

"No, I will walk while I am in the city."

"Yes my lord."

Passing through the Gate Beautiful, I dropped a few coins in the cup of a lame beggar that sat there. He had set in the same place ever since I could remember. Once when my brothers and I were coming back to the Temple from one of our adventures in the city, I picked up a small stone, and when we passed, I dropped it into this same man's cup.

It made a loud clank and the man smiled and said, " - Thank you! Thank you! Bless you my child." We snickered and ran on inside quickly. I, to this day, wonder what the man thought when he looked in the cup and found only a rock.

Later my conscience began to afflict me about it and unknown to my father or brothers I sold one of my favorite neckpieces in the market place and put the price in his cup. I do not think he remembers me, but I will forever remember him. I did not confess to him what I had done, but it was sure a relief and a lesson well learned.

Entering the Temple court, I could see that those who sold sacrificial animals and the moneychangers were opening their booths for the day's business. The booths are built of wood along the walls inside the Court that separates it from the Women's Court and the Court of the Gentiles. Smoke rose and curled into the morning air from the huge stone altar in front of the Temple. Stairs ascended to the Holy Porch whereon sits the Brazen Laver full of water. The smell of burnt flesh filled my nose for a Cohen was offering a sacrifice for a man who knelt before the altar. Another Cohen went and began to wash himself in the Brazen Laver. Several other men were looking over some sacrificial animals as the Temple guards stood watch on either side of the gate facing the Court with uneasy expressions.

I went to the guard near me and said, "I would like an audience with Yosef of Arimathea."

"Who are you," he returned coldly, "a disciple of the trouble maker perhaps?"

"I can clearly tell you are not." I came right back at him.

He glared at me a degree and then turned calling out, "Captain of the Guard!" After a short time a soldier came from the wall guard house and hurried this way.

"What is it," he snapped. His eyes falling upon the guard that called him.

"I wish an audience with Yosef of Arimathea." I answered for him.

I have been here often and never seen the guards so sharp and rude. They, also, must be feeling the tension that permeates the city like some evil spirit wishing to destroy us all.

His look softened somewhat. "Who shall I say is seeking an audience?" The Captain asked trying to be polite.

"Timon of Beitorah in Galil."

"Wait here," he instructed.

While I waited for him to return, I watched dark clouds drift in from the Great Sea. It will bring a late rain either this day or on the morrow. I tried to watch a sacrifice and the people milling around the booths where one may buy sacrificial animals to keep my mind from the thoughts that haunted me, but alas, it was no use.

I again found myself rehearsing the things I had heard at Beithal, the story of Elisheva, the words of the scribe, and those of the prisoners brought beneath my window last night. The vision of the limp blood covered body of the man on the cross and the cold dead star of Yhudah shrouded the sights of the Temple Court. Again, I heard the moan and the crushing thud as the big club hit its mark snapping bones under its blow. I cringed and shook the vision from my mind feeling myself shiver.

"Sir!" An impatient voice behind me said and I turned to see the Captain of the Guard standing there. "The one you seek is not at the Temple, but Alexander will see you."

"Is Nakdimon here?" I would prefer to speak with him."

The man frowned irritably and turned abruptly. "I will see." He tossed over his shoulder and went back into the wall chambers.

As I watched him go, a loud commotion began behind me in the Courtyard. I looked to see what was happening and a large ram had managed to escape the shackles of one of the merchants and was running zigzag around the Courtyard trying to avoid the hands of several men who reached out to catch him. The ram was quick and agile, easily slipping their grasp. Darting here and there he managed to elude their every attempt and after a time even the guards joined the chase.

"Meleu!" The boy called and dropped to his knees. Everyone froze in their steps and stared at him as the ram walked calmly up and gave him a little shove with its horns. Scarcely have I seen such trust in men, much less an animal of the herd. A wide grin formed on the boy's face as he scratched the big ram on the head.

"You are up to your old tricks, again, I can see." The boy spoke softly.

While the boy was busy with the ram, the merchant slipped silently up with a rope and quickly dropped the loop over the ram's neck. The ram began to buck and kick, fighting the rope. Tossing his head, pulling frantically against the rope, but the loop closed tight around its neck holding him fast.

"Stop! Please stop!" The boy called out in an agonizing voice. "You are hurting him." The man paid no attention to the boy's plea. The ram continued to fight for freedom and a hoarse breathing sound came from it. "Stop," the boy screamed. "You are killing him!"

The boy's face twisted with pain and reddened. Then he ran at the merchant, but a man intercepted his onrush, shoving him down hard on the ground. The boy was not about to give up that easily. He scrambled to his feet and made another rush for the man, fists swinging wildly. He was not being very effective but a few of the blows landed as intended. The man yelled for someone to get the boy off. His attack was soon over for a guard grabbed him around the waist. Kicking and screaming he was drug away from the merchant with the rope.

The young lad was not whipped yet, however, for I saw him land a directed kick on his capture's leg. The man loosed him to ease the pain from the blow and the boy ran to the choked down ram who's tongue dangled from its mouth. The boy threw his arms around its neck and instantly the ram stopped struggling. He buried his face in the ram's neck sobbing bitterly, but I could see him loosing the rope. A wheezing sound came from the ram even after the boy's trembling fingers loosed the rope.

The merchant came to them and said coldly. "This man has bought the ram." He waved in the direction of a fellow who came near. "Release the ram and tend to your own business." However, it was apparent the boy had no intention of letting it go. "I demand you release it!" The merchant screamed trying to pull the boy away, but he just held onto the ram. "Release it now, or I..."

"You cannot sell that ram for sacrifice now," I interrupted.

"And why not?" The man shot an angry look at me red-faced.

"Because it is injured."

"There is no spot or blemish on it." He looked at me seething in his anger. "It is an acceptable sacrifice and I have sold it to the man."

"Listen to it breath. It is not a legal sacrifice." I argued.

"Yeah! Well, ...you prove the injury to me and I will relent on my sale. Show us the injury," he demanded swinging his arm to indicate those who stood by.

I could not believe this man intended to sell an injured animal to be sacrificed. No wonder YahShua drove them out of the Temple. I could surely understand his motive. These people were no longer doing this as a service. They had turned it into a moneymaking business serving them instead of the Adonai.

There was no way to show an injury of this kind and I could tell the man fully intended to sell it. "Has money exchanged hands yet?" I demanded to know.

"No, but it is agreed!" The man spit at me.

I, therefore, looked at the would-be buyer. "What is the asking price for the ram?"

"A silver piece." The man answered and said unto me.

Out of the corner of my eye I saw the boy raise his head. He looked at me with tear pools still in his eyes and a spark of hope flashed across his face.

"I will give you two silver pieces for the ram as he stands." Both men stared at me, and a light rumble of voices passed through the throng gathered around. While their eyes remained fixed on me, I drew two silver pieces from my purse and held it out to the man. His eyes went from my face to the coins and he slowly reached forth his hand and took them.

The boy's eyes widened and he stood up. "Thank you, kind Sir," he said with a sniff. Looking down at the ram that stood calmly by his side, he scrubbed him between the horns. Then slowly, sadly, lifted the rope holding it out to me with his small dirty hand.

"Did you raise him?" I ask softly as the people began to drift away for there was nothing else to see. The boy nodded his head and brushing aside a tear that persistently clung to his cheek.

"I have no need of him." I said with a light laugh. "You may have him back." A puzzled smile broke upon the boy's face and he lowered his outstretched hand that held the rope.

"Oh, th-thank you! Thank you so very much, Sir!" The boy stammered, bending to hug the ram's neck again. "Meleu and I both thank you so."

I smiled down at him as he embraced the ram and saw the love that had bonded them together and then I understood the trust of the ram. Even this dumb creature had trusted in the boy's love for him. Enough trust to stop running and come to him, ...and men betray each other's trust to their enemies. What has happened to Israel's love and what is the price of silver compared to life, ...even the life of a rowdy ram? I had bought the ram from the sacrifice, but I had given the boy and myself something more than money could buy.

"That was a fine act my son." A man in a dark robe with short hair and well-cropped beard said to me. I knew who he was immediately, for I had seen him often here at the Temple.

"Blessing Nakdimon." I saluted him my voice showed forth the joy still bubbling in my heart. "Pardon me for this intrusion, but I have many questions that you may be able to answer."

"Questions? Concerning what?"

"The Man, YahShua, called the Messiah." I leaned close and said softly.

He frowned and looked around quickly, but no one was close enough now to hear my words. "Come to my chamber and we shall talk there." He turned to the wall chambers and I went by his side. "You have me at a disadvantage, I am afraid. You seem to know my name, but I know yours not."

"I am Timon of Beitorah, son of Philorah." He neither looked at me nor said anything, only nodded.

In the long hall there was the chamber doors along the inner wall. We passed several young boys wearing light tunics with caps on their heads. Nakdimon just smiled at them in their passing and patted one of them on the head. They were boys sent to the Temple to learn the way of the priesthood and to study the laws of Moshe.

We climbed some stairs and on the second level we went into a chamber. It was a simple room with a writing table and chair, two lounges with a table between them and over in one corner by a small table was a low cot. On the writing table were a few scrolls and several reeds for writing. He had obviously been writing something when the Captain interrupted him for he now put the lid on a container of ink.

"Be seated," He offered a lounge and after we were seated he continued. "So, what are these questions that brings you to me?"

"I have heard that you are one of the followers of YahShua. Is it true?"

He raised one eyebrow and looked thoughtfully at me a degree of time, but remained silent. I perceived that he was testing my patience so I just waited and after a degree of time he said, "I know that He came from Foihim."

"Tell me about Him?" I earnestly sought.

"He said many things that turned the Council against Him. He was a hard Man to understand for He spoke in parables. The meaning of most being hidden from me."

"Did He speak with you?"

"Yes. But, even when I went to Him at night secretly so He would not be afraid to speak openly, He spoke with me in parables."

"You spoke with Him privately? What did He say?" I ask eagerly. The things he said to me were very strange and I am still unsure of their meaning."

"Tell me, Rabbi." I pressed him.

He sighed and reclined on the lounge. "I told Him I knew He came from Elohim as a teacher for no one could do all the things He had done and not have proceeded from Elohim. He simply replied, -'I say to you unless one is born again, they cannot see the Kingdom of Elohim'."

"You do not know what He meant?" I was amazed that a Prushen would not know the meaning of something that came from Yah.

"I am not sure." He opened his palm. "I thought I understood, but in the light of what has happened, ...I do not know." He shook his head thoughtfully.

"Did He not explain it to you?"

"I told Him I was an old man and I did not see how someone old could enter their mother's womb and be born a second time. He just looked at me and said, -'Unless one is born of water and the spirit, he cannot enter the Kingdom of Elohim. That which is born of the flesh is flesh, and that which is born of the spirit is spirit.'" Nakdimon paused and pondered the words he had just spoken. "When," he continued, "I asked Him to explain He sighed, opened his hand to me and said, -'I have told you earthly things and you do not believe, how shall you believe if I tell you heavenly things?'"

"That, ...is hard to understand." I reflected. "Is that all He said?"

"He then began to tell me, -'Elohim has sent His Son into the world that whosoever believed in Him would not perish, but have eternal life.' Yet, He himself perished. It does not make any sense." He seemed to be puzzled at that.

"Did He say anything else?"

"Only that Elohim did not send the Son into the world to judge the world, but the world through Him might be saved."

"The world? Not just Israel?" I questioned. "The whole world? I thought the Messiah would come for Israel, to sit upon the throne of his father David."

"That is the way I understood it also."

"Rabbi, if this Man is truly who He claimed to be there might be a higher purpose in his coming. A purpose beyond what meets the eye."

"A purpose that is beyond me at this degree." He sat up. "I can tell you no more."

"What did He say at the trial?"

"He just said, - 'I have spoken openly to the world, I have said nothing in secret. Why do you question me? Question those who have heard me.'"

"That is all?"

"Yes, that was all." He shrugged.

"If He is from Elohim as He said, then why is there such a cloak of mystery upon it?"

"Friend, you have more questions that I have answers," he said with a frown and I knew it was time to leave.

"Thank you for telling me of these things. I will be going now."

"Very well, Elohim speed." He went to his writing table, picked up one of the scrolls he had been working on and I departed.

On my way back to the inn, I went over everything he had told me several times so I would not forget any of it. The Rabbi was right about one thing. I have more questions than anyone seems to have answers for. I thought about the man so willing to sell an injured ram for a sacrificial animal, completely disregarding the Law of Moshe. I wondered about the elders who willingly turned an innocent man over to the enemy to be put to death and by this committed murder, just to quiet His teaching. They had chosen the way of Cain and not to remember that when a thing is not of Yah it will come to nothing and that which is of Yah will stand forever. I wondered how they thought Yah would not see or, for that matter, not care about their deeds.

I took this opportunity to stop at the market place and buy the items Sarepta and Athera had asked me to pick up. I, also, could not resist buying each member of the family a small personal gift. Just as I was about to leave, my eyes fell upon a small hand harp hanging on a post in front of a store. I could not resist it, knowing Miryam would be delighted.

Back in my room waiting for Yered, I thought on everything I had heard, read in the prophets and things I have seen. I rehearsed again the things the Rabbi told me, trying to put them in some form of order. That proved to be a futile effort and I was becoming more confused all the time. The answers have to be in the Sacred Writings. They just have to be. I went to the table and picked up one of the scrolls, halfheartedly unrolled it, and began to scan it. My eyes fell upon a passage and I read it aloud, "Rejoice greatly, O daughters of Zion! Shout O daughters of Yerushelayim! Behold your king is coming to you; He is just and endowed with salvation. I will cut off the chariot from Ephraim and the horse from Yerushelayim: The bow of war shall be cut off and He will speak peace to the nations."

Peace! What is peace? "Where is peace?" I shouted drawing the scroll back in anger to throw it.

In a flash I saw again the little servant's hand and the crumpled dangling scroll. My intended deed then pierced my heart and I recovered myself in shame. Gently rolling up the Sacred Writing I placed it back with others beside the prussian robe.

"Where is Yered?" I ask aloud, looking out the window.

Silhouetted against the northern horizon I could see the tops of what appeared to be several crosses on the mount of Golgotha. The scene there earlier rushed into my mind and, I imagined that on the cross I could see the humble woman from beneath the window and a faceless Man hanging among a great multitude, YahShua and His many followers. In my vision I strained to see the likeness of the Man, but it remained dark, as dark as my soul felt. I knew that the Romans did not crucify women, but in my vision there were women. Possibly because they still suffer death as He did.

I still have such a strong desire to believe YahShua of Natzeret was the one sent from Yah to deliver Israel. The elders of Israel and those who should know say He is a deceiver and I certainly do not want to be deceived. Even the ones who knew Him tell so many different stories I do not know what to believe. I had never met the Man, yet somehow, I feel a strange kindred with Him. A Man I did not even know has touched my life in a very strange way. Right or wrong I believe He was a good man even if He was not the Messiah, He at least thought He was doing the will of Yah. And in this time when so many do not seem to care about Yah's will, that fact alone is enough to earn my respect. ...I looked down and watched my fingers work the fabric of His robe. Standing there in the seclusion of my thoughts I found a love in my heart for the Man.

The door to my room opened softly and I knew it was Benren, but I said nothing. "May I get you something, my lord?" He offered softly.

This was a welcome interlude relieving me somewhat of the stress of my inward struggle, giving me time to deal with the feelings that ebbed and flowed concerning Him. No longer was it enough to know if He were the Messiah. Now I had to know the Man. I had to understand how He could touch the lives of so very many to the point that they could face the Rock of the Skull and sing the song of victory while they were going. If He were not the Messiah, there was something very special about Him and I had to know what it was.

I had to understand His teachings and know what the words He spoke to Nakdimon meant, what is -' that which is born of the flesh is flesh and that which is born of the spirit is spirit.' If He were the Messiah, the Son of Yah, He, and only He, would be born of the spirit. There is no way possible those people, nor I, could change our bloodline and become of the bloodline of Yah. We have the bloodline of our fleshly fathers, but how on earth do you get born again to get into the bloodline of Yah?

Unless, ...one of the rumors is true about His fornicating with the woman named Miryam Magdalene. Their offspring then would have the bloodline of Yah. No, that cannot be what He meant. Nakdimon, those people under the window, His disciples, even myself could never be His offspring. It is impossible, He could just make blood as he did with Adam. There is nothing impossible to Yah? What had begun as a simple matter has turned into something very strange and difficult to understand.

I must stop this! I feel as though I am going mad. After apparently some time, I forced the thoughts from my mind, answered and said unto Benren. "Yes, a drink of cool water would be refreshing."

"Perhaps even a taste of honeycomb and fresh bread?"

"No, just the water."

"Yes, my lord." He replied and I heard him turn to leave.

"Have you seen Yered this morning?" I injected as an afterthought.

"Yes, my lord. He went out sometime earlier and I have not seen him since."

I nodded and looked out the window again feeling myself getting irritated at him. He knows we have things to do. He is probably off with some young men talking up this idea of driving the Romans out of Israel by force. Oh, the foolishness of the heart of the young.

Benren returned with the water I requested and set about trying to make me comfortable. But, his efforts only seemed to agitate me instead of help.

"Benren, I wish to be alone. You are dismissed," I said frowning and knew my tone was sharp.

"Yes, my lord." He said as he turned to leave.

"I am sorry, Benren. I have much on my mind and am somewhat irritated at it all."

"I understand, my lord."

Yes, I suppose he does. He knows me as well as I know myself. However, I do not even know myself that well anymore. So much has happened, and somehow I know it has changed me, just how I am not sure. While I was thinking on this Benren had slipped away and I was alone again with the thought, the questions and the torment.

Suddenly, the door burst open and Yered greeted me cheerfully, "Good day, Father!"
The shock of the door opening shot through me yanking me out of my thoughts. This annoyed me even more.

"It is about time!" I snapped harshly. "Where have you been?"

The pleasant look drained from his face and his broad grin melted to the coldness of my voice. "I am sorry to have kept you waiting, Father. I have been trying to find out about the disciples of YahShua," he defended.

Standing up from my lounge I looked at the remorse in his eyes and my heart smote me. Why should he suffer for the torment of my soul? Is it not enough that I should be distressed without making everyone around me feel my pain? I took a deep breath and let it out slowly.

"Yered, I am sorry," I said with a wave of my hand. "I am afraid all this has made me anxious and easily provoked. There are just so many things I do not understand, questions with no answers." In my mind's eye, I saw again the flight of the hawk.

"Father, I know Elohim has put it in your heart to find out about the Man, YahShua, and I realize it will not be an easy task, ...but His will shall be done. I am sure He will make known to you the answers in due time. I trust that if we leave the finding to Him and just follow the leads, understanding will come. If there is something you are to know He will surely lead you to it.

Trust! Yes, I must trust, as the ram trusted the love of the boy. I turned to pick up my outer robe folded neatly by Benren before I sent him out. That is what Yah was trying to make me understand! That is the lesson from the incident at the Temple. I have worked so hard to understand. Labored in my mind to find the answers and this boy, ...just simply trusts. Yes, Yered is right. That is what I must do, ...trust, I must let Yah find the answers for me.

"Out of the mouth of babes." I muttered almost at a whisper. When I glanced that way there was a concerned look on Yered's face. He must think me a lunatic talking to myself. "Oh Yered," I laughed lightly, "Do not look so anxious! I assure you, ...I am not going mad. I only made myself a promise to heed the advice so wisely given." I said to him putting on my robe. His boyish grin returned along with the sparkle in his eyes.

I was amazed at such wisdom coming from someone so young. This is the advice I should be giving him. I am the one who should be instructing him, but instead, he is instructing me.

"I have labored and struggled with what you seem to just trust into Yah's hands. I am proud that you have not let all this cause you to lose the simplicity of trust." I put my arms around him and hugged him to my breast.

"Where do you want to go first, Father?" He had enough embracing.

We will go see the man that prepared the Possach for YahShua and His disciples." I kept my hand on his shoulder and turned to the door.

"His name is Aquarial." Yered took up. "He runs a hostel near the southern most wall. I think he is a follower, but because he is a gentile and runs the inn the Romans do not think to look there."

I am always amazed at how many people the streets of Yerushelayim can hold. To make our way through them is no easy task. The narrow descending cobblestone streets were alive with men robed in a medley of colors. Women wore fancy bordered hinations with coins dangling from their Kaffiyeh across their forehead. Children played games and merrily chased in and around the masses.

A throng added to the congestion. A little servant maiden on one side of the street sat perched upon a carved wooden pedestal, harp in hand. The music she was playing was sweet like unto angelic voices. Her master was passing around a cup to receive offerings from those standing by listening.

We stopped with the others and listened for a few degrees. While I watched, I could see in my mind lovely Miryam and her voice drown out that of the maiden. I stood transported home listening to the sweet notes and watched her light brown hair cascade from her shoulder as she brushed it aside with a smile. Something bumped my chest and brought me back. I looked at a man holding out a cup so I dropped a few coins in it before continuing on.

A nearby merchant was enticing people into his shop to buy wares and across the way further down the street two young boys were doing tricks. One is juggling some wooden clubs and the other walking on his hands. A small throng of people stood watching the entertainment.

This intrigued Yered and I had a difficult time getting him to come along.

Then near a spot where there was a general opening, a large press of men was intently calling out taunts while others jeered back at them. Blood splattered cock feathers speckled the ground under the feet of those on the outskirts of the press. I had seen this activity before, but Yered could hardly wait to push through the throng's elbows until we reached the object of all the attention.

Two men, each with a fighting cock stood thrusting the cocks at each other. thus inciting the roosters for the quick, bloody, fight to the death. Two servant damsels dressed in scant Egyptian type garments were passing through the huddle taking lots for or against who would win the fight. A few cages made of reeds were stacked against the back wall containing several other cocks. Feathers lost in previous battles were being swept aside by another servant.

Yered's spirit became aroused watching the two men teasing the cocks so that when one of the maidens came by he reached out and caught an arm.

"A denaril on the red one," He said and placed a coin in the basket she was carrying. She looked startled, then smiled warmly and handed him several small round red wooden disks.

She was a lovely Israelite and I felt her disgrace. Her body exposed to the eyes of lust and her face unveiled as one without shame. My heart grieved. Surely the father of this young girl had no idea the kind of life his daughter would have to suffer, or he would not have sold her no matter how dire the need. My thoughts went to my lovely Miryam, such a delight to me. How could anyone sell into service the daughter of his loins? This was beyond me. I shook my head and groaned deeply inside. Then I was rudely shaken from my thoughts being jostled by the excited throng.

The cocks had been released and there was a puff of feathers as the fury of battle began. It was short but none the less violent for each cock had long spurs with sharp talons that struck deadly slicing blows at its opponent. The loose feathers twisted and curled around blowing against our feet as the cocks beat the air with their wings. Leaving lie there only the ones stuck to the stones by their blood and that of previous battles. This continued no longer than a few degrees of time, until the fatal blow was landed. The triumphant cock strutted around crowing its victory tattered and covered with gore while the owner quickly retrieved it.

The red cock had won and Yered pushed in to gather his winnings. He jingled the coins in his hand as he returned to where I stood waiting. I could see how pleased he was at winning.

"Look, Father," he sought my approval, "I have won!"

"What have you won, Yered?" I raised one eyebrow and turned to continue down the street.

"Five denaris, a week's wages," he answered proudly catching my step.

"No," I returned. "You have won blood money."

He frowned, "Blood money?"

"Blood money is cursed, Yered."

"Ah, Father! That is just a myth." He carefully dropped the coins into his bag.

"You will see." I said nothing more and we pushed on through the crowded streets.

There are many inns and hostels in Yerushelayim because of the Temple Holy Days and the great Feasts. They always draw great crowds, but surely YahShua could find room. Why did He choose to take Posach in a gentile hostel, Yews have no dealing with gentiles? This struck me as very strange. He seemingly had many peculiar ways. It was hard to understand His behavior. He was born a Yew, yet He took Posach under a gentile roof?

"There!" Yered exclaimed splintering my thoughts. He pointed up the street. "There is the hostel I was told about."

I followed his indication and saw a large three-story inn built in the style of the Greeks. Great columns and pillars around about a wide covered porch prominent in that type of construction. When we drew near a sign on the building read, "The Shawan".

In front of the hostel several servants were packing animals, carts and wagons for their trips home. One servant was having some difficulty with the wheel of a wagon that had given way under the weight of the goods piled upon it. I assumed it belonged to a merchant for no one family would ever need so much of the same type of goods.

There were several steps ascending to the arcade porch of the building with a small cluster of men standing on them talking. I made a conscious effort to go up the steps near them hoping they were talking about YahShua. They were, much to my disappointment, discussing the price of a cart. A young servant girl on the porch with long raven hair busied herself sweeping with a hyssop broom. Two well dressed, small boys came dashing down the steps laughing and chasing each other. They ducked under the arm of a man on the top step and ran right between Yered and me with a child's unconcern.

When they darted past, Yered made a swing at their behinds with his sandal clad foot, but much to Yered's surprise the supporting foot slipped on the step and the momentum of the swing landing him bone jarring hard on the step. His face went ruddy replacing his teasing smirk as he scrambled back to his feet.

The two boys, unaware of the incident, raced on down the steps playing, "catch me" around the wagons and carts. Two of the men talking about the cart looked up the stairs at Yered, and the shy servant girl, giggled softly reddening his face the more.

Inside the Hostel we found ourselves standing on highly polished red stained tile with a yellow likeness of the mid-day sun bursting forth, on the floor in the middle of this huge atrium. There were Greeks, Romans, Hitites,

Egyptians, Persians and others milling around and the smell of fresh baked sweet delicacies filled the room.

The ceiling was high with a richly colored tile depiction of a red and gold chariot pulled by high-spirited white horses wearing red and gold barring. A Greek warrior driving them into battle with his blue sagum angrily fluttered in the turbulent white clouds that swirled around the chariot framing the mural.

There were balconies with white marble columns around the mural on the second and third floors. A long winding staircase reaches them with travelers ascending and descending on it. Between the arched columns built into the walls around the room were other murals portraying many Greek conquerors in scenes of battle.

"Father," Yered said softly, "...while you talk with the man I will be looking around and see what rumors I may hear."

"No," I disputed. "You will be filling your belly with the sweet delicacies of Rome." He seemed never to get enough to eat though meals were always bountiful.

He smirked, winked and turned away into the crowd without a reply.

I asked to speak with the owner of the Hostel and was greeted by a Cretan gentile in a hination richly embroidered with gold around the edges.

"May I help you, Sir," he asked pleasantly.

"Are you Aquarial?" I inquired.

"Yes, that is my name. What do you want with me?"

"I would like a private audience with you, Sir."

"Very well, follow me." He led the way and we entered a small alcove where there was a writing stand and a lounge. "I noticed by your speech you are a Greek speaking Yew. We can speak here," he opened a big wooden door carved with Greek arches once inside he closed us in.

"I am Timon of Beitorah. I understand that YahShua, called the Messiah, and His disciples took Pesach here."

"Perhaps. Why do you ask?" His hard gray eyes studied my face.

"I would like to find some of His disciples and talk with them. Are you one of His followers?"

He was silent while he tried to read my soul and I waited patiently, meeting his gaze without a flinch. "I have only heard of some of the things he spoke," he stated flatly and waited.

I was eager to hear what He had said. "Please tell me what He spoke about. It will go no further. I know it is a dangerous time for followers, but I must find out if He was the Messiah and if He has risen from the dead as He promised."

The hardness of his eyes softened and he smiled slightly. "I do not know the answers to your questions. I heard He spoke in the Temple telling stories."

"Tell me, please," I begged eagerly.

"I am told He spoke of a man who bought a field because of the treasure hid in it. Another story is about a steward who knew he would lose his position and he went out and made deals with the people that owed the master of the house money so he would have those he could call upon for help later." The liquid pool of his eyes caught the light of the lamp as he told it with pleasure.

"Then," he was saying, "...some P'rushim and Scribes came to Him and asked, 'Is it right to pay taxes to Caesar, or not.'

"What was His reply?" I leaned forward not to miss a word.

"It is said he replied, 'Why are you testing me? Show me a coin,' and when one of them handed Him a coin, He looked upon it turning it over in His hand.' Then He was said to have asked, 'Who's inscription is on this coin?' and when they replied, 'Caesar's.' He told them,

95

'Render to Caesar that which if Caesar's and to Elohim that which is Elohim's'."

Then began He, also, to upbraid them, saying, 'Woe to you scribes and P'rushim, hypocrites!' He told them of their sins. They were indignant and angry, but did nothing because the people held Him as a Prophet."

"Is He the Messiah?" I asked almost breathlessly.

"I thought so, but Elohim allowed Him to die. This I do not understand."

"Elohim must have a greater purpose in Him than we realize." I returned thoughtfully, more to myself than to him. Then I asked, "Did He raise from the dead?"

"I have heard that, but, have also heard that the disciples stole His body to make it look that way."

"What are your feelings on the matter?"

"If He is alive He will present Himself in time. If not..." he shrugged.

"Yes, ...I suppose you are right. Do you know where His disciples are?"

"Some are hiding, others have gone back home to Galil. That is all I know."

"Galil? Humm, ...thank you! I will take my leave now. You have been most helpful." I made my way to the door. "One other thing," I said, looking back at him. "Why do you suppose He came here to take Posach instead of going to His own people?"

The Hostel keeper looked thoughtful a part of a degree. "By the time of the Posach, the chief Cohanim and P'rushim were looking for Him diligently. I supposed He just wanted to take this last meal with His disciples without being disturbed. It was a great honor to have Him come to me."

"Of course, a great honor."

When I emerged from the Hostel the sun had fled from the face of man and hid itself behind the dark clouds that came rolling in from the Great Sea. Cold bursts of wind made dust, bits of straw and debris dance across the street below and twist and curl up onto the servant's fresh swept porch. On the top porch step in front of the door, Yered sat awaiting my return, the smell of fresh baked goods upon him.

"Well, have you eaten your fill?"

He stood promptly, "I did not hear anything new," he reported, trying to avoid my question, but I pressed him.

"Was it satisfying? Better than Israelites make?"

"It was tasty, Father," he sighed. "But, nothing gentile can be as good as something baked by an Israelite," he confessed. "Will we go see BarArin now?" He asked with a sheepish look.

"Yes," I was satisfied. "A rain is coming, let us hurry. Where do we go to find this zealot?"

"To a tabernae near the Old Pool. If BarArin is not there, he will be before long."

This place was in the Lower City, so we worked our way through the winding down hill streets. The clouds churned and boiled out threats and warnings of impending rain. A woman in loud apparel strolled our way, her long flowing hair blew around a slim lovely face. Her neck was adorned in gold and bracelets of silver charms dangled from her wrists.

"Looks like rain," she said boldly. She looked up into the sky then back at us. "I will offer my hospitality for a price. Would you or the young man like to come in?" She showed a garden gate at the side of a building with her hand.

It took no expert in human nature to understand that she was offering herself to us for a price. I looked away intending to ignore her, but Yered being innocent stopped by her saying, "We have business over by the Old Pool."

"Well, ...you will pass this way on your return. I will be glad to wait for you." She enticed with a jester of movement.

I was about to reprove her when someone up ahead of us called, "Romans! Roman soldiers are coming!"

Yered looked at me quickly and the harlot ran through her gate and slammed it shut. I watched her disappear and then turned to continue up the street.

"It is none of our business." I waved it away. "They mean nothing to us."

The loud rhythmic clank of iron horseshoes against the stone pavement could now be heard. As we proceeded, a patrol of about a half score of Roman Cavalry came into view. The Centurion in the lead rode with head held high, proud and erect. His scarlet lacerna curled in the angry wind pulling and tugging garments in its fury. A few brave souls spit insults at them while others stood breathless and watched, making our going even more difficult.

"Halt," the Centurion called out pointing in our direction. "Halt, there! You, Timon of Beitorah, halt!"

When I heard my name, I froze in my steps. How did the soldier know my name? A rumble of "oohs!" and "aahs!" ran through the crowd. I saw Yered tense and his hand went for his sword, but I caught it while still on the hilt. Yered's eyes met mine and I shook my head slightly. His foolish courage was about to take on a whole patrol of not so imaginary enemies. I felt his hand relax its grip, but the expression on his face changed not.

"Come forward, Timon!" The Centurion demanded with authority. I patted Yered's hand lightly and turned to the man on the big gray horse and began to press through the people to draw nigh unto him. I sensed the tenseness in the crowd and the soldiers alike. The slightest movement could be interpreted as an insurrection and many innocent people standing here could die.

"Please Elohim," I breathed, " ...do not let any die here because of me."

When I drew near where I could see and the shadows of the dark sky was removed from his face, I recognized the Centurion I had met on the road.

"You have been asking questions about this YahShua of Natzeret," he stated and shifted in his saddle. "He is dead and I suggest you not try to stir up the dead.

Has not this Man caused the people enough trouble. Leave it be, man! This is my warning. Leave it be!" He made the words loud and clear so those who stood by would hear and take heed.

I looked deeply into his eyes and saw compassion. Then I understood why this man was different from the one at Golgotha. It was now evident that he really loved the people. He could have just gone on by and let the mantle fall where it will. Instead, he has tried to stop the slaughter of Israelite lives in the only means available to him. I nodded, not so much for my intentions, but to let him know I understood his motive. I would have taken his hand in friendship, but it was impossible there. So, I determined to do it if ever our paths met again.

He turned, signaled to his troops, and they continued on down the street. A whisper raced through the crowd carried on the wind like a bird in gliding.

Yered released his breath with a slight smile as we turned to move one. The people who stood around about moved aside so we could pass through without hindrance.

After we were out of the people's hearing Yered said, "Father, will we not go see the zealot now?"

"It is better to obey Elohim rather than man." I said and was astonished.

An unusual feeling came over me as I spoke. I had no idea where the words came from, but they sounded good even to me. This is now the third time I had spoken something before I thought it. This puzzled me greatly and I wondered if I too had become possessed with something.

"But you nodded in agreement to the Centurion's warning." Yered reminded.

"No, ...I agreed he was right and that I could understand why he spoke it. I did not open my mouth to say, I will not try to find out about YahShua. This, as you have said, Elohim has put into my heart, ...and this I will do."

"We may have to offer the zealot a bribe," Yered informed. "I hope you have brought sufficient." He smiled and felt his bag that hung from his belt. He was proud of his winnings.

The tabernae was dimly lit with a few oil bowls and the smell of wine and fermented drinks perfumed the air. The place had only a few souls and contained several small tables. A scantily clothed maiden with head tilted slightly and one hand resting on her hip stared at us. The low murmur of voices ceased when we entered. All eyes turned to greet us with icy glares.

Yered grinned at the woman and nodded. "Bring us a cup of fine wine, Claudia," he called in a pleasant voice and waved me to an empty table.

"As you wish," she returned gaily.

At this, everyone in the place went back to what they were doing. "BarArni is not here," Yered said softly looking around, "but I am sure he will be here shortly."

The table was of plain wood with stains here and there. The result of spilt drinks, maybe, even spilt blood. I was uneasy with the feel of this place but would tolerate its offensive smell and the rude language of the people if it meant finding some of the disciples. When the servant girl came with the wine she reeked with the smell of sweet spices. It was a welcome relief covering the stench of the tabernae.

"Ten mites," the girl said warmly. She smiled down at Yered batting her long painted eyelashes. I did not like the way she looked at him as he was espoused to the daughter of Ishbak and I was sure this one did not care. Yered reached for his bag pleased to spend his winnings.

"I will pay it." I said to him quickly and drew out its worth for the wench.

He had not yet learned the lesson of ill-gotten gain that sires greed in the heart, so I did not want him encouraged to spend it. When we were alone again I said low, "I hated even the thought of this place and I certainly did not like the way that wench looked at you."

"Ah Father, …the damsel means nothing. She is just doing her chore. Do not pay her any heed," Yered returned lightly.

"Just do not forget who you are," I warned and he gave me an assuring glance.

"Father," Yered spoke after a degree of time. "I did learn one thing while at the gentile hostel. I do not know how important it is, but the one called Yhudah, the betrayer of Messiah, received payment of thirty pieces of silver."

"The price of a slave!" Was that all He was worth to man, thirty pieces of silver? The thought brought me pain. He had done so many wonderful things. Even if He was not the Messiah He was not wrong. It is never wrong to do good or to have pity.

The light patter of rain could be heard on the roof of the tabernae now and a low rumble like the far away sound of many chariots running to battle reached our ears. No one seemed to notice the leak that splashed onto the floor near the wall where a table with several pitchers set containing wine and strong drink prepared for pouring. Finally, the damsel put a pitcher under the dripping menace and wiped up the pool that had gathered there.

It seemed like eternity we sat in this repulsive place. Suddenly, the sound of a tambourine split the air drowning out the low drone of voices and the constant beat of the rain. The wench began to twirl and sway to the rhythm as she held the instrument high over her head, stroking it to bring forth its sound. The nakedness of one leg up to her thighs was clearly visible. Enough to make the men burn with lust while displaying her body with movements. I shook my head and turned my eyes away from her. I was ashamed for her and thought of Miryam now beginning to bud into womanhood.

I knew my father would openly denounce me and Sarepta would be astonished, hurt and unapproachable if it were known unto them that I was in this place. I was thankful we were a long way from home and no one here knew my name. I wrestled with the guilt of even being in this place while Yered watched the wench with awe. This made me somewhat irritated at him and I wondered if he had even given Nebra a thought. If these are the places he comes to find entertainment I will put a stop to it immediately. I watched his face and there seemed to be no shame in it.

"Yered," I said sharply, "…is this where you come to find adventure?"

"What, Father?" He forced himself to look away from the young woman. He did not even hear my words. Now I was really angry with him.

"I said..." My voice raised loud and drawing unpleasant looks from the others. When I noticed it, I toned down my voice, but loud enough for him to hear. "Are these the kind of places you come to for adventure?"

The pleasant look on his face melted and his expression sobered. "No, Father! But, when one hunts a certain creature, one goes where they can be found. I came here because I heard rebels have been seen here. I met Bararin here and we have to win his confidence before he will talk with us. I have never been in a place like this before."

"And I hope never again," I added. "I surely have no wish to be here. I feel it is an insult to my fathers and Sarepta."

"I am certain Nebra would understand although she might dislike knowing of it. She knows I would do nothing to bring shame upon her or our families."

I nodded and my anger began to subside. Impatience was ready to overtake me when Yered's face brightened. "There is BarArni," he declared unto me and went to meet a suspicious looking man at the door.

They talked a few degrees and then Yered led the way to our table calling over his shoulder, "Claudia, bring BarArin a drink."

The man was young, almost too young for the straggly growth on his face, and the uneven cut of his hair gave him an unkempt and dirty look.

"Father, this is BarArni. BarArni, my father." Yered said, before he seated himself at the table.

"Shalom." The man nodded while sitting down. His eyes were close together and very observant. Making you want to grip the top of your purse tightly. The clothes he wore were of the most common kind, wrinkled and dusty. The rain had caught him and this added a rather wretched look serving only to accent the distrust his appearance already stirred in the heart.

"I understand you can take us to some of the disciples of YahShua," I said, anxious to be done with him and this place.

"Well that depends," he returned and moved his fingers slightly. He was every bit a thief.

If the master of the house was only paid thirty pieces of silver, then this one was worth much less. "I will pay you ten silver pieces to take us to the disciples."

He looked eager, but restrained himself. "I do not know," he hesitated. "You might be a spy come from Pilate."

Yered answered this accusation before I could open my mouth. "We are not Romans," his words sounded with resentment, "and we would never betray an Israelite to one of them."

His answer was adequate so I added nothing to it.

"I will have to speak with Barabbas of this." The zealot informed. "He is our leader, you know."

Besides being a thief, the man is a liar. He has no intention of sharing this sudden wealth with Barabbas or anyone else for that matter. I could tell if we did business with this one we would have to cover ourselves well for I was sure he would run out taking everything we had given him at the first opportunity.

The man leaned forward and said further. "I do not wish to offend you, …but I am afraid in these trying times we just cannot be so foolish as to take your word for it." The wench appeared with his drink and Yered pulled the coins from his bag and gave them to her. I sighed and

103

looked at my cup. A lesson in greed would soon be his. "However," the man said after the wench went away, "if you could, maybe, show us something in good faith, it might help persuade him."

Something in faith, Avraham's bosom! More like, something in my hand. "How do we know you even know His disciples? How will you show us good faith in return?" I inquired sternly.

"Hum!" He patted his fingertips together. "Some news maybe! Yes, ...I will give you some news." He took a quick sip of his drink.

"What news? Give it to me that I might see its worth, and if it is sufficient then I will give you five pieces of silver now and five others when you take us to the disciples."

His eyes narrowed and the eager smile faded somewhat but returned quickly. "Ask me a question."

"Which disciples are there with you?"

"Martityahu and Bartalmal," he returned pleased with my question. With the quickness of his answer I did not doubt it. "Well, " his face twisted slightly, "...there are some women too, if you want to count them." He volunteered.

The second mile! I was impressed. "Is Miryam Magdalene there?"

"No," he lifted the corner of his mouth and tilted his head slightly. "I think she returned to Beitanyah, to her brother's the house." Another quick answer and with the confident look that followed I was convinced that this, also, was true.

"Very well! But, ...one more question." I added quickly. "Have you any knowledge of Yhudah Iscariot?"

"Yes," he returned immediately. "He was a Zealot once."

This answer took me by surprise. YahShua had chosen to make a rebel one of His disciples? Somehow I was a bit dismayed. Why did He make a thief and robber a disciple? Surely, he knew what he was.

"Tell me about him." I demanded, using his greed against him.

"He was well known among us and had fought the Roman dogs as well as we until he started hanging around with Shimon and this YahShua. Then, one day he came telling us that this YahShua was the long awaited Messiah who was preaching the Kingdom of Elohim is at hand."

"Who is Shimon?"

"He was one of us also until he began to follow the supposed Messiah."

I nodded and waved my hand in a casting motion, "Go on! Go on!"

"Well," he twisted his face in a peculiar upward lift of the corner of his mouth. "According to Yhudah He would soon overthrow Rome and bring back a throne in Israel. We knew this Man to be causing a big stir among the elders, but we thought Him to be just another Messiah who would, as He did, meet the same fate as the others." He took a drink from his log and then continued.

"Later Yhudah came to us again and told us we were wrong trying to overthrow the Romans by force. That Elohim would use His Son, YahShua, to do it and we should stop fighting and follow Him. No one took heed to his words, but was amazed at the change in him. The next time we saw him he told us, YahShua will reveal Himself before the Posach. Two days later he returned again and talked privately with Barabbas. He seemed to be bothered by something, but still argued with us about our plans." The Zealot looked thoughtful a degree, nodded and continued. "The last time anyone saw him was the day after Pesach. He seemed very upset and had been drinking. He kept murmuring something about not understanding why the Adonai let the Romans take Him."

"His words were, 'I was sure when the Adonai saw they were going to take Him, He would call for His angels and bring in the Kingdom of Elohim'."

He drank again from his cup and removed a trickle on his lip with the back of his hand.

"We jeered and laughed at him," BarArni confessed, "teasing him about how the delivered of Israel was not even able to deliver Himself. Yhose asked him if he had spent the money for betraying his Adonai on the adulteress woman that traveled with them. He got real mad and yelled curses at us and ran away. Later we heard he hanged himself." The rebel shrugged. "I guess he could not live with what he had done."

There was no reason to doubt this story either. If he was a zealot he did exactly what a rebel would do. He tried to force the hand of YahShua to bring in the Kingdom and when it failed, seeing what had befallen the King of Israel, he could no longer bear his guilt. I wondered what became of the money. Did the soldiers who found his body take it? Did he squander it as the rebels teased on harlots and riotous living? I could not believe he had done that as grieved as the man seemed. Surely, it has fallen into evil hands, likely even into the hands of the man who sits before us.

Obviously, Yhudah really loved YahShua for it to drive him to his death or he would have been content with the money. Now the bitter anger in my heart against the man was eased, for this told me something about him. He did not do right in betraying YahShua to the Romans, but now at least I understand his motive. It was not actually the money he desired so much as was to see the Kingdom established. He must not have understood the deeper purpose of Yah, either.

"It is worthy. I will give you five silver pieces in good faith but," I pointed a warning finger at him. "...If you betray me, well... I will give you three days. If by then you have not contacted me, I will know you have betrayed me, and believe me, your fate will surely be worse than that of Yhudah."

He rubbed his hands together and his eyes watched carefully my every move as I took out five shekels of silver and slid them across the table. But, before removing my hand, I added the second warning. "You can find me at the

106

House of Yhudah. Just tell one of my servants when and where we are to meet you. Remember, …three days."

"I will remember." He assured me picking up the coins with trembling fingers. Then looking up at me with those cunning eyes. "Three days," he repeated. Gulping down the remainder of the drink he had been sipping, he arose and departed.

"Look, Father," Yered pointed excitedly, "the bow of Elohim."

"Yes," I nodded.

My mind raced back over the years when I sat in my chamber studying. Yered and Elsan came to me there with excited enthusiasm. Nothing would do them except to lead me, one on each hand, out onto the porch at the back of our home. There to show me their discovery of the sign Yah gave Noach, the man of Yah, hanging high in the blue expanse. I can still see their faces as I set them one on each knee and told them the story of how Yah set His bow in the eternal heavens. About covenant and the promise not to destroy the earth with waters nor every living thing upon it for the sake of man. I have since ceased telling them the story but each time I hear the excitement in someone's voice or see a child pointing at a bow when it appears, I remember the first time they discovered its beauty. I smiled to myself as we started on our way.

The wagons, carts and beasts of burden splashed the water from small pools that had gathered in the low places on the cobblestone streets. Our feet soaked up the moisture splashed upon them by our going and felt cool and refreshing.

Children stood with upturned faces, mouth open, catching the drops of moisture that fell from the ledges of building and porch tops of shops along the streets. A small boy sat in one of the puddles in the road splashing water with the palm of his hand and giggling with delight when it splattered his face. His game was cut short, however, for his mother came quickly and snatched him from the pool as an angry man leading a donkey drawn cart shook his fist and threw curses at her for allowing the child to hinder his progress.

It is a sad thing when bitterness and hatred have so overcome a people that the simple act of a baby boy brings curses and railings instead of smiles of pleasure. What has become of my people? My heart grieved and I wanted to grab the man by his robe and shout into his face, "Harden not your heart against the young and babes least you incur the wrath of Yah." ...Wrath of Yah? Now it hit me like an unseen enemy that lies in wait to subdue, the curse of the Man, YahShua, as He entered Yerushelayim. Curse? No, ...not a curse, I shook my head, ...a Prophesy? Yes! A Prophecy! No wonder He wept. I struggled not to weep for my beloved city and this people myself. The hearts of the people have become evil, ...exceedingly evil, so evil, perhaps, that even the blood of bulls and rams will not cover it. Yah forbid! I shook that thought from my mind.

DAY FIVE

Somewhere in the distance, a cock greeted the dawn and the sun kissed the purple haze reddening its cheeks and smiling bright streamers of gold. It had been a long time since I took to the roof and became one with the wakening of a day and this promised to be a bright and cheerful one. I turned toward the Temple and did my devotions with a thankful heart. It had been some time since I found my heart lightened and unburdened. I was sure the peace I found was a gift from Yah.

Last evening when I retired the sky was still showing signs of the angry clouds that wept out its unrest upon the beautiful city. There had been a few good rumors the servants related to me. I wondered if I would ever find the disciples and if I did, would they know anything more than the confused followers I have already talked to? Would I ever solve the mystery of His resurrection or the meaning of the words He said to Nakdimon? Will He yet deliver Israel and sit upon the throne of His father David. Wait! His Father would not be David, if He were the Son of Yah. Maybe, He was trying to tell us His throne would be in the Kingdom of Yah, not in Yerushelayim. This was a new thought. One well worth pondering. What if His kingdom were not of this place but elsewhere? That would explain why Yhudah could not force His hand. This is fascinating! Perhaps, this is the higher purpose. If so, where is the Kingdom of Yah and how does one get there? How indeed? Now the words of Nakdimon came swiftly to me like a dove in flight. "Unless you are born again you cannot see the Kingdom of Yah."

But, how do you become born again? I frowned. "No! I will not let such heavy thoughts spoil the beauty of this daybreak." I scolded myself, "Trust, you unbeliever! Just simple trust." I struggled to bring my mind under control, but quickly lost the battle. Would the zealot take us to the disciples? Was YahShua of Natzeret the Messiah?

Did He rise from the dead or did His disciples steal His body? Were BarAbbas and the rebels behind it all? Would Yah destroy Yerushelayim and her children? Was I going mad? "Yah in Heaven! So many questions, so few answers." I cried out from the deep. Three days is a long way off.

What shall I do? There is one thing I can do. I will go to the Great Temple and offer the proper sacrifice lest I, too, become sinful in my heart and displease Yah. I will beseech Yah for Yered that he will keep him, for he has wondering eyes. Yes, ...this is what I will do.

Now, the Temple Court was quiet, still very early in the day. "I will buy a sacrifice for Yered and myself, but not from the man who tried to sell the wounded ram less my sacrifice becomes an abomination." My purchase secure, I sought a Cohen to administer the sacrifice. There was one, Alexander, of the ninth year. He stood by the altar his hands folded in meditation.

"Rabbi," I interrupted him. " I have need to offer sacrifice."

"For what sin, my son?" He asked without change of expression or opening his eyes.

"For the sins of my mind and that of my sons."

"Very well." He now opened his eyes. "Give me the lamb and I will do the Law of Moshe while you call upon Yah and repent of your sins." He reached and took the squirming intended sacrifice. I watched as he prepared the bawling little creature, and my heart grieved for it, but blood must be shed to cover sins.

I was about to kneel before the altar for I could not bear to see its death when the most horrible thought struck me. What if this Cohen is defiled? What if the accusations of YahShua were right, or from Yah, and this being why they demanded His death. If this Cohen was corrupt and offered the sacrifice, then I would be cursed and the very evil I seek to avoid will befall me. How was I to know? It would be better not to offer the sacrifice at all than to offer an abominable one.

"Wait!" I almost screamed and the Cohen batted his eyes startled. "I have changed my mind." The Cohen tilted his head pondering my words with a frown. "I mean, ...ah, I must settle some things first, lest I offend Yah."

The Cohen should have no problem understanding this as it is plainly stated in the law, "If you have ought against a brother, first go make peace then come and offer your sacrifice."

I must find peace concerning this thing before I make sacrifice. I have seen so much hatred, bitterness and have heard so much about deceit in the last few days even in the L'vi cohanim, that it puts doubt in my heart about even this. What if it is true? What a dreadful though, but one that must be dealt with before sacrifices can be made. What if our sacrifices are abominations, where do we go, what do we do? What is becoming of this place, this holy place? I felt a sickening in the pit of my bowels as though something much loved had just died. Oh my Elohim!

"Perhaps you should speak to Kayafa. He will help you find the strength to make peace," the Cohen suggested.

"No!" I answered quickly. I knew he was behind the death of YahShua. Then I realized how my rejection must have sounded to the Cohen and his face grew grim. "He is much too busy to bother with one as lowly as I," I explained calmly, trying to soothe him. "Peradventure, I could speak to Yosef of Arimathea instead."

The Cohen threw his head back and laughed. "Well, if you want to speak with him, you will have to go to the ash heap."

"The ash heap?" I felt wrinkles appear between my eyes.

"Why is he there?"

"I do not know. All I know is, after the Posach he went there rending his garments and has sat there ever since with ashes on his head." The Cohen untied the lamb and returned it to me.

It has now been five days since the Posach. Something must be very wrong for him to fast and pray that long.

I sold the lamb back to the merchant having a few words with him when I found the lamb was not worth now what I paid for it only a few degrees earlier. However, my concern about Yosef drove me to settle with the loss, for the merchant was obstinate and would argue for his price for a good while.

The ash heap was outside the city in the Valley of Kidron some ways from the wall. So, I went back to the inn and Benren accompanied me. We took horses and rode out to where the ashes of sacrifices were dumped. As we drew near a deep ravine where it was, I could hear mournful weeping and wailing. I debated within myself whether to disturb him or just return to the city. When we reached the crest of the ravine there below in sackcloth with ashes upon him sat Yosef. He was rocking back and forth in what appeared to be great agony. Much of the ravine floor was covered in great white heaps of ash like the driven snow in the mountain valleys in winter. I decided to return to Yerushelayim and leave him to his mourning and had started to turn the horse when these words reached my hearing. They were weak but forceful. "Oh Israel, He has gone out from His place to make your land a waste. Your cities will be ruins without inhabitant. For this, put on sackcloth and lament and wail; for the fierce anger of the Elohim has not turned back from us."

At his words, I pulled up sharp. Fear gripped my heart as a strong hand grips the reigns of a spirited horse. Suddenly, I was dismounted and finding my way down the steep incline, over deep flaky mounds of oxen and bulls ashes to the place where Yosef bemoaned Israel. My breath was hard to draw and my eyes blurred in the dust of my going. Somewhere along the way through the deep ashes I fell, but was not conscious of it until I dropped upon my knees beside him. Out of breath and unconcerned about the white flakes that clung to my beard I spoke in choking gushes.

"What has... happened, Master Yosef... of Arimathea? Why do you... weep and mourn... so for Israel?"

He turned his thin face to me peering astonished through hollow sunken eyes. His eyebrows seemed oversized and his beard streaked with great long strings of ashes stuck there with many tears.

"Who inquires of this poor miserable soul?" He said with distaste, his voice quivering. "Can one not find peace to die even in the ash heap?"

"I am Timon of Beitorah. Please bare with me, Rabbi, I must know what has happened. When your lament reached my ears, ...my heart died and I now scarcely can breathe. Oh, ...please tell me what has brought you unto death."

"Do you know of the happenings during Posach?" His voice sounded grave in his weakened condition and from his much wailing, but there was love in his piercing gaze, ...love for me. I must be the only man in Yerushelayim who came here to inquire of the reason for his action.

"Yes." I told him. "The Man YahShua, called the Messiah, was crucified and now some have said, 'He has raised from the dead.'"

"Raised?" His eyes widened then he lifted up his voice. "At the very hour He died while I burned incense before the Most Holy Place for Him the curtain veil was rent from top to bottom and the earth quaked. I saw the Glory of the Elohim, the glory that dwells over the Ark of the Covenant of Yah depart the Temple in haste. The veil twisted and rolled in His anger and the table of Shewbread was overturned. The wind of His going blew out the light of the menorah while I myself being struck with horror and fear fell prostrate upon my back, and that not of my own doing." The story gushed out as though it was the mighty

Yarden at the time of rain and left him reeling from weakness.

"The Elohim of Israel has gone from the Temple!" He summoned his strength. "I declare to you, ...He is not there, He has departed! He has left Israel to destruction, ...to the pit of Sheol she will go, bound in chains..." He paused gasping and then continued. "Yes!" He bobbed his head. "The Great Temple will fall at the hands of the Romans. With... With not one stone left upon another."

At these words I, too, fell backward as a dead man and lay there for a good long while. Upon waking, I raised and rent my garments, saying, "Why do the cohanim still offer up sacrifice?"

"Because they refused to believe me. They have said, "It was only the earth quaking that rent the veil exposing the Most Holy Place to the eyes of all who would dare look'. Yet, they went about and secretly repaired the tear."

"Perhaps they are right, Rabbi. That could have happened," I said, hoping against hope.

"No, my son!" He moved his head from side to side drawing a laborious breath. "It was rent from the top to the bottom and not a stone was out of place. The earth shook because of the Veil tearing, not the earth quaking. I saw the Glory depart." His words began to tremble. "Ichabod and again I say unto you, Ichabod."

"What will they do, Rabbi?" I knew he would not last very much longer. He looked so thin and his bones were clearly visible through his skin.

"The elders will try to keep it from the people." He let his head hang low.

"Why, Rabbi? Why would they want to do that?"

"Because of their pride and selfishness!" His words had strength again now, still some fire in them. "They would lose the people's support and, therefore, be without respect and left alone in their sins. The longer they can keep the people in darkness, the longer they have praise and a position among the men."

114

I rent my garments more, throwing ashes up into the air letting them fall upon my head. Lifting up my voice unto Yah my Elohim. I joined the mourning and wailing of Yosef's until evening. Then I arose without a word and climbed back up the ravine to where Benren sat in the shade of a huge rock holding the horses.

When he looked and saw my coming he arose quickly and ran to meet me. "Is it all right, my lord? Has Elohim not forsaken us forever?" I tried to answer, but found the words stuck in my dry parched throat. When Benren saw my distress he said, "Do not try to speak now, my lord, I will bring you a drink of water."

The water was cool and cleared the bitterness of the ashes from my mouth and throat, but I still found words hard to speak. My voice was thick and my eyes were red from the ash. Benren took a cloth and tenderly wiped some ash from my head, face and beard trying not to get any more in my eyes. Then he gave me some more water and while I drank, the words of the Prophet, yheremiah, raced into my heart; "O daughter of my people, put on sack cloth and roll in ashes; Mourn as for an only son. A lamentation most bitter. For suddenly the destroyer will come up on us."

I knew now the prophecy of YahShua was coming to pass and it had already started with the Great Temple. Now I was glad I had refrained from offering sacrifice for it would have been offered upon a dead Altar.

What will the people do without their Elohim? I can already see happening what Yosef had said. -'The elders will try to keep it from the people'. And, they will offer sacrifice that is an abomination to Yah. If He has left Israel, He has left the people and if He has left the people, He has surely not raised YahShua from the dead, and all our hopes are forever gone. Forever gone!

"What of the old man, my lord? Should we try to persuade him to go back with us into the city?" Benren asked.

115

"He will not come, Benren. He is determined to die here."

"Die? Oh, my lord, …should we not stop this?"

"Why?" There was nothing left now, …nothing except to go back home and prepare everyone for the worst. Is this the truth I came seeking? Is this the deeper purpose, to destroy Israel for her sin? Sin so great that even the blood of bulls and goats is not enough to turn His disgust away?

We returned to Yerushelayim in dread for I had rehearsed in Benren's hearing all the words of Yosef and what would befall us.

When we returned to the inn, Yered came running to greet us. "Father, what has happened to you?" He caught my horse by the reigns holding him for me. His eyes round and face pale at the sight of me.

"Come inside and I will tell you the whole truth." I replied wearily and he nodded, steadying me as I stepped down. I said to Benren. "We will rest on the morrow and then return home."

"Yes, my lord," he acknowledged. "Will you go to the bath?"

"I should think so." Yered had answered for me, and I did not feel it necessary to respond.

There were a few people still packing donkeys in front of the inn, preparing to leave and several men sat on the steps watching them. A beggar sat among them holding out a brazen cup for any handout he might get. He was not an Israelite and his right leg was missing just below his hip. Beside him lay a small striped cat and a twisted stick with cloth tied around the extended branch at one end used to support his right side when he walked.

As we ascended the several steps to the porch, one of the men sitting on the steps jumped up quickly yanking Yered's purse from his belt and ran down the stairs into the street.

"Stop! Thief!" Yered yelled and took up the chase down the stairs.

116

They ran past a donkey packed for travel and being startled it began to kick and buck, braying and scattering goods all around on the ground beneath it. Everyone in the area ran to get out of the way of its flying, slashing hooves. A mans servant tried in vain to hold the rope harness on the donkey's head. An angry fellow shook his fist at Yered and the thief cursing them loudly. But, they both disappeared into the crowded street, and I doubted if Yered would have much luck catching him. However, I knew Yered to be one not so easily discouraged, so I went on into the inn.

Inside my room I waited for Yered's return but he did not come. Finally, I went to the window and looked out over my beloved city. As the sky began to dim, I watched the creeping darkness stealing its way into Yerushelayim and knew there was, also, darkness stealing its way into the souls of the people. I felt helpless, sick in heart, and angry with the leaders for letting such a thing happen. If the leaders of a place are corrupt it is certain they will soon corrupt the people. Soon there will be not light, nothing. Only what the evil hearts of the stubborn chief cohanim and elders fool the people into believing exists.

My hand found the coarse material of the blue robe still folded neatly on the table beside the Sacred Writings. I looked down and watched my hand like some strange unfamiliar creature petting the texture of the robe. I had so hoped this Man was what He claimed to be. I was almost convinced that He was the long awaited Messiah. But, even if He was, He is dead and Israel will pay the death penalty for His blood.

They have killed their own deliverer, and in doing so have slain themselves, the innocent along with the guilty. All, ...will pay for the pride of the leaders. It is so sad and I would have wept more, but alas, ...there was no tears left, just that deep inner grief that has not expression.

I looked out the window again and watched the ever-darkening day. I wanted to pray, but there was no prayer in my heart. Nothing was there but emptiness, ever increasing emptiness. Never had there been a time so dark, so bleak and empty. I shuddered.

"My lord," Benren said from behind me. "Do you wish to go to the bathhouse now and wash off the ashes of Israel's sins?' It took some time for his words to register in my mind. Oh, how I wish I could wash off the sins of Israel, cleansing her and invoke the presence of Yah to return. But, no man could do that...

"Yet it was the will of the Elohim to bruise Him, making Him an offering for sin." The words leaped to mind, and so did a sprig of hope. What did that mean? Could it be that Yah is still going to return to Israel? Did Yah foresee this day and prepare Him a sacrifice suitable for the need? If so, why did His presence leave the Temple, and where did He go? Is there still hope?

"Benren!" I whirled around quickly to face him. "There could still be hope. I must know more about this YahShua. I must talk to at least one of His disciples, ...at least one. Yah did not leave us without a way of escape, and I know it lies with this Man, YahShua."

"What hope, my lord? What way of escape?" He sounded anxious.

"I do not know, my friend." I shrugged. "I do not know. But, there is one thing I do know. YahShua is the key. He has to be the key. He has fulfilled so many prophecies, and the thing at the Temple happened because of Him. He has to be the one, ...the deliverance we all sought, ...maybe more even than we ever dreamed. I am convinced now that Yah has a plan, and what a plan it must be. High and far above our thinking or understanding. Just what it is He will reveal in time. I am sure of that."

"Will we not return to Beitorah now, my lord?"

"No, I will stay and find some disciples, ...if the zealot will take us to them. If not, we will return to Galil for I have heard some disciples went there."

I picked up the blue robe and caressed it gently with my fingertips. "The Man was... the Son of Yah. I have no doubts now." I said to Benren.

But, I wondered in my heart if the Kingdom of Yah has been established. Where so ever it is, is that where the presence of Yah has fled? How does one get 'born again' to partake of it. Did YahShua really rise from the dead? What was Yah's purpose in that? If He is alive, is He in the Kingdom of Yah, or is He still here as some of the disciples have claimed. If this were so, will I find Him? Will these eyes behold the Son of Yah and rejoice with joy unspeakable and see His glory?

A short time later, when we came out of the inn on our way to the bath house, there sat a dejected Yered, knees pulled up tight, head drooped. His fingers played with a small piece of leather strap probably left behind by the thief. I sighed deeply, and said to him.

"He got away, did he?"

"Yes," he returned, but did not look at me.

"How much was in it?"

"Four silver shekels and several denarii's." He returned with disgust.

"A small price to pay for a lesson in superstition and greed, I would say." Now he raised his head and looked squarely at me. "I was by your side and my purse was much bigger than yours. Why do you think yours was the one taken?" By his face I knew it hurt his pride to think someone had taken his purse. But, I did not comfort him for I wanted the lesson to sink deep into his heart. Money gained without honest labor is bad money, breeding greed, and it is cursed. I said nothing further.

As we made our way through the streets toward the bathhouse a few lights showed through some windows. Yes, a small glimmer of hope here and there remains. Blessed be Yah!

"Why were you so covered with ashes, Father?" Yered asked while we walked, his curiosity overcame him. So, I told him the story of Yosef of Arimathea. He looked shocked and dismayed just as I had. However, after telling him that I believed there was still hope he looked relieved as I related what I told Benren in the inn.

"So we will not leave Yerushelayim until we talk to some disciples?"

"Yes," I reassured him. "I hope your rebel friend does not forget us."

"Do not worry, Father. He is much too greedy for that." He was talking about the zealot, …but I wondered if he was thinking about his own purse now hanging on some thief's belt.

Up ahead casting a yellow irregular shaped light upon the cobblestone street was the doorway to the Roman bathhouse. It was the one good thing to come out of Rome. Here people could come for ablution freely. There was even healing waters in them like the Pool of BeitZata.

It was getting late, so the place was nearly empty. I liked it best this way. The warm water flowing through heated rocks from the spring outside of Yerushelayim relieved my bones from their ache. It was well refreshing, and I took a turn, also, in the healing waters. I had nothing to heal, but my bottom. I was not used to riding a saddle. Mostly, I traveled in a cisium or a chariot.

The Roman bathhouse, also, had what was called, "A Fog Bath", where the air was heated by water being poured over hot rocks until it filled the room with fog damp with moisture. While I was sitting there on one of the stone benches enjoying it's feeling, I heard a husky familiar voice.

Then there loomed before me the massive build of a man, not fat, just huge. While I stared at him through the boiling fog, I thought of the story of David who slew a huge giant in the plains with just a stone. Here stood a man that surely must be the giant's offspring.

"Sir?" I stood when the fog cleared around his head enough for me to see his face. Without his Centurion's uniform, his body displayed tremendously worked muscles.

"Timon! You seem to turn up in the most unexpected places," he said, seating him wearily.

"So it seems. I do not know your name Sir." I spoke softly.

"I am Appolious."

"May I extend my hand to you in friendship?"

"You want to be friends with a Roman?" His sharp eyes held a look of wonder.

"A Roman who loves my people as I see you do, yes. It would be an honor."

"Then I will accept your friendship." A broad smile broke upon his lips, and brightened his face. "Every man needs friends." He extended his large hand, and I put my smaller one in it.

"I am from Mount Tabor. Are you garrisoned at The Fortress of Antonia?"

"My detachment is here temporarily because of your Holy Days and the Man, YahShua. I am garrisoned at Korazin above KfarNachum."

"KfarNachum! That is not far from my home in Beitorah," I remembered aloud.

Then drifted off with thoughts of Elsan, Miryam and my beloved Sarepta. I wondered how Athera was doing now near her time to give birth. I guess Appolious was thinking of his family back in Rome, also, for we did not speak for some time.

"I miss my family and wish I was there with them at times." I said after a few degrees. "I know you must, also, surely miss yours."

"Yes I do," he replied. "But, I shall be going home on the morrow if nothing happens."

"You are going back to Rome?" I gave him a sideways glance, but his head was obscured by fog.

"No, to KfarNachum. That is where my home is."

"You have chosen to make your home in Israel?" This was not uncommon, and for some reason it seemed right.

"Yes." He turned his head to look at me and the fog swirled away from his face that was wet with the warm dew. "It might surprise you to know I have, also, taken a wife from you people."

"A wife?" I fought to hide my disapproval. Wh-what tribe is she from?"

"The tribe of Dan." He smirked at me.

Did he sense my feelings? I was never good at hiding them. I never like to see a mixed marriage for I know it is not pleasing to Yah, but I realize, also, it happens quite frequently. I looked at him a degree of time.

"How in heavens did you get so big?" I asked to change the subject.

He smiled then his mouth making a peculiar curl. "I used to drive chariots in the races in Rome. You get pretty big handling those half-wild horses." Now he was talking on my subject.

"You might have driven some of my horses then." I told him. "My family raises the finest chariot horses in all Rome. We have a name of renown there."

"Yes!" He made a gesture with his hand. "Yes, of course! I have been trying to place that name ever since I heard it, but could not remember where I had heard it before."

We fell silent again and I could see in his eyes that he was remembering those days with a good deal of pleasure. He is so different from the cold unfeeling soldiers here on foreign duty. It is as though we mean no more to them than a creature of the desert fit only to be crushed underfoot.

"Appolious? Do you know anything about YahShua, the Messiah?" He looked startled at me then sighed. "I told you once I do not know Him and it would be best if you did not inquire about Him anymore."

"I know it is dangerous to speak of Him, but Yah has put it in my heart to find out about Him."

His dark eyes looked puzzled at me a degree through the light fog now gathering about his head again. "I can only tell you one thing about the Man, then we must not speak of Him further."

"Tell me." I was anxious to hear his words.

Once when He was preaching in KfarNachum, I sent to ask Him to come and heal a servant that was dear to me for I had heard that He was going about healing the sick and afflicted. But, being a Roman, I knew it was customary for a Jew not to come into the house of a Roman, so I asked Him if he would only speak the words of healing, because I was not worthy of Him to enter my home. He did and the servant was healed that very hour. That is all I can tell you." He was quiet for a degree and then said unto me. "I do not care what anyone says, the Man was the son of a elohim. What elohim I do not know, but the son of one anyway."

It is widely known that Romans serve many elohim, which are not elohim at all. So, if this man says He was the son of a elohim, I knew He had to be the Son of the living Elohim. This caused a praise to rise up in my heart and by the time I had returned to the inn, taken meat and retired for the night, I was well encouraged.

DAY SIX

Morning brought a fresh sickening to my stomach when I thought upon the things that I had learned the day before. The prophecy of YahShua concerning Yerushelayim had begun already and that at the Great Temple itself. The sacrifices would be empty now for there was no Elohim to receive them. The Most Holy Place was lifeless, the presence of Yah having departed because of the sin of the cohanim, elders and the people of Israel. Their hearts being even so wicked to the point that they would kill their own Messiah. The blood of bulls and goats were not sufficient sacrifices to cover their iniquity, and to heap sin upon sin, now they were going to try to hide it all from the people. So, there will be no national mourning in sackcloth and ashes, and the sacrifices will be an abomination. How great the wickedness of this people has become. No wonder Yah has left us to our destruction at the hands of the Romans. I know the innocent as well as guilty will suffer this punishment, but in my heart, I hope that through the Man, YahShua, Yah has a plan to cleanse Israel once again, and bring back her righteousness as from the dead.

Suddenly, there came a hard demanding knock on my door, and when I opened it there stood two of the Temple guards.

"Kayafa wishes an audience with you and we came to escort you there." One of them informed.

"What does he want with me?" I frowned, wonderingly.

Then I saw Yered come up behind the guards his hand on the hilt of his sword. 'He is determined to get himself or some one else killed,' I thought. However, I understood his actions. The two guards were not giving me a choice in the matter, and Yered was ready if they decided to take me by force. I did not want any trouble with Kayafa and especially with these armed guards. "Very well," I submitted. "Allow me go gather my garments."

"I will go also, Father," Yered volunteered.

The guard said. "Kayafa has not summoned you."

"Where my father goes, I will go." He returned with a set look on his face. The guard scowled, but said nothing further.

We were hurriedly escorted through the streets. Every eye upon us as we went, and some of the people whispered one to another on our passing. A woman on the second floor of a house knocked a potted plant off the window ledge and it smashed onto the ground in front of one of the guards. He stopped, looked up and cursed, waving a clenched fist at her. She quickly pulled away from the window and closed the shutters.

We were delivered to the Counsel of elders through the door on the side. I had never been in here before, but I knew all about it. I could feel the coldness of the place, as cold it seemed as the hearts of those who sit here. Here crimes against the Laws of Moshe were judged, religious questions are discussed and answers arrived at.

We stood in a narrow hall with cedar balusters on either side and beyond the balusters were three rows of benches where the elders sat to hear charges. In front of us was a throne like, high backed chair with two silver cherubim's on each side. Their faces turned heavenward while their upturned wings touched at the tips making armrests for the chair. On the back of the chair were two other cherubim's facing each other, their heads bent toward the seat with wings spread out touching at the tips making a covering over it. The Cohengadol presides over the court from there. Standing beside the chair and to one side was Anan, Kayafa, Yachanan and Alexander. They turned to watch us enter and then Kayafa came over to us.

"I understand you went out to Yosef of Arimathea at the ash heap." His cold hard eyes searched my face for reaction.

"Yes that is right," I replied, studying the engraved lines on his face that comes from much frowning, the nature of the man itself was written there. His short curly hair and beard to match gave a rather ominous look to him.

Kayafa looking Yered up and down. His eyes came to rest on the sword that hung on his side. "Young man." He left off talking to me and addressed Yered. "You must relinquish your weapon or leave the court."

Yered opened his mouth to reply, but shut it again removing the sword from his side. He held it out to Kayafa without a word. It was the move of a man. Without any counsel, he had made the right decision. I was proud of him, and when he glanced at me, I tried to let it reflect in my countenance.

Kayafa signaled for a guard instructing him to take the sword away and return it upon our leaving.

The other cohanim standing by the throne chair watched while Anan seated himself in the judgment chair. Their faces wore a worried scrawl and it was evident from their clothing that they had been here a good long while.

Now Kayafa turned his attention back to me. "What has Yosef said to you?"

"He told me that while he offered up prayers, the curtain before the Ark of the Covenant was torn and the glory of the Adonai departed the Temple. So, now he weeps and mourns for Israel."

"That is nonsense!" He snapped back. "The earth quaked and tore the curtain and the glory of the Adonai did not depart." Now his manner softened and a smile struck upon his lips. "You see, I am afraid poor Yosef has become addled in his old age as these can testify." He swung his arm in the direction of the others who acknowledged his words with nods. "It has been coming on for some time now, but our being his friends tried to keep it a secret, not wishing to shame him. His position here at the Temple is only honorary out of respect for him. He actually has no say in the business of the court. It was the least we could do for him, sad to say. So, you must understand that any words

127

he spoke to you are just the babbling of an old man whose age has rendered him impotent."

He took a long breath and sighed deeply to show remorse, but it was as empty as a newly hewn tomb. "I suppose we will now have to judge him and set him aside from the Council of elders. We cannot have him going about telling this preposterous thing and stirring up the people. Poor fellow! It is a sad thing to have to do."

He looked thoughtful for a few degrees, then opened his hands toward us. "Alas, I must ask you not to spread this absurd idea around. In view of the trouble brought on by the blasphemer of Natzeret. It would certainly not be a good time for the foolish story of Yosef to reach the people's ears. You understand our concern, do you not?"

I understood only too well, and I knew it would be useless to argue with them. People always seem to believe their leaders above the word of an individual. I hoped Yosef was resting in Father Avraham's bosom by now for this would be the ultimate disgrace. They are going to put him out of the Council for the same reason they called for the death of Israel's deliverer.

"Yes, I understand." I assured him with a forced smile.

"Good! Good!" He returned with relief. "Then you will, also, understand why I must ask you not to inquire of this YahShua any further. It is better that He be forgotten as soon as possible." He placed his hand on my shoulder. "This deceiver has turned the world upside down, but with your help the people will soon be brought back to their senses and things will be normal again."

He was instructing me as one would do a child. He could simply make an arrest and be done with us. I wondered why he did not. Kayafa is no fool and his reluctance to act had root perhaps in my wealth. With wealth comes influence and he was not sure whom would be offended if he acted against us.

128

"That will not be an easy task for the disciples will surely not let it die quickly." I reminded him while hoping I was right.

"Oh, I do not think they will make too much trouble." He spoke with confidence and his word bore determination. This bothered me somewhat, but again I thought of Yered's lesson on trust. "They are simple minded unlearned men and have all returned to their homes and businesses." He waved them away with a twist of his hand and then continued, "Only a few zealots who were making use of him for their purposes are left and we will deal with them accordingly."

All this time Yered has been silently listening, but now he spoke, "What if you are wrong?"

Kayafa frowned at him, then retrieved it and smiled. "I suppose that is a possibility, but I am sure we can take care of any problems that will arise."

I held my breath and hoped that Yered's foolhardiness would not cause him to agitate the man. I was relieved to see him nod in acknowledgment to the man's words. Maybe, Yered is matured more than I had been giving account.

Kayafa dismissed us then with a hasty word and went back to where the others were standing. They gathered around and began to speak in low tones. Yered and I exchanged glances, and turned for the door.

The Guard with Yered's sword greeted us as we came through the door of the Council House. He held the sword out with no expression. After Yered took it he returned to his post by the door.

It would be hot this day, for even now the sun burned through our clothing and it was only the third hour of the day.

"What will we do, Father?' Yered asked as we passed through the crowded streets.

"Just as we planned." I returned and Yered looked pleased.

Making our way through the street of the Upper City, two small maidens came pushing through the crowd squealing. I was alarmed at first, but then I saw a boy somewhat older coming behind them. In his hand was a rock creature only about a hand's breath in length. As the little damsels ran past, the boy behind them shoved the creature at them and that brought still further squeals. He laughed sheepishly and that brought a remembrance smile to Yered's lips. I was sure he was remembering the times at home when he, also, delighted in tormenting Miryam and the other maidens. When the lad came near I caught his arm and drew him beside me. The boy's upturned face was sober with wide eyes. I had seen that look many times. He was caught and sure he was in trouble.

"What do you have there?" I asked, knowing very well what it was. He said nothing, but held it up timidly. "Ah," I examined the squirming little creature. "I have been looking for one of those. Would you consider selling it to me?" I now released my grip. I did not want the creature, but I had delayed him giving the little maidens time to escape.

The boy looked astonished for a space of time, then broke into a big smile. "Yes, Sir!" He said with relief.

"What do you want for it?" I asked and the boy shrugged. "I will give you a mite for it."

"A mite?" The boy's eyes widened even further. "Ye, …yes! That, …sum sounds good to me." The boy stammered.

"Good" I opened my bag and took out a mite placing it in his free hand. He stared at the mite like it was some mysterious thing and held the creature up absently without looking. I took the creature from the boy's dirty fingers and felt it squirm in my hand. The boy still stood staring at the coin in unbelief. When we went on a ways, I released the creature and watched it scurry away across the cobblestone.

"Father," Yered ask after a degree, "…what did you do that for?"

130

I smiled, "I took pity on the creature."

"Ah... Father, you took pity on the little maidens, not the creature." Yered corrected sheepishly. I only smiled and we continued our way.

A small throng of people up ahead spoke of something happening. As we approached, we could see a man sitting in the midst of this throng and he was reading from the Psalms of David. He read very slowly and with much difficulty, pausing while he struggled with the words. When we were close enough to hear he was saying; "Then they cr-cried out unto the Adonai in their troub..troubles; He sa...saved them out of their dis..tresses. He br...brought them out of dark...ness and the sh...shadow of death, and broke their ba...nds a...apart. Let them give th...thanks to the Adonai for his lo...loving kind...ness and for His won...ders to the sons of men!"

He looked up showing a row of white teeth with some in front missing. "See," he said to the people with a pleased look. "He has done this thing for me. YahShua put mud on my eyes and told them to take me to the Pool of Siloam and when I had washed my eyes, I could see the water and praised Elohim. Now I can read this in your hearing."

"Who is that man?" I ask a man in a pale blue robe standing by listening.

"He is Eldaher." A young damsel whispered to me from behind while the man I asked stared at me. "Born blind from the womb but YahShua, the Messiah, healed him."

"I know nothing," the man said quickly, glancing at the woman. Then he pushed through the press, disappearing.

While I was paying attention to the man, some legionnaire came seemingly from nowhere, and the people huddled tightly together while the man who was doing the reading slipped away and disappeared.

The soldiers shouted. "Break it up! Have you not heard the words of the city crier this day? It is illegal to

131

assemble in throngs. Go your way or we will arrest you." They began to shove and part the people, and they disbursed in every direction.

I turned to the woman behind me as she was going and caught her sleeve. "Do you know him?" I asked eagerly.

"Yes!" She replied, through her veil. "He was a beggar who sat in the street until the Adonai healed him." She tried to turn away again, but I held her tight.

"N… no!" I stammered. "Not him, …YahShua, the Messiah?"

Her eyes shot quickly at the soldiers and she said hurriedly. "I do not know Him, but Eldaher was healed by Him." I'm sure the disappointment showed on my face though I tried to recover myself. She pulled at my hand trying to release my grip. "He has gone now, …how may I find him to speak with him?"

"He lives in the house of Benjara." She pointed up the street to a door at the top of some steps. "Please release me," she begged still struggling to get away.

I released her, and when I turned one of the soldiers shoved me roughly. "Be gone with you fool," he growled.

I do not know where Yered was while I talked with the woman but, suddenly, he was nearby. I saw him make a quick move, but gathering myself I stepped between him and the soldier. I took his arm and drug him with me down the street in the direction the maiden had pointed. Just when I think Yered has gained some wisdom he becomes foolish again. I wondered if he would ever learn when to act, and when to refrain.

The house sat on a corner and a sign hung on the wall that read, "Rooms Here". I stopped at a fruit merchant's cart on the street across from the house and began to look at the goods.

"Father," Yered turned to me, "…what did the soldiers mean it is illegal to gather in a throng?"

"Pilate has issued a proclamation this very morning." The man who owned the fruit cart answered for me. "Until this trouble about this YahShua is cleared up it will be illegal to gather in crowds."

"Oh," Yered returned with a slight gesture.

I said nothing, but began to choose a few pieces of fruit. It did not take someone with much wisdom to know who was behind that proclamation. If there were no crowds, there would be no preaching and no preaching meant no spreading of the teaching of YahShua. The Council seems to be right in the middle of everything that happens anymore. It is as though you can no longer tell who are the Romans or who are the leaders of Israel. They seem one and the same.

"I will take these." I said to the merchant handing him a few dates and a cluster of grapes.

He told me the price and while I paid him legionnaires came down the street again. "Lets come back this afternoon and let things settle down here a bit." I said low to Yered.

"Will we talk with the man who read the song, Father?" He inquired anxiously. I think the thought of his being blind and YahShua healing him had caught the adventure in Yered's spirit.

"Yes, we will talk with him if he will see us," I nodded. "But not this day."

We returned to the inn where we were staying and some servants were in the hall talking excitedly. "What has happened, my children?" I asked.

"We have some news for you, my lord." Semone, the son of Benren informed.

"Good!" I returned and my look must have pleased them, for they all smiled one to another while a satisfied expression broke upon Semone's face.

"I will go to my room and after a while you may send the ones in with the rumors." I told Semone.

"Yes, my lord." He bowed slightly.

Benren met me at my door. His face showed relief. "You have returned? I was very concerned for you because the Temple guards took you away."

"No Benren! They took me nowhere. I went with them." There was a good deal of difference to me. I loathe the idea of being led away as a common criminal.

"Never the less, I am glad you are safe, my lord," he bowed as we entered my room.

"Semone tells me some of the servants have heard more rumors. After you have seen to my needs, you may go tell him to send them up."

"Very well, my lord."

Shortly there was a soft knock and the servant boy who picked up the scroll that tried my patience in Natzeret slipped quietly into the room. He stood before me, his hands together in front and head slightly bowed.

"Well, speak up lad. What is it you have heard?"

"The elders have bought a parcel of land in the Kidron valley, my lord." He paused shortly. "It was bought with the money of the betrayer, and it will be for the burying of sojourners. The people now call it, 'The Field of Blood,' because it was purchased with blood money."

Then the Prophet Yirmehyaw's words came to me; *"And they took the thirty pieces of silver, the price of the one whose price had been set by the sons of Israel, and they gave them for the Potters Field."*

Ah! So, that is where the money of Yhudah went. I guess they were unaware they were fulfilling the prophecy. The law does not allow them to put it into the treasury because it is cursed. However, I do not see what that should matter to them after all the other evil they have done.

"This is a good rumor," I acknowledged. "It pleases me much."

"Thank you, Master." The boy returned with great satisfaction.

"You may go. Tell Semone to send in the next one."

"Yes, master," he nodded and departed.

Again, there was a knock on the door followed by a servant who stood waiting for me to speak.

"What rumor do you have for me?"

"I have spoken with a lad who went to the Mount of Olives to listen to YahShua teach. His mother had packed him a lunch of two small fish and a few small cakes of bread. When it was time to eat, YahShua said to His disciples, 'Feed the people'. But, His disciples had not enough provisions for such a large crowd, so He called the boy who stood nearby and asked for his lunch." The servant boy wet his lips and then continued.

"When the boy gave it to Him, YahShua blessed it and then handed it to one of the disciples and said, 'Now, feed the people.' So, all the people was fed with the boy's lunch and there were baskets full left over."

"How many people were there?" I questioned.

"I do not know, master, but many, besides women and children. It was a great miracle."

"Yes it was. A great miracle indeed! It is a good rumor, also. I am pleased."

"Thank you, master!"

"Tell Semone to send in the others."

"My lord, Semone said I should say, 'There are no more rumors this day'."

"Very well, You may go." He bowed slightly and went out the door.

If He could do this mighty miracle, He could have saved Himself as Yhudah had said, but He did not. Why? Of course! It was Yah's pleasure to sacrifice Him for sins, our salvation from the impending destruction. It would take much courage to face death because of the will of Yah. Courage! Yes, ...no wonder His followers had the courage to sing the song of victory. They were drawing upon the courage of the Son of Yah.

My Elohim, would I have so much courage? Could I face the cross as He did and find the courage to do so knowing all I had to do was ask and I would be free from it. What courage! What courage indeed!

That afternoon Yered was nowhere to be found so I decided to go myself to see the blind man who was healed although Yered had wanted to go. I made my way back to the house where the blind man who was healed lived.

The street seemed quiet now and no legionnaires were seen. I waited for some time to be sure before I ascended the narrow steps to the door. I knocked and took another look around while I waited. The door opened and a small maiden with large, round hazel eyes looked up into my face studying me. "Shalom little one! Is Eldaher here?" I patted her head and her brown wavy locks bounced to the rhythm.

"No," she reported in a friendly voice. Now an older more cautious voice came from the interior of the room.

"What do you want with him?"

"I am Timon from Beitorah and I would like an audience with him."

A woman now emerged from the depths of the house. She was large with child and not very old. "He is away now." She said quickly and took the little maiden's arm pulling her back.

I could see she was about to shut the door. "Please, tell him I must speak with him." I insisted. She hesitated, so I took the opportunity. "Tell him I will come back on the first day of the week. I am not a Roman, nor an Elder."

"What did you say your name was?" She asked after staring at me a few degrees.

"Timon-bar-Philorah from Beitorah on the slopes of Mount Tabor."

"I will tell him," she agreed.

"Shalom then!" I bowed slightly and went back down the steps.

Back at the inn, I took the sacred scrolls and began to study them further. As I did so it seemed that now I could find a great many prophecies that the Man, YahShua, had fulfilled. Yet, there were so many questions remaining with no answers. There was a small passage about the resurrection that excited me; *"For Thou wilt not abandon my soul to Sheol; Neither wilt Thou allow Thy Holy One to undergo decay."*

It being written by David the Psalmist and I know it did not pertain to him for he has slept with our fathers for many, many years now. It has to refer to Yah's Holy One, His Son. Our hope! Yes, ...hope.

DAY SEVEN

The Sabbath of Yah is a day when all activity ceases. Minds and hearts turn toward Yah to worship and praise Him for His loving kindness. The bright morning sun outlined the Great Temple with a halo of gold. Already, the streets hummed with voices and movement, but this day is different from other days. There was a joyful tone to the percussion of city sounds. Going to the window, I drew in a breath of fresh air cooled by the early dew and stretched my awakening bones. I loved the Sabbath in Yerushelayim with all it's flurry and ceremony. Looking down at the street, I watched the people smile, bow one to another and send forth blessings, no angry faces, curse or cross words could be heard this day. Would it not be wonderful if every day was a Sabbath and everyone's greeting of goodwill and hospitality would display itself forever?

As normal, I fasted breakfast and anxiously awaited the Holy Convocation at the Temple. A Sabbath in Yerushelayim without going to the Great Temple to worship, praise and present offerings unto Yah was unthinkable.

The soft honey sounds of the silver trumps blown by the cohanim caressed the air to signal that the observance was about to begin. I went to the bed where Benren had laid my Sabbath robe with it's elaborately embroidered trim, picked it up, and slipped my arm into one of the sleeves.

I love the pomp, splendor and excitement that fills the firmament of the Temple Courtyard as everyone awaits the cohanim to appear in regal procession and begin the ceremony that lasts all morning. Already, the thrill of it rushed through me and anticipation tantalized every movement of my being.

Suddenly, I was struck with the vision of poor Yosef of Arimethea sitting mournfully in sackcloth with ashes on his head and it turned me to stone. Half in and half out of my Sabbath robe, I stood like a statue flooded by an avalanche of mixed feelings. I felt sad, frustrated and cheated, then anger stole away the joy and excitement. Expectation fell to the ground leaving me empty and with such a sense of loss that I heard myself groan. Yah is no longer at the Temple to hear the songs of praise or see the offerings. It is vain. Empty!

Angrily, I stripped the robe from me and threw it upon the bed, sitting down upon it with despair. The happy sounds drifting up from the street became mocking, tormenting and spiteful. Why are they joyful? They should be mourning, weeping and lamenting. But, they do not know. The cohanim hide the truth and make meaningless rituals. They will still turn toward the Holy of Holies and raise their hands in praise, offer sacrifice and do their service just as though everything is still as it was. They will not tell the people the glory of Yah has departed the Temple for fear of losing them, leaving them to stand stripped of importance, of pride and naked in their sins. They will go on letting the people believe that Yah hears their praise and welcomes their offerings. None will have the courage to speak the truth and the people will return to their homes thinking Yah has accepted their sacrifices, when it is an abomination, bring down a curse upon them. No one will call for a day of mourning, renting their garments and casting dust upon their head to turn away the wrath of Yah. I loathe what the cohanim and elders are doing to the people and with no one to tell them that their efforts are empty. The Temple is empty. No one! No, not one!

"Well here is one!" I determined loudly. Hurt and disappointment enveloped me. I sprang to my feet and ran to the window.

"Why are you going up to the Temple?" I shouted down at the people on the street below. "Elohim is not there to hear your praise and accept your offerings! He has gone up out of the Temple!" People stopped and stared up at me with mouths gaping, eye wide in astonishment.

"The Holy curtain has been rent and the glory of the Elohim of Israel has departed the Temple! Why offer sacrifice in a temple where there is no Elohim! Your Holy Convocations are useless, empty and vain!" While I continued to yell down at them, they waved me away in disgust and turned back to their going.

"Do not turn away! Listen to me!" But none listened. None wanted to hear. The words fell dead upon the Cobblestone Street. "Why," my voice trailed off to a normal tone, "...will you not hear?"

I stood numb, staring at the crowd just passing on by going their way to the Temple. They must think me mad, ...possessed. Suddenly, I felt very foolish. My anger faded quickly into embarrassment, and I shrank away from the window. My heart ached while my mind screamed at me, "You fool!"

Then my fingers came to rest on something coarse and soft. I slowly looked down to find my hand playing with the fabric of the blue robe that lay on the table near the window. For a long time I stared at it, feeling ashamed, sad and miserable. Picking up the robe gently, without looking, I went to the bed and sat down heavily. Tears dripped onto the robe, darkening its blue tint, then burying my face in its softness. I wept bitterly.

I did not know how long I sat there weeping out my agony, praying for my beloved city and the people of Israel. But, when Benren came to bring me a tray, he found me still there. I refused to eat and sat in mourning, a prayer cloth upon my head, beseeching the Adonai my Elohim with my back to the Temple. In all my life I had never prayed unless I faced the Temple. Finally, I arose, washed my face, and called for my meal. Wherever Yah is, I know, He must surely have heard the supplication of my heart. Now it was time to trust, as Yered had admonished. I must trust, just simply trust. I then laid me down upon my bed and slept with a troubled spirit.

Suddenly, I was brought to a sitting position by a sharp ringing in my ears. It was the trumpets from the

141

Temple announcing the evening sacrifice was about to be offered ending the day of Holy Convocation. I seemed mesmerized by its hypnotic notes, and like some trained animal, I found myself mingling aimlessly among the worshippers in the Temple Court. I knew I should not have come for it really meant nothing, yet here I was. Why was I here? Whatever possessed me to come? I had considered myself to be a reasonably wise man, but today I had become foolish, very foolish.

Later in my room disgust filled me for even going. I knew it was empty and vain, but for some reason I went anyway. I hoped Yered, Benren or the servants did not find out. I was glad this tormenting Sabbath was over. It seemed now like a horrible night dream.

DAY EIGHT

The sound of the city's morning yawn played upon my ears. The song of the sparrow on the rampart of the adjoining roof along with bass and soprano voices mingling like music from a festive celebration filled the expanse. But, instead of it bringing pleasure and rejoicing, it brought the heartache of knowing that the convocation will soon cease. Instead of the beauty of a waking city, there will be the forlorn howl of jackals and hyenas. Replacing lively activity, there will be the silence of rubble and decay.

I turned my face toward the Temple and prayed for the City of Yah and the people, but there were heavy weights upon my words and they fell back upon my head. There was really no purpose in this action, for there is no presence of Yah at the Great Temple. However, I did it anyway hoping that where so ever the presence of Yah was He would hear me from there. I then felt very foolish on my knees facing toward an empty Temple so I arose. Old ways are hard to lay aside even when you know they are vain, empty and useless.

"Oh Elohim, no matter where it is, help me find my way to where you are." A country without it's Elohim is dead, but a man without his Elohim is lost, miserable, wretched, and without purpose. It is a thing worse than death.

I went to the Sacred Writings stacked neatly in their rows. Are these empty and vain now, also? I picked one up and lovingly unrolled it to where the writing began, but could not make out the words for the flow that rushed forth into my eyes. I blinked it away and felt the warmth of it upon my cheek. I was just standing there like a mindless thing staring at the blur of letters when Benren spoke softly behind me. It was as though his words were along way off. I did not even hear him enter the room nor approach me.

"My lord?" He repeated again his former words.

I lowered the manuscript, but my actions were as that of honey pouring on a cold winter day. Tenderly I began to roll up the scroll. Slowly, I put it back in its place on the pile from whence I had taken it.

"What is it, Benren?" I found little power to remove my hand away from it as one whom feared it would not be there ever again.

"Master Nakdimon is standing without desiring an audience with you." Now, I turned to look at my servant companion of many years, and I saw in his face a flash of fear. "Are you all right, my lord?" He put out his hand and took my arm. "You look as one who has just seen a ghost." That seemed a proper assessment of the matter.

"Fear not, I will be all right," I assured him. "Tell Master Nakdimon, he is always welcome here at any time and send him in."

"Yes, my lord, but... are you certain you are all right?"

"Quite sure, my friend."

He then bowed slightly and left, going out. I wondered how the Rabbi found out where I was staying, and why had come to see me. The thought came to me. Maybe, he had unmasked the meaning of the words YahShua spoke to him. I knew he was writing them down the day that I visited him. Perhaps, he wants to tell me of his findings.

Now the door opened and Benren held it while Nakdimon came swiftly in, his robe flowing slightly behind him as he moved. "Shalom." He saluted me.

"I am deeply honored that you should enter my dwelling. Welcome!" I bowed slightly. "Take your rest, Master." I bid waving him onto the lounge.

There was an urgent look about him and after seating himself he spoke. "Forgive my intrusion this early, but I have only this day learned that Kayafa had you brought before the Council. What was it about?"

Now that he was here, it did strike me as strange that he, too, was not at the inquiry. However, it not being a trial upon charges, they may have just not called him. Or maybe, he was not part of their little plot to keep the happenings in the Temple a secret. If so, they certainly would not have wanted him there.

"They called me there to find out what Yosef of Arimathea had told me." I explained. "I suppose they found out, somehow, I went out to him in the ash heap."

"The ash heap?" Nakdimon sounded surprised and stood up abruptly.

"Yes. Did you not know?"

"No! All I was told is that he had gone in seclusion to pray. I thought nothing of it because he was very upset at himself for not standing with me against the others at the trial of YahShua."

"Why did he not stand with you? Did he not believe in Him?"

"Not until he saw the way YahShua stood before the council. I found him after they had taken YahShua to Pilate. He was in his chamber sitting in the dark, tears streaming from his eyes. He told me, he was not sure about the Man until then, and by that time it was too late."

Nakdimon went to my window and looked out over Yerushelayim. He stood there a degree in silence. Then took up speaking again, "After the soldiers pronounced YahShua dead and while I was consoling His Mother and the others who were there, Yosef came to the Place of the Skull and stood staring up into the gray lifeless face of YahShua. I went over to him and he kept muttering, 'He is the Son of Elohim. He is the Son of Elohim'. Then he said something very strange, 'The Glory has departed. Elohim has gone from Israel and from His place above the Ark.'"

Turning from the window, Nakdimon began to walk swiftly back and forth. "Yosef was so upset that I am afraid he was babbling somewhat, making very little sense."

He took in a deep breath and let it out slowly, frowned and continued. "He went with me to ask for the body of YahShua from Pilate, who was glad to be done with Him. While we were preparing it for the tomb, Yosef

145

told me the veil of the Most Holy Place was rent at the very same time that YahShua died and the glory of the Adonai left the Temple in haste." He stopped pacing and opened his hands toward me.

"The earth had quaked and the sun had hidden its face, so I tried to tell him that it was caused by the quake. However, he kept insisting the Glory had departed and nothing I said would console him. After YahShua was laid in the tomb, I looked for him but could not find him. He was angry with everyone for not believing him and very frustrated. So, when Kayafa told me he had gone into seclusion for prayer, I thought little of it."

He sighed heavily and dropped his hands limply to his sides. "When did you go see him?"

"The day of preparation. And, I must say his story was hard for me to also accept. I rent my garments and threw ashes upon my head sitting with him until evening mourning for Israel."

"The day of preparation? My Elohim! He's been there for eight days."

I sat and stared at the door as Nakdimon let it slam shut behind him. He had hurried out without another word. I did not get a chance to tell him what Kayafa has said. How he and the others planned to remove Yosef from the council. I then arose and went to the window and looked after him as he hurried out of the building.

"Wait Master!" I called to him. "I have somewhat else to tell you."

"Later!" He returned waving me away without even looking at me.

I watched him in astonishment until he became swallowed up in the throngs that moved like endless streams up and down the street.

"Father," Yered called to me from in front of the inn below the window, "...will we go see the blind man who was healed now?" He stood holding the reigns of his horse looking up at me. He had been up early and out somewhere.

"Ah, ...yes, I suppose so." I returned absently still looking where Nakdimon disappeared into the throngs of busy people. Then I drew back into the room, put on my robe and went down to where Yered was waiting.

Soon the building where Eidaher lived was in sight. Again, we approached with caution looking for soldiers, but saw none. However, we waited for a while near the fruit stand. A patrol of legionnaires happened by, but paid us no attention, and after they were well out of sight, I said to Yered, "Let us go now for they will not be back by for a while." He nodded and we went up the narrow steps to the heavy wooden door. While I knocked, Yered kept watch for soldiers or anyone who looked suspicious. The door then opened and the woman I spoke with earlier bowed slightly.

"Shalom," I blessed the dwelling.

"Enter Sirs," she bid and stepped away from the door.

The shutters were closed on the single window inside the dimly lit room. Over where the lighted candle sat on a table was the man we had seen on the street, and playing on a woolen rug in the center of the floor was the small maiden who had answered the door when I came before.

"Did you wish to speak with me?" The man said staring at us with large, curious eyes.

The woman, heavy with child, went into the corner of the room where a fireplace was built into the wall. She took some water from a large pot hanging from the point of a three-legged stand beside the fireplace and filled a foot basin.

"I am Timon of Beitorah," I said unto the man. "And, this is Yered, son of my concubine." Yered nodded and the man offered us a seat with his hand on a pile of fleece around the low table.

"I am called Eldaher and this is my son's wife, Miryam," he nodded to indicate the woman now beginning to wash Yered's feet. "And this is Sheron." He waved a

147

hand and the little girl playing with a doll made from flax silk looked up at him and smiled.

"Why have you come seeking me?"

"Because you were healed by the Man, YahShua and we wish to hear your testimony," I said anxiously. "We are neither Romans or elders. We just seek truth, and the disciples of YahShua for they know Him best."

"Ah, ...truth." He showed his teeth through his rough, dark beard as his cheeks raised in a smile. "You seek truth. Well, here is truth. I was blind and now I see. That is truth." He looked pleased at his own words.

"But," he continued, "the elders do not want to hear truth. They love lies and are filled with hatred."

"Yes, we know," Yered assured him. "Tell us what happened."

"While I lay begging for crumbs," the man took up the story, "...the Adonai passed by and one of His disciples said to Him in my hearing, 'Adonai, who has sinned, this man or his parents?'. The Adonai answered, '...Neither his parents nor he has sinned, but this is happened to show Elohim's love.'"

The man's face still filled with amazement continued, "So, YahShua spit upon the ground and took the mud, placing it upon my eyes. He said, 'Now, go wash in the Pool of Siloam.' When I had washed, I could see the face of a man looking back at me in the water. I was frightened at first, but then realized what was done unto me. This happened on the Sabbath day, and the elders became angry saying, 'It is not lawful to heal on the Sabbath.' They questioned me for a long time. Even brought in my parents and asked them. After they were satisfied, they told me not to tell anyone what had happened and set me out."

"But you still tell what happened," Yered reminded leaning near. "Are you not afraid they will catch you, and do to you as they did to Him?"

"Haah!" He laughed. "They may seek me and find me, but anything they do will just make matters worse for them. All Yerushelayim saw what He did unto me and the elders know if I am arrested they will lose favor with the people for they would not understand."

"Do you believe He is the Son of Elohim?" I asked. "Can anyone do this? Has ever it been done before? No! But, the Man, YahShua, did it. So, is He the Son of Elohim or no? You must decide that for yourself."

Yered looked at me and then back at Eldaher. "Yes, we must each decide for ourselves."

The man just nodded with a smile and patted his arm. "You are not far away from the answer, my boy. Yes, not far at all."

I wondered once again where Yered's path would lead him. Would he find a place in his heart for this YahShua as I have done? I prayed he would make the right choice when the time came. I believe I have made the right choice, and now I must find the disciples. What will all that bring? What could they tell me? Would He be with them or somewhere in the Kingdom of Yah? I must find Him if He is here.

A commotion arose out in the street bringing Yered and me quickly to our feet. Had we led the elders here?

Then Eldaher calmed us by saying, "Fear not. They are only breaking up a throng which comes every day to hear me read."

"We will go anyway before we draw the Cohanim to you." I answered and said unto him. "Thank you for your time and for telling us your story."

"Wait until they drive away the throng," the man warned. "Miryam will tell you when it is safe to leave."

She went to the door and peered out. After a few degrees, she signaled for us. Bowing, we departed.

When we had gone a space up the crowded street, the sound of music could be heard and it drew Yered like honey draws the ant. "Music!" Yered exclaimed as though I could not hear.

A small throng of onlookers crowded around some people playing and dancing in the open spot where two streets cross. There was several Roman soldiers standing their watch near the inner edge of the press. Beyond them was a troop of entertainers advertising the show at the theater. Yered caught the beat of the music and kept the rhythm with his foot.

"Father," he turned to me after a short time, "I think I shall go to the coliseum and see the performance."

"What if your rebel friend wants to take us to the disciples," I said in his hearing only. "I do not wish to go with him alone."

"He will probably not take us until after dark." Yered told me.

Since he was most likely right, I quickly agreed. "Very well. I will go back to the inn and study the Sacred Writings. You go have a good time. You are probably right about him not taking us until night fall." I encouraged.

I did not want to take him away from enjoying the thing of Yerushelayim, for he will probably not get the chance again since the prophecy of YahShua is already beginning to come to pass.

"After I leave the theater, I will go down to the tabernae and see if BarArni might be there," Yered informed. "And then I..."

Suddenly, the throng erupted into total confusion, frightened people were ducking, running in every direction and there were yells and screams mingled with loud cries of; "Romans go home!" "Death to Pilate!" "Down with Herod!" "Pay, you Roman swine!"

It was really hard to tell just what was happening at first, then it became clear. Several young zealots were pounding the soldiers with clubs and striking fiercely with swords. On the ground lay one soldier with blood gushing from his stomach, quickly pooling around him. Two guards were struggling with a fellow while a zealot ran his sword into one of the soldier's back. A short stout man with a hard looking face jumped upon the back of a soldier, throwing his arm around his neck and sticking a well-placed blade. A satisfied look slowly formed as the

150

Roman's knees became as water and he dropped to the ground.

We were being bumped, shoved and knocked around by the panicked throng and I quickly looked for Yered, who much to my surprise instead of sword in hand striking death blows to the Romans was helping a woman back to her feet not many steps away. Those trying to get out of the way of the slashing blades and swinging clubs had shoved her to the street. As quickly as I could, I made my way to where he was.

"Let us be going from here. More soldiers will be upon us with speed." I said hastily. Yered nodded and we found the going much easier as we flowed with those who were fleeing the scene of insurrection. Soon we managed to turn down a street and mingle with the normal travel. Neither spoke for some time, but my curiosity finally overcame me.

"Yered, why did you not take the opportunity to join the fight?"

"It was neither the time nor the place to fight," He simply replied.

I blinked at him and mused at his statement for a space of time. "That was a wise decision. Unless, …you desire to be a martyr for the cause, …which obviously these zealots do." I sighed heavily. "I tell you though, I think there must be a better way to serve the cause."

Yered just grinned at me with a romantic far away look in his eye. I gave him an understanding smile, shook my head and we walked on. No doubt he was fighting a battle against overwhelming odds in his mind's eye, and most surely winning, maybe even slaying two opponents with one blow. He is arrogant and full of pride. How else would he be doing it?

Rome will not rise up against Yerushelayim unless trouble breaks out that would call for intervention. Already, in Rome, Israel has a reputation of being a place of insurrection, troubling the Senate because our customs are so deeply rooted in the people. The chief cohanim including the elders refused to relinquish much of the teachings of Moshe to fit into the Roman colonies like other peoples have done.

When we were back at the inn, Benren greeted us in the hall and immediately said, "The rebel will take you into the tomb caves tonight. He will meet you at the tabernae."

"Good! You were right Yered." I said to him as we entered my room. "The price of silver has overcome his fears." After closing the door I continued. "When we go to meet him, we must be prepared for anything and remember who we are dealing with here. We will take no money with us. The rest of the rebel's money we will stash somewhere near the entrance to the tombs. If he does well, we can tell him where he may find it. If not, ...then we will not at least be robbed and can go back for it later."

"That is a good plan, Father," Yered agreed. "I will leave my weapon here and maybe they will deal gently with us seeing that we are not armed to do battle."

"Yes, a good idea. There would be too many of them for us to fight anyway."

"Then it is settled," Yered nodded in satisfaction. "How will we hide the money without suspicion for he will be with us?"

"There will be an opportunity somewhere, I am sure."

He nodded and then said, "I will go to the theater and see the players this afternoon if you do not need me any further and then we shall go meet BarArni."

"I have no further need for you. I will just rest and study the Sacred Writings."

"Rest well then, Father." He returned and departed leaving Benren and me alone.

"Do be careful, my lord," Benren cautioned.

"We shall. Now bring me something to eat and leave me to my studies." Benren nodded and bowed slightly, going out.

I was anxious and excited about finding the disciples. I had so many questions and was sure they would be able to answer them. I wondered what kind of reception we would get. Will they think we are spies or will they receive us as dear Elisheva had done? Elisheva, ah yes. When we return to Galil I will bring her news of the happenings here. Surely it will help to ease her mind.

The thought of Elisheva brought to my mind a picture of Sarepta in the cool of the evening standing on the roof near the rampart. Her silken robe blowing gently in the breeze and the slight scent of her perfume mingling with the sweet smell of the fig tree blossoms. I wished with deep longing to be holding her in my arms while we look out across the sprawling valley below. Furrows of rich light green grass cut their way through the enormous expanse of dark green trees. A small spring feeds a sparkling blue stream that winds its way through the valley floor like a dyed thread. What a breathtaking sight from that vantage point on the roof of our home. We have spent much time standing there in the years we have shared together. Sarepta, as myself, loves our mountain home and enjoys the beauty it continually affords us.

My thoughts then turned to Athera, the small Greek maiden who sought refuge with us when she had barely come into womanhood. Her family had fallen prey to a band of robbers on the road at the foot of the mountain. I still remember how frightened she was when my brothers and I found her huddled against a huge rock under a bush crying. Her clothing and soft olive skin torn and bleeding from the thorn bushes she had run through to escape their pursuit. She had fled before their face for some time by the looks of her before losing them in the mountains. She then had wandered lost for many furlongs. Finally, exhausted and frightened she had sought hiding in the bush where we found her.

I loved her the very first time my eyes fell upon her. Sarepta was jealous for some time as we were espoused to each other. In time though, she too began to find love in her heart for the little Greek damsel.

I was pleased that before our marriage she and Athera had become very good friends. About a season after the death of my firstborn, Sarepta began to fret thinking she could no longer bear children. She then made arrangements for me to take Athera to concubine. Sometime later Yah did give me a son from Sarepta and when I was about to set Athera aside Sarepta would not have it. It would not be right in the eyes of Yah she surmised for no man would have her because of me. I thank Yah every time I pray for the two beautiful women that He has given me to love. I wonder if she has birthed the child yet. I wanted to be there when it came, but I was compelled to find the truth of this Man, YahShua.

Sometime later in the afternoon, I am not sure just when for time escapes me when I am deep into study, Benren knocked softly and came into the room. "My lord, a messenger from Nakdimon has arrived."

"Send him in immediately, Benren."

He bowed slightly and went back to the door he left ajar saying to the messenger, "You may come in."

A young boy with a yarmulke on his head, apparently from the Temple school learning under the Rabbis, entered. He bowed and said, "Master Nakdimon sends blessings to you and wishes to inform you that Yosef of Arimathea is in his chambers at the Holy Temple and is nigh unto death. Master Nakdimon has asked that you come."

"Very well. Run and tell him I will be coming," I instructed. The boy nodded, bowed low and then hurried out.

Nakdimon was pacing around in the Temple Court Yard when I came through the gate. I bowed slightly, "Shalom Master. Have they sent for a physician? Will he live?" I asked upon approaching him.

"Only Elohim knows. The physicians are with him now," he returned, a grave look upon his face. "I do not really believe he has the will to live."

Knowing what Kayafa and the others had planned, I secretly hoped he would not. To face the shame of being ejected from the Council of Elders would be a great blow.

Nakdimon led me through the wall chambers, down a narrow hall and near a doorway stood Kayafa, Anan and Alexander along with several others I did not know. I was sure Nakdimon had not told them that he summoned me because upon seeing my coming, a scrawl formed upon Kayafa's face and he glanced at his companions in treachery. I said nothing as Nakdimon escorted me past them and into the dim lit chamber where Yosef laid upon his deathbed.

His eyes closed, his breath rattled and seemed to come only after much struggling. He was stripped of his clothing with bits of ash still clinging to his beard. His long graying hair was wet and slicked back to reveal his leathery wrinkled face. His frail skin covered skeleton lay motionless clad in only a loincloth. Bones protruded like mountains from the floor of a canyon and his long finger twitched slightly, but there was no moan. Two physicians stood near the bed, but were doing nothing.

"In spite of his protesting we brought him here and he kept asking about the young man who came to him in the ash heap. He wanted to see you, and I am not sure he will even be able to talk to you." Nakdimon whispered in my ear.

I drew near bending low over him. "Rabbi, I am here," I softly said, but he did not move nor open his eyes. "Rabbi, it is I, Timon." I waited and then his mouth moved, however, there was no sound. His eyes remained closed but moved under his eyelids.

"What did you say, Rabbi?" I bent closer and put my ear near his mouth. A light rumble of voices could be heard in the hall.

"What treachery... have the elders... thought to do?" I thought he said straining to hear it.

I then whispered into his hearing. "They seek to put you out of the Council, Master."

155

I thought he answered me back, "I... will die... here. They... will not get... that satis...faction." I was uncertain of his words though. I just squeezed his hand and was still holding it when the life went out of him. One of the physicians shoved me back and began tending him.

"He is dead." I said softly to Nakdimon and turned for the door.

In the hall Kayafa caught my arm drawing me aside. "What were his words?"

"I could not make them out." I sadly grieved in my heart. "He is gone now," I said unto him.

Upon hearing that Kayafa released me and looked relieved at Anan and Alexander, then he said unto me, "It is better. I would not have taken pleasure in setting him aside. It is needless now to even mention it, agreed?"

"Agreed," I nodded. However, I wanted to spring upon him and yell to everyone who stood by of his trickery and falsehood, but while I thought upon it, Nakdimon drew me away by my arm.

"I will see you out," he offered.

We were only a short way down the hall when Kayafa's voice reached our ears. "Yosef of Arimathea is dead. We will set a mourning for him on the morrow. He will be placed in his tomb before the evening prayer."

Yes, Yosef was dead, but it would have been far better for Israel if the mourning would have been for Kayafa instead. That which I was feeling in my heart for the man brought me to a shocking realization that the bitterness and hatred was beginning to take hold of me. I could not let this evil befall me, for then I would be no more righteous or blameless than they.

"Oh Elohim, set up a standard against this evil and let it not pollute my heart as it has theirs." I prayed silently as we walked.

"Thank you for coming." Nakdimon said to me when we reached the Temple court.

I realized that we both had walked in silence until now. I wondered what Nakdimon had been thinking. I debated with myself as to whether to tell him the dreadful plan Kayafa and the elders had intended for Yosef, but dashed the thought. It would be no better for Nakdimon to know this than it was for Yosef to know what he knew. I did not want them to devise a scheme to shame this precious man as they had planned to do Yosef.

I was almost back to my room when the trumpets began to sound at the Great Temple announcing to the people of Yerushelayim the death of an elder of Israel.

I thought of what Yosef had said happened in the Holy Place at the precise degree of time that YahShua, called the Messiah, died. What a terrible story these events have to tell. This all happened because the hearts of the chief cohanim, the leaders of Israel and the people had become so vile that Yah was forced to flee from that place where abominable sacrifices were offered. Yah could no longer stand the shame of being called the Elohim of such a people.

So, the Holy Table of Shewbread was overturned defiling the bread of the Temple. The menorah's lights were snuffed out and darkness entered the place of worship. The Cohen was thrown backward, knocked from his service. Yes, the Holy Place quaked. The holy man was cast down even to the ground and all this as the glory of Yah departed the Holy of Holies. The Most Holy Place in all of the world now stands without the presence of Yah. Where did the Presence go? I trust to a place where the heart is pure and undefiled, where love is the first thought and where justice and righteousness dictates paths. If there is such a place, it is surely the Kingdom of Yah.

Darkness came stealing its way into the narrow, almost empty streets as we passed the Pool of Siloam and the Old Pool in the Lower City. The stars brightly twinkled overhead surrounding a silver moon. This was a good night for slipping around unseen. The sound of tambourine music could be heard coming from the closed door of the tabernae. Already, the distinct smell of the place polluted the air, and I dreaded the thoughts of sitting in there until BarArni showed up to take us into the tomb caves.

"Go see if he is in there," I told Yered, hesitating outside the door.

"All right, Father."

While Yered was in the place, I tried to stay as unnoticed as possible. A large brown dog came sniffing around looking for crumbs. His back parts were thin and his ribs showed like ripples on the Yarden in the low area coves. A baby cried somewhere not far away, and the low drone of two men's voices could be heard. The voices became more distinct and louder. Then I saw two men coming around the corner not far from where I stood. They paid me no mind and entered the tabernae. A smell of fermented drink gushed out and rushed into the air drifting past me as the door shut behind them.

I was getting impatient for Yered to return and began to walk back and forth. Suddenly, I saw a patrol of legionnaires. About ten of them were coming down the street. I knew they were going to want to know what I was doing, so I went quickly through the door into the tabernae. I glanced around the room quickly and did not see BarArni, but Yered was talking with the little wench that waits tables and did not notice my coming. He was smiling and then laughed as she tossed her head slightly and batted her eyes him. It was enough for me. I went over and tugged on his arm.

"Come on, we must be going," I said to him sharply and the pleasant look on his face sobered. His eyes quickly searched my face and I knew he could see that I was upset with him. "Shalom, Claudia," Yered bid and the damsel stared at me with a cold look.

She is a disgusting little harlot and I do not suppose she had to guess what I was thinking for I never tried to hide it. I gave her a sharp look over my shoulder as we turned to leave. She should be taken out into the public square and stoned. I wondered how many heads she had turned away from their espoused or wives.

We no sooner reached the outside, than I turned to Yered and in the heat of my anger I spoke, "I do not like the way that woman looks at you! You do not show any restraint around her." My words were harsh and matched my intense burning. Yered's eyes widened and he blinked at me.

"You have shamed me and even worse Nebra with your loose behavior. We will wait for BarArni out here and you shall never go back there again. That is my wish."

Yered lowered his head and stood silent for a short space and then spoke. "I did not wish to dishonor you, Father, and I did not realize I was behaving shamefully." He looked squarely at me now. "I was merely trying to find out if she had seen BarArni this day and when."

"You have not dishonored me Yered. You have dishonored yourself and I have been shamed. Your lack of concern for Nebra is shocking and I am sorely disappointed in you. Sorely disappointed!"

A hurt look rose in his eyes and he looked away quickly, "I am sorry, Father. I did not think I was doing wrong."

"You did not think at all, Yered. That is your problem." I returned, trying not to lose my self-control. "Whatever you do is never done alone. It always reflects on those you love. Remember that!"

"I was sure you and Nebra both would understand my intentions." He defended with a pained look.

"I am not correcting you for your intentions, Yered, just for your behavior. The best of intentions can be soured by behavior," I said, still somewhat sharp with my words. "It is one..." I stopped abruptly as footsteps were heard coming up behind me.

Turning, I saw BarArni appear in the subtle light cast by the open heavens. He stopped and stared at us a moment. "What is going on? Is something wrong?" He asked looking around.

"Nothing for you to be concerned about." I informed.

"It is all clear. We have seen no soldiers." Yered injected in a relieved tone. He was not only glad BarArni was there, but also that the tide of events would take us away from the distasteful conversation we were having.

"Good! Come with me and keep quiet until we get into the valley." BarArni ordered and turned back into the darkness of the buildings. We past through the Dung Gate and out into the Kidron valley.

As we left the city walls behind us, I wondered if there had not been a better way to find the disciples. Maybe, we should have just gone back into Galil and looked for some of them there. Well, it was now too late for that, so I just followed Yered in silence. After a short time we stopped behind a large overhang on our descent into the valley.

"We will wait here for a while." BarArni indicated the place and sat down upon a flat limestone rock that protruded from the side of the ravine under the overhang. Yered looked at me and shrugged. So, we squatted there for sometime, then BarArni arose. "We can go now."

His slim figure bent low, he led the way through the rough gorges cut into the slope of the valley by summer rains. The sheer cliff sides of these narrow gorges were ten to fifteen cubits tall that gave you the feel of a narrow hall.

"Why did we stop?" I asked softly as we moved through the rough terrain.

"To make sure no one was following us." BarArni said flatly. He then placed his finger to his lips and signaled for us to come along.

At a point where there was a deep drop off on the right of us my foot found some loose rock and slipped. I regained myself quickly. Nevertheless, the rocks I had knocked loose rolled noisily off the ledge and bounced several times on their downward path. BarArni stopped and we stood listening for some time. Then he signaled for us to continue on.

Up ahead of us, like a black silent sentry, was a natural cave in the side of the ravine. There were no carvings in the rocks to denoting that it was the entrance to

160

a tomb nor was there a stone to roll into place to make a door.

Once inside the mouth of the cave it was almost pitch black, but a slight glow could be seen further on into the tunnel. Feeling our way along I was struck with the feeling of adventure that I thought I had put aside as manhood overtook me. The cave jetted north sharply and at this place a torch burned brightly sticking out of a hole in the wall that served as a holder. Below it sat a tall reed basket near the wall with several torch handles sticking up out of it. The cave here was about three cubits wide and the ceiling was several handsbreadths over a tall man's head. There was another cave opening on the west wall only two cubits wide and just about one handsbreadth over BarArni' head. BarArni took out two torches and lit them from the one burning on the wall. He then handed Yered one and said, "You go behind and I will lead the way." Yered nodded and BarArni turned to go into the west cave.

When BarArni turned away, I took the small bag containing the money I had promised him and dropped it into the basket where the torches were. It made a slight clank as it hit the bottom, but I covered the noise by kicking the reeds slightly with my foot. BarArni glanced my way then turned back. I looked a Yered and he smiled with a nod.

Just inside this cave entrance was a large room where the dead are lain into wall vault sepulchers sealed with rock and mortar. They were traditionally white washed as a warning to anyone that it contained a body. There were three of these and two open tombs carved into the walls where no one has been lain as yet. These were hewed out so that, the length of the body is lain within the walls. Beyond this room there were several others just about the same. Some caves having more or less sealed sepulchers and open tombs. Then we came out into the night and another gorge went to our right hand and to our left. On the wall just in front of us was three other cave openings. BarArni made no hesitation and entered the one

161

straight across the way from the one we just left. It is impossible to tell how many tombs we went through but there were several crevice crossways.

Inside one cave, Yered following close on my heals tripped suddenly over some obstruction in the floor and lunged forward falling against me. He regained himself quickly and I turned with a frown. In the torch light I could see his face was as white as ash and little beads of moisture laid above his upper lip mingling with the few hairs he had grown to start a mustache and beard.

He blinked at me wide eyed and stammered, "I, …I am sorry, Father."
I just turned and with several hurried steps caught up with BarArni who was now moving rather fast.

Finally, a glow of torchlight could be seen up ahead through a cave opening. Some voices were heard now, but I was unable to make them out. Then we entered a large room scattered with men sitting upon pallets, and before us was a rough wooden table with some benches around it. Three men were sitting around the table with pottery vessel cups in front of them and looked at us when we entered. Several oil pots on stands were scattered around the room providing ample light and a torch burned near another entrance to this room on the far right. There was a set of carved steps going up the wall beyond the table into a hole in the ceiling about ten cubits high and it, too, was lit by torches.

Suddenly, there was a commotion behind me. I whirled around to see two men struggling with Yered. One had each arm and the torch he was carrying swung wildly in the air. They had apparently been hiding against the walls on either side of the door. While I watched, two others caught me one on each arm. I struggled somewhat but could tell it was no use and quieted myself. Yered, however, frightened from our walk through the tombs and now this unexpected attach was kicking and struggling frantically.

Suddenly, in my mind's eye I saw two things; Yered and myself lying somewhere in the valley, our life's blood pouring from us making great pools. Second, Sarepta standing in the doorway of our house looking out toward the sunrise with the sweet sound of Miryam's angelic voice coming from inside singing one of my favorite songs. Then Miryam appeared in the doorway behind Sarepta and they both stood looking. Watching! Waiting! A chill ran through me and I blinked the vision from my mind.

"What is this?" I asked looking at BarArni, but he bore a surprised look upon his face. "You think now that we are here you can rob us?" I yelled. My anger was on the verge anyway still seething from Yered's outrageous behavior. "Well, you are wrong! You will find nothing of value on us. Did you not think we are aware of what kind of people we are dealing with."

"What kind?" A voice behind me inquired.

When the man spoke Yered ceased to struggle and stood breathing hard. The two men holding me turned me to face the table where a short stout man with broad shoulders and hard looking eyes sat staring at us.

"Thieves and robbers," I returned quickly.

"Thieves and robbers, huh?" He scoffed roughly. "How about winebibbers and murderers?" He picked up his cup mockingly with a wide grin.

"That too, I suppose." I acknowledged. This was the man who took delight in choking the Roman soldier before running his sword through him earlier this very day.

He laughed heartily and then said, "Men, we are thieves and robbers, and supposed murders and winebibbers."

He held his cup up, tilted his head back and drank down whatever was in it. Then he swiped the spill of it off his mouth with the sleeve of his tunic and stood up. On his side hanging from a leather girdle was a sword in its sheath. His dark hair lay in tangled strings of waves and his beard had not seen a razor for some time.

"Well, sir," he continued as he came near to me. "You are right about one thing." He smirked and then grew sober. He was a hard man and I could see our death in his eyes.

"We are most definitely winebibbers." He turned himself around waving his arm at the dozen or so men standing around. This drew laughs from them and he reveled in his little joke. He looked at me and raised upon his toes then settled back on the floor. He was enjoying this toying with us, but his antics only served to make the blood in my veins run hotter.

"You think this is funny? We came here in good faith. We have brought no weapons, nor valuables. Is there no honor left in Israel?" I struggled against the retrains of my captures.

"Honor?" He returned bitterly. His lip curled in mockery. "No! There is no honor left in Israel. The Roman swine have seen to that." He spit upon the limestone floor and it rolled and curled in the dust and seemed to take on life like some loathsome creature.

"Release them." He commanded heartily with a wave of his hand. The men who held us were not gentle and the struggling against them did not help. When we were released I rubbed my stinging arms only half-conscious of doing so.

The man studied us a degree with his black piercing eyes. He then turned back to the table and made an upward motion to a fellow who had been seated with him and now stood near the steps. He turned and went up while the man apparently in charge poured another cup of wine from an earthen pitcher that sat in the middle of the table.

"You think we are without honor?" He fashioned the words with his lips. Taking a careless gulp of the wine, he turned back to us. "I am not without honor! You are the one without honor." He shoved the cup in our direction sloshing liquid from it onto the floor without the slightest concern.

"I am a rebel, a zealot, who loves Israel with a passion, enough to live in tombs." He made a casting motion over his head. "Enough to fight and die for her. That gives me honor. You, …on the other hand live in your comfortable home bowing yourself to the whims of the Roman Emperor." He pointed his finger at me around the cup he held in his hand. "No, my brother! You are the one who has no honor."

Now that he was near one of the lamps, I could see what looked like a scar across his right cheek obscured slightly by the short beard he was wearing. BarAbbas! Yes, it must be.

"Who are you and what have you come here for?" He asked after we studied each other a degree of time.

I opened my mouth to answer when three women descended from the upper chambers. One was older and her face spoke of years and wisdom. The other two were younger. The older woman carried a basket of what appeared to be fruit. One of the younger women had another earthen pitcher, while still the other had some more cups.

"I am Timon of Beitorah," I said as the women came to the table and set down their burdens. The one with the pitcher poured wine into the two cups the other young woman had set before her. "This is Yered, son of my concubine."

"Well, I am BarAbbas and these," he swung his arm around the room indicating his men, "…are the sons of Israel. We are not robbers and thieves, but murder we do, if you care to call it that, in the name of Elohim and for the cause of Israel."

He put his arm around the older woman. "This is our mother and these dear ones," he nodded his head at the two younger women, "…are the daughters of Israel." The older woman looked up into his face as he spoke with a pleased expression. Whatever else the man was, …he was a leader of men.

"Come!" He now beckoned to Yered and myself. "Come sit, …have some wine and a piece of fruit with a thief and robber." His words brought grins and few low jeers from his men.

I came to the table seating myself and the young damsel handed me a cup. Yered seated himself beside me and received a cup. BarAbbas took his seat across from us and drank down the wine he had just poured. "Why have you come here?" His words were demanding and the young woman with the pitcher filled his cup again.

"I came to speak with the disciples of YahShua the Messiah who are rumored to be here with you."

A strange combination of looks flashed across BarAbbas' face, then he smiled. "Who told you they were here?"

"BarArni." I replied and my eyes sent him a harsh look.

BarArni became fidgety and fear showed in his eyes. "They were here!" He sounded defensive.

BarAbbas looked at him. "What did you hope to gain by this, BarArni? Do we not have enough trouble?"

"He hoped to gain ten silver pieces." Yered injected shooting a cold look at him. "Five of which he already has received and probable spent."

He winced and said to BarAbbas meekly. "I did not see what harm it would do. I was very careful. No one followed us."

"Fool!" BarAbbas barked then turned back to me. "I was wrong. It appears there is at least one thief among us, but not really a part of us."

"Hey, you can not say that!" BarArni returned quickly. "Do I not fight Roman dogs along beside you? Do I not take the same chance to die as do you? What gain do I get for it? None!"

BarAbbas slammed his fist down hard upon the table both Yered and I both jumped up from the table. Yered's hand went to where his sword would normally be and his fingers felt for it. BarAbbas' wine cup near the blow

166

overturned and the others rocked back and forth wildly. "That," BarAbbas spit, "...is why you are not a part of us." He arose quickly and went over to him. "You do not have the purpose of Israel in your heart."

Grabbing his clothing in a clenched fist, he pulled him down into his face being somewhat shorter than BarArni. "You are nothing! You hear that? Nothing! You are worse than nothing!" He screamed at him while BarArni blinked away the angry spray that came from his words. "You do not give your life like a true Israelite. A true Israelite knows he gains nothing for himself. He fights only for Elohim! For Freedom! For the people and for his children, and their children." He shook him hard by his clothing.

"You make me sick." He roared at him. "Get out of my face!" He cast in his teeth releasing him with a hard shove. BarArni reeled backward, almost falling, but catching himself against the wall with one hand.

"I saw no harm in bringing them to see the disciples." He whimpered.

"Out! Get out of my sight!" BarArni blinked back his words and stared at him. "Get out! O..u..t!" BarAbbas bellowed and pointed at the doorway. BarArni turned quickly and stumbled before he disappeared into the darkness through the cave doorway.

One of the young women turned upright BarAbbas' cup quickly and refilled it while he was still yelling at BarArni to get out. BarAbbas ran his fingers through his hair and took a deep breath, letting it out slowly. He paced back and forth a degree of time clenching and unclenching his fist. Then he looked up at us as though just remembering we were there and returned to the table.

"I am sorry for that ugly outburst, but a man can stand only so much." He picked up the cup and drank heavily from it. He yanked the bench out and seated himself heavily. Yered and I returned to our seats as well. The older woman came behind him and began to rub his shoulders. Love and devotion were in her every movement.

"The disciples are not here," he sighed deeply. He spoke as though unaware of the woman's hands. "They have gone into Galil."

I was not sure whether his sigh meant he was relieved they left, or if it meant he was sorry they had gone, or that the woman's work was satisfying. I was deeply disappointed at the news of their departure. I had so hoped to find at least one and talk with him.

"How long were they here with you?" I questioned.

"About a week." He looked into his cup and then took a drink of it.

"What did they say?"

He looked up at me puzzled and then a smile broke upon his face. "What they did not say would be an easier question to answer. They preached at us most of the time. He frowned.

"About YahShua?"

"Yes." He looked away as though talking about Him bothered him somewhat. "They are peculiar men." he proceeded. "They tried to persuade us to lay down our weapons. They seemed to think that their words would bring deliverance to Israel not the ridding us of the Romans. I must admit we had a few heated arguments about it.

"Did they speak of Him raising from the dead?"

He threw his head back and laughed heartily. "Oh yes. They are convinced that He is alive. They even swore that He appeared to them in the upper room where they were hiding." His eyes sparkled with amusement. "Imagine their talking to a dead man."

Then his expression changed into a scrawl. "Poor fools! The strain of the past few days have played tricks upon their minds." He shrugged as though to rid himself of the thought.

"Was any..." My words were cut short by a loud voice.

"Romans! Romans are coming!" BarArni called as he reappeared in the doorway out of breath.

"How far away are they?" BarAbbas demanded coming to his feet.

"They were at the cave entrance," he reported.

"Go with Ishama and help him with the women." BarAbbas said to him as though there had never been words between them. He had given him an important responsibility, a position of trust, to let him know he was still accepted. It is the mark of a true leader.

"We will meet near the Yarden where John baptized. Go! Go! Everyone go!" He waved them away with a wide swing of his arm. "You, Timon!" He slapped my across the chest with the back of his might arm and nearly took my breath away. "You and your son stay close to me. I will get you out."

"They must have followed us," I determined. "BarAbbas, I am sorry. I should have known Kayafa was having me watched. Now some of these men's blood will be upon my hands."

"And, my sword is at the inn." Yered bemoaned as he stood, but I heard it. Now, I, too, wish he had brought it for if we get caught with the zealots we will suffer as one of them.

BarAbbas looked at me and then took a torch from the wall near the doorway to the right, the one we did not enter. He took off through it at a run and we followed. We ran through tunnels, tomb rooms and crossways. We ran here and there, this way and that, seemingly in circles. I had to stop several times and lean against the wall to catch my breath. We could hear the rush of several footsteps in the tunnels behind us. I did not know if it was Romans or some other zealots making their escape, but it was enough to drive me onward. Everything looked the same. Everywhere we went it all looked alike. Then we stopped at the foot of a wooden ladder that went up.

Yered and BarAbbas were gasping for breath and I felt as though my lungs were going to burst asunder. They seemed unable to receive what breath I was drawing. There was no sound behind us now so we stood there each in his own misery. I held to the ladder to keep from falling for my knees quivered under me and had no strength left in them. Then the sound came again, scarcely were we able to hear it, rushing footsteps.

"Quickly!" BarAbbas gasped as he hurried up the ladder.

The opening was at least seven cubits high and when I tried to make my legs move to step on the first rung they did not respond so Yered took the second place. I summoned all my strength and slowly began to make the climb. Each step took every measure of conscious effort I had left in me.

"Come on, Father!' Yered called down to me as though I was not coming as fast as my aching muscles would allow.

My legs seemed like numb stumps now and about halfway up the ladder, I felt the foot I was trying to place on the next rung slip off. My leg with sure footing was too weak to support the whole weight of my body and crumbled under the strain. There was a tremendous jerk against my left arm and I was swinging only by a handhold on the ladder rung. The cold dark walls of the cave swirled before my face, sweat drenched my body. If I let loose and dropped back to the floor the Romans would be upon me and I would not escape. I made a frantic grab for a rung with the other, but it was not a good hold and it slipped again. The hand I was holding on with was weakening fast for I could feel my fingers slipping. My legs felt like iron now, dead weight and of little use. Then I made another grab out of sheer desperation and this time my hand caught the rail, but almost immediately slipped off again. Just as the other hand came free of the rung a strong grasp caught my wrist. I looked up into Yered's shadowed face. He held on with a grunt. Finally, my foot bumped against the ladder and clumsily found a hold.

"Please, Elohim, give me strength," I whispered.

Everything was a blur and now I was being drug through the hole by Yered and BarAbbas. The soft light of night welcomed me and beyond was the walls of my beloved city.

"Help me with the ladder." BarAbbas breathed and Yered took hold of one side.

I laid there on the ground like water poured out and watched them pull up the ladder. Below the sound of rushing feet filled the cave and while we held our breath they faded slowly into the distance.

BarAbbas came to where I lay on the cool welcome ground. "You are safe now," he said, "...and I must be going." He turned away, then hesitated and turned back to me. "You are not a man without honor, Timon. I was wrong." He patted me on the arm. "Shalom!"

"I, too, was wrong about you, BarAbbas. Elohim speed!" I managed to say between breaths. My heart was pounding in my throat and my lungs screamed in pain.

BarAbbas looked at Yered. "Your father can find his way back to the city from here. Come with me and help me fight the Romans. You have a strong arm and courage. We could use you."

Yered stared at him, and I could see even with just the torchlight, the longing in his eyes. It would not be imaginary enemies he would be fighting if he agreed to go. He was so young, so impressionable. I held my breath and moaned within myself, "No Yered!" I knew I had to let him determine his own path and did not tell him what was in my heart. It seemed to me to be a long time that he pondered the answer.

"No," he shook his head. "I am not sure your way is the way I must go, my friend. Until I am sure, I will stay with my father." His words were definite and BarAbbas grasped his arm as a brother and went away into the darkness.

I let out a sigh of relief and closed my eyes. Sometimes the hardest thing in life to do is to let go, ...just simply to let go. Somehow I had managed to do it and in return Yah gave back to me that which I was willing to lose. The next time I might not get him back, but until then

I will thank Yah for him and be content to have him for the length of time it seems good for him to stay.

DAY NINE

In front of the inn the servants scurried about carrying out Benren's orders preparing for the journey back to Galil while I stood looking over my Beloved City. There was a pain in my heart as I watched the sun's glow brighten the sides of the buildings. I may never again get the opportunity to visit the place I grew to love as a lad seeking excitement and adventure. I wanted so to turn my face toward the Great Temple and pray, but I knew my efforts would avail me nothing. It was hard to imagine the Most Holy Place without the presence of Yah. Now, in the aftermath of all that has happened I found it all so hard to believe. I wanted to think it was just a freakish night dream that now as the morning breaks upon the city, I could rest assured the bad dream was over and everything was as it was in the beginning. However, the bitter taste of the last week reminded me that it was more than a hideous dream. I must this day face the reality of what has happened to this place and to this people.

I wondered what would become of Nakdimon and Eldaher, the blind man who was healed. I was concerned about the zealots. How many died last night because of me and how many are now facing the cross? I saw the heart of BarAbbas and felt his passion for Israel. He was not a bad man. He was just doing what seemed right to him, and for the best interest of the people. I suppose what he is doing could be right, but it seems like such a waste of lives, and the chance that they could really make a change was empty and vain. The coming of the soldiers prevented me from trying to reason with him. It would most likely have been a futile effort. If the very disciples could not persuade him, what chance would I have had. Even I was having a hard time believing that Yah has judged Yerushelayim and this people for their sins by the mouth of YahShua. What if... Maybe, I had missund... If! If! I am so tired of 'ifs', so tired of questions with no answers.

"Go home, Timon! Just get in your carriage and go home." I told myself. But, alas, the restlessness in my spirit told me I would be no better off there than here. At least in my pursuit I might find the answers to a few of the questions. I sighed deeply and hoped that wherever Yah is leading it would be worth the effort. A wise man does not start on a journey without counting the cost, but I did not expect to lose so much to gain, ...Yah only knows what. I have lost my place of worship, will probably lose my beloved city and almost lost the son of my concubine and for what? For what?

"Father?" Yered's voice drifted through the window and I looked down at him in the street below, "I have found the bag where you said and the sum is still in it. Benren said I should tell you everything is ready. Will we go now?"

Reluctantly I nodded my head, "Yes, we shall go now."

The wheels of the cisium squeaked out its song while the horses' hooves set down the beat on the stone streets. A group of children laughed and played in a garden in front of a house while the local merchants were setting out their wares for a day's business. I caught the smell of fresh bread and fig blossoms and watched a maiden with a pitcher on her shoulder going down the street. Up ahead there was the change of guards at the city gate and the officer barked out commands. The troop turned and marched toward us and then upon the call from the officer, made a square corner and then in the direction of their barracks at the Fortress of Antonia.

Passing through the city gate my heart sank as I bid Yerushelayim a sad farewell. I just sat in my carriage and stared into nothingness. I said nothing nor did nothing. Then Yered came to the side of the cisium.

"Father," he scrawled and fidgeted with the reigns of his horse, "...has Elohim forsaken His people forever?"

"No, Yered. Elohim did not forsake His people. The people have forsaken Him. They choose the way of lies and are deceived."

"I have not forsaken Him," Yered returned quickly.

"Nor have I, but the chief cohanim, the elders and leaders of the people have."

"Have Nakdimon and BarAbbas forsaken Him?"

"That they must answer in their own hearts, just as we. If they have not, then they are just blind. The blind following the blind and they both fell into the same ditch and come to the same end."

"That does not seem right to me."

"Elohim is not unrighteous," I assured him with a smile. "When the leaders refuse to walk in the path of righteousness, it is of their own choosing. For Elohim is faithful to make them know He is displeased with their ways. When the people follow these leaders they, too, are guilty, for they close their eyes to Elohim's rebuke and choose to listen to the leaders instead of Elohim."

"What will become of us, Father?"

"Elohim will, as He has in times past, deliver the righteous, but the others will go to destruction."

"Is there nothing we can do?"

"Do the will of Elohim and pray for mercy upon those who do not."

"Where has Elohim gone that I may pray to Him?"

"We will know the answer to that when we find the disciples. Until then just pray in your heart for Elohim always hears the prayers of a pure heart no matter where He is." He nodded in response and then rode back to the front of the procession.

Early in the morning hours we passed through the tiny village of Ramah. It is a farming village with a few merchant stores selling fruit and vegetables. There is a cobbler's shop, a synagogue, and on the edge of the village some ways out is a huge vineyard with a winepress. There is an olive grove and a fig tree orchard with quaint little flat roofed houses scattered among them.

The trees and vines were budding forth and several workers tended to them. The winepress was still now, but would soon be active with workers treading out the deep purple juice of the grape to make the new wine.

At mid-morning we stopped at BeitHal to rest the horses and refresh our water supply. It will be late afternoon before we reach Yaakov's well where we would spend the night. BeitHal looked almost empty now without the many travelers camped by the well. The village was not large, but there were several businesses in the Village Square. The inhabitants were friendly, waving at us with pleasant smiles and warm greetings.

We had traveled some time out of BeitHal when we came upon a man lumbering along the side of the road ahead of us. He wore an old robe such as I had not seen the likes of before. His head was bare and his hair was the color of straw, long and not well groomed. He was going in the same direction as we and kept a steady pace seemingly in no hurry. A walking stick was in his hand that he used to help him along his way. He was traveling light with no pack and seemed to be carrying no source of drink.

I wondered what he was doing out here in this wilderness without provisions or protection from the boiling rays of the sun. When he became aware of us he stopped and turned himself to watch our approach. The tail of his long beard gently blew with the hot dry gusts of wind that sometimes caught the dust stirred up by the feet sending it spinning into the air violently. It was apparent he was wearing a leather girdle to make his going easier, but there were not sandals for his feet to protect them from the ground that burned in the sun's heat. There was something strikingly unusual about this fellow. Maybe, it was the clothes he was wearing.

Yered bowed his head slightly and dismounted by him. I could see they were talking and when we drew nigh unto them, I told Semone to stop.

The man laid his walking stick against Yered's chest holding it about in the middle and I heard the stranger say in the ancient Hebrew tongue. "Young man," his voice cracked somewhat, "...what tongue are ye are speaking?"

I saw Yered frown. "Do you not speak Aramaic, sir?" He said.

Climbing from my carriage I answered for him. "He is speaking Hebrew, Yered." Then I said in the Hebrew language to the old man. "He does not speak good Hebrew, sir. He is still learning the language. He speaks Greek and Aramaic."

The traveler looked astonished at him, but said to me. "He is Hebrew, is he not? Then why does he not speak Hebrew?"

"Yes, he is Hebrew, but Hebrew is spoken very little except among the old ones and some learned people."

"I am Timon from Beitorah." I introduced myself. "This young fellow," I patted Yered's upper arm affectionately, "...is Yered, the son of my concubine."

The old man studied Yered as though he was seeing something others do not. Yered nodded and I continued. "Not being yet well skilled with the ancient Hebrew Language, Yered will be able to understand only the simple things you say." I explained.

The man's eyes were pale blue, sharp and piercing as though he could read the soul. "I am Mikha from Moresheth," he informed.

"He says, He is from Moresheth." I told Yered and he nodded again.

"Do ye have something for an old man to drink?"

"Yes Sir," Yered understood. "There is water and the fruit of the vine."

The man quirked one eyebrow at Yered's Araraic and said, "I will have a drink of water."

Yered called to the servants saying, "Bring a cup of water for the traveler."

Benren appointed one of the young men and he went for it while he climbed out of my carriage and came to my side.

Reading through the Sacred Writings so much lately, I was aware of the Prophet Mikha who prophesied of the establishing of the Adonai's house after our captivity in Babylon. He had told of a deliverer to come from BeitLechem and how His righteous remnant would be blessed in the earth.

I mused over this man speaking Hebrew and having a Prophet's name. He had used the ancient name for the city he said he was from. While I pondered this, the servant brought the old fellow his cup of water.

"Where is Moresheth?" Yered formed a wrinkle between his eyes.

"In the plains of Yhudea." I answered while the man was busy with the drink. This stranger intrigued me. "It has not been called Moresheth for many generations. It is called Marisa now."

"What?" The traveler recovered and looked at me so I repeated it.

"It is?" He looked surprised.

"Yes! It has been called by that name since before the Greeks conquered the land."

"We... well," the fellow stammered, "...I have not been there for a long time."

If he were around when it was called by its old name that would make him, ...many hundreds of years of age! Impossible! It cannot possibly be...

"That would make him hundreds of years old?" Yered looked bewildered. He must have been thinking the same as I.

"What?" The traveler frowned.

"He said, you should be hundreds of years old." I interpreted.

"What do ye have against age?" The traveler became indignant.

"Nothing, sir!" Yered quickly exclaimed. He must have understood or was reacting to the man's tone of voice.

"I will have some wine now." He shoved the cup at Yered.

"Yes, sir!" Yered handed the cup to the boy. "Bring some wine now."

At that Benren asked me, "Will you take some wine, my lord?"

"Yes," I responded absently studying the old man's dress. 'No,' I thought, 'he could not possibly be the Prophet Mikha.'

"Where are you going?" Yered asked the traveler with a peculiar expression.

"Up the road." He returned with an absent wave of his hand.

"You mean, …there is no place, …you are traveling to?" Yered blinked in astonishment fumbling with the words.

The old man's face twisted in irritation. "Does one need to have someplace to go?"

"N, …no, sir! I guess not," Yered stammered.

"Where are you going?" The man tapped Yered on the chest again with the twisted limb he used as a walking stick.

"To Galil."

"Yes. Yes to Galil." The dusty old fellow nodded his head. "Other places as well, a place called Rome. He revealed in a matter of fact way.

"Rome?" Yered frowned.

"Ye will seek a man there held by the rulers by the name of Shaul."

The man is a Prophet! He has told Yered things to come. He has old raiment. His name is Mikha. He speaks Hebrew instead of Aramaic or Greek. This is very strange, …very strange indeed!

By now Benren and the servants had set the traveling chairs and placed the shelter. "The shelter is ready, my lord," he announced.

"Perhaps the Prophet would like some meat." I suggested to Benren in Hebrew.

The man cleared his throat. "Just a little for the journey's sake," he injected with quirked expression.

179

Benren bowed slightly to him and turned to Semone. "Tell the servants to prepare a platter," he ordered and Semone went to carry it out.

Yered walked beside the Prophet opposite me. "Sir?" I do not know anyone named Shaul," he said clumsily.

The Prophet looked irritated at him, seating himself with a light grunt, "You have said that already and I have answered."

Yered opened his mouth to say something else, but closed it again looking bewildered and sat down.

Benren brought a tray with a pitcher of wine and three cups while a young servant maiden brought a platter putting it on the small table placed between us. The tray containing smoked meat, bread, nuts and fruit. Then another servant gave a damp cloth to each of us.

We sat quietly for a while each lost in our own thoughts as the old man ate from the tray. Dust drifted from his clothing with each movement and his manner was crude for he made much sound as he ate. It seemed to me as though he had not eaten for some time.

"Sir," I inquired after a while. "What of me?"

"Ye shall oversee the care of women and children." He replied without missing a bite or looking up.

"Is that all?"

Now he looked up at me pausing in mid-chew, then swallowed. "It is a blessing from Yah. That is enough."

He has used the sacred name of which is forbidden by the elders. I stared at the man a degree, and then I nodded taking a cluster of grapes wet with the water they are cooled in for travel. I pondered what the Prophet meant, but I ate in silence. I wondered if he was aware of the happening in Yerushelayim and if he knew about YahShua. He, being a Prophet, might be able to tell me where I can find the disciples.

"Prophet, do you know of the happenings in Yerushelayim these past few days?" I ventured to ask.

He lifted his head and a far away look filled his eyes and he said with a powerful voice. "The rulers of the house of Israel, who abhor justice and twist everything that is straight, who builds Zion with bloodshed and Yerushelayim with violent injustice, and say, 'Is not the Adonai in our midst? Calamity will not come upon us.' Therefore, because of ye, Zion will be plowed as a field, Yerushelayim will become a heap of ruins, and the mountain of the Temple will become high places of the forest."

I sat astonished as the words of the Prophet Mikha rolled form his lips making the Sacred Writings come alive and ring in my ears as a storm upon the troubled waters of the soul. He knows! He is Mikha! I sat staring in wonder at this man who should long be dead.

"Sir?" Yered spoke with uncertainty. "Will we find the disciples of the Man, YahShua, the Messiah?"

"Ye shall find the man I told ye of earlier," he looked sharply at him, "...and ye," he turned to me, "...will find whom ye seek."

I could not speak for the words refused to form in my mouth, but my soul sang in grateful melody. I will find the disciples! I will find the disciples! I will, therefore, find the answers to my questions. This knowledge filled my mind with serene bewilderment.

We were quiet for some time again, each lost in our own thoughts. I was rehearsing in my mind the words the prophet had spoken. The sun fell all around our small shelter while the light breeze kissed our faces with its hot breath and our body's moisture made our clothing cling to us.

Suddenly, an ear-renting scream split the air. It came from where the servants were resting themselves, and I sprang to my feet like a stone from a sling. The servants were huddled in a small throng so I went to where they were.

Benren pushed though the press coming to me and said, "An asp came up from its hole and has bitten the boy while he stood," he told me. His expression was grave, and I made my way to the young servant boy.

"Has the wound been opened?" I beheld the lad whose face was already blue gray and his body convulsed upon the ground.

"Yes, my lord!"

The deadly asp can kill within a few degrees of time and there is little that can do done. I dropped on my knees near the boy's head and gathered him against my breast. His eyes rolled in their sockets and his tongue became thick as his lips purpled and his breath was quick and shallow. I could feel his body jerking against me and it pierced my heart as a knife. The last task in the world I wanted was to tell the lad's mother of the child's death. He was only seventeen years and very handsome to look upon.

His countenance blurred through my tears and in my mind I saw the vision of him. His arms around the neck of a new colt, looking at it with a proud smile and stroking it with a gentle hand while his voice softly soothed its uncertainties. The vision faded away as the boy's body stiffened, and I knew the end was near.

"Please Elohim!" I called out in my anguish. "...Spare the lad for he is so young and such a delight to his mother."

"Because ye have great love the boy will be spared." The crackled voice of the Prophet rested as the balm of Gilead upon my ears. I looked up at him with hope. The Prophet stooped, touched the lad and his body went limp in my arms.

"For the Adonai Yah would say unto you." The Prophet raised his voice in the power of the spirit. "As I have plucked this brand from the fire and have had compassion upon him, so will I pluck from Israel a brand. A remnant who shall do my will and stand in the last days to show forth the tender loving mercy of the Adonai to a crooked and perverse generation."

The Prophet grew quiet and everyone stood in place for a long degree.

"Is he dead, my lord?" A young maiden companion inquired with a trembling voice.

"No! The Prophet has healed him. He is only resting now." I replied. "Glory be to the Elohim of Israel!" I lifted up my voice in praise, and Yered, the Prophet and all of the servants joined me in exalting the Elohim of Heaven.

"Blessed be the name of the Most High. For he gives life out of death and turns evil into good!"

After the praises subsided, the Prophet declared, "I must be on my going."

Color began to return to the face of the lad and his breathing came with ease now although he still laid limp in my grasp. Semone stooped and took the lad from me and carried him to the carts where the servants rode.

"Sir," I called to the Prophet for he had turned away to go, "...it is much too hot for traveling by foot. There is room in my carriage. Please ride with me until you get to where you are going?" I entreated him humbly.

He turned and looked deeply at me. "I will ride, Reuwel." He stated, and went to my cisium.

'Reuwel', the meaning being 'friend of Yah'. Was I a friend of Yah? What a great honor! I felt very humbled and fought to control my joy. No man has been so blessed! I hurried to catch him and felt as though my feet had wings and did not touch the ground.

In the carriage while we traveled, I told him of the prophecy of YahShua the Messiah, of the impending destruction of Yerushelayim and her children.

He looked at me with little surprise and said, "It shall not be in your time."

I pondered that for a degree and then related to him what had happened in Yerushelayim and how I was seeking the disciples of YahShua who had fled to Galil for fear of the Romans. He seemed very interested in the whole matter and we talked a good long time about it, but he did not prophesy any more.

I took the blue robe out of the compartment built under the driver's seat and showed it to him. I told him of the Centurion who gave it to me. He took the corner gently in his hand, bending his head he placed it to his lips and kissed it lovingly as one would something very sacred.

Then his eyes fell upon the scrolls and he said, "What scrolls do ye have?"

"The Sacred Writings of all the Prophets are there. I looked and found the one written by the prophet Mikha and took it out, gently removing the doe skin cover. Handing the scroll to him, I watched his expression change from curiosity to amazement.

He blinked at me. "Why, …this is my scroll! Where did you get it?"

"He is the Prophet!" My mind screamed and my heart leaped into my throat, but I swallowed it back. How could this be? The Prophet who had written these Scared Words was here in my cisium, beside me, talking to me. I felt dazed and could not believe what I was seeing nor what my ears had just heard.

"My, fa… father bought it from a scribe's widow for a goodly sum." I managed to stammer. "How can it be that you have written these words? They are very old."
He removed his eyes slowly from the scroll and looked at me. "Behold on the day the earth quaked, my tomb opened and I came forth for Yah sent His Holy Son to redeem our souls from Sheol."

This was too much for me. I sat marveling with bewilderment not really comprehending for some time what the man had said to me. It was as though I were numbed, unable to feel, speak or understand anything. Then I sensed the presence of the Prophet leave, and by force, I looked to see him, but he was not there. In the seat where he sat was only the scroll and I blinked at it as something very strange.

"Benren," I reached forward and touched his shoulder. "Where did the Prophet go?"

Benren looked around and turned ashen white. He stared at the empty seat. "I... I do not know, my lord. He was there beside you just a short time ago."

184

"He has vanished," I explained.

"It, …is a miracle!" Benren exclaimed.

Semone said softly. "Blessed be Elohim."

Both Benren and myself choired, "Amen!"

"Stop the carriage, Semone." I commanded, still dazed somewhat and he did so while Benren called out the order to the others.

Yered rode back to me squinting in the brilliance of the afternoon sun and when arriving he looked puzzled. "Where is the Prophet?"

"He has gone," I related.

"It is a miracle," Semone injected.

"He just disappeared," Benren recalled. "He was there talking and then he was not."

"He just vanished?" Yered ask in astonishment.

"Yes, Yered, as though he never was." I reflected a degree. My mind raced back over the whole event, and it seemed like a dream. Then I thought about the servant bitten by the serpent. "How is the boy?"

"Ah, …all right I guess," he returned with an unbelieving quirk to his head.

"I will go ask about him." I climbed from the carriage and went back to where the boy was in the wagon. He lay under upon the spread with his eyes closed. One of the servants, the one who was so concerned about him earlier, was sitting nearby washing his face with a cloth.

"How is he?" I asked, surprised to see him lying there. It brought reality to the happening and I could not deny it.

"He is very sick, my lord." The damsel answered and her eyes showed signs of weeping.

I felt and he burned under my touch. "A fever is upon him."

"Yes, my lord."

"We will stop at the village of Shklem over by Yaakov's well and get a physician for him." I determined. "Do not worry child, he will live. The Prophet has said so." I assured her.

"My lord," Benren caught my sleeve as we were returning to the cisium. "That is a Shamron village." His face held a look of horror.

"I am well aware of that, but the boy is more important to me than tradition. We will take the boy to the inn at Shklem, Shamron or not. Surely an inn will not turn us away because we are L'vites. L'vites are well accepted throughout the land, even among the Shamron. Benren twisted his face into a frown but said nothing further.

We traveled on for several hours stopping occasionally so I could ask about the boy. His condition seemed nothing improved. However, he was alive and I was thankful to Yah for sparing him.

The distant mountains were clothed in dark purple raiment as evening presented itself with a cooling breeze. A white cloud like a halo, crowned the top of the peaks up ahead of us, and below in the valley the Shamron town of Shklem awaited in the distance. The Shamron have little to do with Yews, but will receive me for I am a L'vite. We will find lodging there and stay until the boy is fit for travel.

At the sight of the well, the women of the city were drawing water for the night and servant boys watered a flock of sheep that were bleating a grateful thank you for their efforts. Some distance away, a fleet of camels lay among the colorful fleece tents of a band of nomads. Their humps laid down falling on this side or that as they contentedly chewed their cud with heads held high. Women were tending a campfire and preparing the meal while small children squealed at play not far from them. The men sat under a sheepskin canopy talking with each other.

The village was deserted except those coming or going for water. In the market place a small squad of soldiers rode down the street ignoring us.

Yered called a halt in front of a small inn with the Star of David over the door. He came back to me. "I will find a physician for the boy, father." He assured me.

"Good," I agreed. I turned my attention to Benren as Yered rode away. "Go into the inn and see if there is room."

"Yes, my lord." He climbed down and went into the place while I went to check about the sick boy. He was still with fever and was babbling something that made no sense.

"Yered has gone for the physician." I told the maiden who cared for the boy. "We will soon have him in a room where he shall recover quickly."

"My lord," the damsel said shyly, "if the Prophet healed him, why is he still so sick?"

"Child, a prophet can not heal. Only Yah can heal. The Prophet said, 'The boy will be spared'. This sickness is not unto death. He will soon recover."

When Benren returned he said unto me, "They have room and will receive us."

"Quickly now, bring the lad." I beckoned and turned for the inn door. Semone took the boy in his arms and followed Benren and myself inside.

A woman who apparently runs the inn came to meet us as we entered. "This way."

She showed us the stairs inset in the wall at the back of a small room with only a few tables and chairs. Underneath the stairs was a doorway were many strings of brightly colored beads hung by leather straps from the lintel. Each strand dangled close together making a curtain that would part between any of the strings.

We followed her up to the second level where there were several rooms on either side of a narrow hallway. Several oil lamps sat on a shelf against the left wall at the head of the stairs. Two of the lamps, one on each end of the shelf, sent out a yellow glow as they burned. At the end of the hallway, the beginning of another set of steps continued on up disappearing around the corner.

The woman took a lamp from the shelf and lit it from one already burning and opened a door near the head of the stairs. "You may put the boy in here." She led the way into the room placing the lamp on a small table near a low bed. Semone carried the young boy over and placed him on the bed.

"What is his sickness," the woman asked abruptly.

"He has been bitten by an asp." I informed. "We have sent for a physician."

"How long has he been like this?" Her words were quick as she felt of the boy. "He will probably die."

"No," Semone corrected. "He will live."

"How are you so sure?" He is very sick."

"The Prophet of Elohim has told us he will not die." Benren assured her.

"Prophet?" Her eyes grew large and she looked with expectation at both Semone and Benren, then at me. "What Prophet? YahShua, the Messiah?" There was a hint of hope in her voice. She wanted to hear that it was.

"No," I shook my head, "it was the Prophet Mikha." I watched the hope drain from her expression and she took her eyes away quickly. "Do you believe in the Man, YahShua?" I ventured.

"What does it matter? He is dead." I caught the hint of despair she was trying very hard to hide. I started to answer, but she continued speaking leaving me nowhere to respond.

"Come, I will show you your room." She made quick steps and was at the door, so I just followed her. She was an abrupt and quick person with an air displaying an independent manner. I again started to ask her if she was a follower of YahShua, but before I could speak she said, "The servants may have the common room on the first floor." She went across the hall and opened another door. I opened my mouth to speak again when she looked at me and spoke quickly.

"I think you will find this room to your liking."

She seemed to be a strong forceful woman and I found myself becoming disturbed, for she gave me no room to reply or speak. I studied her for a degree while she held the door for me. I wondered if she knew Him and if she would talk with me about Him, or was she one of those who tried to believe, but now does not?

She tilted her head slightly and returned my gaze. Her long raven hair responded to her movement like a dark waterfall in the moonlight, highlights skipping through it from the hallway lamps. Her slim face was lovely and the green in her eyes was afire with life and expectancy giving her a hint of mystery.

A puzzled look formed on her face and then replaced with a queer smile. "...and no," she took up again her words as though she had never stopped speaking, "I will not lay with you tonight." She showed little emotion or embarrassment, but I felt my face flush and now it was I with the queer expression. I do suppose she could have taken my curiosity of her as an unspoken question, but I was startled at her boldness and taken back that she would even think such a thing. I started to explain myself to her, but I did not get the words out before she spoke again.

"I am sorry! I took your looking upon me wrongly. I am usually good at reading men. Forgive me!" She did not even give me the satisfaction of correcting her. She is the kind of woman a man has a hard time living with.

I was suddenly irritated with her one way conversation and determined to get my say. "I, as..."

I do not know if it was that I was so surprised to finally get to speak or what, but now I found nothing to say. She had said it all for me. Maybe that was the thing that irritated me about her. I had never met anyone who could carry on a conversation with someone without the other person saying a word, but somehow she had managed.

With the lamp in hand she led the way into the room setting it on the small table by the bed as she had done in the boy's room. Beside the table was a comfortable looking bed and near the wall on the far side was another small table with a single lounge by it. Near the small table was a window with the shutters closed.

I shut the door and started to ask her if she was a follower of YahShua, when she spoke again. "Do you want me to prepare you something to eat?"

"Yes," I injected sharply and she blinked at me, "...that will be just fine." I finished somewhat exhausted from trying to find a place to speak.

She opened her mouth to make a reply and there came a knock on the door. It was Yered's usual knock. The door opened and he stuck his head in. "The physician is here, Father." Then his eyes flowed to the woman. There was a degree of silence and out of the corner of my eye the woman's mouth moved again but Yered spoke first.

"I am sorry to interrupt, Father, but I thought you would like to know." Then the woman tried again, but Yered was quicker. "I will see to the care of everything so you can stay near the boy."

This now struck me funny and the irritation lifted as I said with a light laugh, "All right, Yered." He formed a twisted puzzled look, but dropped it quickly and withdrew from the room.

"That was Yered, son of my concubine. He will need a room and a meal, also." I informed, "When you have prepared my meal, bring it into my room and let me know. I will be with the boy." Those were the most words I had spoken since I had entered here.

The woman nodded and went out. I followed her and entered the boy's room across the hall from mine. A man in a dark robe leaned over the sick young lad. Benren and Semone were not here now, only the young maiden who was caring for him in the wagon. I drew near and watched the physician tend to him, and when he became aware of me, he looked up.

"Is he your servant?"

"Yes," I returned. "He will be all right?"

"I think so," he nodded, "but it will take much care. Recovery will be slow, I am afraid. I do not understand why he is not dead. The bite of an asp usually brings death."

"It is because Elohim is with him." My answer seemed to satisfy and he nodded. He took a poultice out of a leather sack tied to his girdle and wrapped it to the boy's puncture wound with a cloth. "Here is something for the fever." He handed me a vile with some dark liquid in it. "Mix it with his water in small portions. It is all I can do for him."

"Very well." I handed the vile to the damsel. "What is the debt?"

"A silver piece will do, and I will check him every day until he can travel. It will be a good idea not to leave him alone until the fever breaks."

"I will sit with him, my lord." The young maiden spoke eagerly and when I looked at her, I could tell she was slightly red behind her veil. "Forgive my boldness." She quickly lowered her head.

I turned my attention back to the physician. "How long will it be until he is able to travel?"

"Several days, I am afraid. He is very sick."

"All right," I sighed.

Taking the coin out of my bag, I laid it in his hand. Benren had entered while we talked and came to my side. I went with the physician to the door. "My room is across the hall there." I showed with a nod. He returned my nod and departed.

I turned to Benren now and said, "Tell Semone he is in charge of the servants, for we will be here some time. The woman is preparing the meal for Yered and myself."

"Very well, my lord." He bowed slightly and left without further delay.

The young maiden and I were alone with the boy now. I leaned over and placed my hand upon him. There were dark circles around his eyes and his lips were swollen and purple against his ashen pale face. The damsel had a damp cloth and wiped him gently to cool his brow.

"You seem to be very fond of this boy." I said without looking at her.

"Yes, my lord, very fond," she returned sadly.

"Are you espoused to him?"

"No, my lord, I am espoused to another," she confessed dipping the cloth again in a bowl of water that sat on the small table beside the lamp and ringing it out.

"Have you spoken to your father about this?" I now looked at her.

"Yes, my lord." She dabbed at his brow again tenderly. "He is a hard man and the dowry is high."

I frowned slightly, but said no more. Some fathers are like that. If she were my child, I would seek a settlement with the espoused to free her. This was one of the bad things about marriage arrangements. However, it does serve to keep mixed marriages from being more prevalent than they already are. There are many Gentiles in Israel now, not that I have anything against the Gentiles. My concubine is Greek, but I would never have thought of marrying her. I watched her minister to him with loving hands. I must see what I can do about this when I return home.

"My child, you have sat with him all the day now." I said to her. "Take your rest this night and then you will feel strong on the morrow to sit by him more. I will have Semone send one of the other maidens to care for him."

"No, my lord! Please allow me to stay," she begged. "We travel not on the morrow and I feel strong enough." I knew she wanted very much to be near when he awoke so I relented.

"Very well, but you must rest when the boy comes to himself lest you, also, become ill."

"I will, my lord. Thank you!"

As my hand found the latch on the door of my room before I entered, I heard a soft movement coming from inside. It was probably Benren seeing that everything is in place and to my liking. Entering without concern I found not Benren, but the innkeeper. She stood near the bed in front of the small table with her back to the door. I must have surprised her for she quickly whirled around looking startled, and I saw something in her hand although she

192

swiftly hid it behind her. She smiled pleasantly, but there was a caught look on her face.

"What are you doing?" I demanded to know sharply, as surprised to find her as she was to see me.

"Nothing, sir." However, her expression bore witness against her. "I have brought your meal."

Her eyes flowed from my face to the tray sitting on the other table. I did not fall prey to her attempt to distract me, and did not take my eyes away from her. I drew close to her without a word and her eyes came quickly back to me searching my face for a clue of my action. Her breath came quick in shallow gushes as I moved. She was caught and it was obvious to her. Uncertainty crept into her anxious expression. I reached around her and took one of the Sacred Scrolls out of the trembling hand she held behind her. She was frightened, and suddenly became like a little child caught in the act of a mischievous deed. She squirmed uneasily, but said nothing as I held the Sacred Writing up in front of her.

"Well?" I demanded sharply and I saw her wince slightly.

"I was not going to take it." She insisted earnestly. "I… I was just looking at it."

I raised one eyebrow and a bit of doubt filled in my mind. This seemed to disturb her and now the child likeness vanished. "I am not a thief, sir," she defended. "I know a woman is not supposed to read the Sacred Writings, but I did not see any harm in just looking at it." Her words were pleading and her face showed a twinge of fear.

I was about to tell her that I believed her, but the expression on her face quickly changed to anger. "That is a stupid law anyway," she flashed. "A woman is just as wise as a man and can understand the Sacred Writings just as well as they."

"Perhaps," I nearly shouted to be sure to speak. "But, Elohim has given the woman a husband to spare her of the weighty things so she will not spoil her beauty," I reminded, somewhat amused at her reaction. Coming from her, this outburst seemed well within character, fitting the strong unorthodox manner she displays. In these days, women were to be gentle, loving and needing the directing, protecting hand of a man.

"Husband," she spit with a toss of her head. "Well I have had five of them and each was worse than the other." She brushed past me in a huff and picked up the meal tray from the table.

"Here is your meal!" She showed a temper setting it back down hard making the pitcher and cup clink together while red spots of wine splashed on the food tray. "I hope you enjoy it. It is one thing a woman can… do." Her eyes flashed in the light of the lamp when her glance caught me watching with a grin, but I quickly hid it.

"Men!" She stomped, clenched her fists and rushed swiftly to the door.

"Wait," I called to her softening my words, and my voice grew serious. "…Please do not go. I would like a word with you." She turned back to face me, cocked her hip placing her hand on it and waited impatiently for me to speak. "What is your name?"

"Neah," she snapped. "I am a Shamron and you a Yew. What dealings do Yews have with Shorans?" Her lips pressed into a hard line.

"That is a beautiful name." I smiled at her, but she did not change her stance or her look. "There is no reason for us to be enemies. Is there not enough Romans? I am not Yew, I am a l'vite. Would you sit while I take meat and talk with me?" I nodded at the table where the platter speckled with wine awaited me.

"Why should I? Do you think you can sufficiently seduce me now!" She tossed her raven hair with a quick jerk of her head.

I was taken back by her boldness. Her words were unfounded and insulting for I had not given her any indication that I desired to be with her. I should ask her to leave, but I felt a deep need to know if she knew YahShua of Natzeret. I must over look her rudeness for the time

194

being. "I would like to ask you some questions and that is all." I held up my hand in self-defense. "What do you know of the Man, YahShua? Are you one of His followers?"

She studied me a degree and tried to withhold the softening of her expression, but she was no better at that than hiding a scroll. After a short struggle, her resistance collapsed and her eyes moistened. "He was the Son of Elohim. Why did they kill Him?" Her love for the Man surfaced.

"The elders felt threatened by the power He had over the people and were jealous of His influence." I ventured to explain.

I offered her a seat, but she hesitated while she searched my face. Then reluctantly she went to the lounge and sat down. When she looked up at me, a tear trickled slowly down her cheek. This was what she had been hiding deep within her heart.

"Why did Elohim not stop them?" She muttered with a frown. Truly she was heartbroken.

"Well," I held up the scroll taken from her still in my hand, "...from what I can understand from the Sacred Writings it all happened according to some foreknowledge of Elohim, some plan. That would explain why He did nothing."

"What plan?" She blinked at me through her long eyelashes.

"I do not know that yet." I sighed and placed the scroll back into it case and placed it with the others on the table where Benren had stacked them. Then I came and sat down beside her.

"I heard that He has risen from the dead." Her words were unstable.

"I have heard that also, but I cannot find anyone who has seen Him. I was on my way into Galil to find His disciples when the serpent bit the boy. Did you know Him?"

"Yes..." Her voice cracked somewhat, but she brought it under control with a hard swallow. "I met Him at the well of Yaakov at the edge of town and He talked with me." She brushed a tear away with a backward stroke of her fore finger. "When I came and told the men of Saklem a prophet was at the well, a great multitude went out to hear Him."

She sniffed softly. "The people entreated Him to remain here and teach us, so He stayed two days and the things He said were like fire in me." She looked away out the window and I could see the thoughts of Him meant a lot to her. She seemed to be reliving the time again as she spoke and something stirred within me. "He has changed my life," she confessed. "I keep hoping He truly has risen from the dead. That is the reason I asked you about Him earlier when you spoke of a Prophet."

"What did He say that changed your life?"

"He said," her eyes took on a far away look, "I will give you water that you would not thirst again'. That was a very peculiar thing for Him to say. There was water in the well, but we had to draw it every day. I wanted to know where I could find this water so I would not have to go there to draw from the well anymore. Furthermore, He was a Yew, but He spoke with me openly." She ran her still trembling fingers through her dark hair, pushing it away from her temple with a sigh and a slight toss of her head. "It was not drinking water He talked about. It was about being filled with the truth of Elohim."

"What is truth?" I ask more to myself than to her. I really did not expect an answer.

"As He taught us," she took up again, "I began to realize that He spoke of truth within our hearts. Satisfying our thirst for Elohim, ...I think." Her eyebrows drew together a short degree.

I was eager to get her reaction. "What is truth?" I repeated.

She pondered my question, then shrugged. "He said unto me, 'Woman, believe me an hour is coming when neither in this mountain, nor in Yerushelayim, shall you worship the Father. But, an hour is coming, and now is, when the true worshippers shall worship the Father in spirit and truth. Elohim is spirit; and those who worship Him must worship in spirit and truth'." She paused and looked at me wonderingly. "Some of His saying were hard to understand."

Well, I do not know what has happened in the Shamron Mountain, but in Yerushelayim the presence of the Adonai has departed the Temple. Is this what Yah meant? Has this prophecy of YahShua come to pass?

"Yes! Yes! Go on." I encouraged.

"Then I said unto Him, 'I know the Messiah will come and declare all things to us'. Then He told me, 'I who speak to you am He."

She seemed to be as anxious to talk as I was to hear, so I related to her about the happenings in Yerushelayim. How the earth trembled the precise time He died and how Yosef of Arimathea had borne witness of the glory of the Adonai departing the Temple.

Her eyes grew wider as I talked and then she blurted out. "I heard nothing of his happening in our High Place."

That was not surprising to me for there was no glory of the Adonai there in the first place for they had not the Ark of the Covenant. Though the Shamron worship Elohim and have their own Temple, the glory of Yah was in Yerushelayim. She looked wonderingly, "If this happened, it would surely be known."

"No Neah." I took a morsel and began to eat. "The chief cohanim and elders are hiding the happenings so they will not lose the people and their positions. Just imagine what would happen if it came to the knowledge of the people that Elohim had fled the Temple. There would no longer be a need for sacrifices, no cohanim would be needed as a result and worst of all Israel would remain in her sin bringing the wrath of Elohim upon her."

"But if He did, as you say leave the Temple, then it is so anyway even if the people do not know it." She reasoned.

"Yes, but the people do not know and the cohanim are hiding it from them. They go right on with the sacrifices just as nothing has happened."

She looked puzzled and then brightened. "So, …now we must worship in spirit and truth."

"I suppose so, but how do you do that?" Neither had a response, but I am sure she was pondering it as well as I.

"What does it all mean?" I thought aloud not really expecting an answer and she offered none.

Indeed, what is the meaning of it all? Yah is trying to tell us something about this, but what? Maybe, the disciples will hold the answers. Surely, Yah will bring us to the truth. Truth, truth is the water of life. I was now convinced that the death of YahShua, His resurrection, if there was, and the Kingdom of Yah have a very important meaning. What that meaning is shall surely change lives forever.

DAY TEN

I looked up from the scroll I was reading to ponder the words, and my thoughts turned to Elisheva whose story fit perfectly with the Prophecies I had just been reading. I could still see her making gestures with her hands as she talked. The thought of her always brings a warm feeling. Then Athera's face came into my mind and I wondered if she had birthed the child, and if Elsan was having any unforeseen problems.

I know Elsan is young to leave with the responsibility of the horses and running a household. However, Themarus has been a trainer for us since my father brought him from Rome. He assured me that if something should come up, he would help in the matter. I wanted to go home but I knew the drive within me to find out about this Man, YahShua, would not let me rest, and I would have to be off again. To go home now would just make leaving again harder for the women, especially Athera.

The door to my room opened scattering my thoughts to the warm morning breeze that drifted in through the open window near the table where Neah and I talked until the night was far spent.

"You are up early, my lord," Benren greeted.

"Yes, I am afraid I lost the fight for sleep."

"You should have summoned me, my lord, and I could have rubbed your muscles to relax you so sleep could come."

"That is all right, Benren. Neah stayed late after you left us." He did not reply, and I knew he did not like it that Neah stayed so late in my room. It does not look good for a married man of my standing to entertain a woman after dark.

"The servant boy is much better this morning, my lord. He came to himself, although the fever is not entirely gone."

"Good!" I nodded with a knowing smile. "Has Yered been up and about?"

"Yes, my lord." Benren's frown subsided and his dark eyes softened. "He is downstairs in the entry room having breakfast. When I am finished I will have yours brought up so you do not have to stop your study."

"No," I returned. "I will go down and take breakfast there."

"Very Well," he bowed lightly.

After Benren performed his duties and had departed, I went across the hall to see how the young servant was faring this day. One of the young servant maidens sat by his bedside, but not the one who loves him.

"Shalom," I nodded upon entering.

"Good day, my lord," she greeted as I drew near the bed.

"How is he doing?" He opened his eyes and smiled at me upon my touch.

"I am sorry, my lord..." He began to apologize. He was still feverish, but coherent.

"Say no more," I raised my hand to quiet him, "take your rest, young man. Everything is all right."

"He is much better, my lord." The maiden reported with a pleasant smile from behind her veil.

"Good." I smiled back at her. "Has the physician been here this day?"

"No, my lord."

"Very well." I turned to go out and the boy said, "My lord, we will find the disciples."

"Yes, we shall my child. We surely shall." I returned with assurance and went out.

"Out of the mouth of babes," I mused to myself as I descended the stairs.

Yered was still sitting at one of the small tables near the north wall when I came down the stairs. There were three other men in the room, and one of them appeared from was a Roman soldier, while the other two were Shamron.

When I came to the foot of the stairs, Neah drew my attention entering through the beaded curtained doorway underneath the stairway. The colorful beads clinked together in her passing and sent a chime of musical notes echoing through the room. She was carrying a tray with a meal and placed it in front of the Prushen. He thanked her politely. At this point she noticed me out of the corner of her eye and turned my way while I pulled a chair out from under the table where Yered sat watching them curiously.

Now Yered turned to me. "Shalom, Father." He quickly stood and waited for me to settle into one of the crude wooden chairs, then seated himself again.

"Good day." I nodded back to him, but my eyes were on Neah coming my way.

Suddenly, the door pushed open and two men entered. One of them was a tall slender man with soft brown eyes, a long pleasant face, and broad smirking grin. The other was a ruddy small built Yew with a mass of hair and a short beard.

"Neah!" The tall man called out a loud greeting in a husky, boisterous voice that did not match his stature or his looks. "You get lovelier each time I see you."

Her eyes shot from me to him and she broke into a pleased smile. "Yosef, how wonderful." She hurried to him in a joyful skip with open arms, and he intercepted her rush catching her in a round swinging motion. When she pulled back, her eyes flowed over him fondly.

"Have you been well?" She gave him an affectionate pinch on the cheek.

"Sure..." His voice trailed off to a normal tone and I could no longer hear what was being said. They talked for a short time before she showed them to a table. The two men seated themselves and Neah turned again toward me.

"Good morning." She greeted when she reached the table. "Would you like something to eat?" She tilted her head in a casual carefree manner. I was about to answer, then she continued. "Yes, of course, I will bring it right out." She smiled then and with her usual swiftness turned and hurried away.

"Did you sleep well, Father?" Yered inquired of me, making a visible effort to ignore her.

"I am afraid not," I sighed.

"Were you worried about the boy, Father?"

"Not really. I just was not very successful at putting things out of my mind." I said with a deep sigh. Then smiled teasingly. "I am surprised you are not out somewhere seeking adventure and fighting some unseen enemy."

"I am thinking about that right now." He looked away contemplating. "I will probably do both."

"My, you are a talented young man." I taunted with a smirk.

"It is skill, Father," he returned with a haughty look. "...Pure skill."

"Remember when one climbs too high it can be a long way to fall." I cautioned with concern.

He just looked confident. "I will remember that when I get too high." He winked, stood, and headed for the stairs. I just shook my head as he went.

Neah brought my breakfast and place it before me. Then leaned near and said softly. "The man whom I greeted at the door is Yosef of Cypress. A L'vi follower of YahShua and a friend of Philip, one of the disciples."

"A disciple?" I looked at him. I was about to ask her to introduce me to him when she said, "I will see if he will have a word with you."

"Thank you." I replied, but she was already gone.

As she drew near their table, several men came in from off the street and stood in a small huddle near the door talking excitedly. Neah changed her direction and went over to them. They talked in low tones for a while. Then she turned again to go on to Yosef's table. She spoke softly to the one she called Yosef and he nodded in response to her words.

The men standing near the door smiled with exuberant looks when they saw his reaction. Neah came to the back of the room where a small counter sat near the stairs on the south slightly in front of the door with the bead curtain. She climbed onto a chair that sat behind it and then onto the counter.

"Listen everyone!" She held up her hands, and when she had everyone's attention, she continued. "Some of the people have asked Yosef," she motioned to him, "...to give us news of the disciples of YahShua and tell us of the past few day's happenings. Let us go out to the tree by the well and hear his words."

He came to her offering his hand and he helped her down. The men at the door hurriedly tromped back out into the street and everyone but the Roman followed. I did not look at Yered, I just followed the throng anxious to hear the news of the disciples.

Under a huge tree near Yaakov's well where many travelers set tents Yosef found a stump used for a seat and stood upon it. A young Prushen came to the door of a tent set nearby. He had short brown hair, no beard, a pious round face with deep-set eyes and a long, large nose. He watched the mass gathering, nearly the whole village came out with us.

"Men and brethren." Yosef began to speak. "The disciples were safe and well when I left them a few days ago. As you all know, Pilate crucified YahShua at the insistence of the chief cohanim and elders. The people giving voice to these murders by calling for the release of BarAbbas at Posach. The chief cohanim and elders of Israel stirred up the people against Him. The Elders are seeking to find the disciples, because they kept company with YahShua. They have told me while they hid in an upper room for fear of the Romans that our Adonai YahShua Messiah appeared to them and ministered unto them. He was hung upon a cross and did as he promised. On the third day came forth from the tomb in victory and is now..."

"Lies! Blasphemous lies!" The young Prushen pushed his way through the startled crowd. "Why do you blaspheme by speaking that name? You are not an Israelite, for you seek to turn the world upside down with this doctrine, and lead these people away from the Laws of Moshe just as that false prophet did."

In the fervor of his anger he rushed forth and laid hold of Yosef casting him from the stump. "These disciples you talk about have stolen the blasphemer's body from the sepulcher, and He is becoming more of a threat now than when He was alive."

Yosef regained himself and shoved the P'rushen rufly. "Who are you to say I am not an Israelite?"

"I am Shaul of Tarsus and a P'rushen." He stiffened in the face of Yosef. "Therefore I have the right to judge this matter, and I am telling you it is wrong. The Man sought to do away with the sacrifices and draw the people away from the Temple."

"He did no such thing!" Yosef yelled back. "He taught love and told you P'rushim of your sins. That is why you hated Him and seek to stop His teachings."

"That is foolish talk!" Shaul gushed forth angrily. "He has received the just reward for blasphemy as prescribed by our laws. Now you ignorantly speak his name to blaspheme Elohim and these disciples are determined to spread His evil doctrine and blasphemy until you bring the wrath of Elohim down upon our heads. It is better for one Man to die than for a whole nation to perish." His voice grew increasingly louder with each word.

Now he looked around at the throng and said, "You know the people called Him king." He waved his hand in a casting motion shouting unto them. "The people worshipped Him in the hearing of the Romans. These are words of insurrection, oh foolish ones! Do you want to bring Israel to her death not only incurring the wrath of Elohim, but that of the Romans as well."

Someone from the back shouted "Roman are coming!"

"See!" Shaul shouted.

Now, Neah quickly step up on the stump. "Leave here and come shortly to the inn and we will hear more. The Romans will do nothing there."

The throng quickly dispersed even as the soldiers were coming, and I saw the P'rushen Shaul speak to the commander.

Soon the inn was full of people. I even saw some Yews there. Yosef went over to the counter and stood upon it. All grew quiet and all eyes were upon him. Yosef opened his mouth to speak when the door slammed open and much to the surprise of the crowd, the P'rushen rushed into the room. This was the last place in the world I expected to see the P'rushen. He had come into a Shamron inn, however, this did not seem out of place for this one.

"Stop, he shouted. "Do not do this evil!" He pointed at Yosef, "You will surely bring the Romans down upon our heads and they will crush us in their hands."

While he spoke Nebra came swiftly up to him. "Enough!" She shoved the man, Shaul, back a step. "This is no place for a P'rushen. We do not need your religious piety here."

She placed both hands on her hips and took a defiant stance. "YahShua was the Son of Elohim and nothing you can say or do will change that, and if we have done wrong then Elohim will judge us, not you. So, just take your religion and leave."

"Do not speak to me like that, woman, nor let that name escape you lips." He was aghast. His eyes blared wildly. "Remember your place and stay out of a man's affair."

I knew that was the wrong thing to say to that woman. I guess, of all the people in the place I was the only one who was not shocked or surprised at her bold display.

"Sir!" She launched at him and he gave way stepping back. "This is my house," she took another step and he moved back some more, "...and I will say what I like." She stepped forward again, "...to whomever I like."

205

Another step and he was now against a table. "Now, I say to you, get out!" She pointed at the front door.

Shaul looked bewildered and I saw him make a tight fist. His large round eyes flashed like lightening, while the muscles in his jaw twitched.

"Neah!" Yosef scolded sharply from behind her. He had come down off the counter. "I do not need your help." He softened his voice as he spoke. "I can take care of this myself. Please stand aside."

She whirled around to face him now. Her eyes shot hot daggers at him, but his countenance changed not, and suddenly the little child was there again in her face. She relinquished her position and did as he told her showing some shame for her actions.

Now, I became aware of Yered standing at the foot of the stairs. I do not know how long he had been there, but when our eyes met he looked uncertain. His hand was on the pummel of his sword. Quickly, I had a vision of him whipping it out and running both of them through. Then, he released it and I felt myself free the breath I had caught upon spotting his hand on the sword.

The L'vite and Yew stood face to face, eye to eye, glaring at each other, but neither spoke or threatened further. Finally, Shaul turned abruptly for the door and walked briskly out.

Yosef said after the door slammed shut behind him. "Everyone go home. I will meet with you secretly this night, and we will worship the Elohim of heaven who has raised His Son from the dead. Go now, friends! Elohim speed!"

"BarNabas," Yosef's said and his friend turned to look at him. "It will be dangerous for us here now. We should go on to Galil."

BarNabas? That must be the name his friends in the following use for him. Nabas means encouragement, - son of encouragement.

Hurrying to where they stood, I could not let him leave without talking to him. "Come! You may use my room to hide in," I offered.

"Yosef, this is Timon of Beitorah," Neah introduced. "Timon this is Yosef and ...ah," She opened her hand toward the other man.

"Yachanan Mark, my mother's sister's son," Yosef inserted.

"Yes," she nodded. "I am sorry, I forgot your name." He just nodded an unspoken reply.

"I am pleased to meet you." I bowed slightly. This is Yered, my concubine's son." I laid my hand upon Yered's shoulder as he came nigh. He bowed slightly to both men.

"I must speak with you Yosef." I entreated him.

"We will speak tonight, come to the meeting."

"Do not worry, Timon, if the soldiers come they will not find them," Neah inserted. Then she turned to Yosef, called BarNabas, and said, "Come I have a secret place and when it is dark you can speak with the people at a place we all know of."

BarNabas turned to Neah, "I do not wish to get you into trouble with the Romans."

"Bah!" She waved away his concern. "The Romans come here all the time. They will do nothing."

"You have been a welcome help to those fleeing Yerushelayim, and your fame has spread abroad among the followers. You are much too valuable to endanger." BarNabas argued.

"Do not worry about that. I assure you they will not find you." She grinned sheepishly and turned abruptly away beckoning unto them.

"BarNabas shrugged in surrender and knew the defeat of argument the persistent Neah. He turned to follow her and I saw in his face the same bewilderment I feel when talking to her. I gave him a knowing smile and watched as she led the way through the beaded curtain doorway.

"Should you not go with them, Father?" Yered asked with a frown.

"There is no need. Shaul will not bother us for we were not involved in it."

"I will go for a ride then." Yered cast it aside.

"You take heed." I wagged a finger at him. "Galil is full of the filth of the Israel, and now with all the trouble in Yerushelayim it has become very dangerous."

"Do not worry, Father." He spoke with assurance.

"Those who look for trouble will find it coming to them on swift wings." I warned with an anxious look. "Be extremely careful."

"Ah, Father, I am just going for a ride, not seeking trouble. I cannot just sit around in this inn for days doing nothing while the boy recovers." Yered defended in a boyish whine.

"Nonetheless you hear what I say, Yered."

"I will be back later, Father."

He was going off to find adventure and I feared that he would indeed find it, but I could say no more. "Elohim speed," I muttered.

"What, my lord?" Benren questioned approaching at my elbow. I did not know where he came from but there he stood beside me.

"I hope Yered is careful." I thought aloud still looking after him. Pulling my eyes from the door to look at Benren. "I will go see the boy," I explained, "...and then I will study in my room. Bring my meal when it is time."

"Yes, my lord." He bowed slightly.

Later that afternoon when I checked on the young servant boy again, his color seemed much improved, and seated by him was the maiden who loves him.
"How are you feeling, my child." I asked upon approaching the bed.

"Much better, master," the boy replied with a weak smile, "I should be ready to travel on the morrow."

"Hardly, but I will see what the physician says about it. You just rest and get your strength back."

"I will, my lord."

I was anxious for nightfall so I could attend the meeting of the followers of YahShua and hear the words of BarNabas. I hoped he would tell me where I could find the disciples. I tried to get into the study of the Sacred Writings, but I found my mind drifting to the meeting and what would happen there. After some time I laid aside the scrolls and went up onto the roof and looked out over the small village.

The air was fragrant with the smell of fruit, dressed olives, spices and new-baked bread drifting up from the village-square. As in any village, the street merchants peddled the products of their fields and the works of their hands. A bakery adjoining the inn made leaven breads and pastries glazed with honey. Knowing Yered, this was the first stop on his search for adventure.

He had not returned and it was beginning to be late. I wondered where he was and if he had slain two imaginary enemies with the same blow. I smiled and saw him in my mind's eye crouching low and swinging his sword in a circular motion to get both opponents.

Then the scene faded into the lovely face of Athera. She may have had me another child by now. I lifted up my eyes and beheld Mount Tabor and could see my house in a vision. It was only about one day's travel from here. I longed to be there. My arms ached to hold Sarepta to my bosom and hear Miryam's sweet voice as she sings the songs of Zion.

I could go home while the boy is recovering, Yered is here with... No! That is a foolish thought. In these times, Yered is much too impulsive to leave in charge. However, I could send him home to bring me news of them, and to see how Elsan is faring with the horses. Everyone there will want to know of our well being. Yes, that is what I shall do. Athera would be very pleased to see him and, maybe, it will keep him from being so restless. He could, also, see Nebra and inform her family of what time the wedding will take place. I nodded to myself with a made-up mind.

Then I noticed a distant hawk making wide circles against the brilliant white of a fluffy cloud drifting in from the Great Sea. Lazily and without effort, it hung in the dazzling blue sky. Watching, I could see myself in its flight and thought of the many circles I had made which always ends back with the Man, YahShua the Messiah. They were not entirely futile, though, for I had met Nakdimon, Yosef of Arimathea and the blind man, Eldaher, who was healed by YahShua. BarAbbas the zealot was a puzzle to me, and the outrageous Neah, a woman who could make men shudder. I had spoken with and sat beside Mikha the Prophet of old, and now met BarNabas who I trust will lead me to the disciples. Some questions had been answered in my heart, but there were the others, so many others still awaiting the light of revelation.

Evening was setting fast and Yered had not returned. I stood looking out the window over the table in my room and listened to the sounds of the merchants as they prepare to go to their homes for the night.

A patrol of legionnaires came through the market place. Some were slumped in their saddle while others wore white wrappings with red stains on them. I strained to see them better. They have been in a battle. There were several horses being led along behind with long lumpy bundles slung across them wrapped in crimson sagums, bodies of the unfortunate who fell in the conflict. I sighed deeply and wondered how many Israelite lives were lost in this battle with zealots or bandits.

The people in the square stopped what they were doing and stood, silently watching the procession of soldiers.

"Blessed be Elohim!" Some man's voice raised from below the window breaking the silence. One of the soldiers drew his sword, broke rank and rushed beneath the window. An agonizing cry pierced the air and I winced, almost feeling the cold iron of his blade. Although I could not see him, I need not guess what happened.

The procession halted and a tired, sharp voice yelled, "Soldier, return to your position." The soldier appeared again in my view sheathing his sword and fell back into the ranks. They then moved on with not so much as a word. There was no little stir in the square that I could not see, but I could hear the people casting up curses to the Romans and beseeching Elohim to avenge the dead.

Already, the stage was being set for the events that would shortly unfold bringing fulfillment of the Prophecy of YahShua concerning Yerushelayim. My heart ached with the pain of the thought and I prayed for the mercy of Yah upon us all.

Benren and one of the young servant maidens entered with my evening meal and were about to leave when a light knock came on my door. Benren went quickly over and opened it.

"May I come in?" I heard Neah's voice.

"My lord is having supper." Benren said in harsh tones. "Perhaps it would be best if you came another time."

"Benren," I scolded, "…allow Neah to enter."

"Yes, my lord," he bowed slightly and opened the door further for her.

Neah gave him a knowing smile as she passed by, and the servant girl went out while the door was still being held open. Benren frowned with displeasure at Neah, but said nothing.

"Would you care for a morsel," I offered.

"No thank you. I have already taken meat." She turned to look at Benren. "I would like a word with Timon in private, if you do not mind." Benren opened his mouth to answer, but she quickly injected, "…which I am sure you do, but it is a private matter I would like to discuss." Benren's eyes darted to my face and he tried to speak again. However, Neah was at her usual self and said with impatience. "Do you mind? I do not have much time."

I knew he would not leave without a word from me. "Leave us, Benren. It will be all right." He scrawled and bowed taking leave.

When he had closed the door, Neah turned to me. "We will go shortly to the thrashing floor of Ishmiabar for the meeting. I will show you the way. We will go out a secret way and stay in the shadows. That Shaul of Tarsus may have the place watched." I had my doubts about that, but I could understand her concern and then she might well be right. I started to answer, but she took my words. "When you have finished here come downstairs and wait in the entry room." I waited a degree for her to say something else then tried to answer, but she again spoke.

"Where we go tonight, you must not speak of it. Many lives depend on its remaining secret." I nodded and opened my mouth. "But, of course," she continued, "I know you would not do that. I am sure you understand the necessity of secrecy." I made no effort to answer her for I knew my attempts would prove unfruitful. "Well, I have much to do. See you downstairs."

I sighed and made a gesture with my hand, but even that was useless for she had already turned to go. Some discussion, she did all the talking and I just sat here. I was not irritated at her this time only a bit unnerved. I shook my head slowly. I certainly am glad I do not have to live with that woman.

Now Benren entered again still wearing a scornful face. "Has Yered returned?" I asked, trying to avoid the subject that I was sure he would bring up.

"No, my lord," he answered and picked up the scroll I had been reading, rolled it gently and placed it upon the others. "My lord," he said determinedly, "I do not like that woman, Neah."

"I know." I answered wearily. "She is not the most pleasant sort of woman."

"No, my lord, she is not!"

"I will go to a meeting of the followers of YahShua tonight. Watch for Yered and when he returns, tell him I wish a word with him early in the morning."

"Yes, my lord."

There was no one in the room when I came down and the short candles which sat in the middle of each table made ghostly shadows dance and play on the walls, I took a chair near the beaded curtain doorway and watched it. I waited impatiently for Neah thumping the table with the tips of my fingers. Waiting always seemed to be the biggest waste of time. There was usually nothing to do and the delay seemed to last forever. I squirmed several times. Not even one soul was in here to talk with, and I had seen about the servant boy before I came down. The physician had been there and said he should rest at least two more days. It has been ten days since YahShua of Natzeret was supposed to have risen from the dead, and now I must delay two more days. Discouragement clutched my soul in its evil grasp and left a feeling of failure.

"Timon!" Neah's voice soft and low reached my ears. Following the sound, I saw her motion for me, obscured slightly by the bead draping.

I arose and went through the beads into a large preparation room. There were two other doorways in here covered with tapestries with a Star of David woven in them. One doorway was across the room and the second was facing us to the right of the beaded doorway we just entered. She pushed this hanging aside and led the way into a room not much wider than the doorway itself. This doorway was under the inset that made up the stairs in the other room. A small shelf graced the wall to our left, and Neah took from it a small lamp that lit the long narrow room with a dim yellow glow. Steps that descend into the floor about a reed into the room and she led the way down them. The light circle from the lamp flowed like golden liquid along the dark stone walls in front of us. Soon we were on the floor of a small storage vault filled with storage jars, wooden crates, barrels and extra furnishings.

As I trailed along behind her staying within the yellow bubble of light, I could not help wondering why she had brought me down here, for there seemed to be no way out other than the way we just came. However, she walked with unfaltering steps right to the north wall and stopped.

Huge cut limestone blocks about three cubits square spread before us. I was surprised to see her pull on an iron ring set into the block on which hung several strings of garlic and leeks. There came a distinct clunk sound and then she push on a block and it easily swung inward. I felt my mouth gape open, and in the shadowed light of Neah's eye, I thought I saw her wink. She did not wait for a reaction. She bent slightly and I ducked through the opening in the thick wall and found myself in a secret room. The block slid back into place with the same ease as she pushed it shut.

This must be the place she took BarNabas and Mark earlier. How many followers had found rest and refreshment in Neah's secret room?

I could tell it was a large place with a fire pit in the center, but to one side. We passed by two low tables sitting side by side some three or four cubits from the fire pit. The light she carried revealed several oil bowls on stand used for lighting scattered around. Now, a set of ascending steps came into view running up the east wall. At the top, near the roof was another huge stone block. This one pulled open having a handhold hewn into one edge and opened quickly as the other had. This brought us out into the stables of the inn where the horses blew at us from their stalls and stomped their feet at our disturbance.

There were container vats of grain, buckets, tools and a pile of dried cut grass where we entered. Harness and other trappings hung on pegs along a wooden interior wall to our right. Neah set the lamp on a small bench opposite the straw pile and went to the open door way not far away which led into a dark empty street. We slipped along the streets and down a winding path, across a barley field into a small shallow ravine where there was a thrashing floor. About twenty men and several women were standing around in small candle lit huddles talking quietly. We went

214

to one such group where BarNabas and Mark greeted us warmly.

"You may start now." Neah said in quick words and BarNabas nodded.

He took a position on a great stone used to grind barley into flour and began to speak. He told once again of the passion of Messiah at the hands of the cruel Romans and how He had appeared in a locked upper room to the disciples where they were hiding for fear of the Romans. He admonished the people not to be discouraged or troubled in heart when persecution comes, saying YahShua spoke on this wise; 'Rejoice, and be glad, for your reward in heaven is great. Blessed are those who have been persecuted for the sake of righteousness, theirs is the Kingdom of Yah and blessed are you when men revile you, persecuting you and saying all kinds of evil against you falsely. I was surprised that he spoke the holy name of Yah so freely. Perhaps the Messiah also used that name freely before them. "Love one another," BarNabas was saying. "Do good one to another and revile not when you are reviled. Be as wise as serpents but harmless as doves. If someone hits you on one cheek, offer freely him the other for vengeance belongs to Yah and he will repay. Be perfect even as your Father in heaven is perfect.'

Never had I heard such a teaching before. I was deeply moved by the powerful influence of the man's words.

"How can we enter the Kingdom of Yah?" Someone behind me called out.

"Believe in Him and by believing in Him, you are believing in He who sent Him. Love Yah first with all your heart and strength and love your fellow man as you love your own life. Yah is love and those who has accepted Messiah has life but those who do not have Messiah do not have life."

My mind reeled under the persuasive words of the man and I found the love for YahShua of Natzeret swelled up large within me until a lump appeared in my throat.

215

Someone who would teach such as this must surely be the Son of Yah and if He is alive as He said, I must find Him and hear Him for myself. The desire to continue my search filled my soul and discouragement melted in its fervent heat.

Then I became conscious of Neah tugging on my sleeve. "Come, we have been called back to the inn. There is trouble." There was an anxious tone in her voice.

"Trouble?" I forced myself to be attentive to her words.

"Yes, come!" She beckoned and started away.

Giving BarNabas another glance, and fighting the wish to stay and hear more, I then hurried to catch her quick steps. When I caught up with her, she began to run and I ran also, through the barley field toward the mellow lights of the village. A hundred dreadful thoughts filled my mind. Perhaps the boy had taken a turn for the worse. No, surely not. I remembered the Prophets words.

Arriving back at the stables, the lamp we had left on the bench was no longer there and in its place was a damp dark smudge. Neah drew her fingers through it and caught her breath. "Oh Elohim!"

In the dark shadow of her face, I saw the fear that reflected in her voice as she recognized the smear was blood. She hurriedly pushed on the edge of the huge block and it moved inward making a pale glow to fall across the stable floor in an ever-widening arch. The oil lamps scattered around the room below leaped with blue flames now, and lying on mats near the west wall were three men. Others sat on piles of fleece scattered about the room and still two others sat on the floor at one of the low table while a short stout man stood near it.

Neah rushed swiftly down the steps and I followed her. A familiar face turned to greet us. It was the face of the zealot, BarAbbas.

"BarAbbas!" Neah called with concern in her voice. He grinned and opened his arms to her. "What happened? Are you hurt?"

His arms went around her and I could see there was something special between them. "Just a scratch." He held up a hand with a bloody cloth wrapped around it. "Yaakov is badly wounded, just as is David and Yachanan." He nodded his head to those on the mats and Neah left him going hurriedly to where they lay.

Now one of the men seated at the table being partly obscured from my vision by BarAbbas rose, and I was sore amazed.

"Greetings, Father." Yered stood with a triumphant look on his slightly smudged face. A cloth tied around his upper lift arm bore the red stains of a wound.

"Yered!" I could hardly believe my eyes. "What are you doing, ...here?"
Despite my wide unbelieving eyes, my mind answered my question. Where else would he be?

BarAbbas laid his bloody hand on my shoulder and said, "He came to my aid while we were being taken to Yerushelayim by Roman soldiers. Because of him, we all stand before you now."

I looked past BarAbbas and saw Yered's glowing countenance, crowned with pride. He had at last confronted an enemy that could fight back, one whose sword was just as sharp as his. My heart plunged and I dreaded the answer to the question I was bound to ask. "You fought with the zealots?"

"Yes, Father." His face grew serious. "I helped free BarAbbas and the others from the soldiers. We hid out until dark, ...then came here."

"He has a fine hand, Timon." BarAbbas tried to soothe, seeing my disapproving look. "You should be proud of him."

I opened my mouth to reply, but Neah drew my attention. "I will need some help with these men. May I have the use of your servants?" I made an attempt to answer, but she continued. "They can be trusted, I am sure."

I waited a degree before answering to give her room to speak further, but she did not say anything more. "They can be trusted." I assured her. "They are all born in my service and would never betray me."

"Good, I will need water to wash the wounds and cloth to wrap them."

Yered, not anxious to confront me, turned for the secret entrance of the storage vault under the inn. "I will get them, Father," he called in his going.

"I am sorry we took you away from your meeting, Timon." BarAbbas stated and offered me a seat at the table with a swing of his hand. "This is Shimon." He introduced the other man at the table.

I nodded and sank down onto one of the piles of fleece that covered the floor around the table. I was glad to sit for I was still shaken from this whole matter. I heard BarAbbas begin to relate to me the story of the incident, but his words faded in my thoughts.

Yered had drawn blood, maybe even killed. Would he now join the Rebels? Was I going to lose him after all? Would he no longer be content to husbandman horses, or has the taste of blood filled him with the desire for excitement, danger and high adventure. He had been showing unusual restlessness ever since leaving Yerushelayim and to a young heart, it is a just cause.

A hand touched my shoulder and brought me from my wanderings. Benren's voice filled my ears. "Would you like something to drink, my lord?"

It took a short degree for what he said to sink in for I was still coming from my thoughts. "Yes, bring some wine." I waved my hand to indicate the table.

"I will have some, also," Yered injected as he seated himself across from me beside the rebel, Shimon, who had been silently sitting there. I studied Yered's face for a clue to my questions, but my inquiring gaze just made him squirm and look away. If he had taken a Roman life it would not be safe for him to travel freely now, especially if they were not all killed and some remained to identify him.

"At what time did this incident happen," I ventured to ask.

"I told you," BarNabbas answered for him, "...it was shortly before dark. We were about two furlongs from here..."

The patrol that came through the village square earlier who had slain the man beneath the window must have been the ones. Now I had no choice. Yered must go home for sure if he has not decided to join BarAbbas and fight for Israel's deliverance. If he has I will try to talk him out of it, but I know it will not be easy because he is just foolish enough to see some glory in the useless struggle, and BarAbbas has a persuasive way about him.

"BarAbbas, ...this fight for freedom serves no purpose except to get young men killed." I began for Yered's sake as well as his. BarAbbas' eyes grew hard and he drew his brows together. It was the same look he had back in the caves when he confronted BarArni and I knew that he was about to erupt into a temper rage.

"There is something the disciples are unaware of that happened in Yerushelayim," I said quickly hoping to finish before he exploded. I saw his muscles tense and I remembered the strong fist that rocked the table at the tomb. "At the precise time YahShua, the Messiah, died on Golgotha..." The right hand on the table near the cup Benren had just set before him clenched into a tight fist. His knuckles were already white and his eyes flashed out their anger. "The curtain," I continued, "between the Holy Place and the Most Holy Place in the Great Temple was rent and the Glory of the Adonai departed from over the Ark of the Covenant leaving the Temple in anger."

"Elohim would not abandon his people. Anyway, what has that to do with anything? I would be angry, too, if they had just killed my son." He strained his words between clenched teeth.

I knew he would probably hit me with that fist and I hurried to finish before the blow came. A strange inward courage welled up within me.

219

"That is just it, BarAbbas! Who do you think Elohim's anger is kindled against, the Romans? No my friend, it was Israel who insisted on His being crucified. Pilate was content to release Him, but the chief cohanim stirred up the people against the Man and demanded your release instead."

Quickly he moved and all I saw was a blur, and then a sting brought a swell of salty liquid into my mouth. I felt myself thrust backward and now saw the large limbs that held up the branches and thick mud of the ceiling. It was very strange, but I was not upset at BarAbbas for what he did. I now realized he did not like to think about YahShua dying in his stead. It hit some spark of guilt hidden deep within him, most likely because he was guilty and innocent blood was shed.

I felt the angry hurt that drove the man to this action and I pitied him. While I lay there beginning to feel a throb now on my cheek, my eyes fastened on a crack in the mud ceiling and I thought it needed repair.

Then there was the shuffle of feet and I heard Yered say, "Lay not another hand upon him."

There was no reply and I looked to see BarAbbas shake loose from the grasp Yered and Shimon had on him and stood staring at me. I sat up and brushed at the place on my mouth where swelling had already begun. Moisture swelled up in BarAbbas' stare as the hardness in his black eyes softened. My mouth was filled with salty liquid and I spit it onto the floor. The throb had now become a dull pain.

"BarAbbas, it was not your fault." My words brought a fresh deluge of blood that trickled out of the corner of my mouth. "It was the plan of Elohim."
Now, Benren was at my side with a cloth and dabbed the blood from my chin and short beard.

"It was Elohim's will for Him to die. What you do not understand is that you will not free Israel by killing Romans."

"What am I suppose to do, lay down my weapon and go home?" BarAbbas growled turning away from the table quickly.

"It is better than to be found fighting against Elohim." I returned through the liquid that persisted to flood my mouth.

"I am not fighting against Elohim," He stiffened. "Elohim is fighting with us, ...to avenge Israel, ...and His Son."

I looked to spit again and Benren picked up my wine cup and held it out. I spit into it and continued. "Look, fighting is of no avail, for the prophecy of YahShua will surely come to pass and that at the hands of the Romans." More blood gushed into my mouth and I felt it spill out with each word. Benren was not just content to sit there he again began to care for me.

As I spoke BarAbbas turned back to look at me. "What Prophecy?"

"YahShua prophesied of the destruction of Yerushelayim and her children the day He entered Yerushelayim as a king." I now pushed Benren's hand away for his concern for the blood was distracting me. "Surely you have heard it."

"...And the Romans are suppose to do this?" Shimon spoke up. "I think so. All through our history Elohim has raised up nation after nation to punish Israel for her sins. Why not now?"

"I do not believe it." Shimon waved it away and went over to the burning fire pit.

"BarAbbas, Elohim has left Israel to her destruction and there is nothing you, or for that matter anyone, can do about it."

"Elohim would never leave Israel to be destroyed!" He shouted back at me and Yered braced himself to intercept his lunge, but it did not come. His eyes flashed at me as he raised the wounded hand tied with a piece of cloth made a clenched fist shaking it in front of him. "And by heavens, ...I shall continue to fight until I am dead or the

Romans have left our land." BarAbbas' hammer like fist came down hard on the wooden table and it left a splatter of blood where it hit. "I shall do what I must do," he spit angrily with a spray of moisture. "Just as you will do what you must."

His words hit me with a jolt. How right he was, ...for now I could see that just as I am driven to find the truth of YahShua, so he is compelled to bring about the wrath of Rome and, therefore, the prophecy would be filled. I did not like the path Elohim had set for my friend, but I could see the necessity of it.

'But it shall not be in your time.' The words of the Prophet sounded again in my heart, and maybe not even in his.

Neah came to BarAbbas now being the same height as he and looked lovingly into his eyes. Placing her hand on his chest, "Calm down," she soothed, "Timon is not your enemy."

She gently took his arm. "Come sit down and let me bandage your hand," she entreated him in tender tones.

He looked deep into her eyes and I saw the anger melt away. This is a very strange woman. She is a follower of YahShua and loves a zealot, forceful and shamefully bold, yet loving, persuasive and intriguing.

He yielded to her wishes and plopped down across the table from me. His face twisted into several expressions and then he sighed heavily. "I am sorry I hit you, Timon. I am afraid I have a rather bad temper."

"I forgive you, friend," I replied. I met his look and a strange warmth came over me.

"You can still call me friend?"

"Yes!" I gave him a painful distorted smile.

He grinned back at me. "An Israelite with honor!"

Benren brought me another cup of wine and I washed the taste of blood from my mouth. Yered and Shimon settled back in their places on the fleece. Then Neah set about cleaning and bandaging BarAbbas' wound while one of my servant maidens tended to Yered.

Then we raised a toast to Israel. We had just finished it, when the stable entrance block swung open. BarNabas and Mark were returning from the meeting and stood looking down at us with a surprised expression.

"Ah, ...come on down," Neah waved to them. "...Join us." They looked at each other and then started their descent.

"This is BarAbbas and Shimon," she flicked a quick hand. "And you remember Timon and his son. Friends, this is Yosef and Mark."

"Shalom," Yosef nodded and I did likewise.

Neah arose then from tending BarAbbas. "Be seated, I will get you some wine."
We know your name." Yosef turned to BarAbbas and smiled as he settled down at the table. Mark settled on the fleece beside him.

BarAbbas looked at bit uncomfortable then brightened. "Unfortunately, I do not know you."

"He is a friend of the disciple Philip." Yered informed.
Then I turned and said, "Yosef, I must find the disciples of YahShua and speak with them. It is very important. There is something I am not sure they know. Will you tell me where I might find them?"

"Most of them are in KfarNachum waiting for the Adonai to tell them what to do now."
"Is YahShua there?' I asked hopefully.

He shrugged, "He told them he would go into Galil before them, so they went there to find him."

"Have you seen Him?" Yered looked at them anxiously.

"No." He shook his head, "but, as I told the people He has appeared to the disciples."

"I must see Him," I returned.

"What is it they do not know that is so important?"

So, once again, I related to them how Yosef of Arimathea saw the glory of the Adonai depart from over the Ark and leave the Temple in anger. I told of how Yosef sat in the ash heap and what the elders had planned for him. I told of his death and how already the prophecy of YahShua was beginning to be fulfilled. BarAbbas' eyes stormed when he began to hear what his anger would not let him earlier. Finally, I think he understood the horror of it. They were all taken back and horrified, rending their garments with loud wails, lifting up their voices. We began to pray and mourn for Israel, even BarAbbas and the servants.

After we had prayed for some time, we each went our own way with heavy hearts pondering how this would effect our lives and change the course of Israel. For when truth comes, there will certainly be change. As for BarAbbas, only time will tell.

DAY ELEVEN

The night had been one I would not soon forget, and in the light of day I pondered the significance of what had transpired.

My face reminded me of the blow I received from BarAbbas with each bite of breakfast. He might not be a big man or have much charm, but when it comes to fighting, he certainly knows how to deliver a punch. He has chosen his course, sad to say, and the end thereof will more than likely be death. It was as though he stopped his ears to the prophecy of YahShua about Yerushelayim being destroyed and her children with her. As the chief cohanim and Elders of Israel, he is determined to continue as though everything is the same. What purpose is there in offering sacrifice on the altar of a Temple where there is no Elohim, or fighting for a cause where there is no possible hope of winning? Yet, they will continue to pour their life into a dead thing. May Yah have mercy upon them, upon us all.

Then the words BarNabas spoke in power at the thrashing floor awakened in my heart and I meditated upon them for some time. A Man that can touch the hearts of men with a teaching and them carry it on after His passing, supports my belief that He was the Son of Yah, the promised Messiah. However, the purpose for His death and the promise to raise from the dead is still unclear. Yes, the mystery, as the gardener has so put it, is something quite puzzling. Why has the Son of Yah been so shrouded in mystery? Yet, important enough to, 'turn the world upside down', in Saul's words.

I was so disappointed to learn from Benren that BarNabas had left for Yerushelayim at daybreak. There were so many questions with no answers, and I did not even get to talk with him about them. Well, I did at least learn the disciples were at Capernaum so I shall go there and find them.

A quick rap sounded on the door and Yered entered, not waiting for my answer. "Shalom Father," he saluted in a cheerful tone on his way to the table where I sat staring out the window deep in my thoughts. I turned and watched his youthful, springing stride. "Benren said you wanted to see me."

"Yes, take a seat." I motioned to the lounge. "Have you had breakfast?"

"No, I came straight here."

"Have some breakfast then." I shoved the tray one of the maidens had sat before me earlier over in front of him. There was still plenty, do to the soreness of my jaw and my appetite not being much this morning due to my concern for Yered and the anxiety about what he will do.

"Looks good." He muttered seating himself. "BarAbbas told me he felt bad about hitting you and asks if you will come down later and have some wine with him."
I watched him take a loaf of bread in his strong hands and tear a piece from it. It seems that only yesterday that hand was small, reaching out to grasp a toy. Now, it grasps the hilt of a sword.

"Yered, did you kill a Roman?" I had to know.

He looked up from the meal at me with mixed expression. "Yes, Father, I did." I looked away out the window at the brightening sky, taking a long breath letting it out slowly. His words hung in the air like a foul odor. The look of disapproval on my face must have prompted him to speak further for after a short pause.

"I took no pleasure in it, Father," he drew his brows together. "It just had to be done. I could not let them take the Zealots to be crucified."

I summoned the courage to ask the dreaded question which weighed upon my heart. "Will you be going with them now?"

"No, I will stay with you." His words were strong and a set look replaced the frown.

I prayed silently that what I was about to say now would not change his decision. "You cannot stay with me, for the Romans will be looking for you. You must return home. It is out of the way and they will not find you there." Disappointment set upon his young adventurous face but I pretended not to notice. "Besides, I have been very anxious the past few days about your mother. It is very near time for her to bring forth the child, and I know it would be much comfort to her if you were there, and the family is probably desirous to know of our well being."

I paused and took a drink of sweet milk. Yahred's eyes searched my face and I thought he would speak for his mouth moved slightly, but he said nothing.

"Tell my beloved Sarepta that I will be traveling to Natzeret and for her to send Elsan to me there. I will stay in the home of the woman Elisheva and inform her of our journey. I want you to take the sick servant to his mother, Yah bless her. I have ordered Benren to prepare one of the wagons for the trip. The boy can lie in the back on a pallet. I will send half of the servants back with you, also. Tell Sarepta to only send one servant with Elsan. There is no need for so many."

I paused to catch my breath and noticed a deep scrawl upon Yahred's grim countenance. There has always been a slight competitive spirit between the two boys though they love each other deeply, and to be replaced by a Elsan was not sitting well with him. I cast this aside also, knowing their nature.

"But Father," he began, "...those soldiers will not remember me long and I could meet you in Natzeret. You know I dislike leaving things I have started for others to finish."

"You have brought this upon yourself, Yered. You are always too quick to act, not giving the slightest thought to the outcome. This will always get you into trouble. It would grieve my heart if I relented and something happened to you because I allowed you to persuade me not to follow my inner wisdom."

I knew he was speaking from his manhood, but I would rather disappoint him than to lose him to the

227

Romans. "Anyway," I continued. "It seems good to me that you and Nebra be married this fall and we should set a date for the marriage with her family. If I am still searching for the disciples, I will postpone my search until after the celebration. Also, remember the words of the Prophet, you have a destiny to fulfill and far be it for me to interfere by using poor judgment." I opened my hand to him. "You must go home!"

When he saw he could not prevail upon me, he arose and went out sadly. His head bent low in the same manner as it was being a small boy when I refused to allow him to go with me to bring in the herd. I felt I had made the only decision available and he would just have to forgive my action. This could prove to be a vital lesson for him. I hoped so anyway.

Later that morning, Benren informed me that everything was prepared for Yahred's departure. So, I arose and went down to the street in front of the Inn where the wagon was waiting and Yered stood nearby with his horse looking grim faced and slumped in posture. As I drew near he straightened himself and half smiled.

"Well, we are ready to leave." He gestured toward the wagon trying to sound pleasant.

"Then Elohim speed and take care of you." I looked deeply into his eyes. Slight tear pools clouded the sparkle normally seen there but he swallowed them back and embraced me.

"Remember me when you pray," I reminded, "...and give my love to your mother, Miryam and Sarepta."

"I will Father." He spoke with a strained voice then cleared his throat as though something was hung in it.

"Yered," I placed my hand upon his shoulder, "...you will never know how precious you are to me. I love you very much."

The pools grew in his eyes and he stammered slightly, "I, ...love you also, Father."

Benren, perceiving the inner struggle we both were having said, "Take care, Young Yered."

He tore his eyes away from mine and looked at Benren. "You take care of Father, also." He told Benren indicating me with a nod of his head.

"I have done so for many years and will continue to do so, young Yered."

He turned back to me. "Well, day is wasting. We should get started." He did not wait for a reply.

Mounting his horse, he motioned to the wagon driver to follow and I stood watching with a lump in my throat fighting loneliness that had already begun to creep in. I will miss him very much. He was a good companion and we have grown close these past few weeks. I hope he will find it in his heart to forgive my decision to send him home.

Near the camel caravan still camped a little ways from the well, Yered glanced back and gave a final farewell with a wave of his hand, then set his face for Tabor. I watched until the small curl of dust kicked up by the wagon and horses engulfed them in the distance.

I sighed deeply and cast the pain of his departure to the wind, knowing it was best and turned my attention to Benren. "We will leave for Natzeret at first light on the morrow." I informed him.

"Yes, my lord." He bowed his head slightly.

While I was instructing Benren, Neah quickly approached. She smiled and there was something very beautiful about it. She seemed to radiate an unusual happiness this morning. If it were not for her quick, aggravating manner, I could certainly understand why BarAbbas finds her appealing.

"Come!" She said in her usual commanding way and put her arm through mine in a jovial spirit. "BarAbbas wishes for you to dine with him." Her voice was low and her clinging near to me insured no unwanted ears heard her words.

I allowed her to guide me along knowing very well any effort to answer or protest, if I had one, would end in futility. "I have prepared a tasty meal." She continued in a normal tone almost before the words of her invitation had escaped her lips. It was clever of her to say that for the sake of those standing nearby but I do not think she did it intentionally. It was normal behavior for her. I shook my head slightly as though shaking the thoughts from my mind and went humbly by her side.

Upon entering the dark lamp lit secret room under the inn, BarAbbas stood up from a well spread table with his big winning smile. "Ah, Timon, my friend! Come and take meat with me."

Shimon was seated across the table from him as usual and beside him were two of the men I saw severely wounded the night before lying on pallets. I gave a quick glance at the wall where they had lain to be sure I was not seeing things.

"Be seated." BarAbbas offered a place on the fleece beside himself. "I was disappointed to find out that you were sending Yered away. I have grown very fond of that lad."

I nodded a greeting to the others as I sat down cross-legged on the sheepskins. "In view of what has happened and the need to see that my sick servant was returned home, I felt it necessary."

"Well, I guess I can understand that."

I could hardly take my eyes off the men who were wounded but now seemed perfectly healthy. I puzzled this while BarAbbas was talking and found my curiosity almost uncontrollable. So quickly, before BarAbbas could say anything else I asked, "What happened to your wounds?"

One answered with a cheerful mouth full of food, "BarNabas healed us this morning before he left for Galil."

I could hardly believe what my ears were hearing. "He healed you?"

"Yes!" The other returned placing his wine cup back on the table. "He said he prayed and fasted breakfast to find the will of the Adonai. Then he touched us saying, 'Rise up, you are healed'. While we were rising, our wounds closed before our very eyes."

A look of dismay was apparently upon my face and a pleased one upon that of BarAbbas'.

"Why are you so surprised, Timon?" BarAbbas injected with a broad grin. "I told you Elohim is working with us in our effort."

I opened my mouth to respond but thought better of it. I did not want to get this small ox of a man mad at me again and to tell him, it was the men Yah moved for, not his cause. It would only roll off him like so much water on a hard stone anyway. He had chosen his course and was reading into this, the first real miracle I had ever seen, what he wanted to read into it. Besides, I was more interested in the miracle itself than the motivation.

"Where is the other man?"

"He left us and went with BarNabas." Shimon volunteered.

"He will be back," BarAbbas interred confidently.

"How did it feel?" I was sore taken by this healing.

"Like a heat." The one called Yaakov reported. "Especially near the wounds."

"May I see the place?"

"It was there." He raised his tunic and there was a red irritated looking scar.

I wondered aloud in amazement. "Why did Elohim heal him leaving a scar?"

"BarNabas said Elohim always leaves something behind as a memorial to bring an important happening to mind in the days to come." Yaakov related.

"Well," the one called John piped in with a grin. "I am glad He left the memorial on you instead of me."

The other responded with a light backhand blow to his fellow's shoulder and a roar of laughter rose with BarAbbas' loud, commanding voice leading. There was an air of unusual joyfulness around the table and I knew that BarAbbas was, as they were, thankful for the act of Yah's love and compassion. It was obvious that BarAbbas really cared for these men.

Enjoying the firmament that permeated the occasion and we ate, talked and laughed together for some time. Finally, I said to BarAbbas, "I leave for Natzeret on the morrow. It has been good and I want to wish you well."

"Aah, what are you going to that place for?" There is nothing there but a few bedraggled old men and some women."

"One very special woman!"

"Oh?" He looked at me with a twinkle in his eye.

"It is not like that." I snapped.

He looked amused a degree and then his face turned thoughtful, then brightened. "Yes," he nodded. "The mother of YahShua. A blessed woman, but I doubt she will be there. She is probably with the disciples."

"Her name is Elisheva. His mother's kinsman, but if His mother is with the disciples, I will see her when I find them."

"Why do you not join us instead? We could use your help. We shall sting Herod and make Pilate feel our lashes as though it was a Roman whip like they use to lash the back of the people." BarAbbas said boastfully.

I sighed deeply and almost felt defeated. He had not heard a word I had been trying to tell him, and now he is trying to recruit me into his rebellion. All my reasoning with him and the punch in the face had not meant a thing. He did not hear or chose not to hear what I was saying. I should have saved my words and my face.

"BarAbbas, you have chosen your path and will pursue it with passion just as I must mine."
"Then I cannot persuade you?"

"No, my friend, and neither can I persuade you." ◇He looked hopefully at me. "No hard feelings." I knew he was remembering the blow he dealt me last evening.

"Yes, no hard feelings." I set his mind at ease and was rewarded with a rough friendly smack on the back.

Later in my room, I picked up the writings of the great Prophets to search them once more. However, my thoughts kept returning to the wounded men lying in their own blood on pallets near the west wall and then to the men sitting across the table from me well and joyful. It was hard for my mind to comprehend what took place. I mused at BarAbbas who as most would see the healing as Yah's sanction of their purpose instead of His pure love.

The very fact that it happened at all spoke to the deep turmoil in my spirit. Even if the cohanim, elders and Israel as a whole had forsaken Him and done despite to His Son, Yah has not turned his back upon those who are truly His. He will surely make a way of escape for this people. At least the ones who seek His will and are disheartened by all that is happening in Yerushelayim. I found a certain amount of comfort in that thought and dwelled upon it for a while.

The door opened softly and Benren entered. He was there to minister to my needs before bedtime. "Benren?" I said thoughtfully not looking at him. "Do you believe in miracles?"

"Yes, my lord," he returned in a matter of fact way.

"Why?"

"Because I have seen some and heard of many more."

"Tell me what you have seen."

"I saw a dead Prophet talking to you while sitting beside you in the cisium," he spoke as he worked. "And, a dying boy given life again at the word of that Prophet."

"Yes," I mused at myself. "…those were miracles, but this thing about BarNabas healing the zealots has struck me like none other. Why do you think that is?"

"Because you bore witness of it instead of taking part in it." He turned his gray head and his lips turned up at the corners.

"Why should there be a difference?" I opened my hand to him.

"When you are too close to something, it sometimes does not have the same benefit. Like being too close to the trees to see the forest."

"But, a miracle is still a…"

The door opened quickly and I came to my feet startled. Four dust covered, hard faced Roman soldiers pushed past Neah who stood with her hand still on the door latch. She rolled her emerald eyes heavenward looking thoroughly disgusted and let her breath out with a gush. The soldiers began to search for something or someone even looking under the bed.

"I am sorry for this rude inter…" She began.

"I will handle this, wench!" One of the soldiers snorted bitterly. "Where is the one who bares the sword. We are seeking him for questioning about an attack upon a Roman patrol."

He stood with a cold icy stare. My heart jumped right into my throat, and the fear that gripped me struck a mighty blow that must have shot to my face. While I was trying to find my tongue he bounced impatiently up and down on the heals of his sandals, frowned and said harshly. "If you are trying to hide him, you will pay the same penalty as he."

"N, …No!" I managed to swallow my heart and lose my tongue. "He is not here! Surely, there has been some mistake. You must be unaware of who I am?" My knees quivered under the weight of my body and I thought they were going to give out letting me tumble to the floor.

"Who you are is of no concern of mine." He cast my words to the wind. "I was told to find the man."

"Yered is the son of my concubine and he is at home with the family on Mount Tabor. He cannot be the one you are looking for now can he?" I reasoned with him and wondered how I came up with that.

His hatred for Yews as they call us was plain to see. The man's jaws tightened and he turned abruptly and said to the others, "Let's keep looking." Without so much as an apology he stomped past Neah on his way through the door. "Come wench!" He spit through clenched teeth.

She closed the door softly with a glance in my direction. I reached out supporting myself with the table and settled weakly back onto the couch. I then looked up at

Benren's who stood wide eyed still staring at the door. The same thought must have entered his mind as mine for he turned now to me.

"Do you think they will send someone to find him, my lord?"

"I surely hope not. Maybe he believed me. Could you feel the hate coming form that man?"

"Yes, my lord," he nodded.

"I certainly pray this is the end of it."

"Hopefully so, my lord. Hopefully so."

After Benren left and I was about to lay me down for the night, there came a knock on the door. When I opened it, Shimon slipped quickly into the room.

"The soldiers are leaving," he said going to the window but staying to one side of it and peering out. "BarAbbas said to tell you, we will be leaving late tonight. He does not want to endanger the woman any further." Keeping his vigil at the window for a degree of time, he now turned to face me. "BarAbbas sent me to find out what happened."

"They just searched the room for Yered."

"How did they know who to look for?"

"I suppose he fit one of the descriptions the patrol gave of their attackers and with our being here this long they surely saw him around."

"Timon, I am sorry your son had to get involved in this trouble, but we all owe our lives to his courageous act. We will always be grateful." He turned to the door without another word and left me standing looking after him.

I sat down upon my bed, but there was no sleep in my eyes. I sighed and reached for a scroll, but my hand refused to light upon it. Instead, it came to rest upon the blue robe. I picked it up and held it to my breast as though it was some living thing, something that could give me strength, courage, and rest the torment of my soul. Courage! Now I thought of those who were being taken to Herod's palace that night beneath my window in Yerushelayim and it was as though I could still hear their

235

song of victory. Courage! I lacked the courage to face four Romans who were not even looking for me. Some Courage! God help me!

A jolt shot through me like a hunter's arrow jerking me out of my thoughts as a soft tap sounded from the door. I took a deep breath to gather myself, laid the robe aside, and went to the door. Neah's face greeted me, but the glow I saw earlier had gone.

"I would like to make amends for the soldier's disturbance, Timon," I started to respond but she spoke quickly. "I am truly sorry."

I waited for a degree to give her room to say more. "It was not your fault, Neah. I have Yered to thank for that." I assured her. Now that I was leaving, I had finally come to deal with her abruptness. "Do you want to come in?"

"No." She shook her head and her raven hair flowed like ebony waves on her shoulders. "You need your rest if you travel on the morrow. I just wanted to tell you what a pleasure your being here has been, and if you are ever traveling in this area again, please stop by for a while."

"I will surely do that."

"Shalom, Timon!" She laid her small hand affectionately upon my arm.

I nodded and she turned away, closing the door behind her. I turned again to my bed.

In a night dream upon my pillow I was standing upon the Place of the Skull and there was the awful scene in all its agony and then I heard Yered call to me in a weak voice. I looked up into the face of a man hanging on a cross, but it was nothing but blackness against the brilliance of the sun directly behind his head. "Yered, …is that you?" I screamed as fear churned within me.

"It is I, Father." I heard him say and I caught my breath. Then I was in a sitting position with my breath coming hard and fast. I blinked and realized I was in bed.

"Please Yah, spare him," I whispered.

DAY TWELVE

There was an excited hum around the servant's wagon as the deep purple sky slowly dawned her golden robe and a cool morning breeze kissed the earth. Benren drew near as I approached my cisium.

"The servants are anxious to move on," he informed, "you have chosen them well my lord. They love the adventure."

"Yes! Well let us be going. We should reach Natzeret near mid-day." I was not looking forward to the dust and heat but it would be worth it to see Elisheva again.

"Yes my lord." He turned to the servants. "Get aboard, it is time to leave."

As my carriage jostled along the rocky road, I rehearsed all that had happened since leaving the small sleepy mountain town of Beitorah. The wonderful story Elisheva told and the rumors of the travelers around the campfire at BeitHal. I remembered the Centurion, Appolious, who gave me the Adonai's robe and the gruesome sight of Golgotha, the tomb of YahShua and the words of the gardener and the cold star of Yhudah Iscariot. It is a sad condition I have found in my beloved city where the anger of the man caused him to curse a child, the deceit of the Elders and the dreadful death of Yosef of Arimathea. The lesson of trust, the healing of the blind man and the...

Abruptly the cisium came to a halt and my thought vanished to the bleat of sheep. It seemed as though we had been engulfed in a flood of dingy white as the sheep flowed around the carriage and the cart. Once in a while I would feel a bump on the bottom of the cisium as some dumb beast tried to go under it. The shepherd stopped and bowed slightly before going on his way surrounded by his herd. As I beheld the sight, I realized that the shepherd of Israel was gone and I knew it would only be a matter of time until like sheep the people would be scattered to the wind. My heart ached for my people and I felt my remorse trickle down my cheek. "What will become of us, Yah? Surely, your Son holds the answer." I must find the meaning of the events that took place in Yerushelayim only a few short days ago.

Sometime later as we traveled Benren drew my attention. "My lord?" He pointed off to the west and there contrasted against the blue hazy horizon dark forms were making lazy circle in the sky. Borne on out spread wings they soared high above the plush green valley floor. Scavenger birds squawking and squabbling over some victim of their delight. These hateful creatures grotesque as they are serve Yah's purpose by cleaning the landscape. Normally you would see two or three but there were many more than that.

"Send someone to find out what it is." I waved to him with distaste.

"Yes my lord." He scrambled from the carriage and went to the servant's cart. A young servant boy took one of the horses and rode away.

I surveyed the cascade of brilliant colored flowers that was now coming into bloom. Tiny golden yellow ones to flame red ones that pointed to heaven like slender fingers and mingled with varied shades of purple. They carpeted the valley in a facet of shapes and sizes as far as the eye could see. The changing green erratic slopes of Mount Tabor as in splendid apparel spread its beauty before us. No wonder our forefather spies spoke of this place as the Garden of Eden flowing with milk and honey. They must have been here this time of year to bring back such a report. This was truly the most beautiful time of the year.

As I took in the majestic sight the small figure of the servant boy appeared to be waving for us to come. I reached forward tapping Benren on the shoulder and motioned for us to go. When the servant boy saw us turn to come he disappeared again below a mound in the landscape. What had he found?

Coming to a place where the land fell away before us the servant boy hiding behind some large bush watched the scene of horror unfolding before him. A large band of rebels were finishing off the last of a squad of Roman Calvary. The few soldiers still standing fought valiantly. The very reason Rome had been able to conquer so many lands.

Romans are brave fearless fighters but obviously this detail was heavily out-numbered. Uniformed red lacerna forms lay in gable fusion mingled with the drab clad of the dead or dying rebels who had given their life for Israel's freedom. Sounds of metal against metal synchronized with the cries of its victims met my ears and then fell silent as the last soldiers crumpled to the ground. A cheer rose from those still standing and then one of the Zealots noticed our coming.

Now the servant boy joined us and we came to a stop near the place of death. The battle had been long and hard, for the surviving Zealots stood slumped shouldered with their arms dangling weakly by their sides.

As I scrambled from the cisium a husky voice sounded in my ear.

"Timon, you are a bit late but I am glad you decided to join us." I did not have to turn around to see who it was. The voice inescapably belonged to Barabbas.

"I did not come to join you," I snapped, surveying the scene.

"Why not?' We have just gained a great victory for Israel and put another lash on Herod's back."

Before I had time to answer, one of the rebels whom I had not seen before said to Barabbas. "Some are still alive."

"Well, kill them for Elohim's sake." BarAbbas boomed at him. "Must I tell you…"

His words faded from my ears as one of the soldiers raised weakly upon his elbow, but having no strength dropped again. His face smashed into the rocky ground and then another moaned somewhere beyond him. I felt my stomach contract and wanted to close my eyes and shake it all from me as one would do a bad thought. However, I knew that was not possible. Then my eyes fell upon one of them only a few paces from where we stood lying face up. This was an officer, a Centurion. He stirred slightly and BarAbbas went to him raised his bloody sword to plunge it into his heart. His head rolled my direction and I could see his face bloody and smudged with dirt. I gasped and almost choked on my own scream.

"Stop!" My shout distracted BarAbbas just long enough for me to catch the downward thrust of his hand and restrain it. Which was no easy task for the little man was strong despite his size.

"What are you doing?" BarAbbas thundered shaking me loose violently, but my attention turned to the dying soldier lying in a crimson pool. I dropped to my knees and could see he had been run through with a blade. I gently removed the helmet and closed my eyes in a groan. I was right it was Appolious on his way back to Capernaum.

"Oh, come on!" BarAbbas spit in disgust. "You are having pity for a Roman?"

I felt myself begin to burn as anger raised within me. Then suddenly, Benren was at my side lifting the breastplate where the blade of the weapon had scored it sliding off to gauge an enormous hole in his side.

"Can you do anything?" I ask anxiously.

"It is bad, but with the proper care he might make it."

"What is the matter with you?" BarAbbas raged. "He is a Centurion."

The anger now came to a full boil and I stood quickly whirled around and shouted in his face. "He is my friend!"

"Friend?" He turned quickly as if to go, but then in mid-step made a full circle to face me again. "He has a Roman friend!" BarAbbas said loudly as though to himself and threw his hands up in the air. His weapon still in hand, he pointed it at Appolious. "He is a Roman Centurion!" His eyes flashed at me and I met those burning daggers without a flinch.

"Yes," I shouted back, "...and Neah is a Shamron and you are a Israelite."

The tight muscles in his jaws moved slightly as we stood glaring at each other. I expected at any degree to feel the wrath of his anger. Seldom, I am sure, does he get the chance to kill a Roman officer, but I shall not let him kill this one.

"Timon, sometimes," He gritted, shaking both of his hands at me in unbelief, "...sometimes you do try our friendship." He then turned away abruptly. At this point he became aware that we were the center of everyone's attention.

"Well!" He looked around at his men. "What are you staring at?" The men shifted uneasily and looked at one another. "He is the man's friend." He spit bitterly. "Gather the spoils and get the horses." He waved his sword. "Lets be going." He turned for Appolious' horse nervously standing a few reeds away. The men scattered to carry out his order and he slipping into the saddle. He rode over and looked down at me still seething in anger.

"Do you mind," he strained the words between clenched teeth, "...if I take the horse?" Using his hand to indicate it.

I made not reply. I just stood and wondered if it was the cause or hatred that motivated him. He jerked the horse's head around violently and sank his heels deep into its side. The horse lunged into movement, ears laid back.

Since leaving Beitorah I have seen brother against brother, evil and deceit in places it should not be and hatred in the hearts of the people. Yah, what is happening to this people. Then the prophecy of YahShua filled my mind and I shuttered.

Because of the seriousness of Appolious wound, we were forced to set camp here. The servants buried the soldiers. The rebels BarAbbas took with him and all the valuables his men scavenged, but they did not come nigh unto Appolious. I did not care what they took but it did strike me how insulted BarAbbas had become when

241

BarArni talked of taking spoils in the cave tombs, yet here he tells them to take anything of value.

He had left without another word to me and I was relieved. I have great respect for the man patriotism, and hated to come against him. It seemed we could not be around each other very long without harsh words. I suppose it is because we have such different views.

The servants made Appolious as comfortable as possible in my tent when it was set. I am very concerned about him. Benren said he still might not survive, but I pray he will. He has a family and is a good man even though he is Roman. The recovery will be very slow so when it is possible I will put him in the servant's wagon and take him home to his wife.

I sent one of the young men on to Natzeret to wait for Elsan. I am extremely desirous to see him and hear the news from home. He is a fine son and I take great pride in him. I still remember the disappointed look in his eye when I told him he had to remain behind and tend the horses. I had confidence in his ability, but it was a great responsibility for one so young.

"My lord?" Benren said softly. "The Centurion needs a physician. I can do no more for him."

"Is it possible to travel with him?"

"It would open his wound again."

"Well, send one of the young men back to Shklem to see if the physician will come here."

"Yes my lord."

While he went to do that, I entered the tent and stood watching one of the maidservants wash Appolious tenderly with water.

Then the scene faded from my eyes and I saw his weary face again as he sat slightly slumped in the saddle looking down at the robe hanging there. I saw him again toss it to me without a word. I remember the look in his eyes and the hint of sadness in the man.

A moan shattered my thoughts like a potters vessel dashed to pieces and he was again lying before me on the cot. His head rolled slightly and I bent close.

"Appolious it is I, Timon, can you hear me?" There was no response so I stood again.

It was nearing evening when one of the servants called that two riders were coming fast. The sun hung low in the sky sending golden streamers through red and purple shroud of clouds. I came to the entrance of the tent and with my hand shading the evening glare I could see it was the servant returning with the physician. I breathed a sigh of relief and went to greet them.

"Shalom!" I saluted. "He is in my tent." I indicated before the physician even unseated himself from the horse.

He nodded and reached for the bag he had brought, and I turned to lead him into the tent but the young lad who had gone for him drew my attention.

"My lord?" He said unto me.

"Yes, what is it?" My words showed the irritation of the delay.

The boy looked sheepish and leaned near and said in my hearing only. "I did not tell the physician he was a Roman. I feared he would refuse to come."

"Very good, lad. I am sorry for my sharp words. You have pleased me well. Now go get some meat and take your rest."

"Yes my lord," he grinned widely.

Entering the tent, the physician stood staring down at the cot where Appolious laid. There was no mistaking his strong Roman features. Upon hearing me come in he exclaimed. "He is a Roman."

"Yes, and he is a good one."

"Hump, a good Roman!" He then bent over the bed and began to examine the large gaping wound in Appolious' side. "What happened? This is very deep. There is very little I can do. It is mostly up to Elohim."

"Is there no hope?" I asked almost at a whisper.

"That depends on how much damage was done on the inside. It looks bad to me. Like I said, only the mercy of Elohim will tell the final outcome."

"Can he be moved?"

"If he lives two days he can travel in the cart, but to move him before that will probably be too much for him."

Another delay, it seems as though Yah does not want me to find the disciples, so many obstacles, so many unanswered questions. What was the greater purpose of the death of the man called, YahShua. Was there a resurrection and if so, where is He now? Will I ever find the truth or understand the purpose of Yah? Then the little sermon Yered gave me in my room at Yerushelayim rang afresh in my ears and I smiled at its memory.

"Trust Timon, just trust." I muttered to myself.

That evening a tremendous wind whipped across the valley making no small disturbance as the servants scrambled here and there securing the camp. One of the camp chairs slammed into my tent near the delirious Appolious scaring the young maiden caring for him nearly half to death. In the commotion that followed the small table by the bed was dumped over and a good deal of the precious medicine the physician left for the fever was quickly drank up by the thirsty ground. When the wind subsided some time later, it had laid the entire camp in disarray.

My eyes had hardly found sleep when the maiden came to my bedside and told me Appolious had wakened. I put on my khiton and went to him. He looked at me as though trying to place me. His face was still hot with fever and his eyes glazed with pain.

"How are you feeling, my friend?" I asked softly.

He blinked at me, trying to sort his thoughts. "Timon?" He spoke weakly.

"Yes, it is I."

"What are you doing here? Where am I?' Then his eyes widened and he tried to raise himself. "My men! What

244

about the men?" The more he talked the more disturbed he became.

I placed my hand upon his burning shoulder. "Take it easy Appolious! You have been gravely wounded and all your men are dead." I hated telling him for it was apparent his men came first, but I knew he had lost men before and would deal with this news as the disciplined Roman officer he was. The head he was trying to raise fell back upon his pillow and he closed his eyes.

"You are in my tent. There is nothing to worry about. I have seen to everything. Just rest now and when you are well enough I will take you home to your family." He just opened his eyes again and looked at me with a grateful expression. The maiden tending him gently lifted his head and placed a cup to his lips. After drinking, he closed his eyes again with a painful look that soon faded into peace.

It was sad seeing him like this. His face flushed and voice quivered from weakness, a mere shadow of the robust, powerful man he was. Sometimes it is difficult to understand the cruel twists of life that we find ourselves in. I knelt quietly beside the cot and said a prayer for him. I knew Yah loved this man who, unlike his fellow, walked in love and compassion and in his position that was nearly an impossible task.

When I returned to my bed, sleep had fled, and as I lay there loneliness crept over me like some slithering, loathsome creature. Yered had left only yesterday and tonight I was alone. Surrounded by servants, I was so lonely I could weep. I wondered if Elsan would come on the morrow or if he would stay a few more days at home.

I missed Sarepta so, the feel of her warm body in my arms. I swallowed the lump trying to grow in my throat. The thought of her took me back to the Celebration of Harvest at the thrashing floor of Yosef-bar-Taddai.

We attended the celebration of our dear friend's harvest each year but I shall never forget that one celebration when at the Dance of the Maidens, my eye fell

245

upon a beautiful young damsel. I was completely captivated by her. Later, I found her sitting on a grinding stone and when I spoke to her, she reddened behind her lacy silk veil. Her eyes, as the water of a deep pool, like unto the sky on a bright day, looked deeply at me in wonderment.

"Next year I shall dance for you," she promised. This pleased me very much and I suppose it showed upon my face.

While we talked, her father summoned me. "I see you have cast your eye upon my daughter," He said unto me. "She is not for you. She is promised to another. Besides, I have two other daughters who must marry before her."

At the harvest celebration the next year the maiden of my delight refused to speak to me. She looked ashamed, and turned her eyes away. However, before the Dance of the Maidens began while waiting for the music, she finally looked at me. My eyes caught hers and held them fast. I did not take my eyes off her through the whole dance and neither did she turn away. I knew she was dancing for me.

After that, I spoke of her often to my brothers and one day before my father they began to tease me about her. Much to my surprise and unknown to my father and brothers their teasing set well with me. I found the memory of her visiting me often, and I began to look forward to the Celebration of Harvest as it drew near.

It came to my knowledge that Yosef had married his dead brother's wife, as is the custom and along with her came three daughters, Sarepta, my delight, being the youngest of them. That year as before she refused to even look at me. I was very unhappy and was about to leave when the signal for the Maidens' Dance reached my ears. I turned myself to see the dance hoping Sarepta would dance for me again this year. Young men are sometimes very foolish. However, I was not disappointed. Try as she did to not look, when the music started her eyes fell upon me and remained until the dance ended.

This beautiful maiden began to fill many of my thoughts being haunted constantly now with a vision of her. I finally went to my father and said unto him. "I cannot put Sarepta from my mind. What shall I do?"

He studied me for a space of time. "She belongs to another. but, if it be the will of Elohim, ...patience has its virtue." He simply said.

The next year at the Celebration of Harvest my father called for me. The Elders were sitting under an olive tree and my father said unto me, "Would you take Sarepta to wife?"

My heart sang and I could not answer fast enough. "Yes, Father!"

Now, Sarepta came that night unto her father and he said to her, "Would you be espoused to BarPhilorah?" He waved his hand at me. Our eyes met and I held my breath.

"Yes, Father." She replied with no hesitation, but shyly dropped her eyes to the ground.

"Then it is done," he declared, and the oath was sworn before the Elders.

Lying here now, I can see the times we were together before the marriage, was always special just as it has been afterwards. Our love continues to deepen for each other. I sighed and turned upon my pillow closed my eyes and went to sleep in the comfort of the thoughts.

DAY THIRTEEN

Morning broke with the smell of dew and the call of songbirds in the valley meadow. The rising sun was quickly swallowing up the low, mystic haze covering the ground. I wondered what the birth of this new day would bring. Would Elsan come this day? What new truth will I be able to glean from the Writings of the Prophets, for in them Yah was speaking of this day?

I pondered the Sacred Writings as they bore witness time and again of the things that I have seen in Yerushelayim and will see as I continue my journey. Something keeps telling me that this is an important time in life, in history. That Yah is at work but just what he is doing remains as obscure and mysterious as does the circumstances surrounding the death of His son and His possible resurrection. The appearance of Mikha on the way here tells me something far reaching happened the day the earth quaked. My hopes are high that I will find the Messiah, YahShua of Natzeret, alive and well when I reach KfarNachum where the disciples have gone to meet Him.

There still is the empty Temple, however, and the deceit of the cohanim and jealousies of the elders. The evil hearts of the people who dawn a joyful face on the Sabbath and pretend that everything is wonderful. Where will it all end? Will Yah have mercy upon this people and relent of the dreadful deed He has prophesied through YahShua concerning Yerushelayim and her people? What of the rest of us who do not live in Yerushelayim? What will be our lot in this impending judgment? I shuttered and tried to push the thought from my mind.

It is unlawful for anyone to travel but a very short distance on the Sabbath day. And no work is don on that day. It is holy unto the Adonai. A devout follower of the law spends that day praying and fasting from food. I turned my face toward the Temple and prayed for some time, then I studied the scrolls of the Prophets and prayed some more.

The Sabbath is also a family time for no one goes to the fields or shops.

Outside the tent I could hear the cheerful voices of the young servants. They seemed to be having a good time. I went out of my tent and watched them play a game of strength where two servants climbed upon the back of two others and a crude form of combat began where the two on top tried to dismount each other. The winner received a cheer from them all and a piece of fruit for a trophy. When a wrestling contest began between two of them, I went back inside my tent where Benren was busy straightening things.

"Benren, I will have a cup of wine." I said unto him.

"Yes my lord." While he poured my cup full of the red fruit of the vine he said, "Do you think young Elsan will be here soon?"

"I do not know, he may stay a few days more at home with his mother before coming. I only hope he does not delay too long for we must take Appolious to KfarNachum in a day or so." Benren did not say anything further and I picked up the scroll I had been reading and went back to my studies.

While I pondered the words I had just read my eyes fell upon a tiny scorpion and I watched it at its innocent play. It had somehow found its way into my tent and now went about exploring the reassesses of its confinement for a way out. I though upon putting and end to it, but it seemed harmless as tiny as it was. Suddenly, I saw myself in the scorpion. Here I was wondering about all of Israel looking for the disciples and was having no more success at it than this little creature finding his way out. I became curiously intrigued with my tiny guest and watch its attempts to find an exit. After a while it turned about and made its way before the opened tend flap, its escape inevitable. I smiled at its persistence and was a little disappointed that it would soon be gone. It was growing din outside and the heat it so loved was waning away. Soon it would dig a burrow in the ground to keep it warm and take its nights rest.

It had almost reach freedom when at that precise degree, Benren appeared in the doorway with a try of fruit, nuts, bread and cheese putting an end forever to its attempt to escape. One large sandal clad foot came down on it and ground it into the hard crusty soil. I winced for it, and frowned at Benren's lack of perception, but then it was only a tiny scorpion. Would someone put an end to my search just as easily, someone like Kayafa or the Romans?

I sighed and looked at the tray, "Has the Sabbath began?" I took the tray gratefully.

"Yes my lord. The sun has well set."

As the new day began the desire to be moving made me restless. I checked on Appolious several times invoking Yah on his behalf and then went to my bed. I lay for a long time waiting for sleep to take me away and listened to the sounds of the night. I heard a horse clear dust from its nose while searching for the short shoots of grass and wondered what song the locus was singing to persuade a mate. I remembered the hawk and wondered if he was making his silent circles on the wind of the cool night air. Would he have a catch this night or would he return to his resting-place with empty talons? It seemed to me that nearly everything was in a quest for something. Is this the way of Yah?

DAY FOURTEEN

My observation of the Sabbath was lacking in enthusiasm, but I still fasted and prayed as usual. However, I turned not my face toward the Temple, but upward toward the heavens. YahShua told the disciples to pray, 'Our Father who art in heaven...' so, if that is where He is, then that is where I shall send my prayers. Where so ever He is, I know He will hear any prayer from the heart.

Appolious has continued his struggle for life, waning in and out of the grip of death. Will he give up the battle in his weakness? He has a lot to live for. His wife and children in KfarNachum, await his return with expectation, unknowing the desperate struggle he now wages to cheat the grim reaper of his daily harvest.

The maiden caring for him had a grim expression. "The wound does not look good, Adonai," she reported.

I stood looking down at what was once a mighty warrior. His dark hair, wet by washing because of the fever lay in small ringlets all about his now thin face.

"I fear his life is ebbing away." She continued with concern.

"He is a fighter. That is what he does best. He will win his battle." I told her and myself.

His mouth moved and a low grunt seemed to reassure me that he was not going to give up. The damsel moistened his parched lips and he moved his head slightly.

"He will make it," I said again drawing strength from my words.

Time passes slowly when you are waiting for something, and I have never been a great waiter. Sarepta has overcome this flaw in my character by being nearly always prepared to go. I can say with pride that that is one woman who does not keep a man waiting long and she has taught that virtue to her children. However, a circumstance cares nothing about my inconvenience. It laughs in the face of my irritation and makes fun of my lack of patience.

DAY FIFTEEN

The day dawned with a heavy haze. One of those days that does no good to a spirit already low. I arose and went to the tent door and looked longingly toward Natzeret. Perhaps, Elsan will come this day and bring word from home. I felt loneliness begin to creep upon me again, but I shoved it aside and went to see if there was any improvement in my ailing friend.

"How is he?" I ask even though I could see myself there was a little color in his face and his fever seemed persisted. Some improvement was what I needed to see. My faith in his strength was beginning to wane.

"He seems somewhat better I think, my lord." The little servant damsel replied with bright eyes.

I nodded and stroked her hair affectionately. She was a sweet child. A man is not to pride himself in what he has for it is a gift of Yah and how can one pride himself in a gift, something he has done nothing to deserve. However, I loved all those Yah put into my keeping and take some pride in them.

I went back to my part of the tent separated by wool hangings and lifted my voice unto the Elohim of Heaven and worshipped.

Sometime in the evening while I sat pondering the words I had just read, one of the servants called, "Riders coming!"

I laid down the scroll, arose quickly and stood in the tent door watching a swirl of dust churn into the air over the heads of three dark figures. Finally, they drew close enough for me to recognize the horses. Elsan sat straight and tall, flowing with the horse's stride, his Sudarin flapping the wind behind him as he rode. With him was the servant boy I had sent to Natzeret and Yhasper, Elsan's personal servant. I came out while they were still a ways off and with joy in my heart waited to greet them.

Elsan gave me a big smile, "Father!" One of my servants caught the reins while he threw his leg over the horse's head and slid to the ground, catching stride with the momentum.

We embraced and I felt the hot wind cool the tears of joy that came while we held each other. He seemed much taller than I remembered. Had I been away that long?

"Let me have a look at you." I held him at arm's length and studied him. "You have grown taller, I think."

His eyes, the same color as his mothers, twinkled excitedly. "...And, you have grown thinner from the looks of you," he added. "Mother would scold you for not eating."

"That she would." I grinned seeing her scowl in my mind's eye. I always told her that frowning would spoil her beauty and she would laugh. Never could she be upset with me long.

"Come into the tent," I put my arm around his broad shoulders, "…and tell me of her and Athera, Miryam also."

As we came through the door of the tent he removed his Kaffiyeh, shaking the dust from his dark wavy hair. Yhasper, who had followed us, took it, his robe and the hination without a word.

"Benren, bring us some wine." I instructed without looking at him nor waiting for a reply.

When Elsan's eyes fell upon curtain behind which lay the Roman and he said, "Is that where the Roman is your servant told me about?"

"Yes, he is desperately ill."

He went to the curtain divider and moved it aside. "Well," he smirked with a twinkle in his eye at the maiden caring for him. "…It appears he is in good hands." She blushed and turned away.

"Yes! Yes!" I caught his arm and led him to a pile of fleece surrounding a small table.

It was puzzling to me that all my offspring's seem to have a wayward eye. I do not remember myself being like that when I was their age, but one never really sees their self as they truly are. Was I like that I wondered, raising a curious eyebrow and seated myself across the table from him.

"Then the Centurion's condition has not improved?"

"No," I wagged my head sadly. Then I brightened as I thought of the news from home. "Tell me of Athera, has she given birth?"

"Not at the time I departed, but Mother said it would be any time now."

"Is she well?"

"Yes, and she sends her love." He brushed back a lock of hair that persisted in hanging on his brow. "She says for you not to worry about her. She is in Yah's hands."

"And your mother?"

"She is having trouble with the infirmity which, as you know, usually appears this time of year. She said, I should tell you, she is well and not worry you with it. She says she misses you extremely and was glad to hear that you are well."

"Yes, I miss her, also, and what of Miryam?"

"Miryam is well, but you have to take that harp you bought away from her to get her attention. I am glad it is Yered who has to listen to her learn to play it."

"Oh Elsan, you know you love to hear her sing as well as the rest of us."

"Sing yes, but play that harp, ...and from sunrise to sunset?" He quirked an eyebrow.

"Stop it." I scolded teasingly and he chuckled.

I told him in detail everything that had happened in Yerushelayim. He was somewhat upset and dismayed by it all, however, I soothed him with what I had learned in the Sacred Writings. He then told me of home and the business and how the Romans came through Beitorah shortly before Yered arrived. This worried me somewhat, but I was sure they probably would not be back for sometime and by then the incident with the rebels would be forgotten.

The day was far spent, while we talked, a long shadow from the doorway of the tent fell across the table, and looking up to find Benren standing there. He came forward meekly. "I am sorry to disturb you my lord, but the young servants wanted me to entreat you to tell them a story."

"A story?"

"Yes, my lord."

"It has been a long time." I reasoned, but I wanted to spend this time with Elson.

"Yes my lord, not since we left Beitorah."

"Oh please do, Father. I miss your stories also."

255

"Will you ever get too old for stories?" I teased.

"Not the stories you tell. They always leave you with much to think about."

"Hum, all right. Tell the servants to present themselves before the table after supper and I will have a story for them."

"I will tell them. Thank you my lord." He bowed slightly and left us.

Appolious is fighting the battle of his life. It is nigh suppertime and he is still alive. This encourages my heart. If he makes it through the morrow, I feel he will have won his fight. He awakes occasionally and the maiden gives him sop and fever medicine. He has lost much weight and has weakened, but I am still hopeful.

In the cool of the evening when the sun had almost hidden it's face behind the veil of the horizon, under the shelter where I am accustom of taking the supper meal, Elsan and I sat sipping a cup of fine wine. I love the peace that comes with the evening. It is as though the affairs of the day have been settled and all has taken their rest. Nothing stirs except a soft breeze that cools with the disappearing sun. While we sat each in his own contemplation, the company of servants came and stood before me.

"We came to hear the story, Master." One bold lad spoke eagerly, then clasped his hand over his mouth and looked wide-eyed at me.

It is customary for a servant not to speak until his Master tells him to speak. However, I have never been one to hold that custom too tightly. Benren does insist upon it, however, especially with the young servants. Benren and I have always talked freely one to another, but he is my personal servant that gives him certain privileges.

"I, ...I am sorry, my lord," he stammered dropping his eyes to the ground.

"It is alright," I eased him. However, I saw a frown on Benren's face. I am sure the lad will be reproved for his enthusiasm. "Sit yourselves down now before me and hear a parable. The servants all scrambled for a place on the ground and look to me with wondering expressions. I shall call it, 'The Parable of the Young Fellow'." I determined thoughtfully.

"Once there was a tribe of woodland dwellers." I started. "They had lived in the woods all their lives, just as their fathers and their fathers before them unto many generations. Every morning they would awaken to the music of the babbling brook and the sweet song of the colorful fowl that dwelt in the boughs of the trees."

"Being a hearty robust people, they would bind on their clothing, lay their broadax across their shoulders and march down to the place of woodcutting. There they would work with pleasant expressions until evening, just as their fathers had done before them. They did not know why they cut, only that it has always been done and the way things would still be done."

"There were laws to live by and rules to follow. No one questioned the laws or the rules they just traditionally obeyed. Those who did not labor and keep the traditions were considered peculiar and rebellious outcast."

"Now, in the cool of the evening, the head of the household would call every member around him and would begin to tell them of the bounty of the Great Forest and beautiful woodlands. He would speak of the joyous life-giving brook and of the fancily dressed fowl. He would mention how many wonderful woodland creatures scampered about and played happily on the forest floor. Opening his hands in pride, he would brag about the lovely house his hands had provided. He would tell the children how fortunate they were and how their forefathers long ago discovered the wonderful woodlands and came to live here."

"Then he would begin to tell them of the stubborn people who remained behind to dwell in the caves of unfruitfulness on the lava lands north of the forest. Their forefathers tried in vain to get the people to come live in the plush living forest where were all the gifts of the Creator."

"The children would listen intently without making a sound as the Elder told of the dry orange clay caves with laws carved upon their walls. About the crude wooden tools the tillers would use to chop the hard crusty soil and there plant the precious seed of life. The children would cringe when they would hear of the fierce sun that scorched their backs as they labored in the heat, hacking away at the sparse yielding ground."

"Then they would all stand and thank the Creator for the bountiful woodlands and for their forefathers who dared to venture into it. Then they would vow deep within themselves never to go into the lava lands of heat and misery."

"One day there was a young fellow not yet old enough to be respected or held in high regard but a thoughtful fellow was he. Catching a breath from his day of labor, he surveyed the deep ugly gashed in the eroding forest floor where all the trees used to stand with majestic living boughs. 'Look what is happening to our beautiful forest! What will happen to the children when all the trees are gone?' He asked an Elder working near by."

"'Do not be ridiculous, foolish fellow, the trees will always be,' he replied with a grunt."

"'Not if we keep cutting them down.' He reasoned, looking around."

"'Our fathers cut trees. We will also cut trees. Enough of this foolishness, back to work with you now.' The Elder scolded."

The young servants set wide eyed and their attention was fully on me. "After several months of serious contemplation, the young fellow came to understand that despite tradition the elders must see the beautiful gifts of the Creator would soon be gone. No one seemed appreciate what the Creator had given or why they were there. The gifts were misused and taken for granted without the slightest thought about why they were slowly disappearing. The bountiful gifts would someday all be gone and the people's land would lay waste, barren of life and without blessings."

"So, being a good fellow and having foresight, he sat about to make the people see what they were doing. That proved to be a bigger task than he had counted on. His words went unheeded and he soon became wearisome to the Elders. Why, it was just unthinkable there would come a day when there were no gifts. It was outrageous and the Elders were furious at such sacrilege, no more gifts, how foolish. So, the Elders stirred up the people against the young fellow and they took up stones, pounding him, until he fled bleeding into the forest."

The children winched as though they too were the victim of harsh stoning. "Hurt, starving, alone and exhausted," I searched each face as I spoke and marveled at the myriad of expressions. "The young fellow sank to the ground with a moan under a tremendous oak. In his ears were the sounds of the woodlands he loved, while all around him were familiar sights and smells, but he found no comfort in them. The confusion, pain and loneliness of his heart had turned all the things he loved into hateful reminders of the cold, cruel stones. He wished for death to ease the aching unrest in his soul."

"There in his misery from somewhere from deep within came a still small voice, hard to hear at first, but as he listened it became clear and understandable. It was soft and refreshing like a gentle breeze on a hot day. 'You are not alone. Arise, take courage and continue on.'"

"He had not heard this voice before, being too busy cutting trees and playing games in the lush forest, but as his soul grew silent, he heard it. He knew the voice had been there all along because it was familiar, as familiar as his own life. He had just been unaware of it. Now the unrest within turned to courage and he arose in the strength of that voice and it guided him onward."

"Only occasionally now did the sounds of the woodlands and the babbling brook distract him from the comfort he had found in the still small voice. Onward he went, nothing seemed familiar where he traveled and sometimes he was sure he was lost, although it did not really seem that way."

Out of the corner of my eye, I saw Elsan arise from the chair beside me and go toward the tent. This was something he would never do without a good reason. I wondered where he was going, but went on with the story.

"As unexpected as was the still small voice, the forest gave way to a dazzling fertile valley. Rolling hills with fruitful trees welcomed him. The air was perfumed with the sweet fragrance of fruit tree blossoms, and every imaginable color and shape of flower greeted him. A soft breeze cooled his cheek like a loving kiss. His heart sang and leaped for joy within him. There would be no hard soil to chop or trees to cut here. This was a place of rest where no labor was needed. All things pertaining to life were here. This was the very face of the Creator."

"Now, his mind raced back to the woodland people. If they could just see this, if they only knew of this place of oneness with the Creator. He was sure they would want to live here for this was Beulah Land, ...home, truly home."

"Yes, it would mean they would have to leave the woodlands and their beautiful houses their hands had made but who would not give that all up just to be in a place like this. The gifts can compare nothing to this place of love and peace."

"'I will go back and tell them,' he thought, '...and bring them here.'"

"With a song in his heart and peace in his soul, his feet hardly touched the ground as he hurried back through the forest and to the people he loved.

"There were warm handshakes and friendly smiles the night he returned. It was as though the old grievances were gone. Even the stone bruises did not seem nearly as bad now. He was excited and anxious to tell of the wonderful new place he had found to dwell. Ah, ...but alas, as he stood to tell of it, the smiles faded into frowns. A place better and lovelier than their forest woodlands, impossible! His words fell to the ground. The people wagged their head sadly and turned away one by one. Soon, he was left standing alone. No one wanted to hear of his discovery."

"He must make them believe. Somehow, he must convince them. So, he went to each one of them to reason with them but they ignored him. They refused to listen, stopped their ears and become angry. Again, he faced their stones and again he fled into the forest."

"'I must try again,' he told himself. 'They are my people.'"

"So, back he came, but they just went about as though he was not there and when one did talk to him, it was only to encourage him to go back to work and forget this nonsense."

"Slowly the peace he had found deep within began to ebb away and frustration quickly took its place. The still small voice seemed silenced by his very own words as he tried even harder to get someone, anyone to listen. It was then that he realized these people were satisfied and content where they were and unless something happened to what they already had, they would never consider leaving or looking for something more."

"Fear grew in his heart for the voice of guidance was silent and that was unbearable. Frighten, he ran from the woodlands. He ran and ran seeking what he had lost. Exhausted again, he fell still beneath his anguish and again found with joy the peace and comfort of his soul. This time, however, it came not as a small voice but as calm assurance and knowledge that brings a deep peaceful confidence."

"In his heart he knew he would have to leave behind all that the loved, all that was familiar and return to the place of the face of the Creator. He no longer belonged to the woodlands of his youth but to a beautiful place far beyond. The inner peace seemed to fill the void left by his friends and woodland home. Never again would he be alone because he now dwelt where the Creator was and that was enough."

I fell silent and waited for some reaction from the servants. They looked one to another and thought upon the story.

"That is an interesting story, Timon." A half-amused voice came from behind and I turned to see BarAbbas standing near the side of my tent, fists folded in a defiant manner on his hips.

"However," he grinned sheepishly, "...had I been a thief or robber, I could have sneaked up and struck you from behind. You should not be so careless."

Only a few feet behind him, sword in hand, Elsan came around the tent.

"That is advice well-given. Do you not think so Elsan?" I said hiding a grin.

"Yes Father, well-given."

BarAbbas spun around quickly and seeing Elsan's sword ready in his hand took hold of the hilt of his sword. "Do you intend to use that?" He asked with little emotion.

"That will depend upon you." Elsan set his face as iron.

"BarAbbas," I opened my hand toward him. "This is my son Elsan. Elsan, this is BarAbbas, the zealot whom half of the Roman army is seeking. He is an obstinate man, but a friend."

"Very well!" Elsan sheathed his sword.

"Not many can do what you just did," BarAbbas relinquished his stance, "...much less live to tell about it."

"Do not worry BarAbbas, your secret is safe with me."

BarAbbas shot him a hard look. "It is a good thing that I am a zealot and fight only to free Israel of the Romans." Elsan held his place, and they stared at each other.

"Enough!" I raised my hand. "Come and have a cup of wine." Then I remembered the servants. "That is all my children, go and find the meaning of my story."

Then BarAbbas turned quickly and took the seat beside me that Elsan had left while I told the story.

"I thought you would be gone by now." I motioned for one of the maidens to pour some wine while Yhasper set Elsan a new chair.

"You never know where you will be from one time to another." He grinned broadly, "...just one of the many sacrifices you make if you want freedom for Israel."

"Tell me BarAbbas." I settled back and picked up my wine cup. "...If your interest is solely in freedom for Israel, why did you order your men to rob the dead and gather spoils?"

He twisted his expression and scowled at my words. Then it faded and he laughed while raising from his chair again. "Do you think my purse is full of Roman coins?"

He jerked his purse from his girdle upon which hung his sword and tossed it onto the table. It landed in front of me with a dull thud and his eyes narrowed coldly at me.

"There! See for yourself the wealth that comes from being a zealot." His words were not loud but resentful.

I made no move to lay my hand upon the bag. I just waited patiently. After a short pause he snatched the bag and dumped out of it two mites and one shekel which rolled on their edge in circles making a musical sound that increased until they finally lay flat on the table top.

"This is the wealth of a zealot." He laughed mockingly, but I caught a hint of seriousness.

I did not see anything to laugh about. His performance made little impression on me and Elsan just looked at him in wonderment. When he saw we were not amused his face sobered, and he leaned toward me.

"Must you always be so suspicious?"

I did not venture a reply, but only looked at him wondering if he had become deranged by all he has been through.

"Humph!" He blew through his nostrils and began to pick up the coins. "Oh yes," he pointed his finger at me while the bag dangled form his hand. "You are the seeker of truth." He laughed lowly almost to himself then dropped the coins slowly back into his bag one by one.

He looked at Elsan trying to read him and then back at me. Two wrinkles appeared between his eyes and then he said, "Many young men have families and there are supplies to buy, …not to mention feeding the poor."

Placing his hands on the table, he leaned on them still holding his bag. "You would not know anything about that now, would you?"

I knew he meant it as an indictment against my wealth, but I just met his iron look with a steadfast countenance. He had no knowledge of me on which to base this accusation.

"Is this what you came here for," I asked sharply, "…to insult me before my son?"

Pushing away from the table quickly he snapped right back. "Nor have I come here to be insulted."

"My question was not meant as an insult. If it sounded that way I am sorry."

BarAbbas took up his cup and drank deeply of it, then settled back down on his chair. "One of my men has just returned from Yerushelayim with news that is very disturbing." He wiped the overflow from his mouth with his sleeve.

"What is it?" I raised up intently.

"One called, Shaul of Tarsus brought before the Council of Elders charges of blasphemy against eight souls. The elders then petitioned Pilate for the death penalty."

"Followers of YahShua." I thought aloud.

"Followers of YahShua, Zealots, what difference does it make. They are Israelites." BarAbbas spit irritably.

"Well, what happened?" Elsan asked impatiently.

"It was granted!" BarAbbas opened his arms holding out his cup to the maiden for another drink. He looked grim. "Golgotha will run red with their blood soon."

"That is sad news. I wish there was something I could do." My mind searched its resources for a possible course of action.

264

"There is nothing anyone can do for them, except make Pilate pay for his decision."

"More blood!" I said disgustedly. "BarAbbas that is not the way."

"More Roman blood, Timon. That is the only thing they understand. YahShua and His disciples tried to love them to death, and that did not do anything except end up with YahShua on the cross and His disciples running for their lives."

"Turn the other cheek they say. Love your enemies they say. Gentiles do not understand that. He took out his sword. "Give them a kiss with this and they will sit up and take notice. We will be a force with which they will have to deal."

"Yes, …and then the blood from Golgotha will reach as far as the Great Sea. The more blood you shed, the more they will require and where will it all end?"

"I do not know. I only know for me, I prefer death to the Roman yoke." He shoved his sword back in its sheath.

I glanced at Elsan. I did not like him hearing this kind of talk, but I knew traveling with me that is exactly what he would hear everywhere we go. Studying his reaction to BarAbbas a degree, I could see he was intrigued, but the glint of excitement so visible in Yered was not there. I was about to breathe a sigh of relief when he said to BarAbbas.

"I can understand that. I feel the same way."

I blinked at him in unbelief. "Enough of this talk!" I bid. "The servants," I swung my hand toward where they made their camp by the cart, "…do not need to hear such foolishness, and it is not pleasant for me either." I had dismissed them, but I knew they were listening.

BarAbbas finished his wine with a quick back sling of his head. I had never seen anyone drink wine as he does. "I must be going." He stood up from the stool.

"It is late." I reminded him. "You are welcome to stay here this night."

"If I leave now and move fast I can get to camp before it is too dark." He went to one of the servant boys sitting nearby, pulled him to his feet by the front of his tunic, loosed him and swatted him gently on his behind. "Go get my horse," he ordered, pointing to the back of my tent.

The boy looked up at him, and then turned to me waiting. I nodded and he ran after the horse.

"How is that cursed Centurion?" BarAbbas turned back to me. "Dead I hope."

"No. He is fighting for life."

"Hump!" Then he turned his attention to Elsan. "You have spirit young man. Join me and we shall make the Roman swine wish they had never come to Israel."

"BarAbbas," I snapped and came out of my chair. "Sometimes, ...you do try our friendship." I used his own words.

He stared blinking at my abruptness, and then burst into laughter. Taking the reins of his horse from the servant boy whom had just returned, he shook his head as though to shake my words away, and climbed up.

"I did not come here to kill Romans." Elsan said unto him giving me a quick glance. "I came to protect my father upon his journey."

I knew from that glance he was telling me, he was old enough to answer for himself and make his own decisions. How right he was, but BarAbbas' brazen way angered me. I wondered if the time he spent not killing Romans was spent robbing homes of their sons.

"Shalom!" He bid loudly with a hearty laugh and kicked the horse hard in the ribs, galloping away.

I watched him disappear, leaving a dust trail for some distance in his going. I sighed and turned to Elsan. "I am sorry I did not allow you room to answer, but he has a way of angering me as none other. I know you are wise enough to make decisions for yourself."

He pushed the persistent lock of hair from his brow and gave me a twisted grin. "Ah, it is all right."

266

"Yhasper," I turned to him, "...set Elsan's cot in my tent. It is large with plenty of room."

"Yes my lord," he dipped his head slightly and went about it.

Elsan and I had another cup of wine before going in for the night and while we sat I thought of the poor souls brought before the Counsel at Yerushelayim. It is sad when our enemy becomes a brother. I wondered to what depths the chief cohanim and elders would go.

Then passages from the writings of the Prophet Yeshayahu came to mind. *"Your iniquities has made a separation between you and your Elohim. Your sins have hidden His face from you, so that He does not hear. For your hands are defiled with blood and your fingers with iniquity; Your lips have spoken falsehoods, your tongue has muttered wickedness."* And again, *"They conceive mischief and bring forth iniquity. The act of violence is in their hands."* He also said, *"Even in My house I have found their wickedness, declares the Adonai."*

When word reaches the people about Shaul bringing the followers of YahShua up before the Council, it will be even harder to get someone to talk about YahShua. They will have more to fear than being unpopular and I can see masses of devoted people like the ones under my window at Yerushelayim, coming to a horrible end. I shuttered and thought of the dream about Yered hanging among the followers or some Zealots on the cruel cross. Will that be his fate? Will he become one of Shaul's victims? Will I?

DAY SIXTEEN

Breakfast was small dove eggs found by the servants, fresh baked bread with honey and wine cooled by the night air. Wild flowers adorned in an array of vivid colors set forth a bouquet of sweet aroma. The sparse but fragrant springs of fresh green grass crushed beneath our feet drifted up added just the right touch to this delightful spring morning. The large yellow sun was now peaking over the rise of the earth threatening to take the coolness from the soft breeze. While we lingered at the table enjoying a final cup of wine, we talked of times past, laughing at things Elsan and Jered did when they were just children.

Elsan talked of his up coming marriage to Anna, who was espoused to him only shortly before I had left Beitorah. I encouraged him to not rush the ceremony but give them time to fall in love deeply. He seemed ready to settle down but Anna was very young and I felt she needed more time at home.

As it was bound to happen, we began talking about the happenings in Yerushelayim and the deceit of the chief cohanim and elders. No doubt that subject was on the lips of a good many, as the day presented itself. The prisoners of Shaul are surely wondering what the day will hold for them. Would they face the tree this day or have the evil minds of the Romans thought up a greater torture. Although, it would be hard for me to think of any that could top the agony of the cross. It is said that Caesar's twisted mind delights in finding new ways to define death.

Yes, I could see how my task was now going to take cunning, careful steps and planning. I would have to be very cautious from now on or I, myself, might find Shaul's hard glare through dungeon bars.

Appolious was still wasting away but fighting valiantly as a true soldier who has had to before deal with nearly impossible situations. However, he was able this morning to take a little broth and wine. A good sign, Benren says.

He looked so thin and seemed very weak when I checked on him again after breakfast. His shallow eyes held me fast. "Timon?' His voice quivered. "If ...I do not make it, ...tell Abigail that my last wish, ...is for her to marry soon." He drew a laborious breath. "Give the boys a father to teach them how to be men." He had spent all his energy now and closed his eyes.

"The boys have a father." I insisted in a sharp scold. "On the morrow I will put you in the servant's cart and take you home to be with them, so stop this foolishness and rest." I am sure to him the battle seems almost too much at times, but I have prayed and feel confident that Yah has heard and will help him to recover.

He forced his eyes open, looked at me a degree, opened his mouth but closed it again. I do not know if his weakness prevented him or if he felt the determination in my words. His eyes shut again and I knelt by his side to ask the God of Heaven to strengthen him.

While I prayed, I saw again the wounded zealots in the secret room under the Inn and how they laughed with joyful tones because of the healing at the hand of BarNabas. If only I could find one of the disciples, he might lay hands upon him and... Foolish, a disciple would not heal a Roman. It is they that killed the Adonai and forced them into hiding. No man heals his enemy. YahShua would not even do that. Then the teaching of YahShua by the mouth of BarNabas that night on the thrashing floor came rushing back to my mind. Yes, perhaps YahShua would heal His enemy. That thought brought warmth to my soul.

Later in the morning, I made mention to Elsan that I would like to stop at Natzeret and see Elisheva but it would not be possible now. Maybe, after I deliver Appolious safely into the hands of his wife, I could turn back and see her.

"Wishful thinking," I told myself. While in KfarNachum I will find the disciples and then, …Yah only knows. Sometime before my search is over I will go see her, I promised myself.

"Why do you not go see her now, Father," Elsan entreated, "…and on the morrow I will come bringing the servants and Appolious. Then we can go on to KfarNachum."

I thought on that a little and agreed with some reservation. I knew Appolious would be in good hands with Elsan, but I still hesitated. Elsan, therefore, urged me, so by noon Semone, Benren and I were ready to leave for Natzeret.

I hugged Elsan and smiled as I looked at him with his deep blue eyes and short dark beard shrouding the comeliness of his round face. He was my pride and I did not mind that he took his features from the mother for he had my determination and was wise beyond his years. I sometimes wonder if he is gifted of Yah. That would please me greatly. When Sarepta conceived him some years after the death of Seth, my first born, I spent many hours entreating the Lord for him to come forth well and healthy. Perhaps, Yah had given me even more than I asked.

We jiggled along the hard sun baked road, the hot wind whipping the heavy canopy top on the cisium. It made dull pops and rumbles that became intensely annoying, distracting my study of the Sacred Scrolls. Eventually, I called for Semone to stop and rest the horses but it was my ears that made the decision.

Natzeret was not much out of the way to KfarNachum and I was anxious to tell Elisheva all that had happened in Yerushelayim. By late afternoon, the outline of the small town appeared in the distance. On the outskirts of the small hamlet, the tents of a Roman garrison obstructed our view. Bitter faces and angry looks greeted us as we passed by. I smiled and tried to act pleasant but they all stood steadfast unimpressed.

I wondered what such a large troop was doing here and I supposed Benren was thinking the same thing for he turned in his seat to face me and said unto me. "Why are they here?"

"I am sure we will find out shortly."

In the market place people were going about with no better expressions than that of the soldiers. Scrawls and frowns were everywhere and tempers seemed short, for we did not even get through the square before two men began to argue and shout curse words at each other.

Soon, Elisheva's house was in sight and I climbed from my cisium, brushing the red dust of Israel from my robe. It made an orange cloud around me that the wind took up in jovial play, sending it spinning into my mouth and eyes. I was finding the task a bit defeating, but Elisheva's friendly voice came to my ears and I promptly forgot the grit between my teeth, and turned blinking through the dust, at her coming with out reaching hands.

"Timon, how nice to see you again." She took both of my hands and bowed slightly. "You look hot and tired. Come and take a cool cup of wine."

"Elisheva." I looked her over. "...Dear Elisheva! I hope you are well."

"Yah has been good."

"Bless be." I praised Him.

She loosed one hand but pulled me along with the other toward the entrance of the house. "Your servants may enter also and take their rest." She instructed and when I turned to Benren, he bowed showing he had heard. "Where is young Jered and the rest of your servants? Nothing has happened to them, I hope."

"Jered has returned home and Elsan, my son, has joined me. He and the servants are with a friend who is gravely sick. They will join me here on the morrow and we shall continue to KfarNachum. We will be taking the ill friend to his family there."

She nodded and pushed aside the woolen curtain to the main room where the lounges and table sat. It was to me almost like coming home. A man of many years reclined at the table and his eyes mirroring the candlestick burning brightly on the table. He was a thin man with a long gray beard, and sharp inquisitive nose.

"Timon," Elisheva spoke in her usual soft voice, "…meet Malcolm, kinsman of my late husband. Malcolm, this is Timon of Mount Tabor. The one I told you about who came during Posach."

"Shalom, Timon." The man set forth and I bowed slightly to him. "Take your rest." He offered me a lounge.

"Why are all the soldiers camped on the outskirts of town?" I ventured to ask.

"Because of the rumors of YahShua raising from the dead." The man cast if off with a quick wave.

"Timon has just returned from Yerushelayim." Elisheva offered as she went for the foot basin.

"From Yerushelayim? Have you any news?" Malcolm looked inquiringly at me, drawing his eyes together intently.

"Much news sir," I returned, settling onto the seat.

I did not realize how tired I was until Elisheva soothed me from my journey with the basin and towel. I opened my mouth anxious to tell of the events that took place in Yerushelayim when a young woman came into the room with a pitcher of wine and some cups. She was not much older than my Miryam. Her raven hair shimmered in the flickering light of the candles.

"This is Rut, my son's daughter," Malcolm informed.

The young maiden bowed her head without a word and went back into the other room. Elisheva following closely on her heels and I heard her say through the reed curtain. "He is the one of whom I told you." I heard no reply.

"There was no small stir in Yerushelayim when I was there for the Posach. I trust that things have quieted since then." Malcolm drew my attention.

"Not really. Much is happening there."
Elisheva returned and settled quietly upon one of the couches and I drank to wash the grit from my throat.

"You would not believe the treachery of the chief cohanim and elders." I said to her. "Not only do they conspire with the Romans but they hide the truth from the people and offer up defiled sacrifices."

Elisheva's eyes widened and Malcolm set himself up. "Speak on," he urged with a wave of his hand.

"Yosef of Arimathea is dead and his death was on this wise. While he offered up prayers as YahShua hung upon the cross, the curtain before the Ark was rent and he was knocked backward, the Table of Shewbread was overturned and the light of the menorah was blown out." I took another drink to help me speak further. "Yosef told me the Glory of the Adonai departed the Temple in anger."

The old man frowned, whaled, rent his garment and raved, "Israel, Oh, Israel!" Then he fell silent twisting the end of his white beard in his slim fingers.

"When he told the chief cohanim and Elders what had happened," I continued, "they went about secretly to repair the veil that was rent in two when the Glory departed, saying the earth quacked and did it. So, Yosef went out after having given his own newly hued tomb for a place to lay the body of YahShua and sat in the ash heap mourning and wailing with ashes upon his head until there was no life left in him. It is sad but it is best he is dead for Kayafa and some of the other chief cohanim were determined to have Yosef removed from the Council, to kill his influence. They were claiming him to be a babbling idiot, too old and not of sound mind.

"Why would Elohim abandon Israel?" Malcolm wondered aloud.

"Because the chief cohanim and Israel have defiled themselves by demanding the death of the Son of Elohim at the hands of Pilate."

"Enough of this blasphemous talk about YahShua." His words were sharp and he drew his eyebrows together tight with a stern look. "He has received His just do."

His words stung in my heart like the bite of an asp. I looked surprised at Elisheva and saw the pain in her eyes. I had made a grave mistake. Because Elisheva believed in Him, I had assumed Malcolm, also, believed. How terrible things must be for her. First, she looses her husband, then her son, and now she must live in this place where she cannot even speak her heart. I felt a slow anger begin to rise within me. She deserves better that this. Poor, dear Elisheva, I shook my head sadly.

This kinsman Malcolm, willing to believe the testimony of Yosef and that the Glory of Yah had departed the Temple, but has turned away from YahShua, who is innocent. He is a very peculiar man.

I tried in my looks to let Elisheva know how sorry I was for speaking my heart in front of him. I seemed to be doing so many foolish things lately. The more I think I know, the more foolish I seem to become.

The pained expression on Elisheva's face faded and she stood, "I will take my leave now."

"Very well," Malcolm said crossly with a wave of his hand. Then He looked at me. "Will you take your leave, also?"

"Yes!" My answer was quick and I knew it showed my anger and as I stood I softened my tone. "I am very tired from my travel."

"Be gone then," he grumped without even looking up at me.

"Shalom." I bid but it was hard to say and he just nodded.

I turned and went hastily out carried by the inner rage kindled by his rude manner.

Once out on the walkway, I heard the woolen curtain behind me rustle as though moved aside. Turning, I saw Elisheva with a sad countenance coming behind me.

She laid a tender hand on my arm and said lowly with no bitterness in her voice. "Timon, pay no mind to Malcolm. He is a sad, confused and miserable man." In her eyes of sadness, I saw compassion where only a degree ago there was pain, what a special woman. I felt the anger in

275

my heart begin to calm as I stood there looking steadfastly into her wonderful warm eyes.

"YahShua, Himself, said something I only now understand," she consoled.

"What is it?" I looked eager, anxious to hear the words He spoke.

"I am told He said, 'Do not think I have come to bring peace on the earth; I did not come to bring peace, but a sword. For I have come to set a man against his father, and a daughter against her mother, a daughter-in-law against her mother-in-law. A man's enemies will be the members of his own household. He who loves father or mother more than Me, is not worthy of Me; and he who loves son or daughter more than Me, is not worthy of Me.'

She smiled, "Malcolm is a good men. He battles the truth within himself."

"Elisheva, you are far more precious than I. How do you always manage to see through other's eyes?"

She patted my arm affectionately. "You and your servants may stay here." She waved her free hand toward the lower manger level. "We shall talk later."

"Very well." I place my hand upon hers.

"I must know the things you did not have a chance to speak," she said eagerly but turned and went back through the curtain.

DAY SEVENTEEN

I had little appetite but forced myself to eat a small amount of prepared cereal and a piece of fruit. I again saw Sarepta as she scolded me for not eating and I smiled to myself letting the thought warm me. Maybe, the questions will be answered in KfarNachum and then I can go home with peace in my soul.

"Please Yah, help me find the truth of this matter and know the reason for this seemingly futile search," I whispered under my breath.

Later in the dim morning light that filtered through the door, I sat staring into one of the Sacred Scrolls. My thoughts were upon Yosef of Arimathea as he sat upon the heap of ashes. His words rolled through the chambers of my heart causing a deep, sorrowful aching. It was so hard to believe Yah had departed from Israel, leaving an empty and desolate Temple. The Glory, not being above the Ark of the Covenant, was almost unthinkable. I could understand very well why the chief cohanim and the elders could not believe his testimony. It seemed so unreal, so unthinkable, I too, wanted very much to believe that it was only the quaking of the earth. But, I knew Yah would not have permitted the curtain to be rent without being His will. Yah is not powerless and it is He who controls the elements. So, whether it was the earth or as Yosef had testified, it was still the doing of Yah and there was some important reason for its happening. I was sure of it but what that reason was, remains a great mystery.

"Timon?" A soft feminine voice tore the thoughts from my mind bringing a freshness as that of the cool wind after a rain. I turned to look at the shadowy outline of a woman, slim and emanating the sweet smell of spices.

"Yes?" I stood.

"Elisheva sent me to ask you to come in and speak with us of your travel."

I squinted in the dimness to see her face. It was properly veiled and her eyes caught a spark of light. It was Ruth the young woman of last night. Then she dropped her gaze realizing that all eyes were upon her.

"Benren." I held the scroll out and he came to my side taking it from my hand. I drew nigh the maiden and she turned for the steps to the upper level.

As she pushed the woolen tapestry aside and we entered, I saw sitting before me two men, two women, Elisheva and a young boy. The damsel I was with took a place by one of the women.

"Timon," Elisheva smiled at me. "This is my family, Philip and Yoel." She indicated the two men. "Nessa, Ester," the two women, "…and little David. You have already met Ruth."

I bowed to each as she called their names. "Greetings!"

"This is Timon." Elisheva opened her hand to me.

"Take your rest." Philip offered a place beside him near the head of the table.

They were all looking at me with excited wondering. I followed Philip's invitation and the one named Nessa poured me a cup of wine from a pitcher already sitting on the table.

"You may speak openly to us for we are all believers," Elisheva assured me.

"Yosef of Arimathea is dead," I started. "He was in the Temple offering up prayers for YahShua of Natzeret, who had been hung on the cross at the insistence of the chief cohanim and Elders. At the precise time He gave up the ghost, the curtain before the Most Holy Place was rent from top to bottom. The Glory of the Lord then departed the Temple in anger, turning over the Table of Shewbread and blowing out the light of the Menorah, while Yosef himself was knocked backward upon the floor.

The women gasped and the men wailed. "The Glory of Elohim has departed Israel! The Glory has departed!"

Tearing their garments apart, they grasp their hair in mourning.

After we bewailed Israel for a while, I continued my story. I told of the plot to remove Yosef from the Council and how the Elders were hiding the truth from the people so there would be no day of national mourning.

"What are we to do?" Yoel asked wide-eyed. "Has Elohim forsaken us? Will He no longer hear our prayers and what of our sins?"

"Elohim will always hear the prayers of a sincere heart no matter where He is. Our forefathers, Avraham, Yitzchak and Yaakov, had no Temple, but Elohim heard them." I assured him.

"I have no answers for the other question," I confessed. "I only know that YahShua is an important part of it, for everything always leads back with Him." He was the Messiah, the Son of Elohim and Israel has slain their deliverer. Why Elohim allowed it, I do not understand but according to the Writings of the Prophets, Elohim foresaw it all and has some purpose in it, a higher purpose, something far more than meets the eye."

"But YahShua is dead, they have killed Him," Philip moaned.

"Rumor has it that He raised the third day, as He promised, and has appeared to the disciples." I encouraged them. Though I, also, tossing back and forth these same questions, just knowing I was not alone strengthened me.

"So that is why the Romans are in Natzeret in such force. If He is alive, He might come here and they are here just in case of trouble. That would, also, explain why many strangers are coming daily," Philip tossed out.

"Then He may still deliver Israel," Yoel hopefully thought aloud.

There was no reason to shatter this hope with the prophecy of YahShua about Yerushelayim. There was nothing that any of us could do about it anyway.

"This is a dangerous time for the followers," I cautioned. "Besides the Romans, there are the chief

279

cohanim and elders that wish to silence us. To make matters even worse, only yesterday I learned, a young Prushen by the name of Shaul of Tarsus has bought some followers of YahShua before the Council with charges of blasphemy. The elders then went before Pilate seeking to put them to death." I took a drink of wine.

"What happened?" The boy injected eagerly and drew stern looks from both Philip and Yoel. The boy was caught up in the story, his eyes fixed upon me and was unaware of their looks.

"It was granted," I nodded sadly. "Now followers will face the cross as He did."
Yoel rose quickly with a great cry and fell with his face to the floor and wept with deep sobs. Philip and I joined him, the women and also the boy.

I do not know how long we languished before the Adonai but while I was prostrate there, I wondered where Meldi was while we talked and why it was so much harder for him to believe than the others.

When we quieted from our praying, I felt a soft touch on my shoulder and looked to see Benren stand there. He bent and whispered, "Elsan has arrived with Appolious and stands without."
I nodded and then arose trying not to disturb the others. When I looked for Elisheva hoping to at least say, Shalom, I noticed Meldi was among us. I made my way past him to where Elisheva was praying and he raised his head and looked at me, his beard wet with tears. I reflected on that a degree and he caught my arm.

"Forgive a foolish old man," he begged hoarsely.

"Peace brother," I smiled. Perhaps, he heard the conversation through the walls or doorway and now believes. He blinked away a tear and with a wide grin showed a row of uneven teeth.

I then caught Elisheva's eye for she had heard the conversation and was looking at us. I motioned for her and went out onto the walkway and waited. When she came through the curtain I said, "Elsan has arrived and we must now travel on to KfarNachum."

"Do come again Timon. I would like to hear more."

"There is nothing more to tell now but before

I return home after I find the disciples I will bring you news."

She nodded, "Elohim speed, Timon, and do be careful."

"You, also, be cautious. The time has come for you to watch who you invite into your house for we have many enemies, even among Israel."

She nodded sadly and muttered, "He has brought a sword." But, I understood it.

Elsan stood without near the cart and when I approached he turned to face me. "Appolious is making the ride well, Father," he reported.

"Good," I patted his shoulder and dust puffed into the air.

I looked into the wagon under the heavy canopy they had spread to keep the sun at bay and there Appolious lay upon a high pile of furs to cushion the ride. One of the servant maidens was busy wiping the gritty red dust from his white drawn face. I touched his shoulder tenderly and he opened his deep set eyes with dark rings around them.

"How are you doing, my friend?" I asked feeling pained for him.

He nodded and wet his lips. "Are we there?" His voice cracked somewhat.

"Not yet, we are in Natzeret, but shall leave shortly. You shall be home soon."

He half smiled and closed his eyes once again. I felt confident of his recovery now, but as the physician had said it would be a long one. There must have been massive damage to his bowels.

"Father?" Elsan's voice showed concern and when I looked at him, he was watching a large patrol of Roman cavalry that was riding toward us. "Why are all the soldiers here?"

"The elders fear a following of YahShua will rise up here for it is said among them that He has raised from the dead and this is His home town." I, too, watched a degree of time, then turned back to him.

"Ignore them and maybe they will pass on by without incident."

Benren now came close and said, "We are ready for travel my Lord."

"Good, let us be going."

I was about to step aboard my carriage when a harsh commanding voice came from behind me. "What is this?"

I turned to see the bitter, scowled face of a Centurion who had just pulled his flouncing horse to a stop near the servant's cart. I did not like the feeling the man gave me, and knew I had better have the right answers or I would be in great trouble.

"Good day Sir." I greeted making an effort to sound cheerful. "I am Timon of Beitorah. Is something wrong?"

"What is this?" He swung a quick hand in the direction of the troop.

"It is my servants and my son, Elsan. We are taking my sick friend to his home in KfarNachum."

The Centurion made a signal and two soldiers scrambled from their horse going to the cart. One of the two roughly shoved a servant boy out of his path and they pilfered the wagon. Then one of them, wishing to look in the furs Appolious lay upon drug the maiden servant from beside him casting her aside with little respect or concern. She landed against the front frame of the cart with a hard thump.

"Sir, I must protest this treatment of my servants," I stepped forward a bit, trying to hide the anger I felt rising within me. "They are valuable assets to me and I do not want them damaged."

The man stared at me with stone expression and then demanded, "What are you hiding, weapons for the rebels?"

282

"No sir! And neither am I a man without influence in Rome. I would keep that in mind if I were you." Some of my anger seeped into my words despite my attempt to restrain it.

The Centurion's expression changed very little. "Return to the column," he snapped to the soldiers without taking his eyes off me. "Be on your way now!" he demanded.

I nodded and as I turned again for my cisium, he said, "We will escort you to the edge of town." Then I heard him say as I climbed up. "Half of the column come with me the other half follow the travelers."

The Centurion took the head of the procession with several of his troop while the others followed and we bid farewell to Natzaret. Even before reaching the edge of the village the sun's heat was penetrating my garments and the hot wind was scalding my face. As beautiful as Israel is it can be a harsh overbearing land.

Before us lies the hill country of Galil with its many dens and natural caves. There the wild beasts raise their young and retreat there after prowling for food in the low country. Worse than that are the thieves, murderers and zealots that hide in it's nearly inexcusable region.

Two ruts cut into the hard dry ground by many wheels and much travel like twin cords of loomed fleece twist and wind its way through the rugged terrain. Some places were nearly unseating and I am sure very painful for poor Appolious although not a sound escaped his lips.

I picked out a scroll and began to read the prophecies it contained. *"Hear the words which the Elohim has spoken against you, sons of Israel, against the entire family which he brought up from the land of Egypt. You only have I chosen among all the families of the earth. Therefore, I will punish you for your iniquities. Surely the Adonai Yah does nothing unless He reveals His secret counsel to His servants the prophets."*

This verified my belief that if it is of Yah it is written in the volumes of the Prophets. YahShua of

Natzeret has fulfilled a good many prophecies concerning the Messiah and I am now convinced that the others have been fulfilled also, although unknown to me. But, why His death and why a resurrection?

My thoughts on the purpose for His death is that YahShua is the supreme sacrifice for Israel's sin, sin so great that the blood of bulls and goats could not cover it. That would make it necessary for a greater sacrifice. Surely He would accept a sacrifice that He, Himself, had chosen and provided. If it was accepted, then why did the presence of the Adonai Yah leave the Temple? The further I go in my search the more questions arise. What is Yah doing and why is there so much mystery in it? Would the disciples know? Would I find YahShua alive and with them? I have absolutely no understanding on the resurrection. There is so much I do not know. Will I ever find understanding?

"Trust Timon, just trust," I scolded myself.

"What, my lord?" Benren brought me out of my thoughts.

"Nothing Benren, I was only thinking aloud."

I had hardly gone back to my study when it felt like the earth opened and I dropped right into Shoel. I gathered my wits and realized that one of the wheels on my cisium had fallen into a large crack in the crusty ground. That tilt made me know it was resting upon the axle on that side. Straining and lunging in their harnesses, the horses' efforts reaped no reward despite Semone's harsh calls and strapping. After some time he pulled them still while they snorted out their frustration still stomping and tossing their heads.

A serpent sunning on a nearby boulder, being disturbed, tested the air before slithering from his resting place and disappeared through the rocks.

While the servants went about getting the carriage out, I went back to check on Appolious. He lay quietly with a slight wrinkle between his eyes. I knew he was feeling the strain and was being weakened even further by the travel but we were now only five stadiums from KfarNachum.

"How are you making the ride my friend?" I asked laying my hand gently upon him.

He stirred slightly blinking at me through the brilliance of the sun which was directly behind me. "Are we there?"

"Only a few stadiums away." I could see the hope fade from his face. "My cisium fell into a crack and the servants are freeing it." I ventured to explain.

He nodded, closed his eyes and wet his lips. At that, the servant girl placed a damp cloth to them and then offered him a cup of water. While he took the water, I whispered a prayer that the Elohim of Heaven would strengthen him for the remainder of the journey. After he had well drank, the servant then offered me a drink from a hind buried deep under the fleece to help keep it from becoming too hot and useless.

I took the cup and watched the servants strain beneath the weight of the heavy hand carved carriage. It rocked a few times under their coaxing, then came up with a squeak followed by a cheer from the servants.

Shortly, we were under way again bouncing and being tossed by the rough ruts etched into the road. This area was extremely rocky and there was no use in trying to read.

There was a steep slope scattered with large boulders on the left side of us, and a mountain ram with his several ewes watched us with caution from its heights. Finally, as though waiting for some unheard or seen signal they turned in one accord on nimble legs and scampered up the hill disappearing over the top.

Between the rough descending slopes, a small glimpse of the Sea of Galil's dingy blue water glistened in the late evening sun. The air was beginning to be heavy with the smell of fish and mucky water.

The large fishing village of KfarNachum was not more than a furlong away now. It is a wild ruthless place with varied sorts of lewd and evil entertainment. Because of its size and importance in the area, a legion of soldiers was garrisoned at Tiberius not far from there.

The Roman fortress serves as an ideal place to send soldiers on leave from their command for rest and relaxation. The high-spirited night-life suited their purpose, and by day the sea offered a water playground.

This did not interfere with the important fishing commerce in the area so vital to Israel for it is too hot for fishing during the day. The fish swim deep well out of reach of fishing nets to seek relief from the scorching sun. Fishing, therefore, took place during the late evening and night hours.

Suddenly, from all around us, men in skins and tattered garments with heavy girdles came from hiding places among the huge rocks and boulders. Bandits and thieves they were and we their victims. I was carrying in the secret compartment a rather large sum of money, and the other goods used in our travel were of the finest quality.

I quickly realized we were well out numbered and Elsan who was in the act of drawing his sword froze. To fight such a large band would be futile and he realized it. By the time Semone had pulled the cisium to a halt the men were already swarming the carts.

"Let them take what they want." I commended loudly for all the servants as well as the bandits to hear, hoping they would be satisfied with the spoils. If we showed no resistance there might not be any bloodshed.

One of the two men who had climbed onto the servant's cart called to his fellows. "Virgins!"

"Three of them," the other reported, catching one of my maidservants by the arm dragging her to her feet.

Because of their status as a servant these men would have no respect for the damsels, so I turned quickly in the seat and yelled at them, "You cannot have my virgins!"

"Virgins!" The other one howled. "Ooo-we!"

I was about to do something foolish again. I could not allow them to violate these young maidens without at least trying to stop them. I opened my mouth to threaten, but my first word was drown out by a shrill whistle. All the thieves looked in the same direction and I turned to see where they were looking. Upon the top of a nearby hill stood a man waving frantically at them. Quick movement by the bandits and they were going for the rocks and boulders again. The one in the servant's cart holding the maiden pulled her against him tore the vale from her face and kissed her. Reluctantly then, he joined the others who could be seen now only between the large boulders as they ran through them.

I was surprised at this unusual behavior and wondered what was coming that persuaded them to abandon their raid. What had caused enough fear in them for them to give up their play with the damsels and all the spoils I was sure they knew I was carrying?

I looked at Elsan, but he was already turning his horse to ride forward. He did not go very far before pulling to a stop. Stretching himself tall in the saddle to get a good look, he then turned and came back fast.

"Romans," he reported, "...about a score of them."

Romans! Yes, what else would have driven the bandits away? "Say nothing of this incident to them." I returned quickly. They might be thieves, but they were Israelites and I had no intentions of turning them over to Romans.

Soon we could hear the rhythmic jingle of metal, and the squeaking leather as the thud of many horse hooves pounded the dry earth. Then the brightly uniformed soldiers appeared near the spot where Elsan had gone to look. The Centurion officer who rode in front showed no surprise at finding us sitting here. He made no effort to stop his troop but rode unfaltering right to my cisium. There he held up his hand and the legionaries came to a stop.

"What is the trouble here?" The Centurion asked with a scowl, but his words were not harsh. "We heard your signal from the hill top," he continued.

I had to do some fast thinking "Ah, yes." I tried not to sound uncertain. "We have one of your officers here." I motioned to the servant's cart. "His name is Appolious, a Centurion and he is gravely wounded."

The Centurion looked pleased, turned in his saddle and said something in Roman to the Captain beside him. This officer has not been here long for he still uses his native tongue. That would account for him not having the usual distraught tone of voice.

The soldier slid from his mount and went to the cart, looked in and then looked back at the Centurion and shrugged, "He looks Roman all right."

"I am Centurion Appolious." I heard a weak trembling voice reply. The Commander turned back to me. "What happened to him? Where are his men?"

"They were all slain by zealots in the wilderness, and he alone has survived," I informed.

"What is your name?"

"I am Timon-bar-Philorah of Beitorah, and I was bringing Appolious to his family in KfarNachum."

"Hump!" The Captain snorted. "Commander, Yews do not help Romans." He informed the Centurion.

The officer looked sternly at him, and he said no more.

Elsan rode to the cart, bent over and took out Appolious' armor and held it up. "He is Roman."

"Does anyone know of an officer by the name of Appolious?" The Centurion asked, looking at his troop. There was no response at first, then two soldiers held up their hand's, "Come forward and identify this man."

While they were coming, the Centurion said unto me, "We will escort you to Tiberius. You will have to answer some questions."

Now what was I going to do? If I am seen with a military escort surely no one will speak to me of YahShua nor answer my questions, not even the disciples.

"I think this is Appolious, Sir." One of the two soldiers called. "He is very thin and nigh unto death."

"A medicus at the fort will take care of him."

"Please Sir," I entreated. "He is much too weak to travel that far and his home is in KfarNachum. Allow me to take him to his home and then I will come to the fortress and answer questions. Appolious is a friend and his life is precious to me."

The captain slowly moved his head back and forth in unbelief, but I hoped to find favor with this Centurion new to the area.

"Very well, we will escort you."

Well, that was a feeble effort at least. It seems as though there is some unseen opposing force trying to keep me from finding the answers to my question.

"Sir?" Elsan spoke up. "The servants and I could take Appolious to his home while my father goes with you to the bastion."

"Ah, come on Commander," the captain blurted out, "...this is some kind of zealot trick."

"Captain!" The Centurion snapped. "I will handle this situation. You just handle the men."

"Yes sir!" He returned quickly.

I looked at Elsan whose pleased expression showed. Did he understand what I was trying to do or did he speak unknowingly?

"Now!" The Centurion continued looking at the captain still irritated. "You take half the men and escort the young man and Appolious to his home and then report back to Tiberius."

"Yes sir!" He thumped his breastplate with a clenched fist and turned to pick his men.

"You will come with me to the fortress." He turned back to me.

"Good!" I nodded, pleased with the commander's decision. At least I would not be seen by the people of KfarNachum in the presence of these soldiers. Somehow things worked out right.

"Trust Timon, simple trust," I scolded myself for my lacking. Then I said to Elsan, "After you have seen to Appolious, find us accommodations for the night."

"Yes Father," he nodded.

The tall towers of the bastion rose above the crest of a hill and soon it's foreboding black walls cast long dark shadows across the rugged landscape as the sun sank slowly behind the western rise. On the top of the towers Roman soldiers stood their post and there was a guard on both sides of the open gate made of heavy logs. As we passed the guards came to attention and saluted the Centurion striking their breast-plates with the fist of their right hand. Inside the fortification there was a hum of activity. Some soldiers milled around while others walked with determined steps. Near the center of the assembly area some soldiers with their horses stood in a ridged straight line while an officer walked back and forth in front of them.

To the left was what appeared to be a series of barracks built in long square blocks and there soldiers, with seemingly nothing to do, loitered on the porches that ran the full length of the buildings.

To the right was another series of buildings with archways that connected their porches and directly in front of us was a large prominent building with huge pillars and steps ascending to a set of richly carved double doors. Two guards with sober expressions stood one on either side of the door.

Before this building we halted and I climbed from my cisium and was escorted inside. The heat from my sun baked garments cooled and I took a deep breath of its refreshing air. Around the room was a balcony where many doors could be seen in its deep shadows. Large round columns supported the hall and on them hung shields from other countries. Before us was an arcade with a raised platform and on it a seat like a throne. The Praetorium was dim lit with oil bowls that hung from under the balcony and two others that sat upon pedestals on either side of the seat. Beyond the throne seat were two doors, one on this side and one on that side with the depiction of Caesar engraved into it.

"Wait here," The Centurion commanded sternly and ascended to the platform going up one of the two steps on either side of the seat and entered the left door.

After what seemed to be a long wait the door opened again and two guards came out followed by the Centurion, an adjunct and the legate.

The legate took his seat and motioned to two guards who came and they escorted me to a position in front of the platform. His eyes seemed to penetrate with the efficiency of a knife as cold as a blade. His lean chiseled features were set as granite and I knew I was in trouble if Yah did not give me favor.

"Who are you?" The legate demanded with a quick wave of his hand. His face scowled with impatience. It was clear that this disturbance did not set well with him.

I struggled to calm my voice before answering. "My name is Timon-bar-Philorah of Beitorah on Mount Tabor."

"I understand you were caught with a wounded officer. What do you have to say for yourself?" He shifted restlessly in his seat.

"We found him wounded in the wilderness." I wanted to answer quickly so he could get back to whatsoever he was taken away from. I felt confident the Centurion would verify my story, but still I wrestled with a deep fear.

"I had met him in Yerushelayim. He seemed to be a good man, so when we found him I set about to bring him home. We were almost to KfarNachum when the patrol found us."

"Why should you care if a Roman lives or dies?" He snarled spitefully.

"I am a L'vite and care for all living." I assured him, but his words quaked inside of me. "I have many business interests in Rome." I opened my hand to him, but removed it quickly before he saw it was shaking.

"What did you say your name was?"

"Timon-bar-Philorah of Mount Tabor."

"I have heard that name before." He turned to his adjunct standing nearby. "Have I not heard this name before?"

The soldier stepped close to the legate and said something softly in his ear. He nodded and turned back to me.

After answering some more of the legate's questions to his satisfaction I suppose, I was released and went out where Benren and Semone were waiting with the cisium. By the time we left the gate of the garrison, the sun was behind the western hills and the hot wind was beginning to cool. Up ahead a Roebuck startled and dashed away with quick agile leaps and the piercing cry of a falcon cut the silence.

As we headed for KfarNachum my thought turned again to the disciples and it sent a surge of excitement though me. My search would soon be over.

Surely, the disciples would hold the answers to the many questions that vexed my soul night and day. Would YahShua be with them? Did He really rise from the dead as He said? Would I get to see this Man who has turned the world upside down. He could reveal the hidden purpose in His death and make known unto me the mystery of the resurrection. Perhaps, He would explain why I am driven to find the answers to these questions and what the words of the Prophet Micah meant that he spoke concerning me.

The heavy damp smell of musty water and fish hung like a cloud over the entire area, and as we rounded a hill there stretched out before us the dingy green of the Sea of Galil. Small wooden fishing boats lined the rocky shore as far as the eye could see. KfarNachum was alive with activity for this time of day the fishermen were shaking out their nets and preparing for the long night of fishing. Masses of men and young boys, up and down the beach, dressed only in loincloth went about their work just as their fathers had done and their fathers before them. They called out greetings with happy voices and made rude teasing remarks one to another.

Further up the beach the tiny lighted windows of the houses and buildings of KfarNachum cast a golden glow into the ever darkening night. The road turned north disappearing into the narrow streets of the town with it's dark box like structure highlighted by tiny yellow lighted squares. As we made our way through the cobblestone streets that opened into the market place, the merchants and shops were closing business for the night.

"Stop here Semone," I commanded and when he had done so, I climbed from my carriage, "I will inquire as to where is the house of Appolious."

A tax collector sat in his booth behind a table counting the day's receipts. If anyone would know where Appolious lived it would be him. He was a large man heavy with flesh. His round fingers struggled to pick up a coin to add to the ones he was stacking on the table in front of him.

"Sir," I interrupted. The task seemed to be taking a good deal of concentration for the man was unaware of my approach, and he was startled when I spoke to him. "I am looking for the house of the Centurion Appolious, do you know of it?"

"Well, you did not have to sneak up on me." The man blubbered drawing his brows together quickly.

"I am sorry, Sir. I did not mean to give you a fright. I am looking for the house of the Centurion, Appolious. Do you know of it?"

"What do you want with him?" His look went from that of irritation to curiosity.

"How much money have you collected this day?" I returned meeting his gaze.

His eyes widened and dropped to the stacks of coins on the table. Then he began to laugh, "I see your point." His round bulging belly giggled in rhythm. After he had regained himself he looked back up at me.

"What was the name again?"

"Appolious, a Centurion who lives in this town."

Appolious?" He repeated as he rolled up a scroll he had taken from the table. "Ah yes!" He exclaimed after a short time. "Appolious! He lives on the road to Dammeaek at the edge of town." He pointed down the street. "What do you an Israelite have to do with an gentile?" A smirk pruned his fat lips.

"Business." I turned to go. He probably enjoyed saying what had been thrown in his teeth on many occasions.

"Would you enter a gentile house?" He called after me.

"I have entered worse." I returned without looking back.

Tax collectors are hated as much and, maybe, even more than gentiles for they are known for collecting much more than is required by law. Something should be done about the freedom the Romans give the tax collectors. They are stealing the people blind.

A Roman style house surrounded by a sandstone fence sat just off the road at the edge of the village. This has to be the place of his abode. The garden gate was still open so we entered. It was a lovely garden with fig trees, a small pond with flowers around it and several benches for sitting. Beyond the garden against the back wall was the large house made of gray granite and black basalt blocks. One of my young men came from the arcade porch and caught the horses by the reins. I climbed from my carriage and he bowed slightly.

"Has Elsan found accommodations for us tonight?" I ask looking up and down the torch lit column porch.

"Yes my lord," the boy replied, "he has said, I should show you the way."

I opened my mouth to reply when one of the two elaborately carved, heavy wooden doors opened and a woman, silhouetted by the yellow glow that came from inside, stood in the doorway. I could not see her features, but she was slim with good conformation.

"Who is it?" She called timidly.

"Timon of Beitorah." I bowed slightly in her direction. "Shalom!"

294

The woman dropped to her knees quickly and bowed her face to the porch. "Would you do me the honor of entering my house?" The woman said meekly. "My husband wishes an audience with you before you go."

"With pleasure will I enter the house of a friend," I answered and went up the steps unto her on the porch and raised her up by the arm. "I am not a king that you should bow to me." I scolded lightly.

"You have brought my husband back from the grave," she offered. "It was for that I bowed before you."

Her dark hair was held in place by a Kaffiyeh fastened above each ear and a string of gold coins that decorated her forehead. She had smooth flowing features and was pleasant to the eyes. Her eyes to the ground with a bowed head she stepped back into the room to give me entrance.

I found myself in a hallway that ran to the right hand and, also, to the left. On both sides of this hall, pillars fixed into the walls arched across the ceiling at intervals.

In front of me was a large room entered through an archway with pillars on each side like the ones in the hall. The room is one step lower than the hall with two highly polished long dark wood tables surrounded by several lounges. The wood on the lounges matched the tables and was covered in wool cloth dyed a brilliant red. From my vantage point I could see some of the red and black tapestry hangings that covered the walls. The floor was polished slabs of black basalt that mirrored the furniture in its surface. Hanging from a tile inlaid ceiling by chains were several shiny brass oil bowls burning brightly, set into a silver maze.

"Come with me please," the woman bade and turned to go down the hall. I followed without a word.

It was a conformable bedchamber with cedar walls and across the room, opened columns revealed an alcove porch. Appolious lay upon a bed of the same dark wood as the furnishing in the reception room. His face was almost the color of the bleached night tunic he was wearing. The long trip had taken its toll on him, but his look was peaceful.

"Appolious?" His wife touched him tenderly. "Appolious, Timon is here."

His eyes opened and he squinted at me in the lamp light near the bed. "You should not have come under my roof, I being a Roman."

"It is a pleasure to enter the house of a friend."

A weak smile tugged at the corners of his mouth. "Thank you for coming my friend," The squint was replaced with a look of relief. "I was concerned for you when I learned they had taken you to Tiberius." He spoke with much effort. "The Legate is a hard man."

"Elohim was with me and gave me favor in his eyes." I touched his hand, "You rest now and I will come again before I leave KfarNachum." Appolious nodded and closed his eyes drawing a deep laborious breath that trembled as he released it.

"Thank you so much for your kindness to my husband." The woman choked and when I looked there were tears in her eyes.

"He is my friend," I returned again, bowed slightly and went to the door.

The women's love for her husband would sustain him now, and I went away with a song in my heart knowing Appolious was where he belonged and I, too, would soon be home with my beloved Sarepta.

That night when I prayed I thanked Yah for delivering me one more time from the Roman grasp by giving me favor with the Centurion and his legate. I prayed for Appolious' recovery and that I would soon find the disciples, whom I was sure would hold the answers to the many questions that remained. I was becoming weary with my search and filled with anxious longings.

DAY EIGHTEEN

Standing on the rampart with the morning breeze blowing cool through her long dark hair, she was lovely in her silken robe. The light fragrance of the sweet spice she wore filled the air around us and I was moved for her. I slipped my arms around Sarepta's waist from behind and pulled her against me. She was warm and comforting in my arms and still the loveliest woman I had ever seen. She turned slowly while I held her and slid her arms up around my neck. She pressed her soft moist lips to mine and I kissed them tenderly. My heart sang with delight...

"My lord?" Benren's voice suddenly intruded the splendor and then I was lying upon my bed looking into his face. I must have looked startled for he said in an apologetic tone. "It is I, Benren, my lord. The fishermen are beginning to come in with their catch and Elsan said you would want to know."

I blinked at him a degree, somewhat surprised to find myself here instead of on the roof of my mountain home. Then his words registered in my mind. "Yes! Yes! Bring my tunic."

I basked in the fading warmth of my dream and felt very lonely. However, soon I would be holding Sarepta again and then it will be no vision of the night. My search is almost over, for the disciples will hold the answers to my questions and possibly I will get to see YahShua, Himself. Excitement sprang alive within as I threw aside the night cloth and sat up.

Several boats set with their bows dug deep into the rocky bank against the blackish green water of the Sea of Galil. The aft of the boats bobbed up and down in the small choppy waves created by those crafts just landing. Others were still coming like tiny dark insects crawling across the black water. The air was still and hard to breathe, being heavy with the morning dew which formed large droplets of water on the cool rocks. The dim light that colored the sky in the east would soon bring the sun and with it, the wind's hot breath.

On one of the moored boats, a boy of about twelve was busy folding nets with the help of another younger than he. The deep hollow creaking of the boat, as it settled even deeper into the pebbled beach, could be heard over the excited cry of the sea birds waiting anxiously for the discards from the fisher's nets. The boys did not look up nor seem to notice Elsan and myself coming toward them.

"Boys!" I called up to them. "Where is the fisherman called Shimon?"

The older boy came to the side of the boat and looked down at us. "He has returned to BeitZaidah for there has been no catch this night." The boy reported casting his hand eastward.

I sighed, my enthusiasm plummeted as a rock slide down the banks of the Yarden on its rush to the Dead Sea at flood time. I was sure the disciples would be here. It is said YahShua called KfarNachum home and here He stayed with His disciples often.

"What of the ones called Yaakov and Yachanan?" Elsan inquired seemingly undisturbed by the news.

"They went with Shimon, only Zavda comes there." A fisherman now appeared beside the boy answered for him, pointing out at a boat cutting a wake on it's way to the shore.

We waved thanks and went down the shore to wait for the father of Yaakov and Yachanan to land. As the craft stabbed the bank a bearded man with wet graying hair, wrinkled sun hardened face tossed a heavy iron anchor off the bow and it stuck with a thud at our feet. His dark eyes scanned us with little emotion and apparently he thought we were merchants.

"No catch today!" He tossed up his hand irritably and turned to go his way.

"Are you Zavda?" I responded quickly.

Now, two other men joined him and I held my breath. Maybe, they were some of the disciples. All three stared down at us then looked at each other wonderingly.

"I might be," the man finally answered. "Depends on who wants to know."

As I opened my mouth to reply, my words became erased by the grinding sound of a boat's bow cutting the rocks as it slid onto the bank. When I looked, all I saw was the ship's hull sweeping to a sharp sloping point bearing down on me. I had to act quickly for the aggressive crescent was closing fast. I turned to flee up the rocky bank but my retreat was hampered as the pebbles under me slipped jamming my knee into the sharp tones. I did not have time to think about that however, for the scraping growl of the bow was loud in my ear. Scrambling to my feet, I ran up the slant where the outline of KfarNachum sat like a stone sentinel guarding the sea. When I had gone, what I felt like was a safe distance, I stopped and turned to look behind me. The gouging sound had stopped and the place where I had torn the rocks with my foot was precisely where the boat sat quietly heaving in it's own wake.

Then I was reminded of my leg by a throb that was becoming a low ache. I found myself unconsciously rubbing the pain with my hand.

Suddenly, Elsan was at my side. I had not even thought about him but he had managed, also, to reach safety.

"Who-oo!" He said almost under his breath. Then he turned to me, "Are you all right Father?"

Before I could answer Zavda yelled, "Yhudah, you crossed-eyes cod! Why not just take her on up to KfarNachum and anchor her right in the market place? Make it easier for that fat tax collector to find you."

"Hah! You crow-faced old sea gull! You are just jealous because I brought in a catch, and that makes me a better fisherman than you."

"I would not be bragging about three fish if I were you?" One of the two by Zavda returned.

"Better than nothing," another voice in the boat that had almost run us down called back, "…which is just what you caught."

Though the tones were harsh in all this shouting and insults I sensed no bitterness. Rival fishermen who have probably exchanged words of this nature for many years but still can have a touch of wine together afterwards.

Elsan stood with a delighted look and waited with expectation for Zavda return, but he just waved him away and turned back into the recesses of the boat.

"Wait!" I rushed at the boat. "I wish an audience with you."

The younger of the two men who had stood with Zavda placed a barefoot on the side of the boat leaned on his leg and said unto me. "What do you want?"

"It is a private matter," I insisted.

His eyes flowing over my garment and then he smiled broadly. "I will tell him." The young man quickly disappeared.

By this time there were only a few scattered places along the shore where a boat did not rest. The absence of piles of fish for the sorters told the same story as that of Zavda. Apparently, only a meager few fish had been caught which put the men in a bad mood. Sharp tones rose here and there over the low hum of voices. Up and down the shore men and boys went about their chores, although they had nothing to show for a nights labor.

A donkey drawn cart led by a dark-skinned Ethiopian servant boy coming from the village road and upon it sat the fleshly figure of the tax collector. He would find little to tax this day. Fishermen busy around their boats watched the approach with scornful eyes.

"Fat Elias is in for a big disappointment." One fisherman remarked between gritted teeth to another as the two men were passing by.

Zavda drew our attention back to the boat as he called down to us, "What is it you want?"

"A word in private with you concerning Yaakov and Yachanan." I yelled back over the constant hum of voices.

"Those two? What have I to do with them? They are of age. I am not responsible for what they do."

Far out upon the water someone shouted and another closer in came to the bow and called ahead as his boat began to turn. Now, one even closer hailed his fellows in front of him, but his words were still unclear. All eyes turned seaward and a sober hush ascended over the crowd as ears strained to here what was being said.

"The fish are running off BeitZaidah!" The voice was clear now. "Kefa, Kaakov and Yachanan have brought in a large catch! It is a miracle!"

By this time the ships still out were turning in the water, and those on shore caused no small stir as men clamored up into their boats to cast off.

Zavda cupped his hand around his mouth and shouted over the noise to the boat of his rival. "Who has no catch today, you ol' sea urchin. The last laugh is on you!" On the ship everyone was to busy preparing to sail and paid him no heed.

"Hey wait!" I shouted, but my call was drowned out.

"Cast off!" He barked with a toss of his hand. By then the anchor was being pulled up by one of the young men while the other who had jumped overboard began to push the boat free into the water.

"Wait!" I tried again waving frantically, but they still paid me no heed.

Soon Elsan, the tax collector and myself was left alone on the shore watching the boats fade out of sight. As they went so did my excitement. Disappointment and defeat took me in its grip. I have never been one to hide my feelings and I guess it showed on my face.

"Come Father," Elsan urged. "If we leave now we can reach BeitZaidah before mid-day."

301

The strength of his voice gave me courage and I turned with a sigh falling into step with him. I glanced at the tax collector when we passed and he was still looking after the boats but had a pleased smile. He is glad for the catch not for the people's sake but because he will surely have a full purse before days end.

Before leaving KfarNachum, while Elsan, Yhasper and the servants prepared for the journey, Benren and I went to call on Appolious. Elsan had said we should leave immediately but I saw no real need to hurry, for by the time we would arrive the fishermen would have already landed their boats, counted their fish, and gone to their homes. Once there I should have no trouble finding the house of Zavdai.

An Egyptian servant girl answered my knock on the door and bid me enter. I was shown into the reception room where another servant girl of Israelite descent from her looks effectuated the act of hospitality. Still another servant brought a refreshing cup of very fine wine while the first disappeared through a door hung with black silk lace.

Abigail breezed into the room, her silk robe trailing her quick steps and greeted us warmly.

"Timon, how nice of you to come," she bubbled forth with much energy, bowing slightly. "I trust you have been made to feel at home."

"Yes, your hospitality is quite pleasing," I acknowledged. "How is Appolious this day?"

"He is much stronger now and on his way to mending, thanks to you. Will you take meat with us?" She kept her eyes from looking directly into mine in the proper manner of a married woman.

"That is very kind, but I am preparing to leave for BeitZaidah. I only wanted to see Appolious before going."

"Surely, …come with me."

She carried herself gracefully and with pride, the quality I am sure that drew Appolious to her. A gold ram's horn fastened to her dark hair over each temple held her jewelry in place and around her neck was another piece liken unto the hair clasps. She smelled of sweet frankincense and brought Sarepta to mind. Suddenly, the loneliness I thought I had left at the inn this morning had returned.

Appolious' eyes opened as we entered the room and a pleased smile gathered on his lips. Abigail stopped at the door and Appolious watched my approach without a word.

"Ah, a smile," I cast forth, "...you are improving fast."

"I would not be improving at all if it were not for you. I owe you my life."

"You owe me nothing, my friend." I returned. "But, to the Elohim of Israel you owe everything."

"Yes, but I am not an Israelite. How could I repay your Elohim?"

"You Romans serve many Elohim. Is it so hard to serve the one true Elohim?"

He looked away out the archway porch. "From where I lie the view will henceforth be of a shrine to the Elohim of Israel."

"Elohim takes no delight in shrines, Appolious, but in a pure heart he delights."

There was silence for a space of time then he looked back at me. "What do you think of Abigail? Is she not beautiful?" His eyes flowed from me to her and I followed his gaze. She blushed slightly and turned away going into the outer room.

"I indeed see her worth my friend and a proper woman at that."

"Have you seen my sons?" He paused to draw strength. "They are quite full of mischief," he assured me.

"Sons usually are," I acknowledged warmly, thinking of my own. "You also have a fine home."

"The land is allotted me for service in the Royal Army." He drew a long breath. "This is where I shall retire. The house has only recently been completed."

We fell silent again and he studied me with interest, and it made me wonder what he was thinking. Finally, he broke the silence. "What will you do now?" His voice was weakening.

"The fishermen have made a large catch at BeitZaidah and the disciples are there, so I am leaving immediately. However, I could not go without seeing you one more time."

He looked as though he would say something, hesitated and simply said, "Shalom, my friend!" His breath was short and I wondered if that prevented him or if there was another reason for him not speaking his heart. I could see he was tiring so I thought it best to leave him. Maybe, there would be a time later for us to speak further.

BeitZaidah is the capitol of Bashan, the tetrarch of Philip, and like KfarNachum, enjoys a lucrative fishing industry. The palace of Philip sets quietly upon a rise overlooking the sea and surrounded on the east by a post with a legion of Roman soldiers. It was well into the last watch of the day when BeitZaidah came into view. From a distance it looked pretty much like all the towns in Israel. Flat topped square buildings, some higher, lorded over by the prominent structure of the palace.

Boats bobbed along the shore in the choppy water with nets stretched out over them drying in the hot sun. The market place faced the sea surrounded on the other three sides by stores and shops. A wide road wound it's way up the hill to the palace and on either side were merchant booths, venders with their goods displayed on wagons, carts and on tables. There was the constant sound of music coming from the various spots of entertainment here and there almost anywhere you would go.

I called for Semone to stop in front of an inn and said unto Benren, "See if there is room for us here while Elsan and I ask about where we can find one of the houses of the disciples."

"Yes my lord." He bowed slightly and scrambled from his seat on the cisium.

There was no lack of people to ask for men and women carrying burdens flowed up and down the street.

Merchants and craftsmen worked in open front shops and stores surrounded by their products. Venders called out the specials of the day from behind their carts that were parked along the walls.

"There," I said to Elsan pointing at a moneychangers sitting just inside the door of his business. "He will probably know everyone who lives here."

As we started across the street we were suddenly engulfed by a herd of sheep driven by a shepherd boy with a tall crocked staff. We were being pushed and shoved as the beasts scurried past our legs with low grumbling bleats. The going was almost impossible and while we pushed our way along I felt something warm and damp land on the top of my foot. I did not have to look to see what it was, the atrocious odor told the tale. I stopped, gritted my teeth and suppressed the desire to yell at the lad with the shepherd's crook.

I looked at Elsan with disgust and he quickly hid an amused grin. He looked away toward the moneychangers, raised upon his toes and settled again while swiping at the small lock of hair that persisted to dangle on his forehead. Then without a word he turned to pass on over to the other side. I came behind thinking it was a good thing he had held his tongue. I was on the verge of lashing out and he would have been the target of my distaste.

Once we reached the other side of the street Elsan turned to me. "I will go talk to the money changer while one of the servants see to your need." His eyes fell to my sandal-clad foot. "How much money do you think we shall need to change for our stay here?"

"A couple of shekels should suffice." I snapped at him with a frown. His mouth twisted to hide a grin. He nodded and I turned back for the carts.

Elsan learned that most fishermen live in the section of town near the sea behind the fish market. Fishermen are thought to be ruffians with a rather rowdy life style as unpredictable as the sea itself. They are loud, boisterous, crude men of the sea. However, this misbehavior is

305

tolerated because fishing commerce is so important to the area.

It was well into the evening hour when we arrived at the house of the man Shimon Kefa. He, his brother Andrew and cousins, Yaakov and Yachanan, sons of Zavda were known disciples of the preacher YahShua of Natzeret. The gate to the house was already shut for the night and the smell of lilac, sumac and honeysuckle drifted up from the garden just inside the lattice.

It took considerable knocking to arouse someone. A young girl not old enough to be espoused timidly peered out at us and then opened the gate. She stood properly veiled but her olive skin was slightly reddened. Behind her a shadowy figure faded into the dark shadows the olive trees cast.

"Shalom." Elsan and I bowed politely. "I am looking for Shimon, called Kefa. He does live here, does he not?"

"Yes," came the timid reply, "but, he is not here."

"Where might I find him? It is very important."

"Aha..." She hesitated looking behind her were the carved tone bench sat empty under the olive tree. She released a light sigh and turned back to me. "I am not sure of my father's whereabouts. Mother would know if you could come back on the morrow."

It seemed that the young damsel had been entertaining a guest who became very shy at our unexpected intrusion. Her sigh signaled the fact that we had unknowingly spoiled a special moment.

"I am sorry for this untimely interruption but it is of the utmost importance that we speak with him." I pressed her.

"Maybe, he can be found at that house." She pointed down the path to where a small fire flickered in the garden.

"Rachel, child, who are you talking with?" A crisp female voice came from the dark archway to the house.

The girl made a half turn and answered. "It is strangers seeking Father."

"Strangers?" The robed figure of a woman appeared like a spirit on the porch. Descending a step, her garments swaying from side to side as she came down the garden pathway to where we stood. "I am the wife of Shimon Kefa, how may I help you?" She was a woman of middle age. Her face showed the marks of hard work that in no way hid her lovely features.

"I am Timon of Beitorah and this is my son Elsan. We are seeking an audience with your husband on a matter of great importance."

"He has gone to BeitAnyah with Yaakov and Yachanan. You look as though you have traveled far. Come! Our home is always open to weary travelers."

"Who is it, Sarah?" Another woman appeared in the pathway. She was much older with sharp clear eyes that seemed to pierce into your very soul.

"They are seeking Shimon, mother." The one who had been talking to us replied.

"My son has gone away with the Adonai and..." The older woman began to explain.

"The Adonai!" I exclaimed and excited joy shot through me. I felt myself become light as light as the time I had been with the Prophet in the way. "Then He was here! He has raised! Where did they go? Oh please, tell me where I might find them." My words gushed out at her and took her back a step. She blinked at me a degree and then smiled warmly. My soul anxiously leaped and the wait seemed to me as though she did not hear my words. "Did you see Him? Did He speak with you?"

"Shimon said He was here this morning, and was going to BeitAnyah where he would see Him again." She injected quickly seizing the opportunity.

I had missed them again. The look of frustration must have shown on my face for now she reached forth her hand and placed it on my sleeve. "You must be tired, come take meat with us."

"I, ...I wanted so to find the disciples." I heard myself mutter. The disappointment was almost too much for me. "Just when I think I will find the answers..." My words trailed off as I realized I was babbling like a fool.

"It has been a trying day." I felt a strong hand on my shoulder. Elsan came to my rescue. "We have accommodations at the inn, but thank you for your invitation. We will, however, be leaving at first light and we do not wish to inconvenience you."

I felt so foolish, like I was the child and Elsan like a father was taking care of me. "Elsan is right." I groped for words. "Our party is much too large and..." I fell silent, my effort seemed ridiculously futile.

"Little Yaakov and BarTalmal are still here, maybe, they could help you." Kefa's wife offered.

"Are they disciples?" Elsan asked.

"Yes! Yes, they are disciples," I entered. "That would be an answer to my prayers."

"Rachel?" The woman turned to the young girl who stood looking steadfast into the ever-darkening shadow of the olive trees her eyes searching. "Show these men to the house of Alfeah."

"Yes Mother." She turned quickly to look at the woman. The mother turned in the direction the girl had been staring with a puzzled expression.

"Hurry now my child," Kefa's mother admonished. "Do not linger for it is quickly darkening."

The girl gave her mother a quick glance and brushed past us with lively steps.

With the thrill of Kefa's mother's words still flooding my heart I turned in step with the girl and Elsan came along beside me. I had hoped to speak with Kefa or at least Yaakov or Yachanan, but now I would settle with a few words from BarTalmal, ...or little Yaakov, as Kefa's wife called him.

The house was small and the gate was still open. The sound of excited voices could be heard inside. Oil bowls set atop posts lighted the tiny garden, and a group of men sat around a small fire while several women went about their chores nearby. After we entered the girl stopped.

"I must get back now," she said abruptly. Bowing slightly she turned back for the path.

Her manner reminded me of Neah back at the Inn in Shklem. I wondered how she was and if the soldiers had found her secret room but the thoughts of her were quickly pushed back for now I felt sure I would get the answers to some of my questions.

The men had not seen us enter being caught up in their conversation. I heard one say.

"Are you sure it was He, Toma?" A big built man with broad shoulders and a husky voice asked. His hair hung in short, choppy locks and he wore a rough beard.

"It was the Adonai." Toma affirmed with a nod of his head. "He took Kefa aside three times and talked with him. It seemed to upset Kefa somewhat."

Toma was clearly the youngest of the three with curly black hair and round face. His dark eyes had an inquiring look about them, but his smile was warm and friendly.

"What did he do?" The third man asked.

I did not have to guess who he was for he was small of stature and his short hair gave him an even smaller appearance.

"Nothing," Toma shrugged, "...you know Kefa, he just sat down and sulked with a frown on his face. I asked him what was wrong and he grunted something about going to BeitAnyah.

They fell silent now and I took the opportunity. "Shalom friends." I drew their attention. The three men looked at us and we bowed slightly. "I am Timon of Beitorah and this is my son, Elsan. I am looking for the disciples of YahShua of Natzeret." Since they had been talking freely about Him, I felt there was no need to hold back.

"Are you His followers?" One of them returned.

It is funny but until now I had never thought about it. Was I a follower? I believed Him to be the Messiah, and I had heard many fine things about His teachings, but was I a follower? Now that the question had been ask, I did not know how to answer it.

"I do not know enough about Him to answer your question."

The three men looked at each other a degree and then one said, "Come and sit by the fire."

The flicker of the fire was welcome relief from the damp, cooling night air and I warmed myself before sitting down. Elsan, however, took a seat beside the one called Toma.

"I am BarTalmal and this is little Yaakov and Toma." He pointed out with the smoldering end of a stick he used to stir the fire.

"I have so many questions?" I blurted out. "Is He the Messiah, the Son of Elohim?"

"Miryam, some wine for our guests," BarTalmal called to one of the women.

"Yes, He is the Son of Elohim." Toma said with assurance.

"He was reported to be Israel's deliverer, to bring back the kingdom and sit upon the throne of His father David." Elsan reasoned with a frown. "None of this has or seems to be happening and you can sit there and say with so much confidence that He was the promised Messiah?"

A confused look crossed Toma's face and he looked down picking up a slender stick leftover of the fire and began to break it into tiny pieces nervously.

BarTalmal came quickly to his rescue. "You speak of Him as though He were dead, but His is alive."

The woman named Miryam brought wine to us in pottery cups on a wooden tray. I took mine gratefully and let its smooth tasty mixture roll slowly down my throat.

Loud and boisterous laughter drifted in from the pathway outside the little garden fence.

"The fishermen are going down to their boats," Yaakov commented. "I am glad to hear their voices carrying a bit more cheerfulness this night." He turned to stare at the dark figures that flowed past the open gate.

"The fishing has been poor lately." BarTalmal remembered aloud.

"Maybe it will be better now after the miracle this morning," Yaakov suggested.

"I doubt it," Toma injected, following the other's gaze.

The other men laughed as though what he said had some hidden meaning and Toma frowned until BarTalmal gave him an affectionate scrub on the head and then he, also, laughed light heartily. The men offered us no explanation. I looked at Elsan who shrugged.

"We heard of it at KfarNachum. What happened?" Elsan asked puzzled.

"We had fished all night," Toma took up the story, "...and near daybreak we started for BeitAidah. As we neared the shore we saw a small fire built and a Man sitting by it. He told us to go back out and cast our nets on the other side. Kefa argued, but at last gave the order. The net was suddenly full of fish almost to the breaking point. The Man was revealed to be the Adonai and He had prepared breakfast for us. I do not know where the fish He had on the fire came from, but they were good. It was a miracle."

They all fell silent pondering it and then I could no longer restrain the question that made the seeming miracle of no importance to me.

"Why did YahShua die on the cross?" I asked.

I knew it was the will of Yah, but I did not understand the purpose. All I have are theories, only theories.

"As a sacrifice for sin." Little Yaakov offered without hesitation. "He came into the world to take away the sins of the world."

"What sins?" Elsan looked perplexed. "Israel, even now under the iron fist of the Romans have always fulfilled

311

the laws of Moshe, and as for the gentiles? He is not their Elohim, they neither worship nor prefer to worship Him."

"Elohim is the Elohim of all created things whether they acknowledge Him or not." BarTalmal reminded him. "The blood of bulls and goats only covered sin for a season, but YahShua can take them away." His voice stressed the word 'away'.

"Nakdimon told me, YahShua said unto him, 'You must be born again'. What did He mean?"

"The thoughts and intents of your heart must come to new understanding, being born, so to speak, of a new way of life." A strange mystic look came over Little Yaakov as his words came forth filling the air much the same way that lightening does when it crackles over your head.

"The way of the spirit of things instead of the actual acts." His voice raised with power. "The laws of Moshe are acts, rituals. Things you must do or not do, but the spirit of the law is what YahShua taught us. Love thy brother! To live it in your heart, not just do it with your hands or your mind. When you were born to your mother, you began to live in the world you were born. So it is with the spirit. You must be born again, into a new world of understanding the spirit of things and live in it, instead of the one you are now. YahShua came to birth us into a new world, a new spiritual life for the Kingdom of Yah is Spirit. The heart, my friends, is the true Temple, the spiritual one, not seen in the world of 'do' and 'do nots'. You see He did establish Israel again as a kingdom but not a visible one. It is a spiritual kingdom.

Something sparked inside me, like a light being lit in a dark room. He too had used the holy name Yah. Suddenly, I understood what had happened in the Temple the day YahShua died. I knew now why the spirit of the Most High had departed from over the Ark of the Covenant. That covenant was no longer valid. A new covenant had been established with YahShua just as the old one had been with Abraham. The presence of Yah was now presiding in our hearts over the new covenant.

My mind went back to the words YahShua spoke to Neah saying, "*Believe Me, an hour is coming when neither in this mountain, nor in Yerushelayim, shall you worship the Father. The hour is coming, and now is, when the true worshiper shall worship the Father in spirit and truth.*"

Excited joy brought me to my feet. I wanted to shout, to run up and down the streets shouting the news. Yah has not abandoned Israel, but has established a new covenant. One that could not be touched by the hands of man to defile it as the chief cohanim and elders had done the Great Temple in Yerushelayim.

Just as quickly as it came, it evaporated in the torrent of questions remaining to be answered. It was as though inside I knew I had just seen the tip of a wonderful thing and my soul though rejoicing, was so hungry for more that it wanted to plunge in even deeper and there was no time for rejoicing now.

"What was the purpose of the resurrection?" I sat down as abruptly as I had stood. Elsan stared at me in unbelief and the others looked at each other with wonderment. However, I had no time to indulge their questioning look. There was so much I wanted to know, to hear.

"We do not understand everything," BarTalmal said apologetically.

"But I must know," I demanded, pierced with disappointment.

"We must know, also. That is why we shall go to BeitAnyah, find the others and hear His words further." Toma offered meekly.

"Wait," Elsan stammered. "I do not understand about this born again." He opened his hands to them and looked frustrated.

"Yes! Yes!" I felt like I had just found a wonderful cup, but it was empty. "Tell us more."

"How do you get born again so you can begin to live in this New Kingdom?" Elsan looked at them one by one.

"Do you believe what I just said is from Yah?" Little Yaakov asked tenderly.

"Yes, it was powerful like the words of a prophet." Elsan acknowledged.

"Do you believe that YahShua Messiah is the Son of Elohim?" BarTalmal injected.

"I, …I do not know." Elsan twisted his expression. "When you do know, you will have your answer." Little Yaakov smiled at him. "For whosoever believes in Him shall be saved out of this world and born again into the world where He dwells."

There was another silence and then we talked for many hours about the things YahShua had taught that they at the time did not understand the full meaning of and was now being revealed.

I related to them the happenings in Yerushelayim, the presence of Elohim leaving the Temple, renting the veil, as told by Yosef of Arimathea. I spoke about the deceit of Kayafa and the plan to remove Yosef from the seat of Elders. The news BarAbbas brought concerning the followers being condemned in Yerushelayim, whom at this very degree may be paying the supreme price for their faith in the man YahShua. I shared with them how I saw the departing of Yah from the Temple as Yah's seal of approval to the new covenant. It was all too wonderful, my mind reeled under the amazement of it all.

Many questions rose in which we had no answers but we rejoiced as we speculated about the purpose of the resurrection while my heart sang a strange melody of an unknown origin.

The night would be one that would stay with me forever, and I knew that Elsan was very near making the decision that all men everywhere must make eventually. The new covenant was not just with Israel, but with all living things. I am told He said, 'I have come, …to save the

314

world.' This then was the higher purpose of Yah that did not meet the eye and why the prophet wrote; "*Yet it was the will of Elohim to bruise Him, making Him an offering for sin.*"

DAY NINETEEN

BeitAnyah was a little over two days travel by cisium from BeitZaidah. The heavy morning fog drifted in from the Sea of Galil rolled silently along the empty streets of the still sleeping town. When the light of day began to penetrate the moist firmament it afford us little help seeing our way. However, this did not seem to hinder the static excitement as the servants went about their work talking happily. They seemed anxious to be on the move again. The spirit of adventure filled them with expectation.

I was finding my search quite frustrating until the talk with the disciples by the little fire in the small quaint garden. The joy that night had sparked in me seemed to grow into a fire through the restless night as I awakened often to relive it over again. I tried to push the thoughts aside knowing the days of travel that were set before me but found the marvel of it all too wonderful.

Even now, as the wheels of the cisium grind the tiny loose pebbles like sand on the cobblestone street, that joy exploded into almost uncontainable excitement. In BeitAnyah I would not only find the disciples but the Adonai YahShua Himself.

Too overwhelmed by it all to settle down in the prophecies, my fingers sought in the small compartment the rough textured blue robe with the stains, His blood, still on the back. It was not of the finest quality and it was far from new but it was the most priceless, precious thing I had or would ever own. I lifted it tenderly and sniffed. Its faint common odor seemed as sweet frankincense and spikenard to me. It was as though my trembling hands were actually touching Him. I folded my arms around it and drew it to my breast embracing it, embracing Him.

When I finally took the robe away, my eyes fell upon a large dark ring of moisture. Then I swiped away the cool stream from my cheek with shaking fingers. There are no words to describe what an impact that feeling had on me

317

but the world around me seemed to dance and sway to the music of my heart. The way it would after consuming much fermented drink.

"Father?" Elsan's voice penetrated the wondrous aura.

He was sitting on his large gray horse studying my face with a deep wrinkle of concern between his soft blue eyes. I blinked at him and found his innocent intrusion irritating and a sense of great loss flooded me. "Father, are you all right?" His voice was so compassionate and soft. "You look somewhat, …unusual."

"I am fine!" He flinched as my words bit at him. "What is it?" I adjusted my tone.

It must have been sometime that we had traveled for now he straitened uneasily in the saddle and said unto me, "There is a small stand of trees." He pointed off in the distance up ahead of us. "It would be a good place to rest the horses and take refreshments."

"Yes," I nodded, feeling quite ashamed now. "See to it immediately."

His expression changed very little as he dug his heals into the horse's side and it lunged into a gallop back out into the lead. When we settle for our rest I will make recompense for my tongue. Yet, I could not help wishing he had just taken the initiative without disturbing me. I must tell him any decision of that nature from now on will be his.

My hands still made the blue robe tremble slightly as I placed it back in its little niche for safekeeping. It is strange how this Man has so moved me, so changed my life. Maybe, I had found the kingdom that Yaakov and BarTalmal were talking about. The new birth YahShua told Nakdimon about.

I only knew the sun was shining brighter than I had ever seen it. The air seemed sweeter and the beauty of the land around me was overpowering. This surely seemed like rebirth to me and it is pure heaven. I found peace in that knowledge and drew in a breath of hot dusty air sighing deeply.

What wonders would the rest of my journey bring? If His death on the cross was to bring this marvelous kingdom, what would His resurrection bring? If it were any more glorious than this, I would not be able to contain it.

Soon, the traveling chairs were set under the low branches of some juniper trees and we were sipping a cool cup of wine. The shade took some fierceness from the hot wind that blew in gusts down the side of the mountains into the valley.

My eye caught a glimpse of a small fox as it scurried from its burrow near a shrub. The horses had routed it out grazing on the green spring grass. Ears folded back flat against its head, with long low strides it shot out across the rocky terrain leaving the horses to snort nervously after it. I thought how beautiful, the sun reflecting from it's slick summer fur. Everything all around me seemed so vibrant and alive.

Elsan moved slightly in his chair and drew my attention. He was so handsome and fair like his mother, not as dark skinned as Yered and myself. His cool blue eyes had a hint of sadness in them. My doing, I supposed.

"Elsan?" I leaned forward and touched his sleeve. "I am sorry for the sharp manner in which I answered you back on the road. I... I did not know how to explain what was happening to me. How does one describe feelings, especially this one? It would make no sense to him. "I have been so caught up in this matter lately and it causes me to react sometimes peculiar. You have done nothing wrong. Please forgive me." It was a pitiful effort but I hoped Elsan would understand.

He looked at me with a tilt of his head for a degree of time and the sadness abated into a smile. "I knew from your look that I disturbed you at the wrong time but the deed was done and there was no calling my words back. Were you praying, Father?"

"No son, I was feeling, ...feeling the closeness of the Man whose robe I held. It was almost as though it was He that I was holding."

"But, you do not even know Him," Elsan reasoned. "You have not seen Him."

"I do not have to know Him, Elsan. I feel Him. I feel Him in the robe, in the words of His disciples, and in the writings of the prophets of old. To feel someone is greater than to know them, deeper and more meaningful."

"I can see that you love this Man."

"Yes," I nodded, "I do love Him."

"It is in your eyes and on your face." His eyes filled with moisture and he swallowed hard. "Is He the Son of Elohim?"

"A wise man said one time, 'We each must make that decision in our own hearts'. It is not enough that I say He is, you must know it for yourself."

Elsan made no reply and looked away across the valley to the grayish-blue mountains against the western sky where peaks rose above a circle of white billowing clouds.

No, I had not seen Him but hope blazed in my heart. He was in BeitAnyah. There I will find Him with His disciples, hear His words and see His face. I will hear Him explain the purpose of Yah for the resurrection and know the Glory of that, as I now know the Glory of His death. Strange how something so morbid could be so beautiful. The Glory of the Elohim of Israel went to reign over a new covenant at the hands of His Holy Son. But, what of the Temple? The altar? The sacrifices? They are empty now and vein now, the blood of YahShua doing away with them. ...Yet, the chief cohanim and elders refuse to recognize it. If they did, they would no longer be needed, of no worth, as empty and vain as their worship and praise. No wonder they fight so hard to keep the people from hearing and knowing the truth.

Then the prophecy of YahShua as He entered Yerushelayim came to mind. This will be the reward for

320

their selfishness, death and destruction, such a waste, such an incredible waste. No wonder Yosef sat in the ash heap. Did he recognize this? Did Yah show him the truth? No, I think not. He might have seen the destruction because of the unbelief of the chief cohanim and elders but he surely did not see Yah's purpose in it all or he would have seen the Glory and not grieved himself to death. No, he saw only hopelessness, just as I did in the beginning, ...what a pity.

"Father?" Elsan broke the silence of our contemplating. "If He is the Son of Elohim, why does everyone, except a few, hate Him?"

"Change is a hard thing, Elsan. It means uprooting, tearing out everything you are taught, everything you believe in and most people are not willing to do that, especially if it is a good thing they have or if it means loss to them."

"Like the chief cohanim and elders do not want to give up the sacrifices and the cohanim service even after the presence of Elohim had departed the Temple."

"That is exactly what I mean. They are so intent on holding on to what they have that they do not look at the greater thing waiting for them."

"That was what you were trying to make us see with the parable of the young man." He nodded and dropped silent again not really expecting an answer so I gave none. He sat staring into his cup.

"More wine, my lord?" Yhasper asked him softly.

"No! We should be moving on, should we not, Father?' He looked at me.

"Yes. You are quite right." I arose, handed Yhasper my cup and caught Elsan's arm as he stood. "You shall make the decision in these matters. If I think otherwise, I will tell you."

"All right Father," he replied, then turning to Yhasper. "Tell Benren we shall leave when all is ready."

It was not long until we could see KfarNachum below with its cord of fishing vessels strung along the seashore like bangles around the neck of a woman. Beyond it, rising into the western sky, the ragged pinnacle mountains of Galil. Never had they looked so peacefully beautiful.

Had the whole world changed while I restlessly slept or was the change in myself? There was the town just as it always had been. The mountains were in their place and the fishing boats still sat awaiting the order to cast off. Yet, they seemed different, unusually serene and magnificent. The change had to be in me. The truth of Yah's purpose for His son had somehow changed me. Yes, truth brings change. What change will the truth of the resurrection bring?

Lately, I had found my thoughts were constantly interrupted with visions of Sarepta, Athera and Miryam. I was sure Yered was having no trouble handling the business, especially with Themarah's expert help. The thoughts of them tugged at my heart. It would be best to satisfy my need to see the ones I loved and then I could go on with peace of mind. Yes, that is what I will do.

Elsan left his position at the head of the column and came to the side of my cisium.

"Father? Will we stop in KfarNachum?"

"Have we supplies enough to last until we reach Mount Tabor?"

"Mount Tabor! Are we going home?" Elsan's voice sounded with disappointment.

"It is on our way, and I wish to see Sarepta and know how Athera fairs. Perhaps, the child is born."

I caught a flash in Elsan's eye that disturbed me. He did not want to go home that was plain, but what was the other thing? Before I could ask about it, he had turned his horse and without another word took his position again in front of the troop. He had not answered my question about the supplies. What had disturbed him about the idea of returning home? I felt a frown form on my face but even this was not enough to take away the joy bubbling deep within and it quickly faded. I will talk with him about it

322

when we stop to rest the horses. If there is not enough supplies he will surely stop in KfarNachum or Magdaia.

As we traveled on, I closed my eyes trying to visualize what YahShua might look like. He could have chestnut hair, long as is the way of a Natzereite, hazel or soft brown eyes. I may have to guess what He looks like and wonder at his appearance, but there is one thing I know for certain, He would have a sweet, peaceful face with a smile that makes you feel warm inside. He would have a sure steadfast manner and gentle hands, the kind needed to feel the grain in the finest wood, and put that to use in His creations. His voice would not be harsh, but carry good so there would be no misunderstanding His words.

"My lord," Benren brought me from my wondering. "One of the horses seems to be limping."

"Hold up," I instructed, "and see to it."

I was aware from looking around that we were well past KfarNachum. Had I been that long in my thoughts of Him? We were almost back to the place where the thieves had stopped us.

Benren raised his voice and called a halt to the procession. Elsan rode back to find Benren examining the left forefoot on one of the horses drawing my cisium. Elsan stepped down and went to inspect the damage to the animal.

I had not realized how hot the wind was, or how dry my mouth was, until Yhasper came to the side of the carriage and held a cup of cool water up to me.

"Drink, my lord?"

I took the drink and wished it were colder. The sun penetrated even the canopy with its heat and my garments felt miserable, sticking to me. There did not seem to be enough air to breath, but taking in more did not really seem to help.

Elsan came nigh now and reported that the horse had chipped his dry hoof into the quick on a rock and would have to be replaced. He had apparently dealt with the thought of returning home. Perhaps, he felt that once there I would not want to continue my search and he would miss the adventure that every young man craves in his heart or he was just jealous that Yered had gone to Yerushelayim and he might not get. Whatever the cause he seems to have settled it within himself.

Our progress now would be slower making it impossible to reach home before dark, not to mention further damage to the horse. However, the desire to get home and the knowledge that the horse could recover faster once we were there made the decision an easy one.

"We will rest the horses for a while here," I determined, "...then go as far as we can before dark."

Elsan seemed moody that night at camp, but refused to speak about what was troubling him. I thought several times about asking him, but he was becoming a man now and it would not be tasteful for me to demand to know his thoughts. Since he did not find much to talk about as we sipped our evening wine I decided the look earlier was that of disappointment and the reluctance to talk was due to a hectic day of travel.

I was not in a talkative mood either for my thoughts kept returning to the little meeting around the fire in the garden. They had expounded many things that YahShua had taught them, such things as it was more beneficial to give than to receive and giving must be from the heart without any thought of recompense.

There was one thing that constantly haunted me about the things they told us He spoke. He had said, it was hard for a rich man to enter the Kingdom of Heaven. I was not rich in any sense of the word, but I had much land holdings and was by no means poor. They had gone on to tell us about a rich young ruler who came to Him and wanted to know how to enter the Kingdom and the answer had been to go sale everything he owned and follow Him. The ruler was young, meaning he had not taken a wife. I on the other hand had not only a wife but also a concubine and three, maybe four children. I could not possibly do what he told the young ruler. I had the care of servants, family and responsibilities. Yet, the story hung in the air like a looming spirit. Was that what I was expected to do?

DAY TWENTY

It was about the fourth hour of the next day, my face reddened by the hot wind that blew in gusts. I sat in my cisium and surveyed my domain with a grateful heart soaring in praise to the Almighty for His bountiful blessings.

We came to the floral covered valley with lively bouquets of blooms raising their heads in silent praise to the Creator. A patch of blue onycha were here and there, patches of golden yellow saffron, several shades of lilies, red and varied pinks, surrounded by the many hues of leafage from light to almost black green.

The familiar churning gurgle of a stream blended harmoniously with the varied pitch of the winged creature's songs. This was home, as refreshing to my mind as the cool drink of the mountain stream, was to my body. The horses blew contented sighs as they drank their fill in the narrow rock strewn creek.

I stood staring into the deep brown face that reflected back at me in the clear mirror like water. Did I know this man, so familiar, yet strangely unfamiliar? I brushed away a role of perspiration on my forehead and the stranger did the same. Had I changed that much in looks? Had the man who looked back at me for forty-seven years fled as the presence of the God of Israel had done from over the Ark of the Covenant.

A voice was calling far off in the distance. I raised my head, squinted in the bright morning sun and watched a rider like a small speck growing larger and larger. The horse's sleek body stretched out under him. Like a blur he came, his arm waving high over his head. As I watched, soon his features began to form into the likeness of Yered.

Elsan, by my side, lowered the hand he used to shade the glare. "Yered!" He let out a heavy sigh, trying unsuccessfully to hide a frown that seemed to shadow this beautiful reunion. When I looked his strong jaw was set and the muscles tightened as Yered's welcoming call reached us.

"Father, you are home!" He trumpeted with unrestrained delight.

In its long stride the horse hit the stream with such force that a shower of water sprayed into the air higher than his head. This sent the other animals that stood calmly drinking into a startled uproar and they yanked the two servant boys with force. With hard jerk on the reins Yered set the horse's back hooves deep into the mud bank beside us. Before it could regain its poise he had both feet on the ground.

His momentum carried him up to us and his arms went around me with a broad pleasing grin and I felt the strength of his youthful muscles.

"I am glad you are back," he exclaimed.

Then turning to his brother, he gave him the same warm welcome. The hug was accepted with tolerated calm but Yah did not seem to notice. Now Elsan began to upbraid him.

"That was real smart, Yered."

He tried to make his voice sound light but its true nature was easily detected. Yered dropped his bear like hug and frowned at him. Yered did not blink or drop his cold look.

"You could have run over someone riding up on us like that, scaring the horses near to death. Beside," He swung his hand toward Yered's horse that was still tramping about. "That is no way to treat one of Father's best mounts."

Yered's eyebrows narrowed and a deep puzzled look frowned on his face while Elsan's words bit at him. For a degree the two boys stood face to face. Then Yered's face brightened into a pleasant grin.

"Ah," he laughed, "it hurt nothing. Have you taken to fretting about everything?"

These two have had their differences at times but there was never any bitterness in their tone or twinges of real hostility. Something had happened between them, probably before Elsan came to join me.

"What is this?" I demanded. "Why have you malice against your brother, Elsan?"

Elsan looked away quickly and Yered answered and said, "There is not malice, Father."

I shot Yered a look and pressed Elsan. "What is it Elsan?"

"Nothing Father."

He turned back to me but did not look into my eyes. I would have pursued it further but this was not the time or the place. One does not air family grievances before the servants, but when we reach the privacy of home I will harvest this crop.

"Oh Father," Yered injected cutting Elsan a sideways glance. "He was just upset because of the water and the horse."

I saw Elsan out of the corner of my eye gave him a sharp look, but he added not to his words.

"Get to the horses then," I ordered, "...and let us be going. I am anxious to get home."

On a large plateau over looking us, as we made our way through the colorfully blooming valley, sat a house made of stone cut from the rugged side of Mount Tabor. Like a proud king upon a throne surveying his kingdom, it's majesty and splendor signaled it's right to ownership. The beauty of it made me catch my breath. Why had I not seen it's splendid grandeur like this before? I had looked upon it often but had never realized how awe inspiring it was.

My thoughts now turned to Sarepta. Would it be possible, ...could it be that at this very time she is watching my return from her place on the rampart? Can she feel the closeness of me as I now feel her? Does Athera's heart race with expectation, but she knows not why? Her face is vivid before me. Has Miryam laid her harp aside and sat with strained ears to hear my coming but understanding not her actions?

The distance between us is only two furlongs but to me it seems endless. The horses seemed sluggish not moving fast enough, while their faces came forth from the recesses of my memory and I examined each one as consolation.

What took only a few degrees of time seemed to take hours but, finally, the elegantly carved stone walls and column porch to the house lay before me. As the horses came to a stop in front of the porch, Jobad opened the door with a wide grin and clamored down the steps to wait impatiently for me to climb down.

"Welcome home, my lord," he burst forth with enthusiasm.

Jobad was a house servant and had seen to the running of the house for as many years as I could remember. He was an old man that years seemed to have forgotten. Clear sharp eyes to see and hands quick to set things in order. He bowed slightly and flitted around me as I made my way up the steps like an excited butterfly.

Coming on a run from the dim recesses of the room, Miryam was the first to greet me. Her dark hair flowed behind her as she moved lightly across the polished floor.

"Father!" She squealed in a high pitched tone and flew into my open arms. Her large hazel eyes sparkling with obvious delight. It was wonderful to hold her close and smell the soft scent of her hair as I kissed her temple.

"Here," I pulled her away, "...let me have a look at you." I held her at arm's length and savored her olive oval face with her mother's nose and a devastating smile. She was strikingly beautiful as a baby but as a young girl she was already beginning to turn the heads of prospective males. I sighed with a twinge of sadness knowing I would soon lose her to another man.

"You have grown more beautiful while I was away."

She blushed slightly and just smiled in a queer way that made me wonder what she was thinking.

"I am so glad your home," she began eagerly, "maybe, now Yered will treat me with a little more respect."

"Yered has been disrespectful?" I frowned at her words.

"Yes, he still treats me like a little child," she whined with a childish pout.

"Well..." I hid a laugh as best I could, "...I will have a talk with him about that."

She poised her head in a proud little tilt and seemed to be satisfied with my words.

While she simmered in her revenge my eyes had become adjusted to the dim interior of the receiving room and I surveyed the familiar surroundings. The walls were decorated with gold and blue tapestry wall hangings. Near the entrance wall a long receiving table prepared with two foot bowls and spices for the water for guests. In the middle of the room sat two fragrant cedar tables with matching lounges covered in a deep blue fabric and hanging from the ceiling a configuration of several silver bowls full of oil burned with the welcoming softness of home.

High arched doorways on either side of the long wide room led into the deeper recesses of the house. Directly across the spacious room was the multi-column, covered terrace. Beyond the expanse of the terrace is the well-groomed family garden. A winding path making its way through fruit trees, patches of colorful flowers and an open cistern where water springs forth in a pool. Benches scattered here and there at comfortable locations to offer a place to contemplate the day or spend a lazy Sabbath.

The soft subtle sound of rustling silk and quick steps on the gold variegated blue floor covering caught my attention. My heart leaped and filled with wondrous warmth as my eyes fell upon my beloved Sarepta. Rushing to greet me her steps was more like a run than a walk and she gave a little skip wanting to let it out but remembering her dignity she withheld herself.

Across her forehead she wore a string of coins, two gold ones flanked on each side by three silver ones, and fastened to her shiny brown hair by golden fig blossoms just above her ears. Her light green silk robe hung loosely around her and made the blue of her eyes more striking than usual. Her round beautiful face seemed aglow with obvious pleasure illuminated by the wide smile that had stolen my heart those many years ago.

I sniffed deeply of her sweet fragrance as my arms drew her against my breast. "Sarepta, My love!" I breathed softly into her ear. Her clinging to me for a long degree spoke to my heart of her longing. I held her and time seemed to fade into eternity.

Reluctantly she pulled herself away slightly and looked up into my eyes. We made love to each other with such a deep swell of feelings that words could not measure it.

"I have missed you my husband." Her words were soft and sweet to my ears. "Are you well?"

"Yes my love! H…" I had almost given Elsan away by asking her about her infirmity, but instead I said, "Have you been well?"

"Of course!" She dismissed my question as she would a servant.

I smiled to myself sensing she knew she had hidden nothing from me. She turned abruptly, clapped her hands and a servant girl appeared at the door on the left side of the room. She bowed to her mistress and stood awaiting her instructions.

"My husband has returned." Her words filled with pride. "We will take meat on the terrace. Prepare something special."

The girl nodded understanding that something special meant my favorite delicacies. She bowed slightly, turned and disappeared again.

"Sarepta, how is Athera?" I took Miryam in one arm and Sarepta in the other guiding them on into the room.

"Athera is in travail. I was with her when the servant said you had arrived."

"Then I am in time," I stopped. "I will refresh myself and go to her."

"And I will go practice a song for you, Father." Miryam determined and started away.

"No Miryam!" Her mother caught her up short. "You will come with me and help attend Athera."

"But there are servants to..." Her voice trailed off as she caught my sharp look. Letting out a heavy sigh, she turned toward the door.

Falling in step Sarepta slipped her arm around her daughter and said, "I think it is time for you to attend a birthing."

In my spacious bedchamber, Benren attended me and I was beginning to feel refreshed. At home the frustrations of my journey began to melt slowly away and peace settled in to make union with the deep seeded joy still lurking in the inner court of my heart. I could hardly wait to tell it, but first there was Athera.

The cool yellow silk bed drape blew softly in the wind that came from the arched terrace walk-way and lying beneath it's canopy was the small frame of my little Greek damsel. Beside the bed sat the birthing chair already prepared for use. When her eyes fell upon me, the twisted look on her face was immediately replaced by a bright smile.

"You came for the birth of the child," she sounded pleased.

I bent low over her and brushed her cheek with a kiss. "Yah knew I wanted to be here," I replied tenderly. "Do you have much time?"

She shook her head and winced, reaching wildly for my hand. I helped her to find it and felt the pressure of her pain. I had to look away from the anguish of her face as tears rolled down into her hairline from eyes squinted tightly shut.

The mid-wife chambermaid tugged at my sleeve. "The child is coming." She said in a hasty voice.

I knew that it was expected of me to leave the room, but my heart wanted to stay. Sarepta gently took my arm and turned me toward the door. I went out with a backward glance and waited for the sound of new life. I knew there were three attendants and the experienced hands of Andora, but I could feel that old familiar fear creeping in. What if there was no sound, as with Sarepta's first? What if something went wrong?

I took a deep breath and longed to bow myself toward the Great Temple and pray for the child. But, of course, there was no point in it, for Yah was not there. Where was He, …in Heaven? Where was this Heaven?

I leaned on the baluster, lifted my eyes to Heaven and prayed for the child to come forth strong and well. Like I told Yered and those in the house of Elisheva, Yah will hear the prayer of a sincere heart, no matter where He is.

Suddenly, I sensed a presence near me and turned to see Yered standing silently beside me. His eyes were closed and his lips moved ever so slightly. Was he praying also? I raised my hand to lay it on his arm when a baby squalled unhappily from within the bedchamber. My hand still poised in mid-air I felt a sense of relief rushed through me. I looked at the door and let out the breath I had been secretly holding deep within and then looked back at Yered who turned to grin at me.

"Looks as though I arrived at the right time." Elsan's voice reached us from the hall as he came into view.

Then from further down the hallway a rumble of excited voices where the household servants stood waiting. It was not a long degree but seemed to be before Sarepta emerged from the room. One look at her face told the story. Her eyes were ablaze with excitement and she smiled widely at us.

332

"My husband," She drew near and placed a soft dainty hand on my arm. "...It is a beautiful daughter."

"Is she all right?" Yered asked my question before I could utter the words.

"She is fine and Athera is well also, an easy birth." Her eyes sympathized with the fading fear she must have seen in mine.

"Alleluia!" Elsan trumpeted.

"We shall see the child, then celebrate the birth." I ordained.

Sarepta nodded approval and turned in the direction of the servants, walking briskly down the hall.

When I turned my attention back to Yered and Elsan who was standing near there was a peculiar quirk to their smiles. I looked from one to the other and frowned questioningly. Both bore the same look as though they shared an unspoken word and had agreed.

"What is this look on your faces?" I demanded calmly.

"Oh Father, another girl." Yered breathed almost at a whisper and a slight groan escaped Elsan's lips at the mere mention.

"All right you two, she is your sister."

I knew their words were only meant as a tease, for I had spoiled Miryam on every hand and had told them that girls were born to be spoiled, while boys were born to responsibility and inheritance.

I guess, I not only lived up to my words but over did it somewhat for the females in this household definitely are spoiled. Come to think of it, it is not all my doing. They also contributed to their condition.

"Now, now!" I mused. "It is not all as bad as that." Andora opened the door to the bedchamber and all eyes turned expectantly. She beckoned to us and we drew near.

"You may come and see the child now," she said quietly.

Inside the room, the silk draperies around the bed were fully drawn but the distorted small figure of Athera

333

was lying there still and silent. A soft squeaky sound came from the small bundle of swaddling cloth Miryam was cradling in her arms. She turned with a radiant aura smiling down as a tiny hand waved uncertain in the air.

"She is so beautiful, Father," Miryam crooned in a soft tone and came to us with her precious cargo.

I gently pulled the cloth back and peered down at the small rosy infant that squirmed with a terrible face at life's awakening. I thought that at that moment I could actually feel my heart enlarging just enough to fit this small part of life in it and pride soared like an eagle in upward flight. There was no distinguishing features or recognizable likeness, but I knew that would quickly change. I caught my breath in pleasure and felt a smile warm me.

"Come on, Father, stop gloating and let us see our sister." Yered complained softly at my elbow.

"My lord?" A weakened voice from behind the yellow silk called softly and I left the child to her brothers and went to the bedside. Gently pushing back the curtain I sat down easy on the edge of the bed. Athera looked so tiny in the width of the bed and her hand so frail as I held it in mine.

"How are you, my sweet." I bent and kissed her gently.

She smiled up at me, her eyes following my face as I raised from the kiss. "I am all right. Is she not beautiful?"

"As beautiful as her mother," I traced the line of her forehead and my fingers played aimlessly with one black curl, "...but, you must rest now. I will come and see you later."

She nodded and I kissed her eyes closed, stood and pushed through the silk. The room was empty now. They had left me alone with Athera. I, therefore, went out into the hall where the two boys stood glaring at each other.

"What is this?" I asked approaching. "We have just had a new birth and it is a time for celebrating and here you stand defying each other. What is the matter with you two?"

334

"Nothing!" Elsan growled, turned and walked away.

Now, I looked at Yered. He raised his eyebrows and drew a deep breath.

"Well?" I demanded.

"I only said that Anna would produce beautiful children also and Elsan became angry with me and told me to stop talking about Anna and remember Nebra."

I opened my mouth to speak, when Sarepta came down the hall. "What is wrong with Elsan? He brushed past me just now without a word and he seemed very upset."

"Some disagreement with Yered." I returned and Yered took the opportunity to turn away and go.

"Nothing serious I hope?" She looked after him with a frown.

"You know the boys. They are always into it for some reason."

I saw no need to worry her with the unusual hostility that seemed to be in their arguments lately. I knew they would handle it in due time.

"Here, now," I scolded teasingly. "What is this?" I ran a finger across her scowl. "You know you are not supposed to do that, ...ruins your beauty." The frown was forced away as she smiled up at me and I drew her into my arms holding her tightly.

At the evening meal on the terrace, there seemed to be an uneasy truce between the boys. I told of my journey, the happenings in Yerushelayim and about our exciting meeting with the disciples. How the presence of the Adonai left the Temple, to preside now over a new covenant somewhere in the Kingdom of Yah and how one must be born again to understand its significance. Miryam sang a beautiful song accompanied by her new harp and we discussed at length the business of horse husbandry and what possible higher purpose Yah had in the resurrection of YahShua, the Messiah.

DAY TWENTY EIGHT

On the eighth day, which happened to fall on the Sabbath, as is required by our law the child was brought into the synagogue to be named, circumcised if it is a boy. I handed the tiny bundle to the Rabbi who declared in the hearing of the elders that her name should be Hanna. It is said that if a child's day of dedication fall on a Sabbath that the child is special in the sight of the Adonai. Abidad administered the rite and I stood there wondering if even this was any longer acceptable with Yah. I knew the Temple worship was empty and vain, but surely Yah was still accepting children. I had known the Cohen for many years, he was a good man and incorruptible in his service.

"Yah!" I cried out within. "Accept my child into the family of Yah." Family of Yah? Yes, that is where she belongs. In the bloodline of Yah, born again. Could one so small be born again? She was innocent of sin and needed not a sacrifice. What would this new covenant mean to a child? I groaned silently, more questions with no answers. Then there was once again the strong pull to understand, to seek the answers. I would soon have to be off to search again for the answers as the tormenting questions came rushing back over me like the torrents of Yarden. Why did YahShua do miracles? Why was the fact that He was the Messiah, the Son of Yah being shrouded in such mystery? What was the purpose of the resurrection and what will it mean to us? Will Yah still somehow deliver Israel?

What about the prophecy of YahShua? Why was the fact that He was the Messiah, the Son of Yah being shrouded in such mystery? Will Yah still somehow deliver Israel? What about the prophecy of YahShua concerning Yerushelayim? What does Yerushelayim mean to those who do not live there? Will I ever know why I cannot rest these things and leave the understanding of them to the... No, the chief cohanim and elders of Israel do not seem to even care about finding the answers. They do not even

337

seem to know there is anything happening to raise questions, much less needing answers. It is all so baffling. Will I ever find understanding?

On the way back from the private chamber, the night breeze flowed down the length of the corridor tugging gently at the tassels of my hair. The night was black and quiet except for the muffled sounds of music coming from the interior of the house. I stopped at the baluster that looks out across the valley, drew a deep breath of the fresh mountain air and wondered just how to tell Sarepta, Miryam and Athera I had to continue my search for the truth. I sighed, raised my eyes heavenward watching the stars twinkling above. They seemed so close that if I reached up I could surely touch them.

My father had not returned from Rome, so a messenger was dispatched to inform him of the birth of the child, to give him a report on the business and well being of the family. I had hoped he would be here upon my return but something pressing must have come up. I smiled, or maybe he was just enjoying the Roman spring festivals and the grand arena events.

It is unlawful for one to travel or do any work on the holy day. Therefore, the day is spent fasting, praying and visiting. I took the opportunity to tell any who cared to listen about the happenings in Yerushelayim and about the plan of Kayafa against Yosef of Arimathea. Some, but not all, understood the deeper purpose of the death of the Messiah and the departure of the presence of the Adonai from the Temple. Those who did not understand or chose not to accept it left the room with much indignation.

Then I frowned, Elsan and Yered's arguing had become very annoying and seemed to be heating up instead of getting better. The last argument was over, whose fault it was that the gate in the holding stalls was not locked, letting the two big studs at each other. I could not believe they would come to blows, but never had I seen Elsan so full of anger. Not at Yered's accusations exactly, but some deep under lying resentment that he has been unable to deal with. Once, I thought, I even saw a flash of hatred shot through his blue eyes. I wish he was a man that would talk about his problems, but even as a small child he would bear the burden alone until I confronted him. I guess now that is what I will have to do.

I took a deep breath and let it out slowly. There was no putting it off any longer. I had to return to the celebration. It would be unforgivable to stay away too long. I walked slowly along drawing my fingers along the top of the baluster.

On down the column walkway a sharp harsh voice rose and fell. It was unmistakably Elsan's and it flowed through the bedchamber window just in front of me.
"Oh Yah," I thought, "They are at it again."

But, as I drew near it was a girlish voice that replied. It was not anger filled, but strong with a hint of defense.

"I do not care," Elsan was saying loudly by the time I was close enough to hear. "He makes eyes at you all the time, and he is supposed to be married next fall."

"Why are you yelling at me about it? Do you think I encourage him?" She demanded.

It was Anna, no missing her voice either. Who were they talking about? If one of the servants or guests has acted unseemly toward his espoused they will have me to deal with. I stopped at that thought. I did not intend to listen to their private talk, but if something was amiss in my household I wanted to know.

"No, of, …of course not," he stammered.

Then I heard the sound of sandals drawing near the window in wide strides and Elsan's distorted shadow grew long stretching across the walk in front of me. He was coming out here and I would be found listening. I caught my breath and quickly looked around for a place to hide. No! I determined not to hide. If I am caught, I am caught. He was almost to the window when his shadow stopped lengthening.

"It, …it really hurts, you know, when it is your own brother, someone you love."

I clasped my hand over my mouth to muffle the gasp that almost betrayed me. But, the worst thing was the stabbing pain that shot through my heart like a hunter's arrow. Yered? Surely, he was not speaking of Yered.

Now there was a soft movement and another shadow joined the first on the walkway floor. "Elsan, I pay him no mind, neither should you." Her voice was close to the window.

"How can I close my eyes to it," Elsan's voice was angry now, "…when he looks at you that way and with Nebra sitting there beside him."

There was a short silence then Elsan spoke again in a choked voice. "He has betrayed Nebra, sinning against you, …and me, also."

"You speak as though he has violated me. He has not so much as touched me with his hand."

"He lusts for you, violating you in his heart."

The last shadow moved slightly and touched the other on the face. "My love!" Her voice was softly sweet and barely audible. "I grieve for the pain in your heart, but it pleases me very much that you are jealous."

They were silent as the two shadows become one. I supposed he was holding her.

I had been too busy with the guests to notice the scene Elsan was talking about, but I had seen it before, …that night in Yerushelayim with the winch at the tabernae. Now I fought to control the anger that pushed the pain of Elsan's words from my heart. How could he do such a thing? How could he dishonor his brother and shame Nebra this way? I only pray that Nebra's father did not see this tragic scene. I was bitterly ashamed of him. His sin was not only against them, but Nebra and Yah as well. How could he have done this? Why would he do such a thing? I pressed my lips into a tight line. This will not continue under my roof. I will stop it and fast. Where had I failed?

What did I do wrong that Yered would commit such iniquity?

"Elsan," she spoke again now, "tell your Father."

"No," he rejected vigorously, "…he has enough to worry about. I will take care of this myself."

Enough to worry about? Does he not understand that he comes first? Nothing, except Yah, is more important than he. Maybe, he has always felt that way. That could explain why I have to draw things out of him. He thinks his troubles and problems are bothersome to me. That hurt almost as much as what Yered did. Adonai Yah! I thought I knew them, but I guess I did not really know them at all.

Their shadows cast on the walkway floor by the lamps inside the room pulled apart. Then she reached up, brushed aside the twig of hair that always plagued his forehead.

"I must go," her words being forced, "Father will be looking for me and if I am found here, ...he, also, has a temper."

The shadows melted together again and then slowly moved back into the room. I stood like a stone statue the scene Elsan talked of replayed itself again and again in the imagination of my mind and each time I felt a new stab of pain. To think that Elsan could not come to me with this problem. There was something wet dropping on my feet, splashing onto the stone polished floor. My eyes were stinging. I angrily brushed the wetness from my cheek and found it took great strength to move, all this had struck with a crushing blow. There will be no need for Elsan to know what I determined in my heart to do for he might misunderstand my intentions.

Yered entered the room wearing one of his famous smiles. He looked cock sure of himself. Any other time I would have admired it, but now it disgusted me. My look must have given me away. I never was that good at hiding my feelings, but this time I was not trying to do so. His face sagged and eyes narrowed in a faltered step.

"What is wrong Father?"

341

"Why have you sinned against your brother and Nebra?" I asked flatly in harsh words.

"Sinned?" He looked shocked.

"Yes! Did you think you would not be seen, the way you looked upon Anna to lust after her and shaming Nebra even with her there watching?" My words were sharp and spiked with angry disgust.

The color drained from his face while his eyes widened in horror, then it flushed reddening.

"I, ...I was not lusting after her," he stammered after he finally caught his breath.

"Do not add to your sin by lying." I sat my face like stone against him, but it was more to hide the aching sadness in my heart.

"Did something happen before Elsan came to join me?" I demanded sternly. "The truth now."

"I, ...I meant nothing by it," he sputtered. "I was only teasing him."

"Tell me." I fought the stinging tears that tried to rush forth.

"I found him and Anna in the garden. They were embracing and she became embarrassed upon seeing me and fled away into the house. I said to him that if I were not already espoused to Nebra I would take her away from him. He became furious and would not let me explain. He just said one look was more than any words. What did he mean by that?"

"You do not know?" I frowned.

"No." He shook his head. He looked bewildered and I wondered if he could look so innocent had he really looked at her the way Elsan said.

"He meant your look told him you were not teasing." I dropped my harshness, but the anger was still in my words. "How do you explain your behavior tonight?"

One eyebrow rose and there was a puzzled look. "Tonight?"

"Do you not think your looking upon Anna would go unnoticed."

His jaw tightened and he looked uncomfortable, then he dropped his eyes. "I think she is beautiful, …lovely to look at. Is that wrong?" He shifted his weight and shrugged. "I like to look at lovely things," he offered. "The beautiful trees, big mountains, our valley…"

"Elsan's valley," I reminded him. "You have a part of it only if he agrees. Remember that when you are tempted to commit fornication in your heart with his betrothed." I snapped at him coldly and meant to sting. He was too old to take a stick to, but I had thought about it.

His face twisted under my words, but he continued to stare at his distorted form reflected in the shiny floor.

"You have made your brother an enemy, insulted Anna, disgraced Nebra and dishonored me in the eyes of my guests. I will not even dare mention the embarrassment to Anna and Nebra's families with your lewd behavior."

"I meant no harm, Father," he defended. "I did not intend my look to be an insult or to do sin against Anna or anyone else." He raised his head and looked past the column walkway out into the night.

"Well, you did, …no matter what your intentions were! How can I go back and sit before them now? Because you have done this shameful thing, I must go now from this room, rend my garment before Yah and cast dust upon my head.

He responded by squinting his eyes tightly together. "I did not intend to shame you, Father." He wagged his head slowly and looked down again.

I sighed sadly. "Your sin is very grievous and could destroy many lives…" He looked up at me and there was a strained redness around pleading pained eyes. "…But, the saddest part of all is that you have sinned against Elohim."

He gasped, gave me a pitifully sick look. "Oh no Father, not against Elohim! I would never do that."

"But you did, Yered!" Now I was aware of the dampness on my own cheeks as a trickle slid down from Yered's eyes.

343

"I did not know…" His voice choked off and he took a step in my direction.

"Did you think you could sin against man and not sin against Elohim also."

"Oh Father!" He dropped on his knees at my feet, pulling my legs against his breast. "Father help me," he sobbed deeply, clinging to me. I placed my hand lovingly upon his head and we wept.

Looking down at him kneeling there, I marveled at his great love for Elohim. He took my sharp words for the sins against his brother, Anna and Nebra, but the thought of sinning against the Elohim of Heaven had brought him to his knees. Pride rose in my inner being for I know now, his love for Elohim will sustain him throughout his whole life, even through grievous sins, such as this.

"Tell me what to do," he begged looking up with tear sodden face. "Please tell me what to do."

"You should go seek Elohim and find forgiveness, and ask that He hide these things from the eyes of the people, but you must determine in your heart to repent and never to look upon another woman no matter how beautiful she may be. Your eyes are suppose to be for Nebra and her only, but since they are not I will find out for you what will be the price to break your betrothal.

"No Father!" Fear replaced the hurt in his face, and he raised to his feet. "I love her."

"How can you love her when you have eyes for others?"

"They mean nothing to me. I admire their beauty only, but Nebra is more to me than any."

"Can you keep yourself for her in your heart? She deserves faithfulness and reverent love."

"I can Father, I will be faithful, I swear it."

"Well… it really depends upon whether Elohim will hide your sin from her or her father. If they ask, I cannot deny, nor lie and will submit to their wishes. Do you understand?"

"Yes, Father. But, ...what about my sin? There is no sacrifice now?" He gripped my arm and I saw shear terror flash in his eyes. "How may I get forgiveness or persuade Elohim to hide the sin?"

"It is true there is no sacrifices now to offer, but something deep inside me makes me to know that Elohim will hear a sincere repentant heart. There is a new covenant. We do not understand it all yet, but YahShua' death was the sin sacrifice. Plead with Elohim in behalf of His blood. That is all we can do."

"I will go for the cohem," Yered determined and turned to go.

"Wait!" I called after him. "There is no need for a Cohen if there is no need for a sacrifice. All that remains is for us to pray from our hearts. Yes, ...pray, fast and pray."

"All right Father. That is what I shall do."

Yered went to his room and after I sought the Adonai on his behalf, I rose, dried my eyes and washed my face. Then I returned to the celebration to find that Serepta and Athera was beginning to get anxious about my long absence. Many of my guests were asking about me. After some time it was apparent Yah had heard our prayers for no one, including Nebra's father asked to speak to me privately about Yered's lewd behavior. However, Nebra seemed strangely withdrawn. Finally, I mentioned it to Serepta who promptly went to her. Serepta reported that she was despondent because her search for Yered was unfruitful, so I went to her.

"Yered is in his chamber." I explained.

"Is he sick?" she asked.

"No, he is seeking Elohim."

She nodded and went back to sit with her family. I worry some about her being so young. Well, both she and Yered are young. Perhaps it was foolish of me to mention their marriage. Let them have a few more years to mature, I told myself watching her take a bunch of grapes from the servants tray.

The evening breeze had a chill but it felt good to be alone after being in the crowded reception room. I took Sarepta's hand and we walked in the garden for a while without saying anything. Serepta began to sneeze and I moaned sympathetically. I should have known it would bring on one of her attacks. She tended to the sneezing and smiled up at me with a slightly reddened nose.

"Now do not look at me like that," she muttered reassuringly, "...I am just fine."

Her smile always did strange things to me and in the starlight her hair took on a soft halo. I sighed deeply.

"On the morrow when all the guests depart, I must go to BeitAnyah," I told her.

"On the morrow?" She sounded with disappointment.

"Yes my love, I must find out the purpose for the resurrection and see YahShua."

"But, on the morrow?" she pleaded.

I found the words hard to say, so I pulled her into my arms, stroked the silken strands of hair that hung down her back, and pressed my cheek against her forehead. How could I make her understand something I did not understand myself? She will just have to trust my judgment.

While we were still standing there in the shadows, Yered came out of his chamber onto the porch to Nebra. They talked a short time, embraced and she went quickly to her room. I will not tell Yered that her father did not approach me about the incident. It will be good for him to wonder about it for a while. He will find out the answer himself in time. I knew I should not tarry long for the sake of my guests, but the desire to escape the endless questions and loud throbbing beat of the musicians held me in place. I sighed again, telling my feet to move, but they defied me.

I was not one for long enduring celebrations, but Sarepta had pointed out in her usual calm persuasive way that it was only being hospitable to our friends and relatives. After all, I had returned from my trip and they

346

would be anxious to see me, and then there was the birth of the child. Sarepta had sent for her family and was anxious to show off the gifts that I brought her from Yerushelayim. Athera could proudly display the child and Miryam found such pleasure in performing her songs at these celebrations. It was good for the boys to spend some time with the families of their soon to be brides. All in all, her reasons were pretty convincing and I found little room to argue with them. I did have at least a peaceful stay at home and I would soon be traveling on to BeitAnyah. That thought brought a joyous stirring that had almost subsided since I had been home.

DAY TWENTY NINE

Shortly after my guests had all departed, on the twenty-ninth day after the resurrection, Elsan, myself and a small company of servants once again bid farewell to our mountain home and set our face toward BeitAnyah. The brilliance of blazing hot sun forced a deep furrow between my eyes and I watched a flock of birds in the distance take to flight. In their midst, I saw again the hawk and smiled to myself. I had one over on the hawk, now. One of my circles had netted me some of the answers I was seeking and a deep joy that was beginning to surface as the wheels of my cisium turned. I wondered with excitement what lay ahead in BeitAnyah. Would I finally get to see Him?

Elsan seemed in good spirits and I was relieved to see him come from the house with Yered at his side. Maybe, there had been restitution before we left. I hoped so anyway, but would not pry into it, for I did not want Elsan to know I had taken it upon myself to settle the matter. If Yered had told him I would surely find out in time, in which case I would admit it, otherwise it would never be mentioned. In any event, I had learned some wonderful truths from the trouble. One being, there was some wondrous power in the blood of YahShua, a sacrifice for

347

our sins and another, that Yah heard and answered prayer from his place where the presence of Yah had gone to preside over the new covenant. The disciples at BeitZaidah did not know the answers to my other question but surely when I find YahShua and the other disciples they will have the answers.

I sighed. Maybe, I could discover something from the scrolls. I reached into the compartment to take one out and felt the soft fabric of the blue robe. I drew it out. I had intended to leave it at home but Benren had brought it with the scrolls without even asking me about it. Apparently, some where in his mind the scrolls and the robe was unspeakable. I stroked the coarse fabric and wondered how Appolious was coming along on the road to recovery. Poor Appolious, he had no idea the significance of the robe. I smiled and returned it to it's place and draw out a scroll.

In the fading light of day, as the sun's influence on the wind began to loose its power, we set out tents. Having gotten a late start that day, it put us still a day's journey by horse from Shklem. We took meat as usual under the shade of the heavy woven canapé and found the evening cup of wine very relaxing. I was somewhat travel weary, having been spoiled by the comfort of home, but my spirit soared with anticipation of the things to come.

I looked at Elsan, who stared out across the hills of Shamron toward our destination. I knew he too was anxiously looking forward to the rest of our journey, adventure was in his eye. As I studied his defined features, set jaw and pleasing round face, I wondered if he had settled things with Yered before we left. They did come out of the house together. I wanted very much to ask, but could not risk his knowing I was aware of the problem, that had been his plight the past few weeks. If only he would talk to me, Maybe, I could coax it out of him.

"Elsan, when would you like to be married?" I ask trying to sound natural.

He tore his eyes from his vigil and looked at me thoughtfully. "I thought you wanted me to wait for a while."

"It was not an order, merely a suggestion."

He dropped his eyes and sloshed the wine in his cup around watching the velvet swirls. "Perhaps, we shall set a date when I get back."

I nodded and held my cup out while Benren poured wine into it. He seemed content not to talk about it and I decided not to press it.

"Father, ...he hesitated and I held my breath, "Yered said Yah has changed him and there was a look about him that was very strange. Did you notice it?"

"I am afraid not. In our preparation to leave, I was quite busy with last minute instruction and shaloms."

"How is it possible that this Man YahShua has the power to change people?"

"I believe it is because He is the Messiah. He has fulfilled many of the prophecies and I am quite sure the others also, although unknown to me."

"Will we find Him in BeitAnyah?"

"That is my hope and I am sure the answers to my questions lie there, also."

"It is hard for me to believe that He actually raised from the dead, even though the disciples we met in BeitZaidah say so." He looked out across the rolling countryside again.

Strangely enough, I was having no problem believing He had risen, but understanding the purposed for it was what bothered me. At first, I thought it was to bring back the throne of David, but I see no sign of it happening. YahShua seems content to only show himself to the disciples. This puzzled me and deepened the mystery.

DAY THIRTY

It was dusky when we began to see the welcoming lights of the town of Shklem and around the well of Jacob the servants and women were drawing water for the night. The market place was empty and only the sound of our horses' hooves and the grind of our wheels could be heard.

However, the Inn of David seemed to be alive with activity. Nearly every table was taken and the small frame of Neah hustled about the room flitting from one table to the next. When she looked up at our entering, she smiled brightly and hurried to greet us.

"Timon? How are you? Come on in and find a seat." She jested with a swing of her hand.

I waited for a degree before answering her, remembering her ways, "Shalom Neah. Do you have accommodations for us this night?"

"For you, always." She took my arm, then looked at Elsan mildly. "And, who is with you this time?" As I opened my mouth, she continued. "Do not tell me he is another son?" I just nodded and smiled down at her. She turned to Elsan, "Welcome to my house." Then she looked back at me. "He does not look as much like you as Yered does."

Someone at one of the tables called her name and she glanced around at him.

"I must attend to my guests," she went on in a gush. "Find a place and I will get back to you as quickly as possible." As usual, before I could even respond she was dashing off across the floor.

"Whoo-o!" Elsan muttered raising one eyebrow.

"That is Neah and she is famous for one sided conversation. I see two places over there." I indicated a table near the west wall.

Shortly, the place began to clear and Neah came to our table. "Did you enjoy your meal?" She asked with a sigh setting down in an adjoining chair. She looked at Elsan, tilted her head slightly and smiled at him. "I am Neah."

350

Elsan smiled back and cast me a sideways glance. "Neah, this is Elsan." I injected quickly.

"Your eyes are very unusual," Neah remarked. Then turning to me, "I have seen to your rooms. When you are ready I will show them to you. Your servants have been settled into the common room and I have taken it upon myself to tend to your breakfast. I am anxious to hear your news. Did you find the disciples?" She drew a long breath, letting it out in a gush. "I am sorry. Where are my manners? Surely, you must be tired. Come, I will show you your rooms."

She stood swiftly and Elsan batted his eyes at her abruptness. I suppose I must have shown some reaction also for she always catches me off guard.

In my small but comfortable room Benren's grim face told me he was not pleased that I had chosen this inn for the night. As he went about seeing to my needs, I gave him instructions for an early departure on the morrow. He seemed to brighten upon hearing that and I smiled knowingly at his concern.

Neah came in after he had gone and we talked for some time about what had happened since I was here last. She told me BarAbbas was in Yerushelayim and there had been more arrests at the hand of Shaul of Tarsus. However, Pilate was reluctant to carry out any executions unless they were connected with the Zealots, much to the dismay of the chief cohanim and elders. I told her about the meeting with the disciples at BeitZaidah and the revelation of why the presence of Yah left the Temple at Yerushelayim and that I was on my way to BeitAnyah to find YahShua and the other disciples. She seemed excited about my confidence that YahShua was alive and I saw hope spring up in her eyes.

DAY THIRTY ONE

The next stop on our journey would be BeitHal and we would have to push hard to reach there before dark. The road wound it's way like the trail of a serpent through the mountain country of Yhudea. The cisium would rock violently when one of the wheels fell hard into one of the deep ruts made by many carts and wagons. The travel seemed long and the sun did its work to weaken and drench us in its relentless heat.

Finally, we set shelter at the sixth hour to rest and take meat. The wine had not kept good and was warm but we welcomed it to wash the dust from our throats.

While we sat under the shade of the heavy woolen cloth, Benren came close and said, "My lord, two men approach."

We watched two figures coming toward us. One was extremely tall with a short black beard and the other was average with a rather expensive robe. We stood as they drew near and I bowed slightly to them.

"Shalom!" The tall one greeted with a friendly wave. The other only nodded.

"Welcome brothers. Sit under my tent and have some wine. It is warm I am afraid, but none the less refreshing." Then I said unto Benren, "Bring our guest some chairs and something to eat." He nodded and went away.

"I am Parmenas of Archelats," the tall one informed, "...and this is Nicanor of Phasaelis."

"Timon of Beitorah and this," I opened my hand to Elsan, "...is my son Elsan."

Benren and Yh74asper set some more chairs and brought out another tray, poured their cups full of wine and took their leave.

"This is a rather large troop. May I ask where you are going." Nicanor opened the conversation.

353

"We are going to BeitAnyah to find YahShua and the disciples," Elsan supplied.

I winced and shot him a quick scolding look. The tall thin man smiled at me having apparently noticed my action and shook his head. "Do not be afraid, we also are followers."

"But," the other continued, "…you should be careful who you speak to of YahShua. It is a dangerous time."

"Now Nicanor, how can we spread the wonderful news if we go around afraid to speak. Where is your trust in Yah?" Parmenas scolded mildly.

Nicanor shifted uneasily in his chair and looked at Parmenas with a lifted brow.

"What is this good news?" Elsan questioned searching Parmenas' face.

"Do you not know of the events of the Posach?" Nicanor widened his eyes now at Elsan.

"Yes, but I am afraid I find it all a little hard to believe," Elsan countered.

"Ah yes," Parmenas nodded. "But, you must believe. With Yah all things are possible."

There was a short silence while we all thought about that. Then I asked my guests, "Are you looking for the disciples also?"

"Yes. We will find the disciples and join their efforts to comfort the followers who are in prison and to encourage the others to stand fast in faith." Nicanor revealed.

"Are there many followers?" I asked.

"Yes, but they are in hiding for fear of persecution."

"Have you seen YahShua?' Elsan injected. "Will YahShua be there?"

"No we have not seen Him but we hope to when we get there." Parmenas stated.

"Then we can travel together for we also seek Him," I invited. "Travel will be much faster in my cisium."

They looked at each other and nodded in agreement. Then we spent much time talking about YahShua, what He taught and why we believed He is the Messiah. Elsan, however, did not say anything, only listened.

The sun had fled behind the purple mountains of the western sky and darkness was creeping over the small farming village of BeitHal as we entered. Being only one Inn in the town, we stopped there for the night. The accommodations were comfortable but small and as I lay upon my bed I prayed for Yah to help us find YahShua and for Elsan to believe in Him.

My new companions did not seem to understand why YahShua had not manifested Himself to the world any more than I did. My new friend said he told the disciples that he could have called ten thousand angels to come to his aid. Yet he went willingly to the cross. What great love he must have had to be willing to lay down his life like that. The mystery surrounding the Posach events still remained and I wondered what Yah was doing, if anything, to bring about the fulfillment of the other prophecies about the Messiah. Would Yah yet bring about deliverance at the hands of the Messiah? Apparently he had the forces of heaven to do it with yet I saw no evidence that Yah was going to destroy the Roman yoke or establish the throne of David again.

My new friends did help me understand that the miracles were done to prove YahShua' words and to show the power of the Kingdom of Yah. They were signs to those who did not believe. Suddenly, I felt I had missed a great deal by not seeing Him for myself.

I sighed deeply and closed my eyes. Tomorrow we would reach Yerushelayim and I felt the increasing joy of expectation as we drew closer to YahShua and the disciples. Somehow, I knew Yah would bring about something spectacular and I wanted very much to be a part of it.

DAY THIRTY TWO

About the sixth hour of the day we began to see the gable towers of Herod's Palace and the elegant walls of Yerushelayim soon appeared. I had not expected to see her again and my heart rose up into my throat at the sight. Then I remembered the words of prophecy YahShua spoke concerning those precious walls and her children and groaned deeply at its thought. The Temple was empty and full of deceit, the people had cried out for blood and now Yah was giving them blood to drink. I quaked inside and suddenly became sick and weak.

Elsan was then beside me but when I became aware of it he just rode along silently. I guess he decided he did not want to face my sharp words this time so he was waiting for me to notice him. Seeing me look up, he studied me a degree before speaking. There was pleading in his eyes and he struggled to contain himself.

"Father, will we stop in Yerushelayim or go on to BeitAnyah?"

I looked at Parmenas riding beside me and then to Nicanor who had taken the Benren's seat in the front beside Semone.

"Some of the followers in Yerushelayim may know where we shall find YahShua and the disciples." Parmenas reasoned.

Nicanor agreed with a nod so I said unto him. "We will stop at Yerushelayim."

His eyes brightened and surged with excitement. "Will we stay the rest of the day?" He burst forth no longer able to contain it.

I smiled at his youthful zeal but knew that I too wanted one more chance to enter the gate and be swallowed up in the pomp and splendor of my beloved city.

"Yes, Elsan. Ride on ahead and find us a hostel. We will meet you in the market place near the Bridge Gate."

The hostel Elsan found was a large three-layer building built into the dividing wall separating the upper from the lower city. It was only a short way from the Theater and my window allowed me a view of the seats and the Pool of Siloam in the distant left. It's bluish green water glistening in the lowering sun. To the left the walls of the Great Temple towered over the court of the Gentiles and I watched tiny figures ascending and descending Solomon's Porch. From my lofty height on the third floor, I could pick out the cohanim by the dark contrast of their robes against the stone steps mingling with the fusion of other colored vestries.

It felt good not to feel the ground moving under me and I would have enjoyed the peaceful solitude of my room more if the excited anticipation had allowed me to do so. But, the restless joy deep within seemed to demand some kind of action.

I signed and turned from the window. Eldaher quickened to my mind and I knew if anyone would know where YahShua and His disciples were it would be the man healed of blindness. That would be a good place to start. Then I could stop at the "The Shawan" and see if by chance the Adonai had returned to the upper room. Yes, and Nakdimon might know something if persuaded to talk. Anyway, it would an answer to the restlessness and give me something to do this evening.

Yerushelayim had not lost its timeless charm and gripping magnitude but there was something in the air. A sense of anxiety permeated the whole city. Perhaps, winds of change that promises a storm. The whole place is unknowingly bracing for something, echoing the restlessness of my heart, but being filled with some awesome dread instead of joy.

On the street, the people seem edgy and quick with a sharp word. The soldiers appear tense, on the verge of sudden action. An eerie lack of the usual laughter and cheerful voices in the masses that move too and fro

357

signaled a silent warning. An uneasy shutter flowed through me and I struggled to shake it off.

The man, who sells fruit from his cart, was still standing across the street from where Eldaher lives. He was still calling out his chant, holding up a bowl of fresh dates. I stopped there and looked at his fruit shaded from the blistering sun by a colorful cloth canopy. I waited for sometime. There seemed to be more patrols than I remembered, but immediately after the next one passed I dashed across the street. Pausing a degree to let a damsel with a pitcher on her shoulder pass, I climbed the narrow steps and knocked urgently. I gave a quick glance around while waiting by the door. When it opened just slightly Miryam peered out through the crack.

"Shalom! Do you remember me?" I asked hastily.

There was a short pause, then she blinked at me and nodded slightly, "I remember."

"Is Eldaher here? I would like an audience with him."

"No, he is not here. Please go away," she retorted and shut the door.

I stared at the closed door wondering why she seemed so frightened. I pose no threat to her. I knocked again but there was no answer, so I hurriedly returned to the street.

Eldaher had apparently gone underground like most of the followers. Finding someone who would talk to me seemed to be a difficult task. I did not really expect the owner of the Hostel to be much help either, but I had to try.

Inside the large atrium of the hostel there was the bustling activity I remembered from my first visit. The gleaming yellow symbolic light rays smiled up at me bursting forth from the golden globe set into the red tiles of the polished floor. The Greek chariot still raced across the ceiling in the churning clouds of white while people in fancy henigans, each with the style of their native country, ascended and descended the wide circular stairs. A choir of languages and tones hummed in an endless drone with accompanying soft music supplied by a small group of musicians on a platform against the wall. I did not notice them when I was here before. Glancing around the room, I caught sight of Aquarial in his royal blue robe trimmed in embroidered gold. He was talking with what appeared by their dress to be an Ammorite and an Egyptian. The look on his face was pleasantly courteous. The corners of his mouth slightly raised as he listened with interest to what was being said.

Making my way to him through the scattered press I noticed a small company of men in dark heavy robes nestled together near the curl of the stairs. What was peculiar about them was that about a span of the unmistakable him of a cohem garment could be seen below the outer robe. If they were in disguise the cohanim pride was showing. With a quick glance I picked out the piercing eyes of Alexander, one of Kayafa's companions in deceit, watching me cross the floor. A fleeting thought questioning his possible reason for being here floated through my mind but was quickly dissolved as I drew near the circle of men.

I waited quietly where Aquarial could see me and when he looked up I nodded, smiled and continued my wait. Shortly he dismissed himself from the men and came to where I stood.

"Shalom my friend," he greeted.

"Shalom Aquarial. I would like a word with you in private, if you do not mind."

"This way." He swung his hand for me to proceed him, but he quickly fell into step with me.

"It seems you have a full house."

"So it is. Ah, …Timon, is it not?"

"Yes," I nodded. "I was unaware the cohanim frequented here."

"Oh, …you noticed that. Well, they have only recently taken interest in my place." He placed one slightly crooked finger over his lips and said with a twinkle in is eye. "They think they are hid." Then he leaned close for me only to hear, "They think they are spies."

He laughed heartily and opened the heavy door with the Greek warrior carved on it. Leading the way into the private room he offered me a richly covered lounge.

"Have you found the answers to your questions?" The hostel owner said seating himself across from me on a matching lounge.

"I have found out that YahShua is the long awaited Messiah and why the presence of the Adonai left the Great Temple at His death, but the purpose for the resurrection is a mystery."

"Then He is alive?" Aquarial drew to attention.

"The two disciples I met in BeitZaidah told me that He is, but I have not seen him myself. I was hoping He had come here and you could help me find Him. That is why I came back to Yerushelayim."

"No, I do not think he would come here. "But what is this about the presence of the Adonai leaving the Temple?"

"Ah yes, …well, you would not know about that. The chief cohanim and elders are trying desperately to keep it quiet. At the very hour YahShua died, Yosef of Arimathea was offering up prayers for Him before the curtain in the Holy Place, and the Glory of the Adonai rent the curtain, exposing the Ark of the Covenant and the Glory of Yah left the Temple in haste."

A questioning look fell across Aquarial's countenance and he raised one elegant eyebrow thoughtfully.

"I know you are not an Israelite," I continued. "And this will be hard for you to understand but it is the will of Yah. The death of YahShua, the Son of Yah, brought by the sacrifice of His life a New Covenant. Not established with the blood of bulls and goats as the first was, but by the divine life of Yah." I heard myself say the words but they did not come from my mind and it startled me. I was unable to restrain because the power thereof was too great. "The presence of the Adonai left the Temple, the Ark of Testimony, to preside over the New Covenant of the heart.

360

YahShua told a woman of Samaria that the time was at hand when men would no longer worship in the temples made with hands. But, they would worship Yah in spirit and truth, in the heart, fulfilling the promise Yah made to King David many generations ago when it entered his heart to build a Temple unto the Adonai. It is written in the Torah that it shall come about when David's days are fulfilled and he slept with his fathers that Yah would set up one of his descendants to establish his kingdom forever. Yah is actually going to dwell with men on the earth.

When I fell silent we both sat amazed and dumbfounded for a short time. I pondered the things that came forth from my own mouth, my being vibrated with the truth of what was said. The New Covenant seat was in my heart and the joy I felt there was a witness of the presence of Adonai. That is why YahShua said, 'The Kingdom of Yah comes without observation.'

I lifted up my voice and praised the Elohim of Israel, worshipping from the New Temple where His presence dwelt.

"Blessed be the Elohim of Israel," Aquarial muttered softly after a degree.

"I was told there is a large following here," I was finally able to speak, "...and YahShua might be meeting with them. He is supposed to be in BeitAnyah. If I do not find Him here I will go there. Do you know where the followers meet?"

"I have heard that they have met in times past in the dry cistern in the north part of town."

"Thank you my friend. Perhaps, I will go there this night and see if they meet."

"No Timon, you cannot. Even now the chief cohanim are being told of your visit here and you would just lead them to the followers."

I had not thought of that and the disappointment must have shown on my face for Aquarial smiled knowingly, sighed and rose from the lounge. He, also, must have known my determination to find YahShua because he turned to me and added. "It is rumored that YahShua stayed in the home of Elazar when in BeitAnyah."

I nodded and rose to face him. "The blessing of Adonai be upon your establishment."

"The Elohim be with you, Timon."

"Elohim of Israel is with me, and I need no other. Thank you very much my friend," I bowed slightly.

The day was far spent when I emerged from the hostel and the travel was catching up with me. I debated with myself whether I should go on to see Nakdimon or wait until morning. After much deliberation my body convinces me to return to my room and take meat. I thought that perhaps Nicanor and Parmenas might join me.

When I arrived at the hostel Benren greeted me in the hall. "Young Elsan is waiting for you in your room, my lord."

"All right Benren. Go see if Parmenas and Nicanor will take meat with me. I have some news."

"Yes my lord." He bowed slightly.

Elsan stood up from a lounge that reclined near a small table along the south wall as I entered.

"Shalom Father."

"Now, where has your adventurous heart taken you this evening?" I said unto him mildly.

"Too and fro," he returned. "There is something I think you would like to know. None of the disciples have been seen in Yerushelayim since the Posach but it is said that YahShua, himself, has appeared to as many as five thousand followers in the slopes of Mount Olive. Two cohorts of soldiers went out to them and broke it up. YahShua disappeared out of their midst and the multitude hid the disciples and allowed them to slip away. There were a few arrests but most were sent home after the Romans and temple guards were unable to lay hands on YahShua or His disciples."

"On Mount Olive?"

"Yes, Father."

"Very well, it is good news, but I understood the followers meet in a dry cistern. From whence came your rumor."

"I over heard some men talking in the market place."

Before I could say another word, Benren entered the room with a wash basin to tend to my needs. "Parmenas and Nicanor have agreed to take meat, my lord. They also have news."

"Join us Elsan for they will also want to hear your news."

"Alright, I will go to my room and freshen up," Elsan determined and straightway departed.

"I have made preparations for you to take meat with your guests on the roof." Benren informed. "It will be much cooler and it is a nice evening. Shall you wear your guest robe or just a common one."

"There will be no need for the guest robe these men are my friends."

"Yes my lord."

The soft and cool breeze carried the night sounds up to us playing upon our ears. The meal had left us somber and peaceful as we each entertained our own thoughts. Mine was upon the events that had brought us together this night. Elsan had related the story he had overheard in the market place while I told of the followers meeting in the dry cistern. Nicanor said that he heard that the followers were hiding in the tomb caves in the Valley of Kidron. Now the decision remained as to which story was right and where we should go.

"It is my opinion," I broke the stillness, "...that going to the tomb caves is not a likely prospect without a guide because it is dangerous and we can get lost quickly."

"That leaves two," Parmenas sighed.

"I will take one of the horses and ride out to Mount Olive if you would like." Elsan opened his hand toward us. "It is far too late to walk there. The meeting would be over by the time you arrived. If they are there I will find out when and where the next meeting is before I return."

"Yes, that is good and Nicanor and Parmenas can go to the cistern." I added. "It is not wise for me to go because I am sure the Council is having me watched. However, I know someone who can find out if the followers are meeting in the tomb caves."

"Who, Father?" Elsan looked intrigued.

"A Zealot who owes me something." I smiled slightly.

"It is good. Let us be off." Parmenas stood anxiously.

Soon we each departed with our own mission. Somewhat refreshed from the meal, I found even at night the streets which are usually empty had more troop movement than normal and there was an eerie quietness in the air. Making my way through the narrow streets under the watchful eye of a large round moon and its twinkling companions, I stopped in front of the door to the tabernae where a soft yellow slit of light spoke of life within.

Even without opening the door, the distinct odor reminded me of what awaited inside. I drew a deep breath of fresh air and pushed the door open. The disgraceful winch was hovering over a table where two men set talking in low voices while two more from another table looked at me with interest.

At still another table in the darkened corner a lone figure slumped over a cup of wine sullen in his misery. His darken silhouette held familiar lines and I half smiled at his desolation. BarArni will always be an undoubtedly miserable person for his greed will always leave him empty. But, he was just the man I wanted to see.

I took a silver piece out of my bag as the winch turned her attention to me. Leaving her two customers she glided toward me with a pasted smile.

"Good evening," she tossed. "What can I get for you?"

"A pitcher of wine and a cup," I returned dryly. "Bring it to that table over there." I pointed to where BarArni sat, still unaware of me.

Resting her hand on one hip, she tilted her head slightly and let her black eyes flow over my face. I tried to hide my distaste behind a half smile. Finally, she nodded and turned swiftly away. Obviously her memory had failed her.

BarArni must have been searching deeply for a plan to gain riches, as he did not notice me until I dropped the silver coin on the table in front of him. His dull eyes sparked to life and he quickly looked up at me with a questioning expression.

"I have ordered some wine, may I join you?"

"Ye, …yes." He cast a slim hand toward the bench across the table from him. "Welcome! Welcome!"

I had just seated myself when the winch came with the pitcher and cup. I very deliberately and slowly placed one finger on the silver coin lying in front of BarArni and slid it to her. BarArni's black eyes followed the coin until the damsel picked it up. Then they darted back to me, clouded with greed and his mouth twitched slightly.

"How can I help you, friend?" The words formed slowly.

I smiled, poured some wine in my cup and then into his. After taking a sip, I drew out my bag and took another silver piece from it. His eyes followed every move of my hand with expectation.

"I hear," I placed the coin on the table in front of me and fingered it while I spoke, "…the followers of YahShua and even He, Himself may be meeting in the tomb caves. Is that right?"

The winch returned with the change, deposited the coins upon the table without a word, turned and went back to the men at the first table. BarArni watched her go letting his eyes slide over her rounded hips. Then, as though he remembered the coin, he turned his attention back to me.

His fingers moved in rhythm on the side of his cup as he watched me play with the coin.

"That might be right." He muttered in a distracted tone.

Covering the coin and the change with my hand, I slid it halfway between us, left it there and picked up my cup taking another sip.

"Many of the followers hide there." He looked up at me. "But, YahShua is dead."

"Do the followers meet there?"

"No." He shook his head slowly.

"Do you know where they meet?"

He shrugged, "No."

"If you do find out where they meet, you can find me at the Wall Hostel."

I took another drink of wine, stood and went quickly out. I was almost all the way back to the hostel before the stench of the place was no longer in my nostrils. I hoped I would not have to go there again.

DAY THIRTY THREE

Brightness flooded my eyes although they were still closed. Opening them, I squinted in the harsh light of the morning sun. I lay in a warped square of brilliant gold that flowed across my bed from the window. The heat that comes with the sun bathed the distorted golden blocks making a distinct difference in the temperature. I stretched and yawned. The prominent sound of my beloved city was singing its wakening melody in my ears and called me from my sleep.

This day I would go to BeitAnyah. The thought brought the quiet joy surging into activity. Though yesterday had brought disappointment I felt sure this day would find fulfillment with answers to my questions. Hope was alive and vivid in my heart nudging me out of bed with insistence.

The previous night at the hostel Elsan was awaiting my return. He had not found the followers on Mount of Olives and gave a miserable look when he reported it. And, then when Parmenas and Nicanor came back some time later unable to find the dry cistern, my disappointment was hard to hide.

Now, in the light of a new day I found courage and inspiration. While raising from my bed, the door opened softly and Benren peering in smiled and then came to see to my needs.

Breakfast seemed dull compared to the excitement stirring deep within. I ate quickly unaware of its taste. I was anxious to be about my business.

There was a sharp rapid knock on the door but before Benren could answer Elsan breezed in. "Good day Father," he called cheerfully. Coming in with me still sitting on the lounge, he paused to peer out the window. "It is a beautiful morning, is it not?"

"This day may hold unexpected surprises for us," I chimed.

Taking in the strength of his youthful exuberance, I watched his profile as the rays of amber sunlight cast a soft halo around him but I did not need to draw from it. This day I felt alive, vital and youthful myself.

What will we do this day, Father?" He caught my excitement and turned to smile at me.

"First we will go to the Temple." I put my arms in the robe Benren held out for me. "...And then we will go to BeitAnyah."

Turning to Benren I said, "See that the cisium is ready when we return."

"Yes my lord."

Ascending the steps to the Royal Porch it seemed stiflingly unchanged. The sights and the sounds were just the same, as though nothing had happened, nothing at all. I fought a strange urge to yell at everyone that things had changed. The people are coming and going without concern. Dead to the wonderful change Yah was working in the world all around them. Dead! Ironic as it seems, it took death to see death. And, out of that death came life, if you look for it, but no one here is looking.

Passing through the Court of the Gentiles, the old excitement, the expectation was gone. I gave Elsan a sideways glance. His eyes darted here and there taking in the sights and sounds around us. To him it must seem very exciting. Once in the heart of the Courtyard, he turned completely around so as not to miss anything. I wished I could share the experience with him, but sadness was all that I could feel. Something so wonderful had come to naught.

At the 'Gate Beautiful', the lame beggar still lay holding up his cup asking for alms. His hair was in disarray and his robe was thin and worn. A weary scowl was hidden behind his unruly beard and his eyes searched the faces of those passing by with a complacent interest. This man had been there as long as I could remember. The same man who had received the rock in his cup in my act of mischief long ago. Pausing, I took a denari from my bag and it made a

368

loud clink as I dropped it into the cup. A smile spread across his aged face.

"Elohim bless you, my son." He answered the sounds.

I wanted to say something, ...do something. My heart went out to him and I opened my mouth, but closed it again without a word.

Elsan who was about to go through the gate ahead of me somewhat noticed my delay and turned to watch me. I did not know what to say to him either, so I said nothing.

Once inside the Women's Court Elsan said thoughtfully. "Father, why does not Elohim do something about people like that?"

"Elohim is not unjust, Elsan. He has not spared man of injustice to make us appreciate justice, wrong to make us appreciate right, bad to appreciate good. I assure you that those like that have a greater reward in Paradise to make up for what they suffer here. I think Elohim wishes to remind man just how vulnerable he is so he will not live life too proudly and become arrogant."

The Captain of the Temple Guards was the same one I had spoken to before, still frowning, still hostile in a polite way. When I had made my wish to speak with Nakdimon known to him, he shot me a sharp look but departed quickly.

While we waited, Elsan drifted away to watch a sacrifice. He seemed totally engrossed in it and the activity of the Cohen. He had seen it many times before, but there seemed to be something this time that particularly interested him. It was as though he had never really seen one before.

I turned away, because sacrifices always seemed so brutal. I never did get used to seeing it, and it seemed even harder now in the light of its futility. So, I busied my mind with thoughts of the small boy who fought so forcefully for his beloved ram. I smiled as I still saw the determination on his tear-streaked face and the small, trembling hand holding out the rope to me. I drew a deep breath and let it out slowly.

"The lesson of trust" I muttered to myself and watched a man lay a young bawling lamb over his shoulders holding two legs in each hand while it struggled.

Then the guard returned. "Come with me," he commanded in a voice of authority. I decided to leave Elsan to explore the Temple Court Yard and went with him.

I knew where we were going. It was all still very fresh in my mind, but I followed quietly. Arriving at the door he knocked and let me in without a word. Then closed the door softly leaving me alone to stare at the back of Master Nakdimon at his writing table. Finally, he stood, turned and smiled tolerantly.

"Ah, the seeker of truth," he greeted gruffly.

"Shalom, Master Nakdimon. I…"

"Yes! Yes! I know, " he interposed. "You are sorry to bother me, but there are some questions you are sure I have the answers to. Well, unfortunately," he waved me to a lounge, "…there is nothing more I can tell you."

"Perhaps there is something I can tell you." I countered a bit irritated at his insolence.

He blinked at me with little expression, probably thinking I could tell him nothing he does not already know and he may be right. Surely I am not the only one who has found the meaning of the death of the Messiah and the purpose for the presence of the Adonai leaving the Temple. But, if he has knowledge of it he has made it clear that he has no intention of talking about it. I do not remember his being this difficult when I was here before or when he later came to my room. Maybe, the things happening around him have effected him. I suppose everyone will be changed some way by the things going on now, whether for better or worse.

"So," he was saying, seating himself on a lunge across from me, "…what is it you came to tell me?"

"I believe that YahShua of Natzeret is the Messiah," I began.

"And…" he injected tautly.

"And that He is alive as his disciples say."

He raised one bushy eyebrow and studied me for a degree. "So they say."

"This much I know for sure." I decided to tell it all. "Yosef of Arimathea was right. The presence of the Adonai did leave the Temple. YahShua, the Messiah, has established a new covenant by His own blood instead of that of bulls and goats thus making the old one empty and void. So, the presence of Elohim went to preside over the New Covenant. Poor Yosef only saw the presence departing, but did not know why or where it went."

"What makes you so sure of this?"

"YahShua told a woman of Shamron that the time was at hand, and now was, when men would not worship in Temples made with hands, but in the heart and in spirit and truth."

"A Shamron?" He scoffed.

"Yes a Shamron," I persisted. "Remember what He, Himself, told you. 'He came that the world through him might be saved.'"

"Yews have no dealings with the Gentiles." He waved it away.

"No, but YahShua, the Messiah, did." He pondered my words moving his fingers on his short beard at each corner of his mouth. I knew I had intrigued him. "The world would include the Gentiles, I believe." I added as a second thought.

There was a flash of light through his dark sullen eyes, hope perhaps. He looked thoughtful.

I opened my mouth to ask the question I came to ask when a knock came on the door. Nakdimon got up slowly struggling to bring himself out of thought and went to it. There were two Temple Guards waiting not so patiently for him when it opened.

"Kayafa wishes to see your visitor." One of them informed him stiffly.

"When we are finished, "Nakdimon snapped.

"Now!" The guard shot back.

Nakdimon turned halfway around and looked at me. I saw the concern in his eyes, then the apology. I stood and came to the door.

"Shalom," I bowed to him.

"Blessing." He laid a shaky hand on my shoulder.

I had no idea what was going on here, but I could see how it had effected Nakdimon. I knew there was no way to avoid trouble without complying with Kayafa's wishes. Apparently, I was not the only one being watched.

I was shown into Kayafa's private Temple chamber by one of the guards. It was roomy with a fine table to entertain guests and his writing stand was large with many scrolls and several ink bowls. I saw no bed, but there was another door in the room of rich cedar and the room was scented with it.

Kayafa reclined on one of the lounges beside a table with a large basket of fresh fruit in the middle. He stood as I entered.

"Ah, …come, Timon." Kayafa gave me one of his deceitful smiles. "Take a lounge," he indicated with his hand, but he chose not to sit back down.

"I must admit," he watched me seat myself, "…I am quite surprised to see you here. I was sure at our last visit we had come to an understanding." He began to pace up and down the length of the table beside his lounge and chose his words carefully. "It is not an easy task to put to rest the heretic teaching of this deliverer. Of course, you understand the importance of letting it die, but there are those who still insist on seeking after this blasphemer." He opened his hand toward me. "This is foolish. The man was just another false Messiah and has paid the penalty for His sin. You know as well as I, the Man is dead." He stopped pacing and drew a long breath letting it out in a gush before taking up his strolling again. "So, also will those who

372

persist in keeping His demonic teachings alive. I do not suppose you have heard," he cast his hand in my direction, "...that Pilate has given the death penalty to such insurrectionists."

"I have heard he is reluctant to carry it out," I defied him.

"Well, you are wrong." He shot back at me.

He stopped, turned and studied my face for some reaction. I tried desperately to hide any. Not being good at such things, I prayed that I could succeed this time. His eyes drifted slowly from my face to the basket of fruit on the table. Then he turned abruptly and took up his stride.

His tone went back to its usual false pleasantness. "Because it is of a more religious nature, he was hesitant to crucify offenders." He showed patience. "He will soon relent when he sees these fools persist in causing trouble." He opened his hand toward me.

"I know this sounds like extreme measures, but I am sure you can see how dangerous to Israel it is for this teaching to continue. Elohim has given the cohanim the responsibility to keep the laws of Elohim pure and that is a task we do not take lightly. Anyone who is foolhardy enough to be found fighting against Elohim will pay the extreme penalty of the law."

He stopped as though thinking about what he was about to say and continued after a short pause. "I know, ...you are much too wise a man to be deceived by any of this, but asking questions about this matter only encourages the simple minded. Oh, I realize you mean no harm, but unfortunately there are those of the Council who might think differently. Unless you are ready to risk facing the Council I suggest you leave this matter to those qualified to deal with it."

"I see, ...therefore, you have suggested well." I appeased him.

"I thought you would understand once you were fully aware of the facts." He looked pleased. "Well, I will not detain you any further. Enjoy your stay in Yerushelayim."

Standing, I nodded, "Rabbi." I then turned to the door and went out.

I would have liked to continue my visit with Nakdimon, but in the circumstances I decided it was unwise. Already, Kayafa's was restricting my movements by spying. Maybe, I can find some freedom in BeitAnyah. I doubt that Kayafa will have me followed out of the city.

Out in the Courtyard Elsan was leaning against the chamber wall. He straightened himself as I came through the doorway and hurried to my side. His face was creased and solemn.

"Why did you not wait for me, Father?" He asked dryly.

"I thought you would prefer to see the sights of the Temple," I said absently. As we walked along my thoughts were upon Kayafa, who was determined to stomp out the teachings of YahShua. Fighting against Yah, what a laugh. He certainly is in for a surprise when he finds out that it is he and the Council who are fighting against Yah. It is they who, according to YahShua, will pay the supreme penalty. I did not understand why Yah was not revealing his Son openly. Why is the resurrection kept so secret?

"What did Master Nakdimon say?" Elsan broke into my thoughts. "Does he know where we might find YahShua and the disciples?"

"I did not get to ask him before Kayafa summoned me."

"The Cohen gadol? What did he want with you?"

"To warn me the Council will not hesitate to put the death penalty upon those who keep the teachings of YahShua and to let me know he is aware of my asking questions about Him."

"Put to death?" He looked at me with wide-eyed expression. "Does that mean we shall give up the search?"

"No. His hands are still tied for the time, but it will not take him long to find a way to get that authority. It means I am now aware of the price it may cost to keep looking. I have made my choice long ago. Elohim is doing something very wonderful and I want to be a part of it. I am not foolish though. What I do now will be very discrete." I looked at him. "You may return home if you like."

"No Father, I will stay with you."

"Then you too must understand the risk?"

"I understand." He nodded and then continued. "It is for my own sake I stay. I must know for myself about this Man who can change lives."

I smiled knowingly at him and knew YahShua, also, had affected his life, but did he believe now? Only time would tell that.

"Father?" Elsan spoke after some time. "Why does Elohim allow the sacrifices to continue if YahShua has brought in a New Covenant that does not require the blood of animals?"

"Why did He allow our forefathers to wander in Sinai for forty years after they refused to go into the land of Canaan?"

"Because he wants obedience, but He will not force it upon us. Obedience must be willing. Man is made in the image of Elohim, which means we have a will. Like the big stallions at home. You want them to perform without breaking their spirit. Without spirit they do not perform to the peak of the ability with which they are born. The idea is to direct their will not destroy it, thus they become valuable."

"How long will He allow this to continue?"

"Perhaps forty years." I shrugged.

"Why forty, Father?"

"It seems to have been proven in the past, the number of days or years allotted for decision before Elohim intervenes. Elohim does not administer punishment without giving man a space of time to repent. He is not unjust."

"What if they do not repent?"

"They will die or be destroyed. Elohim let a whole generation die in the wilderness because they refused to go

375

into Canaan. Remember I told you of the prophecy of YahShua that the city will be destroyed and her children with her."

"Yes Father, I remember." He replied thoughtfully and fell silent.

When we returned to the hostel Elsan and I, along with Semone and one of the young men, set out for BeitAnyah. It was only a short ride so we took no supplies.

The small town of BeitAnyah was nestled in the foothills of Mount Olive not far from the Garden of Gethsemane. For such a small farming area, its market place seemed overly crowded. A sea of humanity like waves moved up and down the open square. The few shops and merchants seemed to be thriving in the almost festive fervor that prevailed. Even a small camel caravan had just arrived at the far end of the street and was causing quite a stir. Music was coming from somewhere inside one of the shops and the smell of fruit and fresh baked goods added to the spirit charging the firmament.

In front of what appeared to be a small bakeshop, a merchant went about wrapping a loaf of bread for a customer who had chosen something from the display table just outside the door. The man who was wrapping his sale was short and with only a span of wild sprig like hair on his head just above his ears. His neatly trimmed beard seems a strange contrast giving him a rather humorous look.

Elsan began to concern himself with the sweet bread and pastries on the table. I smiled, remembering the look on Yered's face when we had visited the hostel where the Adonai took Posach with His disciples. However, I could not blame Elsan for his interest, as they did look good and it was near the sixth hour.

After the merchant received the price for the man's bread, he smiled up at me then his eye's fell away to look at Elsan. "Would you like to buy something?" He asked with an understanding twinkle in his eye.

"Yes," I answered for him. "Elsan," I touched his shoulder with the back of my hand, "...would like some sweet bread and I would like to know where I can find the house of Elazar."

He smiled taking up a loaf and beginning to wrap it. "He lives around the corner there and three houses down but if you are looking for the Adonai He is not there this day."

This day! 'He was here,' my heart shouted, but as soon as it came the emptiness of missing Him again entered. "Where is He?" I returned with little hope.

The man gave a friendly shrug holding out to Elsan the bread and replied. "It is very mysterious. He comes and goes without notice. That will be two mites."

Elsan paid the price, took the bread and I bowed slightly. Then we went back to where Semone waited by the cisium.

The press around us created an air of expectancy to match that which I had inside. YahShua might not be here this day but it was as though I could almost feel His closeness and I wondered if others could feel it also. Could that be why there were so many people here? Had they come to see YahShua? I must find Him.

"I will go see Elazar," I informed Semone and then turned to Elson.

He had just broken the bread and handed some of it to the servant boy still sitting astride one of the horses that pulls the carriage. The boy grinned and took the bread with a slight bow of his head.

"Do you want to go with me or would you like to stay here and look around?' I asked him.

"I will come with you, Father."

The house was of the common sort with a door against the street. After several attempts to raise someone we turned back for the cisium. A sense of confusion and loss over took me as we headed back for Yerushelayim. Elazar had gone under ground with the followers. Now what? Where shall I turn now? I had not spoken with Nicanor or Parmenas that morning and now I wondered how they had filled their day and if they had better success than we. Maybe the servants have heard something.

Entering Yerushelayim again, I wondered if I should look for the abandoned cistern but thought better of it. I would probably be watched. So, there was nothing to do but wait. Wait! I hated waiting, such a waste of time but there seemed no alternative. If I began to ask more questions I would be in trouble with the Council. This thought added to my distress and I gave a weary sigh. Would I ever find the other disciples? The answers to my questions weighed heavy upon my mind? If I do find the disciples will YahShua be with them? The burden of my search had worn me down and the short rest at home which I hoped would help, had not. By the time I entered my room I was so disheartened that I had to force the lump in my throat back down several times.

"Benren," I said unto him dryly, "...see if Nicanor or Parmenas will take meat with me and Elsan this evening."

"Yes my lord."

"I do not want to be disturbed until then, unless there is news of the followers. I wish to meditate and make prayers." Benren nodded and then I added hopefully. "The servants have heard no rumors of YahShua or the disciples?"

"No, my lord."

A breeze was cooling the rooftop as we sat down to meat driving away the heat that remained after the lowering of the blazing sun. Soft voices from the streets drifted up to us as the throng that filled the market place began to disburse. The city was settling down for the night. Evening was always my favorite time of day. Man and even nature began to cease from its labor.

Parmenas and Nicanor arrived and by their expressions I could tell they had not found out anything of importance. I had just begun telling them about my visit to the Temple and Kayafa's summons when Elsan joined us, and the servants began to serve our meal. The good company helped make the meal pleasant and the weariness of the day melted away slowly.

After supper Parmenas announced that he and Nicanor were going again to see if they could find the dry cistern and Elsan decided he would go once more to Mount of Olives and search there again. There was nothing I could do and that did not set well with me. I could go to my room and study the Sacred Writings but my heart was not in it so I had another cup of wine and watched the stars bring out their light and speckle the blackness of the sky.

"I always marvel at the work of Elohim's hand." A voice spoke behind me. It was deep and coarse, but very familiar. The suddenness of the words made my heart jump slightly, but when I recognized the voice I relaxed.

"BarAbbas, you have a way of turning up at the most unexpected times." I complained lightly but did not turn to look at him.

"That is how I survive, my friend." His presence came from the shadows of the night and he seated himself in one of the chairs. "Do you have any more wine?"

"I will bring some my lord," Benren's voice answered from nearby and his steps faded away.

"I heard you were in Yerushelayim." I said to BarAbbas.

"I heard you were still looking for the followers of YahShua." BarAbbas countered.

"Yes. I suppose BarArni told you I was here."

"I knew before you went to see BarArni. I have eyes everywhere."

"Everywhere?"

"Yes." He smiled sheepishly and tossed me a glance. "We are about two thousand strong now and we are planning an attack on the palace soon. We have become a force to deal with."

"You will only succeed in getting many young men killed," I shot back angered at his lack of discernment. "...And bringing the wrath of the Caesars down upon our heads. You stand no chance against the Romans."

He did not choose to reply, but sat quietly looking at me in the darkness. "How is that miserable Roman Centurion?" BarAbbas ask, but without bitterness. I knew the question was meant to turn the tide of conversation away from his plan, but there was almost a concern in it also. I wondered if he had a change of heart toward Appolious or if the concern was for his men.

Benren came with the wine and he drank deeply of it, then held out the cup for more. Benren filled it again and I studied BarAbbas's features. Deep shadows hid his eyes and his expression was masked by the darkness, but there seemed to be something about him, I could not determine. Maybe it was his manner, maybe something else, but he seemed less defensive and more controlled.

"There were some disciples in the cave tombs this day visiting with the followers hiding there." He looked at me now and held up his wine cup in somewhat of a salute.

I flicked my hand in acknowledgment, but his words were what interested me. "Then, perhaps, you may have heard where they will meet next. I would like to go. Was YahShua there?"

"YahShua," he laughed. "Friend, YahShua is dead and His disciples will have their share of it as well if they live by what they teach."

"What do you mean?" I frowned at him a little irritated at his mockery. He was behaving more like BarAbbas now.

"Why do you not know? They are going to change the world by turning the other cheek and praying for those who despitefully use them." He scoffed swinging his wine cup away from him in a light jester. Drawing it back quickly, he drank down its contents and held it out again in expectation. Benren accommodated him without hesitation.

"Fools," he growled. "They refuse to join me and continue to preach love, ...even for the Romans. I have nothing against love, you understand, but love will not conquer, and unless we act, the Romans will keep us in bonds until there is no true Israelite left to stand for Elohim.

Even you, yourself, have seen how they have influenced the Council and controlled the cohanim."

"You are wrong BarAbbas. It is the Council that is behind the happening, not the Romans." I insisted. "Only this day did Kayafa make it clear to me that he planned to obtained authority to stone those whom Pilate has been reluctant to punish, because of religious matters. It was not the Romans who cried for the death of YahShua. It was the leaders of Israel. It is not the Romans who are bringing the followers to Pilate, it is the cohanim and Prushim, ...namely one Shaul of Tarsus."

BarAbbas jumped up quickly, "What are you, a traitor? Speaking against Israel as you have."

"No, BarAbbas, I am not! But neither am I blind." I stood to face him feeling at a disadvantage sitting down. "I do not like our country controlled by Gentiles any more than you, but I know the sin that lies at our own door."

"Sin can be covered by sacrifice," he stormed, waving his cup aimlessly, "but, the Romans must be driven out, and it will take blood to do that."

"Yes, the blood of YahShua not the blood of men," I shouted back at him.

"You sound like the disciples. Are you one of them?"

"I wish I were."

He opened his mouth to say something else but closed it after a short pause. Turning abruptly, he shoved his cup toward Benren and waited impatiently for him to fill it again.

"We are arguing again," he finally said, his voice under control, watching the dark liquid pour into the cup.

"We are men of different views," I reminded him at a normal tone.

"But friends?" He held his cup up to mine touching it lightly.

"Yes," I nodded, "...friends."

His white teeth flashed in the dark and he drank the wine. Setting the cup down hard on the table, he turned into the shadows and was gone.

I took a deep breath and let it out slowly. He was headstrong and obnoxious but, ...I knew he would die for me, just as he will for Israel someday and that made me sad. I remembered our first encounter and smiled at the thought of it. Then my mind took me to the hidden room beneath the inn where I had angered him until he hit me with his fist. Ours is indeed a strange friendship.

"Do you want more wine?" Benren asked softly.

"No. I will finish this and go to my room."

"Very well."

Suddenly, there was a commotion below in the street. There were shouts of men and the sound of clashing metal. When I went to the rampart and looked down two soldiers were getting to their feet. Others stood as in a state of confusion while two others were chasing a figure in a dark robe down the street. Then the others regained themselves and hurried off in the direction of the chase. I held my breath and watched until they were out of sight. I knew in reason it was BarAbbas they were chasing and I prayed he would escape.

DAY THIRTY FOUR

A Man in dazzling apparel stood before me the brightness of Him made me hide my eyes. He spoke no words but I knew his intent. Looking with great effort behind Him, I could see many women and children. He opened His arms to them as though to show them to me. My heart reached out to them then, as they looked at me with expectation.

Suddenly, the scene was jerked away into darkness and I opened my eyes. I was lying upon my bed and there was a confusion of voices outside my door. Then with a loud thump it sprang open and four Roman soldiers entered, upon much protest by Benren. His effort ignored, he was swept aside in annoyance by the strong arm of one of the soldiers. I sat up wide eyed and my heart jumped, as two of the guards came near, taking off as a stalled horse racing wildly. I opened my mouth to speak but no words came out and then I was being drug out of bed, one soldier on each arm.

Before I could loose my tongue to protest I was being propelled toward the door in a rude ruthless manner. I heard some strange shaky voice demanding to know what was happening, in the same words that were in my mind, but they seemed to fall on deaf ears. In my nightdress with no shoes upon my feet I was being unceremoniously half dragged and half carried from the hostel. I heard Benren's voice somewhere making protest and I was then aware of faces, many faces, some frightened, some sad, some astonished, others gawking. Buildings drifted past me in slow process and I could feel the iron grip of the soldiers on each upper arm. My feet finally found the cold stone street and it sent a chill through me. I could feel myself shaking. Was it caused by the coldness of the street or fear? Where were they taking me and why?

"Oh Yah!" I cried out within or was it? Had I spoken it? The early morning throngs with low murmurs and curses were parted for us by one of the other soldiers.

We went up a long set of steps, through a gate, a large enclosure where many glaring soldiers jeered and laughed upon our passing and on into a large cold room.

As my eyes adjusted to the darkness of the room I became aware of a raised judgment seat against the back wall. It was made of stone and the tall backrest was inlaid with colored tile. On either side of the raised platform, upon which the seat stood, was two huge braziers of brass on individual stands, heat burned bright with leaping tongues of fire. The eerie shadows they cast on the walls, seat and floor seemed to dance like ghosts to an unheard tune. Column archways ran the length of the room on each side. Beyond the ones on the right were several doors and on the other side the light of the morning sun gave a golden cast to a covered porch.

Brought to a rough halt in the middle of a polished red tile floor bearing the seal of Rome in white. The two soldiers released me and my knees almost gave under me. I was trembling and felt my stomach lurch. Now, I realized that only the strength of the two soldiers had kept me from succumbing to the fear that gripped me, turning my attempt to breath and walk into painful labor.

Someone moved softly to my left and I jerked my head to see a man in a white Roman tunic with gold embroidered trim. His sandals of leather were laced to the knee with gold cords. Around his neck on a thick gold chain was a large amulet, like a giant golden coin with the inscription of Caesar. Other chains of gold complemented the larger one and added an impressive value to the otherwise bland garment. Sneering cruel lips curled upward in a mock smile and accented a brown chiseled face crowned with short forward combed light hair. I met the cold demanding stare of shadowed eyes and my already weak knees trembled threatening to deposit me in a heap at his feet.

384

Pilate! "Oh Yah!" I cried out from my inner being.

"So," an angry voice came from him, but his mouth hardly moved, "...what have we here?" He came closer to examine me further with piercing green eyes. "A zealot?"

My mouth had dried up like a pool beneath the sun and when I opened it to deny, not a sound would come forth.

Pilate waited. Then turning impatiently to the soldiers. "Take him away," he commanded with a wave of his hand.

I closed my eyes, swallowed with much difficulty and drew strength from the tiny seed of will power that had grown inside of me and with it a spark of courage.

"I am not a zealot." I managed with surprising sharpness as the soldiers laid their hands upon me.

Quickly, Pilate raised his hand, the soldiers stopped and he flicked them away with his fingers.

From somewhere deep inside strength began to grow, very small, very comforting.

"So you do talk?" He studied me a degree. "If you are not a zealot," he turned away from me, "...then what are you?"

"A follower of the blasphemer." A cold familiar voice spoke from the shadowy columns from where Pilate had just come. Kayafa moved into the light of the braziers, "That is my jurisdiction, I believe." He smiled at me with contempt.

"You have no jurisdiction!" Pilate turned on him venomously. "Remember that." Then he motioned toward Kayafa and said to one of the soldiers. "Show him out."

Kayafa seemed not the least bit perturbed by Pilate's outburst. He just gave him a smug smile, bowed slightly and said, "Shalom friend."

Pilate whirled about and took a few steps toward the raised platform, stopped abruptly and turned back to me.

While the confrontation between the two powerful men had taken place I had time to gather my wits and draw from the courage, as small as it was.

"Do you know the man BarAbbas?" He said unto me in a controlled voice.

"Ye, …yes," I bobbed my head slightly. Realizing I had to do better than that, I struggled to find words. "Who does not?" I opened my hand to him.

"Where is he?"

"How should I know?" I replied weakly.

"Last night I almost had him in my grasp." He clenched his fist tightly together in front of him as though he might cause BarAbbas some pain by doing so, and glared at it with pure hatred. "…But the fool soldiers let him slip through their fingers again. He is a slimy serpent." He let the words slither out.

BarAbbas had not been caught. I breathed a silent sigh of relief.

Releasing his fist now he shot hot arrows at me. "He came from the hostel where you were taking meat on the roof. If you are not a zealot what was he doing there?"

The words of his accusation pounded in my ears with the same violence as that of the beating of my heart. What could I say? I could not betray BarAbbas to this Roman, but dare I lie? Either way I am condemned. The reality of the situation dawned on me and shook me to the core. Then the scene at Mount Calvary appeared before me, the cry of agony, the breaking of bones. Yah help me! I felt the spark of courage going out.

"Well!" Pilate demanded sharply.

"Is, …is it my fault he was at the hostel?" I fumbled. "Do I direct his actions? I did not invite him there."

"He came to you while you were taking meat on the roof." Pilate pointed at me.

"No," I shook my head.

BarAbbas came well after we had finished the meal. That was no lie. Elsan, Parmenas and Nicanor had already gone.

"Did you see him?" Pilate demanded angrily.

"Yes," I found courage to say. "He was in the street with your soldiers. I saw him escape."

"You saw him escape." Pilate repeated spitefully. "Where were you?"

"On the roof." I tried to steady my voice.

"What were you doing on the roof?"

"Having a cup of wine in the cool breeze before I retired to my room. I heard the turmoil in the street and when I went to the rampart I saw the soldiers chasing him."

"He was not on the roof with you while you took meat?" He spit at me.

"No." I returned stiffly, some courage coming again. I was so thankful he had worded his question so I would have a true answer.

"You lie!" His eyes blazed at me.

"I do not lie," I shot back with surprising aggressiveness.

He turned and looked away out to the balcony, where the sun cast yellow light on the stone floor.

"Are you a follower the so called Messiah?" He demanded to know without looking at me.

"I am a husbandman." I informed flatly, my voice still a little shaky.

"A husbandman," he repeated sarcastically. "Of what?"

"Horses, ...horses for your chariots."

He turned now and surveyed me a little in disbelief, his eyes flowing over me. Following his gaze I looked down at myself. I did not blame him for his doubts. There I stood in my night cloths, no shoes and hair undone. I looked more like a beggar than anything else. I felt very foolish at that degree. Summoning what little courage I could find, I raised my eyes and looked into his.

"My name is Timon-bar-Philorah of Beitorah on the slopes of Mount Tabor," I began weakly, "...and I would apologize for my appearance, however, your soldiers have made that unnecessary."

Slowly, as I spoke a plan began to form in my mind. It was not much of one but it might turn the tide of events. With the plan, my confidence built and now the quaking stopped.

"I wish we could have met under more desirable circumstances but, unfortunately that did not happen. I would have liked to have presented you one of my finest stallions as a gift. Now, I can only hope to have it brought from the hostel stable by one of your guards for your inspection."

He looked at me a degree, blinked thoughtfully and sighed. "Very well, I will send for it."

"Tell my servant I have sent him for a horse."

Hopefully, my gift will appease and he will believe my story. Benren will send my personal mount thinking it is for me. He is by far the best with me and a fine animal. Pilate should find no fault with him.

"Why are you in Yerushelayim?" Pilate brought me from my thoughts after having spoken to one of the guards.

How shall I answer him? To tell him I am looking for YahShua and the disciples would be as condemning as telling him I am a friend of BarAbbas. Well, almost as condemning. No follower has been put to death yet, but if what Kayafa said was true it will only be a matter of time. Perhaps, Yah will help me just this once more.

"I came to seek the truth." I answered.

"About what?"

"YahShua." I returned without hesitation and with remarkable calm.

"Then you are a follower of this man?"

"First one must know what they are following to be a follower."

"And, this is what you seek to know?"

"Yes."

"How do you propose to do that? The man is dead."

"The disciples say He is not."

"They lie. One does not rise from the dead, and I know He is dead. His disciples have stolen his body out of its tomb to make people believe that."

These were the words of Kayafa, and I could see the sway he had over this man. "Why should His disciples lie?"

"To keep His teachings alive."

"Or, …they tell the truth." I challenged very simply. "Israel's Elohim is the Elohim of impossibilities. Surely you know our history."

"Fables," he pointed out.

"To you perhaps, but to me it is truth."

"Truth," he scoffed and waved me away. "What is truth?"

"Truth is the cornerstone upon which a man builds his life."

He snorted crudely, "Truth!"

He swung about and looked back outside. There was a short silence then he turned back at me quickly.

"Truth? You seek truth? Well, here is truth. An evil man found guilty of murder was freed while an innocent Man died. What truth did the people of Israel seek that day? What was His crime that made Him so dangerous and worthy of death? The truth, …none! Yet, they called for His death and I had to wash my hands of His innocent blood, while this murderer torments me even now. Furthermore, the followers of this Messiah persist in keeping a bleeding wound open."

Suddenly, I was seeing Pilate the man, not the procreator. A man torn with grief and bitter at the injustice of the people. His reluctance to carry out the death penalty on the followers of YahShua spoke of a man with firmness. But, his position is his life and as such, he must make compensations that do not set well with him. Power has its own hell, I marveled. I did not envy him. He is as much a victim as is this nation. This man is not my enemy only his position and power. If only BarAbbas could see it.

"Truth is what each man makes it," he was saying. "What truth do you seek? That the dead lives? And, if this is true, of what value is it to a people that does not want truth? Why seek a truth with no value?"

He fell silent now and stared at the floor in deep thought, a troubled look upon his face.

"Truth is truth," I opened my hand toward him. "It cannot be defiled by man. It is what man does with truth that makes the wrongs. If it is truth that Elohim raised YahShua from the dead, that truth will stand no matter what man chooses to do with it. YahShua was innocent, that truth stands and what people want to make of it does not change it."

His eyes gave no light as to his thought, but a slight smile flashed across his lips before fading into the stiff line that is the door to the sanctuary behind which the man lives.

Shortly, the soldier returned with the horse and though Pilate did not make much of it, I could see he was pleased with the gift. I was brought a robe and then released with little ado. This surprised me in the fact that I had confessed to him that I was seeking YahShua and the disciples. However, the Council would have to be the one to bring charges against me, as it is a religious matter. That is very likely the reason he released me in spite of the efforts of Kayafa to prove me a zealot. I am sure he was behind this whole matter. Nevertheless I will not prolong my stay in Yerushelayim more than I have to.

Elsan and the servants were waiting at the hostel anxious about me and wanted to find out what happened. Still a little unnerved, I told them the story and how Pilate had opened up to me. While I was in the midst of that, Parmenas and Nicanor too had come to find out what had happened for the whole hostel was talking about it. After rehearsing it again for their benefit they told me their news. They had finally found the dry cistern and were waiting nightfall to go see if there would be a meeting taking place. We talked of the death of YahShua and it's purpose. About the resurrection and what possible purpose it held.

Eventually, I was left alone and took some time to thank Yah for delivering me from Pilate's hands, and to ask forgiveness for not being completely truthful by omission.

It was still morning I reasoned and after we take meat at the sixth hour, we shall go to BeitAnyah once again to seek YahShua and the disciples. There I will stay until nightfall then slip back into Yerushelayim and go with Parmenas and Nicanor to the cistern.

Until now, I had little time to meditate upon the dream I was having when the soldiers came to take me. There was the man clothed in a light. I could not see his face, but I was sure he was an angel. But, what of the women and children who looked at me with expecting eyes? What was I to give them or do for them? It was something Yah was asking of me, but what? Then the prophecy of Micah came to mind. Had he not told me the same thing? I would care for women and children. Where? Why?

"Elohim," I moaned. "I just find a little peace in one place and a hundred more questions in another. When will it all end?"

My thoughts were disrupted sharply by loud angry voices in the hall outside my door. Upon opening it I saw Elsan with his sword out holding at bay two Temple guards. They had drawn their weapons also and were on the verge to do battle.

"What is this?" I demanded.

"Are you Timon-bar-Philorah?" One of the guards demanded to know.

"Yes, I am he."

"Your presence is required at the Council of Elders." The guard informed sternly.

"Do not go with them, Father." Elsan shot me a quick glance still holding his position. "You have done nothing wrong."

"And, you will slay them both where they stand? Their blood not dry before the Romans march you off to the 'Place of the Skull' to face the tree as a murderer? No thank you. I will go with them."

"But..." Elsan started to argue.

"I will have no blood shed because of me." I retorted sharply. "Put away your weapons."

Well, now I knew. Kayafa had brought the charges, and now I would stand before the Council. He was determined to rid himself of me. He knew, as well as I, there would be no end to my search until I had satisfied the desire that drove me. Oh, what did I expect? I knew the price, and now I must pay. I sighed and wondered at the peace that I maintained.

"If you will allow me to get my robe, I will go with you." I told the soldier who had been doing the talking.

I retrieved my robe from the bed where Benren had laid it and went back into the hall. The soldiers still with weapons drawn stood waiting. Then Eason who had dropped his guard turned and stood looking at me with deep lines in his face. His eyes moistened and he blinked away the hurt in them, replacing it with a determined look. I suppose he read the pain in my heart, as I looked with much love upon my son. A lump formed in my throat and such a helpless feeling flooded over me. I knew this would undoubtedly be the last time to see his youthful face with that stubborn lock of hair that always seemed to be hanging down on his forehead. I could do nothing but gather him into my arms and hug him to my breast. I felt his strong muscles strain under my hold and I knew he was trying hard to keep his composure.

Then my gaze, over Elsan's shoulder, fell upon faithful Benren standing behind the two guards. When our eyes met he looked down at the floor and swallowed hard. Semone stood near him and comforted him with a soft touch on his arm.

I searched deeply for the courage to turn away. Finally, I released Elsan and looked lovingly into his mournful eyes.

"No matter what happens, you must not act foolishly." I counseled with a wavering voice. "It will be up to you to see to the servants and take care of things here. Use wisdom in whatsoever you do, and do not act hastily."

His lip trembled slightly and I thought he would reply, but he just nodded his head. I knew if I did not go now, they would have to drag me away. Forcing myself to look away, I turned slowly and went with them.

The Council chamber was not empty this time. The sets on both sides of the balusters were occupied with Prushim, Tzdukim, scribes and cohanim. All were aged men, ...some with heavy beards while others were short and well groomed. All were elders who showed the wisdom of years in their faces. They stared at me as I was ushered into the middle of the room to stand before the cynical eyes of Kayafa. He sat upon the judgment seat like a king on a throne, glowering down at me with satisfaction. A slight smile curled his tight lips and he silenced the soft murmur that rippled through the elders with a raised hand. When all was quiet, he raised his voice so all could hear.

"What is you name?"

"Timon-bar-Philorah of Beitorah." I managed to say with a voice much calmer than I really felt.

"You have been summoned here to answer questions concerning charges of blasphemy," he informed dryly. "I have appointed an elder to represent you. If you have any objections to my choice, it is your right to choose another."

I grimaced as Alexander stood for my approval. Kayafa was shrewd and had chosen a man he knew I would object to, so I would have to select another. The only other person in the room I knew I could rely on was Nakdimon. However, if I chose him to represent me, being a just man, he would do so at his own detriment and we might both be found guilty, which I am sure Kayafa is counting on.

A sick feeling gripped my stomach, and my heart pounded angrily in my ears. I swallowed quickly several times trying to get a grip on myself.

"Yah help me!" I begged inside. "Do not let my enemy triumph over me."

I glanced around the room. Surely, there was someone I could pick other than Nakdimon. Most of the eyes of the elders were hard, cold or in different. It seemed that the decision had already been made in most of their minds. Kayafa had woven his web well. I was ready to give up and let things stand. There was no reason to put Nakdimon in a dangerous position and let Kayafa try to catch him in his speech. Then my eyes fell upon the soft lines of a compassionate face and I pointed at him with a shaky finger.

"I choose this man to represent me." I determined, forcing the words through my tight dry throat.

He stood slowly his lips curled up slightly at the corners and then nodded at Kayafa in acceptance. Kayafa's eyes narrowed slightly, but he waved the man forward to take the first seat beside him on the right and Alexander relinquished the position shooting hot daggers at me with his dark eyes. However, Kayafa quickly released his eyebrows and looked confident.

"Let it be recognized that Elhizhar has been chosen to represent Timon-bar-Philorah." Then he turned his attention to me. "What is your business in Yerushelayim?"

The trembling in the midst of my bowels began to spread and soon my legs shook beneath me. I felt my face burn with the rush of heat as every eye was upon me waiting expectantly.

Somehow I knew I would not get off easy this time. If I told my reason for being here, it would be just what Kayafa wanted to hear, but making up a lie would probably not work either. The thing about lies is, that it takes many to prop up one and inevitably it would become obvious. It would have to be the truth or nothing and the truth would condemn me to the stoning pit. As I stood there looking back at the wondering eyes all around me struggling to deal with the idea of the stoning. I swallowed hard, the moisture in my mouth being thick and my throat paralyzed with fear.

"I, …ah, I am seeking the truth." I finally managed with much difficulty.

"The truth about what?" Kayafa asked with amusement using precise movement to place his fingertips together.

The smug serpent thinks he has me. Well, …maybe he has, but I will not give him the satisfaction, also, of making me look like a fool. Anger began to replace the fear, and I felt my face harden and the embarrassment began to drain away. From somewhere in my inner man an amazing transformation began to take effect. Like a creature knowing there is no hope, I threw caution to the wind. I found courage somewhere, and my head came up defiantly to look into his mocking cold eyes.

"About the Messiah, YahShua the Messiah." I answered with such a calm voice that I surprised myself.

Kayafa raised an eyebrow and a small murmur fluttered through the elders.

"YahShua of Natzeret was not the Messiah of Israel, nor is he the son of Elohim." He gestured, opening his hands. "Everyone here knows that." He tossed his arm in a circle around the room.

"But, what if He is?" I shot back with anger showing in my words. "He has fulfilled many of the prophecies."

"If He was the Messiah," Alexander–bar-David came to his feet, "…do you not think we who hold the laws of Moshe would know. How dare you…"

"You do not have to defend the action of this Council." Kayafa stopped him with a sharp rebuke, holding up his hand. "Ignorance is a fools folly."

"Yes, and the blind leading the blind all fall into the ditch together," I returned amazed at my own tongue.

The court erupted into a storm of voices making jeers and shouting curses at me. I knew I had just sealed my own doom, but somehow I was oblivious to it. It did not seem to matter anymore and I wondered if they would take me out immediately and stone me. It took Kayafa some time to silence the outburst and regain a measure of order again. When he had eventually obtained relative quiet, his lips curled up into a cynical smile.

Now, I cursed myself also, realizing I had played into his hands and had in effect condemned myself with my own mouth.

Elhizhar then stood up. All eyes turning to him and there was a deathly silence that lasted only a short time, but seemed to go on for eternity. When he spoke his voice was soft but with authority and distinct.

"There is no law that I am aware of that says a man can not disagree with the decision of this court. This court is not on trial here so let us get to the matter at hand."

This statement was directed at me as much as it was to the elders and I recognized the truth in what the man was saying. Obviously, so did Kayafa for he now turned to me.

"Are you a follower of so called Messiah of Natzeret?' He demanded to know.

"You first must know what you are following to be a follower." I offered without hesitation.

"Why are you seeking the disciples of this Natzerene?" He persisted.

"To find the truth."

"To find them, to hear the teachings of this blasphemer and become a believer?" He insisted.

"No," I shouted. "Just to…"

"You are already a believer then?"

I could not deny the fact that I believed in Him. The love I held for the Man burned in my heart. I realized to deny Him would be a fate worse than death. I would be found against Yah, His will and the purpose for giving His Son as sacrifice for sin and I, myself, would be as guilty of His death as they were.

"I…" My words faltered. "Yes, I believe in Him."

The words burst forth in me and my heart flooded with joy. He was the Messiah and my heart sang the song. Words tumbling into my mind, the words of those who sang the song of victory under my window that night, and my song joined theirs and I suppressed a shout of delight.

"Do you believe He is the Son of Elohim as He claimed?" Kayafa thundered at me.

"Yes, I believe," I shouted. "I believe!"

There was instant chaos, everyone tried to talk, shout, curse and revile at the same time and I did not even care. I could only feel the sweet presence of the Man, YahShua, and it flooded every fiber of my being until their angry words were as the song of angels. If their words had been stones, I would not have felt their pain. I just stood there and watched Kayafa try in vain to bring order, but they would have none of it. Finally, he seated himself and sat staring at me with a merciless expression. Even that did not quench the fire of praise that burned in my heart. He had gained my condemnation, but I had gained the victory and the thought of that brought a pleased smile to my lips.

At that Kayafa stood, like an arrow shot from a bow and made another attempt to quiet the uproar. This time he was able to bring a measure of quiet. Then he silenced the others as he began to address the elders.

"By this man's own admission he has confirmed his blasphemy by seeking the Man who clamed to be the son of Elohim and His evil teachings. Need we hear any more?"

A low rumble went through the elders and some heads were shaking while accusing eyes shot daggers at me. Kayafa held his hand up and waited for silence again.
"Not to be accused of being unrighteous, I will ask for the witness to be brought before the Council so we can hear him."

He signaled the Temple guards standing beside the side door and one opened it while the other went out. Shortly, He reappeared and at his side walked BarArni looking pale faced, lips pressed into a hard line. Whose two large eyes glanced around the room and then came to rest upon me. There was something in them, maybe, an apology but I was not sure. Then his eyes darted to Kayafa setting with ease now in the judgment seat.

"Your name is BarArni and you are a thief by profession, is that not true?" Kayafa asked snidely.

He shifted his weight and answered with a shy nod of his head, dropping his eyes to the floor.

"Do you know this man?" Kayafa pointed to me.

BarArni turned slightly and looked at me with a strained face, fear in his eyes. He nodded again but refused to let his eyes meet mine fixing them on my garment.
He was a pitiful looking man who was as much a victim of Kayafa as was I. Suddenly, I felt sorry for him and wanted to let him know I was not upset at what he was about to do. He was probably trying to keep from going before Pilate for some act of thievery or for being a zealot.

"How do you know him?" Kayafa called back his attention.

"He found me in the tabernae and wanted me to take him into the tomb caves to meet some disciples that were staying there."

"Did you do this?"

"Yes, but the disciples had already left there. I did not know it."

"Was that the only time you met this man?"

"No. He came again to ask me to find out where the disciples were to meet with the followers."

"Did you give him that information?"

"No. I did not know and could not find out."

"Do you swear before Elohim this is true?"

"Yes. I swear. It is all true."

"Elhizhar, do you have any questions for the witness?" He opened his hand toward him causally.

Elhizhar slowly lifted himself from his seat and looked at the Council of Elders. Then his gaze slid to my face, held a degree and then went quickly to BarArni.

"There is no use in these questions. What this man may know is of little importance. I am sure a vote would be more in the interest of this court."

"Well put." Kayafa waved away the guard holding BarArni. "Take the witness out." When the door was closed

398

behind them Kayafa turned again to the Council. "Those of the Council who find the charges against Timon-bar-Philorah to be accurate and wish to vote guilty signal by the raising of a hand."

It was so quiet while the count was made that the breath of life that flows through my nostrils could be heard. While this group of men was deciding my fate I stood with such a deep peace that I found the seriousness of this misguided Council almost laughable. Kayafa was right about one thing, "Ignorance is a fools folly." Men do unusual things under such circumstances and all I could do was stand there and suppress a desire to laugh at their folly, with the praise to the Adonai in my heart.

"...Take him away." I heard the last part of what Kayafa had just said, but I knew the result without having to hear it.

Now, I could contain no longer and burst forth with praise and worship. Two guards led me from the Council House of the Sanhedrin. Two others joining them outside and took me along the Temple wall.

"Father?" Elsan's voice reached my ears and then he was there trying to get near me, but one of the guards shoved him back. I strained to turn to see him, but the guards who held my arms jerked me back around and into step. The remaining joy was suddenly jerked away and replaced with the pain of great loss.

"Elsan, look after your mother and the family. You are the head of the house now." I called to him and felt the tears cool my cheek. "Tell them not to worry. I am in Elohim's hands." I choked.

He ceased his struggle to get near me, and stood watching them lead me away through a gate and onto the Royal Porch. I was quickly taken along the back wall of the Temple porch and into the Fortress of Antonia.

The two soldiers roughly shoved me through a door where another soldier stood waiting. When I was inside the third guard closed door with a loud clang sliding iron bar into place. This was a small room bare of any furnishings except for a stone bench built into the west wall.

"Remove your garments down to your loin cloth." Shoving me by the shoulder one of the soldiers shouted.

"I demand an audience with Pilate." I returned, gaining my balance. "You have no right to hold me like this."

The soldier moved quickly and I only saw the slicing hand out of the corner of my eye before I felt the stinging blow that jerked my head violently to one side. "You are a prisoner of Rome," he said between clenched teeth. "Say it!"

I blinked at him still shaken from the blow. I had done nothing to deserve this violent act. What was happening to me? I did not understand.

"Say it, fool!" The soldier drew back his hand again.

The low aching throb in my cheek raced to my thoughts now and I flinched at his raised threat. "I am a prisoner of Rome!" I stammered.

"I have no rights!" He coached.

"I have no rights." I heard myself repeat and felt sickly isolated. Helplessness overtook me, the reality of my situation slammed into my mind with a violent force with a blow greater than any fist could inflict.

"I will not speak unless spoken to." He continued with a strong voice.

I swallowed hard, but no longer feared the fist. A greater fear had taken hold of me. I was cut off. I had lost all. Not just my rights, but freedom and worst of all my family. "Oh Yah!" I groaned inside, but with my mouth I was saying the words I had just heard.

"Now, get your things off," he snapped, lowering his hand.

I moved to do as he instructed, but my body sluggishly responded to my mental commands as though I had little control over my actions.

"Quickly now!" The other soldier prodded me with the end of his whip.

Stripped to my loincloth, the next thing I knew I was descending narrow winding stairs, one guard in front of me, and the other with the whip behind me. The stairs were lit by torches fastened in a hole in the wall just above our head. Below was a floor laid in irregular shaped sandstone. The round stairway ended at this floor in a small room, most of which was a holding cell, with several men and women in it. A woman's scream came from behind a heavy wooden door and the other women began to weep softly and whisper the name of YahShua. They called for mercy and spoke words of forgiveness.

Suddenly, the sound of sliding metal drew my attention and then I felt myself being jerked into a dark narrow hall with an iron bar doorway. In the dark hall were was a step-down. Now a familiar song began in the cell behind me. Just as the followers beneath my window, it began weakly but grew in power. They were singing a song of victory, prisoners of Rome facing the tree or the stoning. Yah, where does such courage come from?

As I was escorted down the hall, the air was thick and musty, but the worst part was the song of victory was swallowed up by the sad mournful sounds of misery and despair that drown out the singing. Both male and female voices raised in a choral of weeping and wailing. In another room, this one large, with prisoners hanging around the wall by shackles. They had no garments to cover their extremities and stood in their own waste. The stench in this place was sickening. Some slumped with bent heads supported by their chains while others watched with round staring eyes. One slumped man moved slightly and a light groan escaped his lips. I could not believe the human misery I was seeing before my eyes.

"Move on!" The gruff voice of the guard with the whip commanded, and I was shoved toward another heavy iron door with a small barred window in it. Beyond the door was a hall, one to the right hand and one to the left, lined with more iron doors. In front of one of the doors on the left the soldier in front of me stopped, lifted a heavy iron bar hinged by a coupling on the left side. It swung upward as the soldier's strength demanded and held in place. A high pitch squeak came from the door as he pulled it open with much effort. He then turned, caught my arm, and thrust me forward through the door. It was extremely dark and I raised my hand to my eyes blinked several times. The door behind me slammed shut with a loud bang. That sound echoing through me like thunder through a mountain valley its judgment final.

The only light in here came from a narrow bar-like slits fixed into the high ceiling on one side of this large stone room. Then I began to make out the forms of many people, and the faint sound of trickling water some where near by.

Huddled close together against the back wall was a group of people. Women sat in a little cluster nearest the wall looking at me with wide, frightened eyes while others clung to men, hiding behind them. The men wore dirty loincloths and the women short tunics tied with ropes around the waist. No one moved or made a sound. Every eye was upon me.

The sound of water seemed to grow louder and drew my attention away from the little throng. A hole in the wall not much bigger than a man's finger shot forth a small stream of water that splashed into a trench in the floor. The trench was about a span wide and it ran the whole length of the right wall disappearing into another hole on the other side of the room.

Out of the corner of my eye I caught a glimpse of a rat scurrying along the wall. It stopped, raised upon its hind legs, sniffed the air and then dashed into the hole where the water leaves.

There was nothing else in the room except the smell of mildew and dampness. My trembling legs grew weaker and threatened not to hold me. Then someone moved in the small group. I felt them more than heard them. Quickly, my eyes jerked to see a man get up with slow motions and come toward me.

"Do not be afraid, friend. We will not hurt you. We are prisoners also." His voice was soft and filled with compassion. "I am Yaakov." He informed with a weak smile.

He was not much older the Elsan with matted hair and a short straggly beard. His face was distorted and swollen, one eye almost closed, but he had pleasantness about him. My eyes left his face and I looked beyond him to the others.

"Come on over," he answered my look, "...and meet the rest."

I wanted to go with him, but my limbs seemed like tree roots and held me in place, shaky as they were. It all seemed so unreal. This just was not happening. Yet, the tremors inside me told me that it was indeed happening even if my mind refused to accept it. Yaakov must have understood what I was feeling, for he gave a warm smile that twisted somewhat because of the swelling.

"It is all right," he reassured me taking my arm gently. "We are all the same here. You need not be afraid."

Now he drew me along with him and for some reason I was loosed and went. There were about twenty of them. I scarcely heard their names for my mind was still numbed by it all. A few weak smiles here and there behind straggly beards and frightened hollow eyed acknowledge me. Pale faced women nodded shyly as my eyes followed Yaakov's introduction. In their stares I saw my own confusion and fear. Then a strong oneness flooded over me as I realized I was one of them and it brought a strange calm.

Yaakov went to take his place against the wall and I was left standing alone. Sitting down, he pulled his knees up and rested his arms across the top of them. A sudden coldness replaced the warmth of his presence and I sought it again by following him. I lowered myself slowly down beside him and looked around the room. It was an empty, desolate and cold place.

I leaned my head back against the stone wall and closed my eyes. I do not know how long I sat there. Maybe, I slept. But, I jerked when a warm touch on my arm startled me. My eyes flew open to reveal the serene face of a man. My mind sought a name but it brought nothing but frustration. I gave up the search and just looked into the dark liquid pools of his eyes.

He must have read my expression for he said softly, "My name is Yosef. What news do you have from our brethren?"

"News?" I frowned and then slowly I realized he thought I was a follower. Well maybe I am. I certainly believe in YahShua, but I never followed Him. "None," I muttered.

"You are not a follower then? But, ...why are you here?"

"A follower?" I shrugged. "I am a seeker."

"What do you seek?"

"YahShua and His disciples." I answered weakly.

He smiled and nodded. "Then you have not come from the brethren." He said with understanding. "I was hoping for some news about their well being."

"Do you know anything?" another seated nearby asked with a rasping voice. "Why were you put into prison?"

I drew a deep breath and let it out shakily. Looking around, I could see some of them had been here a good long while. Every eye seemed to be turned upon me waiting with expectancy.

"Kayafa is trying to stop the furtherance of the teachings of YahShua and anyone that talks too much about Him or searches for His disciples are under suspicion of blasphemy and after stern warning, if they do not stop, are considered dangerous to the future of Israel. I was seeking the disciples for I believe that YahShua is with them."

404

"Then you are a believer." Someone said, but I was not sure which one.

"Oh yes, I believe YahShua is the Messiah and I know the purpose for His death, but the reason for His resurrection remains hidden, therefore I sought Him, for He, holds the answer."

"The purpose for His death was to get rid of Him." A slight man with short chopped hair cut the same length all over said with distaste.

"That was the Council's purpose, but Elohim had another purpose in allowing it." I answered and said unto him. "Do you not know that if Elohim had wished He could have stopped it all."

"If YahShua wished to do so, He too could have stopped it. He told us so Himself." An older man injected with a weary smile.

"What was the purpose of Elohim in His death?" Yaakov inquired with interest.

"You are followers and you do not know?" I was astonished.

"There is much confusion since His death." Yosef spoke softly. "Please tell us what you know."

So, I began with the visit to Elisheva and told of my search. About finding BarAbbas in the cave tombs and Yosef of Arimathea in the ash heap. I told them of the plot of Kayafa to remove Yosef from the Council and what had happened in the Holy Place the very hour YahShua died upon the cross. How BarAbbas brought the news of how the followers are being brought before the Council for blasphemy by Shaul of Tarsus.

I did not, however, tell them that Kayafa had plans to force Pilate to give him the right of the death penalty in cases calling for it by the Law of Moshe. I did not see any use in adding to their sorrow, nor did I mention the prophecy of doom for the beautiful beloved city. If they knew already no one said anything and I left it at that.

I was about to tell them of our talk with the disciples at BeitZaidah when there was a noise outside the big door. This seemed to signal something, for everyone got up quickly and went to huddle around the door. I too went to see what was happening. The iron door groaned open and a man wearing a tunic with spots on the front of it carrying a large pot pushed his way through them with ugly grunts. He carried over shoulder was a small bag containing something lumpy. Two soldiers stood in the doorway to prevent anyone from taking advantage of the situation and trying for an escape.

The man sat the pot onto the floor, relieved himself of the bag, turned and pushed between the two soldiers and left. A soldier shoved a metal tray and a cup into one of the men's hands. Then they closed the door without a word.

A faintly familiar smell ascended from the pot and a woman produced some more trays from somewhere and began to pass through the throng handing them out.

She was not quite as old as myself and gave me a shy look as she handed me one of the trays. She had a pretty face with smooth features, but her dark eyes were filled with sadness and the weak smile showed the trouble in her spirit. She seemed so vulnerable and meek, but a set expression spoke of an inner strength

Yah, how do the women stand it? Thrown together with these men, no privacy. How humiliating it must be for them. I wanted to say, "I am sorry", but what good would that do?

Now my attention was drawn to what was happening at the pot. One of the women was pouring a watery liquid into the trays with one of the cups while another took from the sack and broke crisp dry bread and handed it out. I watched a woman with a strained frown, pour sop into my cup and another woman with a trembling hand place a piece of bread on my tray. This one seemed very young and I wondered where her family was. Where did they all come from?

The whole process took place in silence. No one spoke and no one began to eat until all had their trays and were seated again. Then the older man whom looked to be the elder of the group, held up his bread and raised his voice.

"We thank you, Elohim, for this meal and we ask your blessings upon it. We pray that our brethren wheresoever they are may be filled and kept in safety by the power of the blood of YahShua, our Adonai. Amen!" The others echoed his amen and then they all began to eat.

The sop had little taste and the bread was nigh unto ruin but if one was hungry it would somewhat satisfy. However, I had no appetite and found it hard to eat. I had taken my seat beside Yaakov who had befriended me. He seem interested in eating either handing his tray to another man with a smile. The man who had been gobbling down his bread and sop looked up at him. His expression softened into a smile and received Yaakov's offer without a word. Then Yaakov leaned his head back and sat with his eyes closed. I did not see his mouth move, however, I was sure he was praying.

I looked at the watery liquid in my cup and thought about the fine meals we have at home and knew I could never set at one of them again. This sent a pain through my heart. The thoughts I kept suppressed of Serepta, Athera and the family leaped to mind and I shoved the tray away quickly and leaned my head back against the wall with a low moan. My hand with the tray bumped into the fellow who sat to my right and he took it from me with a grateful look.

After a degree of time I rolled my head against the wall and studied Yaakov's features. He was not handsome, but his face was full of character. "Yaakov, …what happened to your face?" I asked with sympathy, trying to fill my mind with something other than the misery of my situation.

He looked at me, smiled and said, "Tried to be a champion."

"A champion?"

"Yes." The man on my right answered for him. "They took one of the women prisoners away and the guard was being rough with her. He tried to persuade him to be gentle."

"Well, it worked did it not," Yaakov insisted. "He could not very well beat me and harm the damsel at the same time."

I could not help but laugh slightly at his logic.

After the meal was finished and the women had washed the trays, stacking them neatly near the water hole, something very strange began to happen. One of the young damsels began to sing softly, then another took it up, and before long everyone was singing.

I did not know the song, nor did I feel like hearing it, much less singing. However, as I sat there the sound began to lift my burdened heart and soon I found it pleasant. After a while I heard the words coming softly from my mouth and soon I too was singing. It was a song of triumph and love and forgiveness. Then another song of praise and worship began. The joy I thought was gone revived itself and there in the blackness of the prison, I sang the song of victory with praise in my heart. My mind went back to the happening below the window at my hostel and I remembered the words of my prayer. I had prayed to find the courage to sing the song of victory in the face of death.

Finally, the old man looked at me and said, "Tell us some more news."

So I took up the story again where I left off, telling them of meeting the disciples at BeitZaidah and how there I began to see the purpose of Yah for the death of YahShua, but still I had no answers to offer about the resurrection. We talked for many hours and none could add to my knowledge. Finally one by one we began to fall asleep.

DAY THIRTY FIVE

It was the Sabbath day and in the Temple the Holy Convocation was just beginning for it was the sound of the trumpets that aroused me from my sleep. I lay upon the hard, cold, stone floor and in my mind's eye I could see the ceremony being effectuated. The cohanim were dress in their finery mingled with the milling throngs in the Courtyard and the smoke from the Alter of Sacrifice ascending to color the blue of the heavens a dingy gray. I could imagine even the distasteful smell of burning flesh. Empty sacrifices! Dead services! Vainly the people stand in unknowing reverence. What a deception? What a lie?

I blinked away a tear that rolled warmly from the corner of my eye into my hairline. So much I had trusted in, believed in, was gone. And, here I lay without hope waiting the day of stoning. Why do they not get it over with? Is not death punishment enough without the torture of waiting for it to come? Do they not know that the consummation of the punishment, after this, would be a blessing not a curse.

Yaakov stirred beside me and I rolled my head to look at him. He, too, was listening to the muffled sounds of the activities of the Sabbath Temple service. As though he sensed my looking, he turned his head toward me and we shared a degree of oneness. I could see the rare sadness in the lines of his slightly swollen face and I loved him. Now aware of the others around us my heart went to them also. Yes, I loved them. I loved them all. Now I understood why Yaakov willingly gave his evening meal to them and why he had fought for the young damsel being treated roughly by the guard.

I arose and bowed my face to the floor and prayed with much weeping and groaning that the Elohim of Heaven would deliver us from our prison and that the teachings of YahShua the Messiah would not be snuffed out by the evil cohanim and elders. While I prayed I again heard the words of BarNabas in the thrashing floor and they

409

mingled with those of the disciples at BeitZaidah. All the rumors of YahShua and teachings raced to mind and filled me with the wonder of them all. I lifted my voice praising Yah for sending His Son unto me.

Here in the prison cell the Sabbath day, also, was unlike other days. We joined our voices and sang Psalms of praise and deliverance, of trust in Yah's goodness and the songs of victory. Most of the day was spent in this manner and by the time for the evening meal there was an unusual air of peace and gratefulness. Out of our distress we found joy, out of darkness we melted together in love and I knew if Yah did not deliver me I was a richer man than I would ever have been by having lived to a ripe old age. I do not suppose there is another place in the whole world that could have touched me as deeply and moved me as much.

If I ever leave this place alive I will never again look at things the same way.

"Elohim help me to be strong and not feel sorry for myself." I whispered. Looking at each face I found myself, …hidden behind fearful eyes, etched in the deep furrows of their faces.

DAY THIRTY SIX

When I awoke I was stiff and every bone in my body complained of the lack of comfort it endured that night. The joy of the Sabbath was gone now and it was mid-morning or that is what I thought anyway. It was hard to tell. We were given more sop and bread. I was hungry although I did not feel like eating, but I managed to swallow down most of it. There was never anything left either in the pot or in any tray. If you did not want it there was always someone who did. It was not the kind of substance that satisfied the needs of the body, therefore, it was never enough.

There was nothing to do but walk around the room or just sit and visit with those around me. That, however,

410

became dull and before long I just let my thoughts ramble. Painful as it was I thought about home with the mare and colt racing across the meadow heads held high in the wind. The lovely view from the rampart of our large wonderful home built on the side of the mountain. Then I brought before me the faces of those I had left behind. My first thought was Sarepta with her blue understanding eyes so full of love and for an instant I though I caught a whiff of her spices. I groaned silently and my arms felt the emptiness of them. I smiled as I saw Elsan once again swipe away that persistent lock of hair that always plagued his forehead and marveled at the manliness in him. I have no doubt that he is well capable of taking the responsibility of the family while Father is in Rome.

Again I saw the confident battle of Yered as he fought his unseen enemies and remembered the glint of adventure in his eye. Finally I looked in my mind's eye and saw Miryam with her harp and though I could hear her psalms. Hanna, "Oh Elohim!" I grieved within realizing I would never see her make the first smile, take her first step and wear her first festive robe. The agony of knowing I would probably never see them again did not quench my need to remember them. They are all I will have and so like refreshing water I drank in my memories and savored the sights I could recall of the beautiful valley.

Again that evening, as before, Yaakov gave his meal to one of the others. I knew he had to be hungry and was amazed at his sacrifice. One meal of sop and a crust of bread would not keep the body alive and I wondered if he was that unhappy or if he just cared more for the others than for himself. After studying him for some time, I came to the conclusion that it had to be the latter case. He was never irritable like the others and could bring forth a warm smile when it pleased him. He must have an abundance of love in him, quite like I imagined YahShua to have. I envied him in a way for I found my words sharp and felt a constant wrinkle between my eyes.

My heart grew heavier as the day wore on and even the pleasant sound of the water splashing onto the stone floor began to irritate me. Then, as was the custom, one of the maidens began to sing and to my dull soul sweet release and joy accompanied the songs. My frown melted and strength swelled up within me to keep me through the long cold night.

DAY THIRTY SEVEN

As I sat against the wall, I thought of the events that lead to my present condition and wondered how I could bear another day in this hell. The bleak reality of where I was and my eventual fate bore down upon me with unbelievable heaviness.

A commotion arose beyond the big iron door. I assumed it was time for the usual pot of sop and dry bread. But, when the door opened we were not greeted by the usual hard-faced man in his stained tunic, but by a squad of soldiers. They entered carrying spears and shields pushing us backward with force. Then they stood aside for a small impressive looking Centurion to enter. He stopped in the midst of his men, stretched himself to his full height, raised upon his toes, then settling again back on the floor. All the time his gray eyes searched our faces and his hard chiseled looks held no expression. Then with a heavy voice that did not match his stature he pointed out three prisoners. One of which was the young damsel who hands out the trays.

The two male prisoners went forward bravely, but the young maiden stood stiffly in her place. One of the soldiers came and fiercely caught her upper arm and out of the corner of my eye I saw Yaakov make a slight movement. Immediately, I thought of his face. That thought was pushed aside quickly by my own sudden rise of anger.

The soldier jerked the woman toward the door and she did not resist. Instead she looked around quickly at Yaakov halting him in his steps. Her face was twisted in fear, but there was a peace hidden beneath it that touched my heart. Some emotion flashed through her large brown eyes. I did not recognize it, but then quite unexpectedly she began to sing softly as she had done on previous evenings after the meal. Yaakov took up the words and we all joined in as the door slammed shut. We continued to raise our voice loudly. However, the song dwindled away shortly and we stood silently.

No one asked where they were being taken and I wondered if they knew. Perhaps, they did not ask because they did not want to know. Everyone returned to his or her usual place without a word, but I sensed a hollow emptiness among us and I wondered if they also felt it. The silent gloom that fell lingered on through the day.

Although the old man's prayers over the mid-morning sop was for the three prisoners that were taken from us, an understanding silence prevailed as each, I am sure, pondered their fate. A fate we were all sure to follow eventually.

That evening after the meal there was a reverent silence. Our little song leader's place was empty, and each person sat staring into the face of his or her own thoughts. Finally, a timid female voice rose shakily from the small water girl in uncertain notes. Yaakov took up the refrain enforcing it and soon the others joined in one by one. The undefeated spirit of these people gripped my heart and I let my voice mingle with theirs. I was proud to be a part of them. I was glad to know in the face of death there was a song to be sung, praise to be offered. While we sang I remembered the words told to me of YahShua, "Blessed are those who have been persecuted, ...for theirs is the Kingdom of Heaven."

DAY THIRTY EIGHT

The next day was much the same as the other days. Mid-morning sop with the time afterwards being spent

413

talking about YahShua and His teachings or some event in the life of one of the prisoners. Between which came silent interludes when each drew out personal thought from their memories. The day seemed long with nothing to do and I found it extremely depressing for I am a man of action. Waiting always came hard for me. At home idle time was spent with a family member or studying the Sacred Writings.

My thoughts turned to Elsan and I wondered what he was doing. Did he return home to tell Serepta and Athera of my plight, or is he still in Yerushelayim? Did Parmenas and Nicanor find the followers of YahShua or the disciples? I wondered if Kayafa would devise some evil plan to get rid of Nakdimon. Had BarAbbas and the zealots made their attack on the palace of King Herod?

I did not want to think about what would happen to me. Yet, in weak moments I wondered how I would act when it came right down to facing the pit. Would the courage I felt now flee while the stones beat the life out of me? Could I sing the songs of victory and praise then? How long will it be before they come for me? There was one thing I found particularly disturbing and that was the idea of going to my death without seeing YahShua. During the last part of my search it had become almost an obsession to find Him, or at least His disciples and now...

Shortly after the evening meal while we were singing praises to the Elohim of Israel we heard the bar being lifted from the door. Every eye turned to look as the words of the song died on our lips. Were they coming to take one of us? Would someone go to rest in Father Avraham's bosom before the sunset this day? Who would it be? A stab of fear shot through me, but I repressed it. Although I was the last to arrive that did not seem to mean anything. The time they took prisoners before the choice seemed to be random.

The door was quickly drug open and a squad of soldiers marched into the cell. In the midst of them came a tall, slim Centurion. He was a ghastly sight and I sucked in a deep breath. It was, much to my surprise, Appolious. He stood proud and erect, his uniform hung on him showing the weight he had loss. He swayed slightly, eyes set deep in their sockets, face stone hard and pale against the dim light that flooded in behind him from the hall outside the door. He let his gaze slide over each face and then rest upon me.

"You," he pointed at me. "Come with me." His voice was harsh and sent a chill through me.

He was my friend, but he was a soldier first. What a cruel turn of events that he would be the one to deliver me up to the stoners. I squinted in the dimness to catch a look at his eyes hoping to read something in them, but there seemed to be no emotion there. Surely, he had not forgotten me. He could have chosen another, but I found myself stepping toward him. His look did not change as two guards pulled me between them.

I heard Yaakov send up a quick prayer and others did likewise. Then Appolious turned abruptly and led the procession of guards that marched me along through the doors. There was no song this time from the prisoners, but I could hear their prayers as we climbed. We went through the torture chamber and I felt some tenseness go out of me. They were not stopping here. On up the steps, we pasted the holding cell. The prisoners stared with many faces pressed against the bars. None made a sound and the silence stabbed at me like the point of many spears. One soldier nudged me forward for I had slowed as I caught a glimpse of the familiar face of the song leader that was taken from us earlier. She smiled at me and wiggled the fingers of her right hand that clung to the bars. I wanted to say something, but what could I say? I just returned her smile with a pitiful one of my own.

I was pushed along toward the short flight of stairs that lead into the receiving room where Appolious halted the squad with an up-lifted hand and turned to one of the soldiers. "Prepare him," he commanded without looking at me. Then he did an about face in ridged military fashion and went for a door to the right. As he went I saw a faltered step and hoped he was having second thought and would turn back. He did not, but disappeared from sight without so much as a backward glance.

The sun had nearly gone down and the sky was beginning to gray, but the brightness still stung my eyes and I shielded them with my hand. As I faltered the soldiers on either side of me paid no attention, but the one behind gave me a shove. This was the courtyard of the fortress of Anthonia. A light cool breeze tugged at the tassels of my hair and I caught the pungent odor of my own body.

My heart pounded in my ears and a tight fist seemed to grasp my chest making it hard to breathe. This was it. I was being taken to the pit. However, suddenly the soldiers stopped beside a post with two pegs in it about two cubits over my head. Hardly realizing what was happening the soldiers took my hands, bound them and stretched me until the ties hung over the pegs leashing me to the pole. What were they doing?

The smell of horses played in my nostrils accompanied by the squeaking jingle of boarding gear and the sound of clomping hooves. High over head a falcon squawked and I caught a glimpse of it in flight. Wings spread unmoving, it caught the wind soaring in its silent circle. Ah yes, the hawk. What a strange thing to think about. Some soldiers behind me laughed and those who had bound me to the post now moved away. Pilate's judgment hall was in front of me and soldiers were ascending and descending the steps. Upon the balcony, a lone figure stood silhouetted dark against the building. The golden ornament around his neck caught the light of the fading sun and reflected its remaining brilliance.

Suddenly, a sharp crack split the air and a stinging pain coursed across my back. A cry escaped my lips and then before the pain subsided there was another and then another. My mind screamed out its agony, or was it I that screamed? Again and again I heard it and then a voice deep inside me spoke louder than the scream I was hearing and drew my attention to it with force. "Blessed are you when

416

men revile you, and men persecute you, …rejoice and be glad for your reward is great."

I felt my body slump my strength was poured out as if a sacrifice, and I was now hanging from the post. The building before me swayed back and forth while the agonizing fingers of pain in my back pierced through me. The sounds in my ears became dull and darkness descended upon me quickly. The last sight was of the man on the balcony fading into the darkness of the building.

DAY THIRTY NINE

My eyes opened to a dim light and I blinked to recognize it. I saw a table upon which was a candle burning in its dish, beside it a stack of scrolls and a familiar blue robe. I lay upon my stomach and could hear the sounds of the city softly in my ear. Where was I? My mind quickly reenacted its last memories and then found the remembrance of the table. I must be in the hostel, but, how? What happened? Was this a dream? I moved and in doing so brought the stab of it into my back with such force that it nearly took my breath. The sound I heard must have been my own moan for a shadow fell across me.

"My lord?" Benren's voice soothed my anxiety. "Do not move," he was saying. "Rest, my lord, rest even yet for a while."

I relaxed then upon the bed. Benren was there and I was satisfied. I closed my eyes for they were filled with heat.

A soft sound, …voices fading in and out, then they became understandable. My eyes were hard to focus. I blinked several times and watched the candle with no flame and the pile of scrolls come into clear view.

"How is he?" A low voice inquired.

"Weak from the loss of blood, but he will be all right." Benren's voice informed.

I could not see who he was talking with, for I still lay upon my stomach. I had no knowledge of how long I had laid there. Then I became aware of something damp upon my back. I felt no pain but there was a dull throb. Then Elsan's voice reached my ears.

"Elohim is with him, thank you for coming."
"I need no thanks." The strange voice replied. "He would do the same for me."

Appolious! Yes, I recognized it. There was concern and softness in it now, not the hardness of the man who came to the prison. The prison! I saw it now. He had brought me forth and the punishment I received was far less than what Kayafa had in mind. How unhappy he must be to find that his plan had failed. He will no doubt try again, but the next time I will be ready for him.

Later, I learned from Benren that immediately after the trial Elsan left Yerushelayim on a fast horse and went straight to Appolious. It was a wise decision although one I myself would have not considered. A Centurion does not carry that much influence. I do not know how he did it but somehow Appolious was able to persuade Pilate to let me off with just a lashing. Maybe, it was because of my business in Rome or because of the gift I had given him. No, it was none of that, it was because Yah had mercy upon me. Only He could have given Appolious favor with Pilate.

Appolious was still a sick man, but he had risen from his bed to come to my aid. He must have rode hard to get here and thus the faltering steps. That thought brought deep warmth and a lump to my throat and in vain I tried to swallow it. We have a warm friendship that will endure through the ages.

After a while Benren brought me warm sop and bread. My tray in the prison came before my eye and I thought to shove it away. However the smell of it was pleasing and so I relented. The sun was bright and it was the heat of the day. A servant stood near the bed and waved a large fan made of woven wool and the stir of the air was comforting.

418

"How long have I been here?" I ask and heard my own voice tremble.

"It is but the ninth hour my lord." Benren replied while he put cool ointment on my back. "Take your rest now. You are very weak from your ordeal."

He need not tell me how weak I was, nor how painful my back. That I could feel for myself.

By the time for supper, I was able to sit up and take meat. My fever was small now, but my back reminded me not to move too fast. I thought of those in prison. I suppose I will think of them often and wonder about their well being. Had others been taken? Were they singing the songs of victory? Suddenly I felt a great loss. I will miss them, all of them. Will they miss me? They must think me dead by now. I wished there were some way that I could let them know or maybe give them some hope. Hope! Our only hope lies in YahShua the Messiah, both theirs and mine. No, not just us, but for all Israel, for all mankind everywhere.

DAY FORTY

Early in the morning Appolious came and seated himself heavily upon one of the lounges. "There is news among the officers that I thought you would like to hear." He told me.

"What news?" I asked anxiously. If Appolious, as weak as he was had come here before returning home what he has to say must surely be something important.

"Kayafa was well put out with Pilate for letting you go after just a lashing. There was a heated confrontation I understand. Kayafa has a powerful influence with the people as you well know from what happened at the trial of YahShua. Pilate is forced to appease him or be in danger of the Senate in Rome thinking him incapable of his position." Appolious paused and sighed deeply. There was a worried look upon him. "I am afraid," he continued, "...things are going to get worse around here in the days to come."

"YahShua has prophesied this." I remembered aloud, then realized Appolious was not finished. "Oh, ...ah, go ahead."

"Well," his tired face took on a grim expression, "Pilate has persuaded Rome that punishment for religious crimes should no longer fall under the jurisdiction of the state, but be handled by the Sanhedrin according to the Laws of Moshe. Pilate is to make the decree at the celebration of Shavuot. The maximum penalty will be death by stoning. This will mean that the leaders of Israel without Rome's interference will punish the followers of YahShua, who are found guilty of blasphemy. I was not sure whither his concern was for the followers or just for me but I loved him for it.

Anger shot through me and I found myself cursing Kayafa and his evil treachery. Now many Israelites will die at his hands and I being his unwilling tool to give him this power. It would have been far better had I remained in

421

prison and suffered as the rest. How my heart grieved for the people and for the evil I had brought upon them.

"I know how you must feel," Appolious spoke softly after a degree. "But, you must not blame yourself. It would have happened anyway sooner or later and, as you have said, YahShua prophesied this."

"Yes, but did I have to be the one to bring it about?" I realized my words were bitter, but at this time I did not care.

"Perhaps your Elohim had a reason for sparing you." Appolious reasoned with me. "Do not be too hard on yourself. Each of us has a fate to follow and there is none who can resist."

"No." I rose angrily and paid for my actions with many fingers of pain shooting through my back. Hesitating only a degree, I went to the window and looked out upon Yerushelayim. "Life is what we make it."

"Then what of the prophecies? Are they sure and steadfast or can they be broken?"

"Prophecies are implemented by the foreknowledge of Yah not by fate."

A hawk's shadow soared along the face of the building across the street and I looked up. Squinting in the brightness of the morning I saw it's dark shape against the intense blue of the sky. It made a lazy circle and then swooped down out of sight.

"What ever you call it," Appolious was saying, "...there are times when a man has no say over what will happen. I think you are being too hard on yourself."

"My circles have not been meaningless," I replied distractedly.

The hawk did not reappear, so I turned to look at my Roman friend. He had stood now and I knew he was anxious to be off for KfarNachum.

"I have a long way to go my friend. Shalom." He struck his breastplate with his fist.

"Until we meet again." I bowed slightly.

Benren then went to the door with Appolious, opening it for him and they both departed. I had gained some strength after spending needed rest in bed. I could not just lay here. There were things to do, place to go. I had not yet found the disciples or seen YahShua. I called for Elsan to come to my chamber. My back was no longer hurting, but was stiff and sore where the stripes lay. However, the desire to find YahShua was becoming almost unbearable.

While I waited Benren entered saying, "Parmenas is without asking an audience with you."

"Bid him enter," I returned. I was still feeling my weakness and went to my bed and sat down.

Parmenas gave me a bright smile as he rushed into the room. There was an unusual lightness about him and I sensed this visit was special.

"Good day Timon," he saluted. "How are you feeling this day?"

"I am somewhat weak, but fine."

"I have wonderful news."

"Take your rest and tell me about it." I offered the lounge. "Benren some wine."

"No." He stopped him with an up lifted hand. "I have no time for it now. Last night at the meeting of the followers there was a rumor that this evening there is a meeting of the disciples and YahShua will surely be there."

"Wonderful!" I straightened and hardly noticed when I winced. My heart racing wildly and I found renewed strength. "Where is it?"

"We were unable to find out where is to be held, but Nicanor and I are off to see some of the followers we have become aquatinted with. Peradventure, one of them will know."

Some of the excitement subsided upon hearing this but I was encouraged. Maybe, Nakdimon would know. I could go see. However, I would only do so as the last resort for I did not want to be used again. Kayafa would like nothing better than to use me against him. There is Elazar, …maybe he is no longer hiding with the others.

"Good," I said unto him. "Elsan and I will go to BeitAnyah to the house of Elazar, the friend of YahShua. One of us may find out where it will be." I turned to Benren. "See to the preparations."

"Yes my lord."

"I will take my leave now," Parmenas said in his excitement and departed as Benren went out.

When Elsan entered he smiled and asked of my well being. I was impatient with all the fuss and said without answering his question. "This day we shall go to BeitAnyah and find YahShua and the…"

"But, you are not well enough to travel," Elsan cut in.

"I am well enough," I snapped back at him, "…and I shall go. If you do not wish to go, I shall go alone."

He opened his mouth to reply but I held up my hand and silenced him. "I have instructed Benren to prepare my cisium. It is but a short ride and there is no danger of tiring in that time. Do you wish to go or not?"

Elsan took a deep breath and let it out loudly. "I will go," he said simply.

I do not know if it was a sigh of defeat or just indulgence, but either way I was sure he was not pleased with my decision.

It was about the fifth hour when we came into BeitAnyah. The streets were as crowded as usual and there was a strange expectancy in the air. The merchants called friendly greetings to the people passing by and a small shepherd boy with a tall crook, stood in front of one of the shops eating a cluster of grapes. A small lamb rubbed his leg and bleated its impatience.

The sun was busy doing it's work upon us when we found ourselves outside the home of Elazar. A man of full age wearing a drab colored tunic opened the door at our knock. His hair looked somewhat out of sorts but there was a kind face filled with lines of generosity behind the short, scraggly beard. His dark eyes were soft and they smiled at us below thin bushy brows.

424

"Shalom," I saluted. "Is this the house of Elazar?"

"I am Elazar. Why do you seek me?"

"We are looking for the Messiah." I spoke boldly, but only because I had knowledge of the man. He was known as a friend of YahShua.

His eyes flowed over me taking in my garment down to my feet. Then they trailed across to Elsan and went up him and meet his gaze. Then they drifted past us to my cisium sitting in the street. When he looked back at me there was no suspicion and a smile now showed itself on his lips.

"Welcome friends." He opened the door wider and stepped away for us to enter.

After closing the door he led the way up a few steps against the wall on the right of the door. To the left of the stairs could be seen a rail fence and the bleat of a lamb drifted up to us.

At the top of the steps a faded rug hanging over an entranceway he shoved aside and held while Elsan and I filed into a small room. It had a slab wood floor with cracks between each slab and the movement of something could be seen on the lower level. Some kind of animal, a cow perhaps or the sheep we heard coming in. A worn woolen rug covered the central part of the room. In front of a fireplace sat a table and four rough wood chairs. Hanging on the west wall was a tapestry of a shepherd watching his sheep, but it was too small for the wall. Beside the fireplace was a clay jar hanging from a three-legged stand. To the back of the room an open doorway showed a preparation room with a table against the far wall cluttered with jars, a large bowl and pitcher. While I looked, a woman appeared by the table with a bowl and poured water into it from the pitcher. Her dark shiny hair picked up the light of some candles that hung clustered together over head in a black hammered iron holder swung upon a small cord.

"Take your rest," Elazar was saying and pulled out chairs for us. We seated ourselves and Elazar looked into the preparation room following my gaze.

"That is my sister Marta," he offered.

Now the woman came into where we sat and began the act of hospitality. She did not look directly at us nor did she speak. She must have a husband somewhere. She was just a little younger than I was and her face was becoming when she smiled.

"Marta, these men came to inquire of YahShua," Elazar informed. "Will you bring them some wine when you have finished?"

Elsan had been looking upon our host with much curiosity while we talked. "Were you really dead?" He blurted out not being able to contain himself any longer.

"Yes," Elazar laughed. "I was dead for four days."

"I find that hard to believe," Elsan was honest.

Marta finished her duty, arose and went back into the preparation room leaving us alone.

"My sisters and all BeitAnyah are my witnesses." Elazar assured him.

"…And, YahShua raised you from the dead?" I spoke wonderingly. It was more of a statement than a question but he nodded his answer.

"What happened?" Elsan asked eagerly leaning forward.

"As I remember, Miryam and Marta were standing by my bedside weeping and then the next thing I knew I was in a cold place with a cloth over my eyes and a voice was calling my name. But, the voice was not just in the cave where later I realized I was, but everywhere, …filling everything. It seemed to be outside, inside, in the tomb and in my bones. It was with great power and my body obeyed it, although my mind did not understand what was happening."

"That is incredible, …unbelievable," Elsan stammered.

It was not as much a shock to me as it was to him but I knew how he felt. It was the same way I felt when I realized that the prophet Micah was sitting beside me in my cisium. He had told much the same story.

"It is a miracle," I muttered coming from my thoughts to see Marta had returned with a tray and was pouring us some wine from a pottery pitcher. When our goblets were filled she left us again.

"But, how is that possible?" Elsan began then his voice drifted away into nothingness.

"Because YahShua came from Yah." Elazar opened his hand to him.

"You are using the Holy name of Elohim," Elson stammered.

Elazar showed the missing teeth with a big grin. "Yes, the scriptures says we are to declare His name. Elson blinked at him unbelievingly. "I know! I know! It is against the laws of the elders," Elazar waved his hand as though to dismiss it. "But, YahShua said it is Yah's commandment."

He paused and reflected upon that for a degree and then continued.

"You were telling us of your resurrection," I reminded him.

"I was in the tomb for three days and you know by then rot would have begun. However, when I came forth and the grave clothes were removed I was whole. No sign of perishing. YahShua said, 'whosoever believes in me shall not perish, but have everlasting life.'"

"Do you have everlasting life?" Elsan stared at him in awe.

He just shrugged. Perhaps, he had never thought of that or, maybe, it was something he did not understand. He had no answer for that question.

We all sat lost in our own thought and wondering for sometime. Apparently Elazar was as mystified as we were. Certainly in the heat a body is well under way to decompose in three days, …yet here sat this man who was dead, alive, whole and well. Would he really live forever and not die again? It was definitely something to think about. What did YahShua mean by ever lasting life? "Did the same thing happen to YahShua?" I wondered aloud.

"No it was different," Elazar answered with a start.

427

"Different? Elsan repeated in bewilderment.

"How was it different?" I asked and felt a surge of joy.

"He is… It was…" Elazar sought for the words. A scowl twisting his usually pleasant face. "When He showed himself to the disciples in the upper room," he began, "the door was barred for fear of the Romans and YahShua just appeared in their midst. He had a body." Elazar frowned deeply, "…because He had Toma put his finger into the wounds and told him, He was no ghost. Yet, He appeared in a locked room and after encouraging the disciples disappeared again." He fell silent.

Apparently, he had never thought about it before from the look on his face. It held almost the same shocked look as Elsan's and probably mine. Excitement churned in my bowels and a heady joy filled my entire being. I sensed I was on the verge of understanding the purpose of Yah for the resurrection of YahShua. There was something very special about it, even more special than the promise of everlasting life.

To have everlasting life was to live everlasting, eternally. There was no doubt that Yah could do this and that is what was in His mind with that promise. To live everlasting, never die in this body, being kept by the power of Yah, everlasting power and everlasting life. Even as Elazar now sits before us in his flesh and blood body. Would he live eternally, have everlasting life now that death has been broken over him?

YahShua, on the other hand, had a different kind of resurrection as Elazar was pointing out. What did it all mean? What was Yah trying to show us?

"Not only does YahShua come and go by the power of this new life, but He can change His appearance." Elazar began speaking again as though he had not stopped to consider the revelation. "I remember two of the disciples telling of a stranger who traveled with them for several furlongs and when He would go His way, they invited Him

428

into their house for meat. There He revealed Himself to them plainly as YahShua, the Messiah."

"He must truly be the Son of Elohim," Elsan confessed a little shaken by this revelation.

I knew he had been struggling with the idea of YahShua being the Messiah, the Son of Yah for a long time now, but I did not realize how far he was from being convinced. I doubt if anything other than this man's testimony would have reached him. Some people are just skeptics I suppose, but then he did not search the Sacred Writings as I, and had little knowledge of the prophecies, except those told him.

"Yes," Elazar was saying, "...he is the Son of Yah. That must be the answer."

"But, he was born of woman just as we and had a fleshly existence," I reasoned. "His resurrection should be not different from yours unless there is something greater here Yah is trying to get us to understand."

"Before His death when He referred to Himself, it was as the son of man," Elazar confirmed, "...but, since His resurrection he speaks of Himself as the Son of Yah."

"The blood of the son of Man was poured out at the cross and in His resurrection He laid down His humanity and became deity. Yah in flesh." Elsan spoke as though his words were just thoughts, but there was miraculous truth there.

"And," I continued for him, "the life of the beast is in the blood. The blood line."

Now, I began to see that the death of YahShua bought man more than just forgiveness from sin. And, His resurrection means a new form of life could be ours, a new creation life. Not bound to the restrictions of this world but access to the realm of Yah. Yah had not only freed us from sin, but also made it possible for us to ascend to a higher form of life. It was deep and would take much thought and many hours of meditation to understand the fullness of this revelation. But, I knew that at that moment we had embarked upon a new understanding and as BarTalmal has said, change our way of thinking. What it all means is yet to be completely understood, but wonder and excitement filled me.

The knowledge of the Adonai flooded my whole being with joy unspeakable and I was full of His glory. Praises suddenly sprang forth and we worshipped the Yah of heaven for His faithfulness and the peace that His knowledge brings, peace, such joyous peace. This was what I had been searching for. The purpose for my whole life lies in this revelation.

We talked for sometime about it all and then I related the story of Yosef of Arimathea to Elazar. He was shocked to anguish to learn that the presence of the Adonai had gone from over the Ark of the Covenant, however, he became soothed when I explained the purpose for it and where the Presence had gone. We talked of the cohanim and their refusal to tell the people what had happened. We discussed Kayafa's determination to stop the teachings of YahShua and about his plot to put Yosef forth from the Council and my imprisonment. I told of the decision of Pilate to put the punishment of religious matters in the hands of the Council. The followers of YahShua would certainly pay the supreme sacrifice for their faith.

As the day began to wind down, I found myself weary from weakness so Elsan insisted we return to Yerushelayim immediately. We were about to take our leave when Marta appeared at the door with a delicious meal. It would have been rude to leave after it was prepared. As we set about to eat, the door sprang open and a beautiful woman quietly entered with a glowing expression. She paused a degree upon seeing us. Then came over to Elazar and kissed him affectionately on the forehead. Her startlingly dark eyes went to the frown on Marta's face.

"I, …I am sorry I am late," she stammered lowering her head.

"Where have you been? Elazar asked with a raised eyebrow. "You were gone almost before sunrise."

"Need you ask?" Marta mumbled, but there was no bitterness there.

Her expression changed at Marta's words and the glow disappeared somewhat. Then she looked at Elsan and lastly at me, but said nothing.

"This is my sister Miryam," Elazar waved a hand at her. "Miryam, these men are inquiring about the Adonai." Elsan smiled brightly at her and I almost elbowed him for he was staring.

"I am Timon of Beitorah," I supplied, "…and this is Elsan my son."

Miryam wore a scarf over her head, but was unveiled. She bowed slightly to us, "The disciples are in Yerushelayim," she offered and turned back to her brother. "I have been with them nearly all day. It was so good to see them all again, they are all there."

"Where in Yerushelayim?" Elsan asked quickly apparently out of his daze.

"In the upper room." She looked surprised as though we should know.

"Where the Posach was served? I pressed her.

"Yes," she nodded as she turned to follow Marta. "They are waiting for the Adonai." She tossed over her shoulder before disappearing into the preparation room behind Marta.

Suddenly, my weariness was revived and I felt a surge of strength. Joy filled my breast and I found praise ringing in my heart.

"Tell Marta she sets a fine table," I turned to Elazar, "…and thank you for your hospitality. We must be going now. I have need to speak with the disciples."

Elazar arose and followed us to the door. "You are welcome in my house at any time. Shalom!"

"Shalom," I echoed and Elsan nodded.

I had finally found the disciples and would soon have the answers to the questions that still remained and, perhaps, even see YahShua. This thought thrilled me and I knew my trembling was not just from weakness. There were many questions. Questions that I was sure only YahShua could answer. It seemed that every time I found the answers to some of the questions. More questions arose. I wondered if I would ever find the answers to all the questions. Life would lose its meaning if that were possible. I suppose I will spend my whole life seeking answers to questions, but that did not bother me. I had found the peace of Yah and His purpose for that which happened forty days ago in Yerushelayim and for now that was enough.

Entering Yerushelayim, I instructed Semone to go straight to the 'The Shawan'. It was an appropriate place for them to hide for the chief Cohanim and elders would never think to look for them at a gentile Inn. The day was long spent when we came to a stop in front of the building. As usual there were servants unpacking animals and people of the surrounding countries coming and going.

Inside the large reception room people were ascending and descending the stairs. Small throngs of gentiles were clustered here and there, but there was no sign of Aquarial.

"I will speak with Aquarial," I spoke softly to Elsan who was at my side. "You talk to some of the servants and see what you can find out."

"Elsan nodded and separated from me and I went looking for Aquarial, but he was no where to be found, so I caught one of the servants by his arm when he passed by.

"I am looking for Aquarial." I said to the small Greek boy carrying a bundle.

"He is in there," the boy pointed to the heavily carved door. "He is very busy and does not want to be bothered."

"Thank you." I released him and turned to go to the door.

I received some awkward stares standing by the door knocking on it. I seemed to be the only Israelite here and I supposed there was much speculation as to why I was knocking on the door, but there was no answer. I was turning away to leave when Elsan came quickly to my side.

"The disciples are not here." His words were between quick breaths. Catching my arm before I knew what was happening, he was hurrying me along toward the door. "They have gone to Gethsemane for evening prayer and YahShua will surely be there."

"We just came down that road. We should have seen them. Are you sure they said Gethsemane?

"That is what they said and I ask two different ones." Elsan insisted turning for the door. I caught his step and we went hurriedly to where Benren and Semone waited by the cisium.

Shortly we were bouncing swiftly along the road that would take us to the gate of the garden. It seemed I felt every pebble in the road and because of our hurrying, my back took up a throb in time with the clomping of the horse's hooves. When we arrived, there was no indication of anything happening. No one was in sight. My heart sank and I sighed deeply wondering where the strength would come from to search the garden.

Elsan had the answer and it suited me well. "Father, I will go see if they are there and then I will come for you."

I suppose he could see the strain on my face and I nodded settling back into my seat. I was tired almost to tears and my legs were shaky under me. Frustration was beginning to take away the excitement and the joy was melting into disappointment. Again, I thought of the hawk's circles, always circles. Was I fooling myself? Would I ever really find the disciples and YahShua? Was my search as the flight of the hawk?

Waiting for Elsan to return was almost as hard on me as going myself to search. I have never been one for waiting. I made a deep sigh fidgeting with my robe and thought if he did not quickly return I would call for him.

Then he was there and the look on his face told me everything I wanted to know. He had found no one in the garden. He did not bother to say it. He just went to his horse, mounted and turned to me with a questioning expression.

I could not speak for the words would have been drowned out by bitter sobs, so I just waved weakly and he looked at Semone, motioned for him to follow, and turning for Yerushelayim.

This was it! I had had enough! After a few day I will go home and forget it all. There was no use in fighting against Yah and apparently finding the disciples and YahShua was not His will. I was tired, too tired to go on. I had suffered much and had learned much, but still it all seemed so lacking. Perhaps it would never be complete, but it would just have to do. I was at the end of my rope. There was no where else to go, no where else to look.

Now I shook myself. Why was I thinking such thoughts? While there is life, there is hope. On the morrow when I am rested, things will not seem so bleak. I must trust, simply trust. Pushing everything from my mind, I tried to empty my thoughts, just not think of anything.

The crawl of the cisium wheel on the rocks and the clomping of horse hooves on the hard dry ground filled my ears. A slight breeze came up and cooled my face. Looking heavenward, a dark cloud was beginning to grow overhead in the dulling blue of the evening sky. This was a very curious sight and it was a distraction to the fierce throb on my back. Clouds do not just form in a clear sky, they rolled in from the Great Sea. Oh, there were high level storms on the top of the mountains, but they usually remained high. Mount Olivet was to the right but it was not high enough for storms to brew there.

While I pondered this strange occurrence a sound was coming to me on the wind. I strained to hear it. Praise? It was praise! Somewhere upon the Mount there were people offering up praise to Yah. Elsan must have heard it also, for just then he halted the cisium and we all sat listening. There it was again. Praise! Definitely praise!

I looked at Elsan and when his eyes met mine he broke into a wide grin and shoved the stubborn lock from his forehead. He dismounted while I scrambled from the carriage. Without a word to Benren or Semone, Elsan tied the horse and we both turned to go up the mountainside. It was a fairly steep grade and in my weakened condition I found it took all my strength to pull it. My legs wobbled and I fell to my knees, but Elsan came back to me. He took my arm lending his strength to mine.

It was only a small rock but under my unsteady foot it dislodged, I went down pulling Elsan on top of me. Pain shot up my arm as my elbow stabbed into the ground and my back scream in the sudden stop. A sudden bolt of defeat shot through my breast stealing the rest of my breath. Elsan who had retrieved his footing tugged on me. It was more his youthful power than my ability that finally brought us to a shallow ravine. Beyond it was another even more impossible grade, very high and forbidding, but at the top of it a press of people was singing praises to Yah.

Their words gave power to me and with much effort and Elsan's help I found myself making my way up the final slope and now I could hear a Man's voice.

It was soft but distinct. The wind grew tearing part of His words from my ears, but I could hear the love in them.

I knew this was YahShua and I had to see Him. There was a large throng of people pressing in on Him, but I had to get to Him. I do not remember what happened to Elsan or just how I managed to do it but somehow even in my extreme weakness I was shoving people aside and squirming between elbows. I ignored the frowns and sharp rebukes. Then someone pushed back and I tumbled into a sea of sandal clad feet. I had no strength to rise so I pushed my way between feet and legs on my hands and knees. Suddenly, there was a strong hand on my arm, then another took hold of me and I was upright, but I ignored them tearing loose and pressing still closer. The only thing I knew was I had come this close to Him and I was not about to be turned away now.

He was saying: " ...I am sending forth the promise of My Father upon you; but you are to stay in the city until you are clothed with power from on high."

As I emerged through the main press of the crowd I could see a Man standing upon a flat place His hands stretched out toward the people and His face aglow with the power of Yah. He had on a glorious white robe that shone against the dark clouds. I had to reach Him. Only a few people stood between Him and me, but when I brushed past one of them, he caught me and held me tight. I struggled to be free from him, but I was no match for him. YahShua turned to look at the commotion and I was suddenly stilled from my struggle by a strong feeling of love that flowed through me when our eyes met. They were aglow like embers of a fire, filled with peace and love and in them I saw understanding.

All my weakness fell from me like a heavy burden. My heart pounded in my ears and scarcely could I breathe. Paralyzed by the majesty of the sight of Him. I stood transfixed staring into the Glory of the only begotten Son of Yah and knowing He was pleased with me.

While I watched, the wind whipped my hair wildly, stinging my face and I blinked in its lashes losing contact with His gaze. Pushing it away impatiently I saw Him look up into heaven, raise His hands. There was a tremendous rush of wind and He began to ascend, rising toward the churning black cloud. As he went his countenance began to change and emanate brightness, so bright that we had to hide our eyes from it and then it was swallowed up in the dark clouds. He was gone. We stood staring up into the churning cloud with mouths gaping. No one spoke nor moved as the cloud shrank slowly away.

Then two men appeared at the spot where YahShua had stood and spoke with a loud voice. "Men of Galil, why do you stand looking into the sky? This YahShua, who has been taken up from you into heaven, will come in just the same way as you have watched him go into heaven."

And I, Timon, am a witness of these things and declare now unto you that all the scriptures have been fulfilled.

"He who has an ear, let him hear what the Spirit says to the churches."

Epilogue

The rest of the story of Timon can be found in 'The Acts of the Apostles', chapter six, verses two through five.

"...The disciples said, it is not seemly or desirable or right that we should have to give up or neglect preaching the Word of Yah in order to attend to serving at tables and superintending the distribution of food. Therefore, select out from among yourselves, brethren, seven men of good and attested character and repute, full of the RuachHaKodesh and wisdom, whom we may assign to look after this business and duty. But we will continue to devote ourselves steadfastly to prayer and the ministry of the Word. And the suggestion pleased the whole assembly, and they selected Stephen, a man full of faith and full of, and controlled by the Holy Spirit; and Philip, and Prochorus, and Nicanor, and Timon, and Parmenas, and Nicholas, a proselyte from Antioch. These they presented to the apostles, who after prayer laid their hands on them. And the message of Yah kept on spreading..."

TERMS AND CUSTOMS

CUSTOMS

The customs of the people of the Bible land is very difficult to understand and I have not attempted to bring light upon all of them. That task I will gladly leave to the experts in that field. However, I have presented some simple explanations that seem important to the story.

Birthing Chair – A chair with arms and a hole cut in the seat. The woman sat on the chair and the baby was caught in a blanket when it came. It was though that this position helped ease the birth and the child's head was down, allowing better drainage of the fluid in its nose and mouth.

Espoused - A ceremony in which a male and female child were promised by the parents to each other for marriage when reaching the proper age. It is the male child's decision, after coming to age, just when the wedding between the two was to be consummated. However, if he took too long and the parents of the girl wished, or if there had been a violation of the ceremonial covenant, the contract could be broken and a divorce granted by the Elders of the community.

Languages – Although the learned and scholarly people spoke and wrote Greek, the common language among the masses was Aramaic. Aramaic is a sub-language of Hebrew, much like American with all of its slang words is compared to English. The New Testament was translated into Greek by scholars. The ancient manuscripts were written in Aramaic. Aramaic is the language used by the disciples and YahShua. Thus I have chosen to use the Aramaic names in this writing. The word for the son of Yah is YahShua(ya' shu' a') .

Names

Aramaic - As found in the Bible

Yah - God - This name was considered by the Pharisees too Holy to be spoken through human lips.
Elohim - Substitute word for Yah. This name was accepted, but later even that became taboo
Adonai - Lord. The Messiah was never called Lord. It is Greek and a substitute.
RuachHaKodesh - Holy Spirit
Anan - Annas
Bartalmal - Bartholomew
BeitAnyah - Bethany
BeitHal - Bethel
BeitLechem - Bethlehem
BeitZaidah - Bethsaida
Cohen/cohanim(plural) - Priests
Cohenhagadol - High Priest
Dammesek - Damascus
Elazar - Lazarus
Elisheva - Elizabeth
Galil - Galilee
Kefa - Peter
Kayafa - Caiaphas
L'vi - Levi
Marta - Martha
Martiteah - Matthias
Martityahu - Matthew
Mikha - Micah
Miryam – Mary
Moshe – Moses
Nakdimon – Nicodemus
Natzeret – Nazareth
Posach – Passover
P'rushen/P'rushaim(plural) - Pharisees
Shaul - Saul or Paul
Shavuot - Pentecost
Shimon - Simon
Shklem - Sychar

Shmuel - Samuel
Shamron - Samaritan
Sukkot - Feast of Tabernacles
Tanakh - Holy Scriptures
Toma - Thomas
Torah - Law of Moses
Tz'duken/Tz'dukim(plural) - Sadducees
Yaakov - James
Yachanan - John
Yahudah - Judas
Yarden - Jordan
Yerushelayim - Jerusalem
Yeshayahu - Isaish
Yews - Jews
Yhudah - Judah
Yhude - Jude
Yirmehyaw - Jeremiah
Yitachak - Isaac
Yosef - Joseph

Libation - A ritual act of hospitality which consisted of the washing of the feet of a guest or traveler who enters an Israelite house. It was performed by the servants of the rich, or by the woman of the house. Also, a ritual bath for priests to fulfill holiness.

Nazarene/Nazarite- A special cult of people, set aside from the others, under a covenant to deny self and serve the will of Yah. The sign of such a covenant was for them to never cut their hair or beard, even from birth.

Passover - A feast called by Yah to be celebrated on the fourteenth day of the first month of the old Israelite calendar. It was to commemorate the feast ordained by God in Egypt when all the first born in Egypt were slain. Yah commanded the death angel to pass over all of the houses that had the blood of the sacrificed lamb applied to their front portals on that fatal night.

The feast started a seven day period, holy unto the Adonai, now called Passover, but then called the Feast of Unleavened Bread, which was celebrated on the fifteenth day. The purpose of this festive week was to remind the Israelites of their haste to leave Egypt and was consummated on a holy Sabbath. Leaving in haste meant having no time to wait for the leaven to rise, thus the bread was unleavened and eaten with bitter herbs to represent the hardship of their journey to the land's border.

Servitude - A person sold for goods or money by the head of the house into service to someone for a specified length of time. This custom usually befell youthful unmarried children, especially young women.

Time - A day was marked from sunset to sunset, but daylight hours were calculated from sunrise to sunset by use of a sundial or water clock. So, the first hour of a day was right after sunrise and the sixth hour was noon. Each hour could not accurately be divided as it is today because the summer days were longer than the winter days making an hour longer in summer than in winter.

Veils - A sheer net or silk square of cloth, attached to the headdress and worn over the face of a young unmarried woman while in public. She was not to expose her beauty or innocence to the lustful eyes of men. For a young maiden to be without a veil was shameful and a reproach to her family. These girls, referred to an 'maidens' and 'virgins', were highly respected by men of all ages. Veils were worn from the time female came into womanhood and were discarded after a marriage was consummated, the husband then becoming her covering. If, however, the girl was allowed by her family or her master who held her in servitude to go unveiled, the shame is more upon the family or the master than the maiden.

Wives & Widows - Married women wore no veils, but did not look directly into the eyes of any man except her father, husband or sons. To do this was considered flirting and was shameful. Widows could look directly at a man to show her eligibility for marriage and to suggest her attraction to him. Women past the flower of their youth, beyond child bearing age, were not under any restrictions.

TERMS

Many of the terms in this book are Bible based and I have made no effort to explain them. I have only given pronunciation to names and approximate values of money. For those who need an explanations of terms to give meaning and depth to the book, these are the ones I used:

Ablution - Washing with water, hence, bathing.

Adjunct - An assistant to a commander or high ranking officer.

Atrium - Large hall with column pillars.

Arcade - Arched, roofed or covered passageway.

Balusters - A series of short pillar-like columns supporting a rail.

Bastion - Garrison or Fortress

Brazen - Brass

Centurion - A Roman army or Calvary officer, captain over up to one hundred men.

Chief Priest - Held the highest seat in the Council of Elders. They were of the tribe of **Levi**, descendants of Aaron and obtained the title through service or birthright, as **Caiaphas**, the office of High Priest. They were highly respected among their brethren as leaders of religious importance and, as such, had much power of persuasion over people.

Chiliarch - A Roman army or Calvary officer, commander of up to one thousand men.

Messiah - The meaning of this word is 'The Anointed One'. This, unlike always thought, is not a proper name. It is a holy title held by someone anointed into the service to Yah, such as prophets and/or deliverers in the Old Testament.

Cisium - A variety of horse drawn carriage; some had four wheels and could carry a driver and two passengers. Some were elaborately decorated. They were made of wood, some being richly carved and of the finest woods.

Coins - A denaril was a coin worth about eighteen cents. A mite is the smallest of coins and was worth about one cent. Shekel was the weight of gold or silver. A silver shekel is worth about eighty-four cents. A gold shekel was about twelve dollars.

Concubine - A servant girl or a woman, given by the wife to the head of a household as a second wife, but not with the same social standing as a wife. These never took ceremonial vows and were sometimes resented by the wife. Therefore, they were never referred to as a wife. Their offspring received part of the family inheritance only if the man of the house wished it. A concubine was in subjection to the wife, liked or disliked, and in second standing with them in everything. Because they were sometimes despised in the eyes of the wife, their lot in life was usually hard but they might find some protection in the husband if she pleases him. Often their offspring were adopted by the wife as her own because she might have been barren or sickly, without strength to bear children unto her husband, but this is not always the case. Some husbands had several concubines. This was not an Israelite custom but was picked up from a pagan nation sometime in the early history of Israel.

Cubit - About eighteen inches.

Degree - A slash of time on the sundial equal to about one minute.

Elders - These were city officials, or Councilmen, made up of chief priest and high Pharisees, Sadducees and scribes, which under the Roman dictatorship was only a representative of the people with no real power of their own in civil affairs.

Ferrule - An ornament made of precious metal to hold the hair in place.

Furlong - One eighth of a mile.

Girdle - A cloth worn about the waist to hold the loose tunic close to the body to aid in movement, which contained pockets for the storage of useful items.

Handbreadth - About three inches.

Herod - There were several Herod's in the history of Israel and were all rulers of Palestine.

Hin - About six quarts of liquid.

Hination - Outer garment, sometimes elaborately decorated and colored. It was worn over the tunic, especially in the case of a woman.

Hostel - Hotel

Ichabod - The glory has departed.

Kaffiyeh - Also known as the Sudarin which was a yard of material folded diagonally and used as a scarf to cover the hair. Unlike the turban, which was rolled around the head, this was worn flat and held into place by a cord. These cords might range from braided camel hair to gold. Women usually wore coins held together by copper couplings. The wealthier the woman's husband, the greater the value of the coins. It was considered unlucky for a woman to loose any of her coins. Therefore, the woman in the Bible who searched diligently sweeping the house carefully looking for a coin was probably looking for one of these.

Lacerna – As short cloak that hung down the back to the thighs attached to the shoulders of a Roman soldier's breastplate. It was used for cover at night and in cold weather could be wrapped around for warmth.

Legate – A high ranking Roman Officer over a Legion of men equivalent to a General.

Legionnaire - Members of a Roman Legion, the Army of Rome that was stationed in a foreign country.

Levites – Members of the tribe of Israel from the line of Levi. This tribe was the one designated by Yah as His inheritance in Israel. They received no land like the other tribes of Israel, but could buy or were given land holding in all the other tribal lands. Only the lineage of Aaron could serve in the Tabernacle and later the Temple. From his lineage came the priesthood and those who were set participates in Temple rituals and worship. Other Levites did mundane service, such as cleaning, maintenance and Temple guards. Service time was usually four years. When not in service they lived as most other Israelites.

Log - A measure of liquid about one pint.

Medicus - A member of the Roman Army Medical Corps.

Menorah - Israelite candlestick of the Temple and synagogue, which had seven branches of equal height. This candlestick was used as representative of the churches in the book of Revelations. It is my opinion that the last candle called Laodicea is now flickering out.

Pharisees - A high order of a religious cult, much like modern day deacons that do not belong to the priesthood. They held seats in the Council of Elders and were supposed to be strict upholders of the law, both civil and religious. By the time YahShua arrived upon the scene of history they were lax and followed only the rules that pleased them, but demanded others to fulfill all the laws and sought punishment for those who did not. On the most part, they looked as though they were fulfilling the laws, but were deceitful and hypocritical.

Praetorium - A parade ground, court or hall where the commanding officer viewed his troops and received visitors.

Procurator - An official of Rome accountable only to the Senate or Caesar, usually a high ranking officer no less than a Legate.

Reed - About eleven feet.

Robe - Outer garment worn over the hination while in public and varies in richness of material or color according to wealth or position in the community. Royalty usually wore scarlet or purple. These dyes were the most costly to obtain.

Sabbath Day's Journey - About half a mile.

Sadducees - A religious cult equal to the Pharisees that differed on doctrinal issues, but were highly respected and held seats in the Council of Elders as did the Pharisees. The main doctrinal difference between them and the Pharisees was that they did not believe in resurrection. They, like the Pharisees, had degenerated from the high standards of the law first followed by their founders.

Sagum – A longer version of the lacerna worn by Roman Officers. They hung to below the knees.

Scribes - Considered lawyers and experts of the Laws and were the ones recognized by the priesthood for the copying of the Sacred Writings, the Torah, from old worn out scrolls to new ones. This was a religious act to them, very tedious and precise, sometimes taking a whole lifetime just to make one copy. These, too, have chosen not to see the failure of the leaders of Israel to follow fully the laws of the Torah.

Score - Twenty.

Span - About nine inches.

Stadium - About one mile.

Taberne - A place of entertainment equivalent to a tavern. The place known to be frequented by criminals, thieves, rebels, harlots and assorted low life.

Torah - The sacred scriptures known to us as the first five books of the Old Testament.

Tetrachy - Territory or providence ruled over by a representative appointed by a government.

Traveling Chair – A stool made of a crossed wood frame with a heavy woven wool clothe for a seat. They could be easily carried or folded and store. Much like the folding campstools we have today. Some more elaborate chairs had backs as well.

Tunic - Also called a khiton worn next to the skin as an under garment.

Yamaluk – A beanie like that we see worn by Jews today.

Zealot - A rebel full of zeal for a political opinion or law. Zealot was a name made famous by the resistance movement against the Romans in Palestine.

Shalom!